GIRL IN A RED SILK SARI

SHARON MAAS

Storm

Previously published as *Peacocks Dancing* by HarperCollins in 2002, *The Lost Daughter of India* by Bookouture in 2017 and *Lost Daughter of India: Girl in a Red Silk Sari* by Karna Books in 2023.

Ebook ISBN: 978-1-83700-054-8
Paperback ISBN: 978-1-83700-056-2

Cover design: Rose Cooper
Cover images: Shutterstock

Published by Storm Publishing.
For further information, visit:
www.stormpublishing.co

ALSO BY SHARON MAAS

World War Two Historicals

The Last Agent in Paris

The Children of Berlin

The Soldier's Girl

The Violin Maker's Daughter

Her Darkest Hour

Those I Have Lost

The Quint Chronicals

The Secret Life of Winnie Cox

The Sugar Planter's Daughter

The Girl from the Sugar Plantation

The Small Fortune of Dorothea Q

Small Days in Guyana

The Girl From Jonestown

The Girl from Lamaha Street

The Far Away Girl

The Indian Collection

Of Marriageable Age
The Orphan of India
The Mahabharata: Sons of Gods

GLOSSARY

Arati – A Hindu religious ritual of worship, in which a flame is offered to the deity.

Beti – A familiar North Indian pet name for a young girl.

Chaat – A savoury snack.

Charpoi – A bed consisting of a wooden frame strung with interlaced cords or webbing.

Crore – ten million in the Indian numbering system; ten *lakhs*.

Dupatta – The shawl of a sari, worn over the shoulder.

Idly – Savoury rice cake, popular as a breakfast food.

Laddu – A typical Indian sweet.

Lakh – One hundred thousand.

Namaste – A customary Hindu 'palms-together' greeting.

Nimbu pani – Sweet limewater.

Paan – Tobacco and slaked lime wrapped in betel leaf.

Paapaa – A familiar South Indian pet name for a young girl.

Paise – Smallest monetary unit in India; 100th of a rupee, no longer in use.

Payasam – A sweet dish and a type of pudding similar to semolina.

Pranaam – A respectful greeting.

Puja – A Hindu worship ritual.

Puri – a deep-fried bread made of unleavened wheat, often served at breakfast.

Shalwar kameez – Traditional Indian combination dress consisting of specific wide trousers (shalwar) and a long tunic (kameez, or kurta).

Vibhuti – Sacred ash used in Hindu ritual worship.

Wallah – A suffix used in many Indo-Aryan languages, to indicate a specific profession or trade.

ONE

MADRAS, 1997

Asha

'Come, girl.'

Mrs Pandian's voice was a command, her grasp on Asha's wrist that of an eagle's talon securing its prey. Tight fingers dug into her skin. Claws that pinched.

It hurt. When Asha resisted, Mrs Pandian only tightened her grip and yanked again. She pulled her up the stairs. Asha stumbled and Mrs Pandian tugged again, jerking her forward.

'Look where you're going, girl!'

Asha hurried to keep up. Mrs Pandian only walked faster, hurrying her along the upstairs hallway. The tiled floor felt hard and cold on the soles of Asha's bare feet. Inside, too, Asha felt hard and cold. She had felt hard and cold ever since the day of the accident. The day Amma and Appa died.

Mrs Pandian pulled Asha through the door to her dressing room; a room Asha knew well, because she cleaned it every day, along with all the other rooms in the house. How long had she been here, in this house, with the Pandians? Asha had lost count of the days. Perhaps eight, perhaps ten.

All she knew was that it was in Madras, a long way from home. She had been to Madras before, with Amma, visiting Janaki at university here. She remembered. Janaki was now in America, far, far away. And Amma was dead. Neither of them could help.

God couldn't help either. Prayers couldn't help. But prayers were all she had, so she prayed. All the time. *Amma, Janaki, God, help me, help me!* Prayer changed nothing. But it was like a rope to cling to when you were drowning. Asha clung to the rope.

There were two women in the room, standing next to the long vanity table with its large three-part mirror. They smiled and gestured for Asha to come closer. Mrs Pandian let go of Asha's wrist and pushed her forward. The smiling women grasped a hand each and pulled Asha forward, pushed her down to sit on a stool before the mirror, chattering away as they touched her face, lifted her chin, held up the long plait that trailed down her back.

'Come paapaa, come! We will make you beautiful!'

'Such a pretty girl! So fair!'

'What lovely thick hair!'

'Make her as beautiful as you can,' said Mrs Pandian as she left the room. The smiling women held up small vials of paste and powders next to her cheeks and then, chattering in Tamil, with the occasional English word mixed in, the women began to apply make-up to her face. Thick, gaudy green eyeshadow on her eyelids, bright red lipstick on her lips, thick pale paste and rouge on her cheeks. Fingers prodding and patting.

'Oh, lovely!' said one of the women, beaming as she inspected Asha's face.

Asha stared vacantly into the mirror. She did not say a word. Her eyes teared up. Her mascara ran.

'Do you think purple or green eyeshadow?'

'Green. It will go so well with those amber eyes.'

'Such beautiful eyes!' said the other woman, staring into Asha's teary eyes. 'Don't cry, paapaa. You will ruin the make-up. All will be well.'

She turned Asha's head back and forth all the better to admire her, like the movable head of a doll.

'Now for the hair!' said the first woman, and started to unplait Asha's heavy braid.

The other woman was rubbing some kind of paste together in the palm of her hand. When Asha's hair was free and hanging down, the woman plunged her hands into it and scrunched the long black locks, all the while exclaiming, 'Such gorgeous hair! You are so fortunate, paapaa, to have hair like this! Your hair is your fortune!'

When Asha's hair had been coiffed into an elaborate up-do, decorated with pearls and shiny jewels and ribbons, one of the women held a mirror up behind Asha's head.

'See, dear! See how lovely your hair is now!'

Asha stared into the mirror, her expression unchanging. She did not smile. She did not nod. She did not speak. But her eyes were moist with tears she could no longer shed.

Mrs Pandian entered the room and came over to inspect her.

'You have done a wonderful job!' she said. 'You have brought out all the beauty of this girl. It's amazing what the right products can do. Now it's time to dress her.'

She held out a bundle of folded red fabric.

'Here, I have brought the sari. Be most careful. It's real silk.'

'Let me wash my hands first,' said one of the women, and moved over to a sink in the corner. 'They are full of oil.'

Both women washed their hands thoroughly with soap, then returned. They took the bundle of cloth from Mrs Pandian, exclaiming all the time, 'How lovely! Oh, she will look delightful!'

One of the women held a bundle of fabric by the edge and let it drop open.

'What a beautiful sari! She will look like a Bollywood star!'

'Get her dressed,' said Mrs Pandian. 'The petticoat and the blouse were made to her measurements. The sari is the smallest I could find but should still fit if you tuck it in properly. Don't take too long. Then bring her downstairs. Mr Pandian is eager to see her.'

Asha stood in the middle of the room wearing a red sari blouse and a red full-length petticoat. One of the women held the sari against the petticoat and started to wrap it around Asha's waist. 'Raise your arms, dear!'

She did as she was told. The sari was far too long. The woman tucked the extra fabric into the petticoat waist, chattering in Tamil all the while.

She then folded the sari into pleats and tucked them into the waistband. She pleated the pallu and lay it carefully across Asha's shoulder. 'Now for the jewels,' said the woman.

When Mrs Pandian returned, Asha was wearing not only the sari but glittering jewels on her nose, long sparkly earrings, and a heavily jewelled necklace.

Mrs Pandian nodded. 'Exquisite! This girl is truly special. Take her downstairs.'

Asha was led by one of the women downstairs and into a gaudy living room with many plush sofas and armchairs. Mrs Pandian led Asha into the room, took her to a sofa and told her to sit down.

A photographer came in and took photos, camera flashing. Asha looked petrified.

'Smile! Smile! You must smile!' said Mrs Pandian.

Asha put on a false smile.

'Stand up!' said Mrs Pandian. Asha stood up. More photos were taken. The camera flashed again and again and again.

'Turn right! Turn left!'

She complied, a smile fixed in place as if tattooed onto her face.

Mr Pandian, a paunchy middle-aged man, entered the room.

He looked Asha up and down, touched her, moved her face this way and that by the chin. He circled her wrist with his fingers.

Finally, he gave his verdict: 'She is too thin. You must feed her up. But she's quite ravishing. She will be a star. Get the photos developed. I'll fax them to Rajagopal.'

The cold, hard feeling closed like a vice around Asha's heart. An invisible fist of eagle's talons tearing into her very being. She could hardly breathe. She felt faint; her knees gave way but Mrs Pandian was right behind her, yanking her upright. She held her still, an arm solid around her waist. Asha stumbled, sank again, and looked up with pleading eyes at Mrs Pandian.

'What is happening? Why am I dressed like this? I don't... understand... I don't want...'

'Don't worry, dear. Just trust us.'

TWO

CAMBRIDGE, MASSACHUSETTS, 1965

Caroline

Caroline snuggled deeper into Meenakshi's lap, her favourite place in all the world. Meena's whole body was a cushion, soft and yielding, and when you cuddled into her it moulded around you and held you safe. It was the best place for a five-year-old to spend a summer evening, swaying gently in the rocking chair on the back porch, Meena's arms around her as she held the book.

The backyard smelt of summer: of sun and moist earth from the water sprinkler gently waving to and fro. The sounds were of summer too. Birds twittered in the chestnut tree in the centre of the backyard, squirrels scampered across the branches, chattering among themselves. The sights and sounds and fragrances of a leafy Massachusetts neighbourhood surrounded them.

Meena didn't smell of America. Meena had her own distinctive smell, and Caroline breathed her in. She smelt of India, sweet and spicy all at once, a thousand secret aromas all mingled together. It was in the fabric of her saris and in her hair; in her skin, dark as a hazelnut and shiny as silk. It wafted, too from the pages of that book, which Meena had brought with her from India when *she* was a little girl, the same age as Caroline was now.

It was a big book, the biggest book on Caroline's shelf, with over a thousand pages. They had been reading it for months now, every day a chapter, and it might be a year before it was finished, and that was fine with Caroline. She hoped it would last forever.

It was the sort of book that took you on a voyage far, far away and made you live in another place and another time, and become another person while you were away. It was the sort of book that created vivid pictures in your mind so that you were actually *there* and *then* and *among* those people and even *turned you into* those people so that they weren't foreign anymore because you *became* them.

Meena's voice was perfect for the story. It was languid but strong; Meena was never in a hurry to get to the end of a story and close the book. She read as if she had all the time in the world, and probably she did; she could put on a man's voice or a girl's voice or a demon's voice or the voice of a god, and make you believe that very person was speaking. She could give you goosebumps, and make you quake in fear. She could transport you into that person's soul.

Right now, Caroline was in India, a young prince disguised as a simple priest, and he was about to win the hand of the most beautiful princess in the world, Draupadi.

"'*Arjuna strode over to the bow, head held high,*'" Meena read, in her strongest book-voice – her royal voice, Caroline called it.

"'*As effortlessly as Karna had done before him, he raised it; the kings gasped. He picked up one of the glittering arrows, took aim at the golden fish spinning high above, released the arrow. With a silver streak almost invisible to the eye it pierced the eye of the fish, which tumbled to the ground. A roar as thunder filled the arena; furious, fuming, the assembled kings waved their fists and screamed insults into the arena; but Arjuna was unmoved.*

"'With three wide springs he leapt onto the royal dais and stood before Draupadi, holding out his hand. Dhrishtadyumna helped his sister to her feet and placed her hand in Arjuna's. Conch moaned and trumpet blared as Arjuna led his bride away: like a young celestial with a heavenly apsara...'"

'What's an *apsara?*' asked Caroline, and Meena replied in her normal voice, 'A divine dancer.'

The chapter over, with much effort Meena pushed her cushiony body to her feet, grasped Caroline's hand and led her indoors, through the kitchen where Lucia was cooking the evening meal, into the hall and up the stairs to Caroline's bedroom to get her ready for her parents' homecoming. Her three older brothers were still outside, at friends' homes, playing baseball on the street, climbing trees; the things boys did after school. They'd be in soon, too.

Caroline's father was a lawyer; he worked extremely hard and sometimes he didn't make it home for dinner. But her mother, a doctor, always did; and it was her mother who, after dinner, would give her her bath and put her to bed and read her a story. But those stories were never as real as the ones Meenakshi told from memory, or read from books: stories of Indian kings and queens, heroes and villains and gods disguised as animals or beggars; cows who could fulfil desires and deer who could speak and monsters who could change shape at will.

If you asked Caroline what she wanted to be when she grew up, she'd say, like many a little American girl, a princess. But Caroline would be no Disney princess. She'd marry a prince like Arjuna, and ride to her wedding in a howdah on an elephant's back wearing a fabulous sari adorned with real jewels; and her palace would be in India.

Caroline was in love with India before she could even write the word. She could point to it on the globe, and she'd tell anyone who asked that *that* was where she'd live when she grew up. Adults would laugh indulgently, and pat her on the head, and tell her she was dreaming, but Caroline knew it was destiny. She *would* grow up to marry an Indian prince.

Caroline grew into womanhood and her childish dreams faded, along with the comforting memory of soft-bosomed Meena with her never-ending tales of swarthy kings and queens and the eternal battle between Good and Evil. Swept up in the dramas and emotional rollercoaster of her teens, Caroline learned that the world stood open to her, that she already *was* a princess of sorts. She could do whatever she wanted, become whoever she wanted to be. She had the choice.

Indulged by wealthy parents, spoiled by older brothers, folded in the safe and cosy arms of Cambridge high society, she wanted for nothing. She dated boys, fell in and out of love, dressed up for Halloween parties. Visits with Grandma and Grandpa Mitchell on Cape Cod, family gatherings around the Thanksgiving table, and the Christmas tree, weddings and christenings, vacations in the Caribbean, trips down to Florida every now and then to see Great-Aunt Janey: that was Caroline's life, and she loved it.

Yet as the years passed something happened, something changed. It started with a boyfriend, Samuel, who didn't quite pass muster with her parents.

Sam had an untidy beard, and he came from less than prime stock. She was seventeen when she met him, he nineteen, in his first year at college, and not at Harvard either, but at Boston U, and studying politics; and his parents were ageing hippies. He had been born on a farm in Ecuador while his father was on the run from the Vietnam draft, had grown up on a series of alternative-lifestyle farms and communes in South America and, later, in Vermont, California and Arizona.

She liked him a lot. She didn't love him, but she loved his mind.

Sam put new, revolutionary ideas into her head.

Sam told her about the World Out There: about the Amazonian Indians whose habitat was being eroded by greedy corporations tearing down the rainforest. He told her about the rape of Africa: about Apartheid. He opened her eyes to the plight of blacks on their own continent. And right next door, here in America, too: in Boston's South End and Roxbury. About the Boston busing crisis of 1974, about racism and oppression and crime caused by poverty and lack of opportunity.

'You're a white princess,' Sam scoffed, 'living in dreamland in your pretty Queen Anne mansion.'

He made her feel guilty; it was a good and healthy feeling, so she listened. Feeling guilty made her feel, incongruously, noble and virtuous.

He told her about the oppression of women in the Middle East, and Pakistan, and India.

'India!' interrupted Caroline. 'I used to have an Indian nanny – Meena was her name. She practically raised me when I was a little girl – like a second mother. Oh, I loved her so much! I love India so much! It's so *romantic!*'

'India, romantic?' scoffed Sam. 'I've been to India. My parents took me when I was just a kid. They took me along the Hippie Trail: through Europe and Turkey and Iran, Afghanistan, Nepal. We lived in India for a year. It's a basket case, Caroline. Millions of people in abject poverty, hardly scraping together enough to survive. They are exploited and downtrodden. The women are nothing but chattels. India is anything *but* romantic.'

Sam opened her eyes to the misery of millions, billions of human beings who shared the planet with her, but did not have the random – it seemed to her – good fortune of being born to privileged white parents in America.

Caroline began to think, to explore. And even when the relationship with Sam broke down – deep down, he resented her privilege, and mocked it just a little too much – she continued on the trajectory he had launched her on.

The seed Meena had planted so long ago, hidden in the depths of Caroline's soul, stirred, and yearned for nourishment. India called. And though she was not ready to go there yet, she decided to flout her parents' will and, instead of studying law at Harvard so as to join her father in his practice, or becoming a doctor like her mother, Caroline chose a different path altogether, one that would allow her to plunge into an Indian world, even if only academically, for the time being at least.

Meena had created a paradisical India in her mind, a charmed land of flowers and birdsong and breath-taking landscapes, snow-capped majestic mountains and sparkling lakes, fabulous royal palaces, kings and queens dripping in jewels. A storybook India.

As she reached adulthood and became involved with liberal politics, and especially through the influence of Sam, she had come to understand that this India was a clichéd, one-sided version of a complex country; that the *real* India was far more multifaceted; that great misery and ugliness existed there, side by side with incredible beauty and sublime ideas.

Against her parents' advice she chose South Asian Studies for her Masters. As the subject of her thesis, she chose *Kinship, Customs and Continuity in Tamil Family Structures: Village Traditions and Marriage Practices in South India.*

Because India still fascinated her. *One day*, she swore to herself, *I will go there and see for myself.*

THREE
CHANDRAPUR, GUJARAT, INDIA, 1968

Kamal

Kamal tried not to breathe; he was sure they'd hear him if he did. He could hear the drumming of his heart, loud and erratic, and it seemed to him the whole world must be listening, watching for him. He crouched lower in the hamper, hugging his knees, curled into a ball with his head tucked in, exactly fitting the circular shape of the basket. He was glad that he was so small, so supple. Like a cat, they said, loose and limber and able to crawl into the smallest spaces and jump from the highest windows, landing like a coiled spring and sprinting off before they could blink twice.

That's why they never caught him. That's why when Her Royal Highness Rani Abistha – known to Kamal as Daadi, Granny – sent them for him he was able to wriggle loose and run, and that's why Daadi tried all the more to bind him to herself, and keep him imprisoned within the Chandrapur Palace walls. But such bondage, for Kamal, had the effect of a whiplash, urging him to escape, stimulating his ingenuity so that, short of winding him in thick chains, Daadi remained the loser. He smiled to himself, thinking of Daadi's rage, and then her panic, when he turned up missing. She'd punish him, to be sure: but he could handle that.

He had placed a cloth over himself so that if someone did happen to open the hamper, they wouldn't notice he was there; they'd be deceived into thinking the hamper had been sent back with its contents intact, rejected by the caretaker. At first he squeezed his eyelids together as if, by shutting out the world, the world would also shut him out – at least the little world of Chandrapur Palace which he knew so well, every tiny corner and crevice so that he could find his way blindfolded through the labyrinthine passages and staircases; led on by the pungent smells, the sounds, the shape of the cobbles, the smoothness of the stones beneath his bare feet, the texture of tapestries and curtains, the senses of touch and hearing and smelling refined to such perfection he could almost abstain from the sense of sight.

With the passing of each second his excitement grew, but also his anxiety. The more time it took to load the cart and coax the bullocks into movement, the more dangerous it would become for him; he had to make sure everything outside was *normal*. Cautiously he opened his eyes to a slit. It was dark inside the hamper but not fully dark: slabs of daylight glinted between the strands of wicker. Curiosity won over caution: carefully he adjusted his position, pushing his face right up to the hamper's side, aligning his right eye with one of those daylight cracks, and peered out.

Everything seemed normal. In the greyness of the first morning light there was the usual courtyard bustle. Punraj, wearing only his loincloth and a turban, trotted across Kamal's limited line of vision, bent slightly forward under the weight of the rice sack he carried on his back. Punraj's body, black as ebony, glistened with sweat although the sun was not yet out; it was a long way to the storeroom at the back of the complex and this was certainly not his first sack. Kamal smiled to himself. He wished he could call out to Punraj, and share his secret; Punraj wouldn't mind and Punraj wouldn't talk. Punraj was a friend, a forbidden friend, one of the many forbidden friends Kamal had made among the palace subordinates.

He couldn't see much through the slit, and after Punraj there were a few seconds when all he could see was the red-brick building at the back of the courtyard. But he could hear the familiar morning noises and knew therefore that he had not yet been missed, that everything was as it should be.

Then, the high-pitched cries of a child as a goat ran across the fine strip of courtyard revealed to Kamal the white nanny goat that Kamal had named Wendy. Wendy was being chased by six-year-old Bibi, Punraj's daughter, another of Kamal's forbidden friends. Bibi wore a long red skirt, and she raced zigzagging behind Wendy, squealing in excitement, thrusting out grasping arms that the little goat neatly evaded, before she, too, disappeared from sight. Silence again.

Kamal smelt the smoke from fires lit in the kitchen at his back, and his mouth watered as he heard the sizzling of ghee as the cooks began to fry the breakfast puris. He heard the clang of buckets being let into the well to his side, the creaking of the pulley, the gush of water poured into clay vessels. The chatter of a hundred servants; the strident calling of a peacock on a faraway roof.

He felt another prick of impatience; it was time to get going. Else they would... there! The bell for breakfast rang out and Kamal bit his lip in nervousness: he should be long gone because if he didn't come for breakfast it would certainly be noticed. And they would start the search for him while he was still within the palace and would certainly find him. He felt his spirits sink – had everything been in vain? Every day for the past week he had watched and waited and every day the bullock cart had left well before breakfast began.

The empty hampers were loaded in the blackness of predawn, which was why it had been easy to slink through the vacant corridors, mount the cart and climb into one of them, covering himself carefully before reaching out, groping for the propped-up lid and closing it over himself. Once hidden all he had to do was wait.

Today, though, driver-*wallah* was taking his time. Kamal knew that on every other day he had sat on the freshly swept earth outside the kitchen drinking tea and sharing gossip with some of the male servants who breakfasted at this time, before the day's work began. They sat in a circle around a small brazier, wrapped in layers of cloth for warmth since the mornings were chilly at this time of year, murmuring to each other, pouring their tea from curved-lip cup to cup to cool it, raising their chins and opening their mouths to receive the milky brew.

On previous days Kamal had watched, hidden, and on every day well before now the men had stood up and shaken out their clothes and dusted themselves off before separating to go about their various tasks. Driver-*wallah* would return to the cart, settle himself on the wooden perch between the rumps of the two bullocks, call out *hey-hey*, prod the slothful animals several times on their backsides, and the cart would rumble off long before the bell for breakfast began its rigorous, joyous pealing. The bullocks would pause at the huge grid of gates let into the palace walls. Watchmen swathed in heavy wraps would draw back the many bolts and turn the many keys and unwind the many chains before heaving the massive gates slowly inward, letting the bullocks and the cart pass through. The gates would close again, be bolted, chained and locked. The bullocks, the cart, the hampers were Outside.

Kamal, in all of his ten years, had never once been Outside.

And then Kamal breathed out in gratitude, for the cart swayed to one side with the weight of driver-*wallah*'s ascent, and the bullocks shifted, the cart creaked, and he heard the familiar cry of *hey-hey*, and they were off. He heard the grating of gates opening, and then they were Outside.

Near the *chowk*, the marketplace, the cart came to a halt and Kamal climbed out unseen. He jumped to the ground and, following his senses, drawn by the noise and smells and whirls of colour, made his way to the bazaar. What a world! A world teeming with fruit and vegetables, some of which Kamal had never seen, much less tasted. His nostrils absorbed a thousand different aromas at once, some so sweet he stopped simply to look, and, because he was hungry and had had no breakfast, his mouth began to water as he stared at a man cutting open a big round fruit and pulling it apart into soft, slippery, translucent sections, bright yellow and luscious.

'What's that?' he asked the vendor, who laughed out loud.

'You don't know what a jackfruit is? Where are you living, little boy?'

He ran away, down the row of fruit stalls till he came to the flower vendors. Here the fragrance was intoxicating. Kamal looked right and left and all he saw were flowers, piles of garlands and baskets of roses; a girl his age was sitting on the ground before a basket of tuberose blossoms threading them expertly into garlands with quick, nimble fingers. Vendors coming with full baskets and going with empty ones, for it was still early, the stalls were still being replenished, and Kamal alone had nothing to do but stare.

A woman handed him a single lotus, in full bloom, on a long straight stalk. She smiled at him, kindly.

'Take it,' she said, and shooed him away.

Having seen all there was to see in the bazaar, holding his lotus he wandered up and down the surrounding lanes, the hunger in his stomach gnawing more and more insistently. He found himself in a narrow alley where the road's tarmac crumbled and the shops on either side all seemed to sell nothing but rusty nails. Another lane was unbearable because here every building was a tea-shop and outside every shop pans of oil sizzled on open fires and golden puris swelled up into crisp balloons, emitting the aroma of breakfast that invaded his nostrils and sank into his belly and screamed there for succour.

Kamal's pockets were empty. He had not thought to bring money; even had he thought of it, he would not have known where to get it. He had never handled money; he'd had no need to. And now, though his clothes were of silk and the chain around his neck and the ring on his finger were of pure gold, he was as poor as the poorest beggar – *those* he had seen everywhere – because he could not eat silk or gold. At this thought something clicked in his mind and boldly he approached the boy – not much older than himself – frying puris outside the next shop. He eased the ring from his finger and held it out.

'Would you accept this ring as payment for breakfast?' he asked hesitantly.

The boy stared at the ring and then at Kamal and called to someone in the black interior of the shop. A man came out, wiping his hands on a grubby cloth, and, looking Kamal up and down, said, 'Where did you get that ring, boy? Did you steal it?'

'No, of course not,' said Kamal angrily, and then remembered that no one knew who he was, and so added in a milder tone, 'My grandmother gave it to me. It is mine. I would like to eat but I have no money. Would you accept this ring as payment?'

'Yes, yes, of course,' said the man then, and showed Kamal a bench at a long table where three other men were sitting eating. Kamal slid in and waited to be served.

One of the men, dressed in white pyjamas and a white cap and a black waistcoat, looked keenly at him and said,

'Are you a fool, or not?'

'Why should I be a fool?'

'To pay for your breakfast with that valuable ring. Look, don't do it. Come with me afterwards and I will show you where you can sell it for a good price. I will pay for your breakfast. You can pay me back when you have sold the ring.'

'Very well,' said Kamal gratefully, and ate with more appetite than he had ever done in the palace, for the simple food tasted more delicious than the most sumptuous feast Daadi had had prepared for him alone.

The shopkeeper was not happy with this new arrangement. When Kamal and the man got up to go he spoke some sharp words, but the man simply left the money on the table and strode off, Kamal running behind him, thanking him profusely.

'It was only my duty,' said the man, brushing off Kamal's gratitude. 'A boy like you must be careful in this town: there are wicked people just waiting to rob you. Look at your fine clothes, your jewellery! Why do you walk around looking like a prince in his palace? Where do you come from? What are you doing on the streets at this time; shouldn't you be at school?'

Kamal felt he could trust this man and told him his name and his story. The man laughed and wished him luck.

'I hope you enjoy your day,' he said. 'Goodbye. It was interesting meeting you.'

'But aren't you going to show me the jeweller's shop? I have to sell my ring and give you back the money!'

'Don't worry about the money,' said the man. 'It was my pleasure to buy you breakfast. But go home now. Here's some money. Take a rickshaw and go home.'

He handed Kamal three rupee coins, and before Kamal could thank him once again, he turned and walked away. Later, Kamal believed the man was a form of God, sent to help him.

· · ·

After his meal, Kamal wandered up and down more streets at random, still grasping the lotus, which he thought brought him luck. He found himself in a part of town where the colours were reduced to black and grey, the streets teeming with human and animal life. There were beggars sitting at the roadside, their clothes black and caked with grime. There were children, infants with limbs bent backwards and eyes oozing pus and swarming with flies. There was a dog with half its head missing, walking around with its brain hanging out. Pigs in the gutters, eating human waste. A stench of offal pervaded these lanes; Kamal felt on the verge of vomiting yet still he walked on, observing, wondering, asking himself questions that could not be answered.

He had never in his life seen sights such as these; he had not imagined such misery could exist in the same world as the palace of Chandrapur where he had grown up. He wandered through the town for many hours.

It was afternoon when he found himself in a potholed street, wider than the others, lined by ramshackle buildings. The strange thing about this street was that there were so many women on it. The women sat or stood outside the open doorways; they sat in the dust or on mats or on *charpais*, or they leaned against the doorframes, laughing, chatting with each other. They combed and plaited each other's hair; they gathered around an open tap and walked home carrying full buckets of water in their hands or on their heads.

Some of them held plates of food in their hands and ate; others nursed babies; a few crouched on the ground cooking over an open fire, or washed pots and infants over stinking gutters. They glanced at him as he walked past but quickly went back to whatever they were doing. There were one or two girls among them, some not much older than he himself. There were several small children. But there were no men. A woman in a faded purple sari grabbed his arm and pulled him into a doorway, where several other women were sitting on *charpoys* chatting.

'Where do you live, boy?'

'In Chandrapur Mahal.'

At that, they all burst out in raucous laughter.

'In that big palace? With the fake queen? Are you a prince, then? Is that why you are dressed in fine silks?'

'Ah, little prince! You grace us with your presence! Should we bow before you? How can we serve you?'

'Ay, little prince, do you have a job for me in the palace?'

'Will you make me a patola-silk sari, boy?'

'Only royals wear patola silk, girl – you think you are a royal?'

'Ay, maybe I will marry a royal and then I too will get to wear patola silk!'

'Go home to your fine palace, boy, and your patola silk. This is not the place for you.'

'Yes, go home. Shoo! You need to be saved from the likes of us. We will only lead you astray. We are bad women.'

They all laughed again, and in the space where they stopped talking Kamal found his voice.

'I don't know the way home.'

'Ah. The little prince is lost. No worries, boy. We will make sure you reach home safely. Hey, you! Baldev, come!'

Baldev was a boy of about ten, sweeping a doorway across the street. He came immediately.

'Take this boy back to the palace. He is a fine prince; got lost and stepped into a cowpat. He doesn't know the way home.'

'But don't steal from him on the way back, hey! He will give you some baksheesh when you get him home. He is so rich.'

The boy called Baldev led him home through the labyrinth of streets, and Kamal gave him the rest of his money. And so, an hour later, Kamal found himself outside the gates and the sentries called out in relieved astonishment, and, it seemed to him, the entire palace household came running out into the courtyard, calling out to him how much he had been missed and where had he been, and what a naughty boy he was, and how angry Daadi would be, and why was he clutching a limp lotus.

'Your Daadi is angry with me, too, Kamal,' his friend Hanoman, Teacher's son, whispered. 'She thinks I helped you out. Look!' He opened his hands and showed Kamal the thick red welts across his palms. 'She beat me to tell her the truth. But I didn't know! I didn't know anything!'

Kamal's filthy clothes were peeled from him by clucking servants. He was bathed and perfumed and bedded for the night. They threw away his limp lotus.

'Your Daadi says she will see you tomorrow,' came the message just before he fell asleep.

FOUR

Kamal and Caroline

When Kamal was twelve, Daadi sent him to the well-reputed boys' boarding school at Kodaikanal. The school was strict, but there he found freedom from the golden cage that was Chandrapur Mahal. His years there flew by, as happy times always do. He found friends and independence. He found hobbies; he discovered a talent for both music and acting. He learned to play the piano tolerably well, and the guitar, and sing along. He joined a theatre group and discovered he was particularly good at playing dastardly villains. He was the brightest student in his class and could take his pick of the best universities in the world. He wanted to go as far away from Daadi as possible. He chose the Massachusetts Institute of Technology, in the USA.

Daadi, of course, had been strictly against his going abroad. They had a hot discussion, with her extolling the virtues of the Indian universities in Calcutta and Bombay and Delhi. But in the intervening years a subtle change in the balance of power had taken place, and Daadi knew now that there was nothing she or anyone in the world could do when Kamal had made up his mind. She accepted defeat on this issue with something very much like grace.

There was still the business of what he would study. He chose engineering. She pleaded with him to take up economics, business studies, law, degrees that would fit into her plans for him, but he refused. She begged him to at least let it be *textile* engineering, which would come in useful when he took over the silk business, but no, stubborn as usual, Kamal had set his mind on *civil* engineering. And, he told her, he had absolutely no intention of going into the silk business.

Daadi shrugged and accepted defeat. It was a pity but, after all, the family business ran itself. She had placed good and trustworthy men in charge, and with only a minimum of supervision the profits were good.

The market for patola silk was still thriving – patola silk was royal silk, and although there were no more royals in India, there were plenty of millionaires who behaved and dressed like royalty. They had also expanded; they had purchased a struggling silk company in Tamil Nadu and built it up. They had moved on to a lesser, but still exquisite, quality for their top range, and more commercial qualities for the export market, and profits had only increased in the last few years. People would always want silk; women would always want to wrap themselves in fine garments. The future was rosy.

In his final year at MIT, Kamal received a bulging envelope with a long letter from Daadi that made his blood boil.

'Soon your studies will be over, my son,' she wrote, 'and no doubt the offers of work will be flooding in. It is time to start looking for a bride for you. As your parents are no more it is my duty to initiate the process.

'In the envelope you will find the biodata of five options. All beautiful ladies with good connections. I have already negotiated with their parents. I have decided we will not demand a dowry as we are modern people, but the connections are important.

'My favourite is Miss Bhattacharya – a lovely girl and her father owns a chain of retail fabric outlets all over the North. They are from Delhi. She is having an excellent education in economics, which she will complete at the end of this year. She is perfect for you but if you prefer one of the others I am quite understanding. All of them are extremely suitable, it's just that Miss Bhattacharya is the best, though perhaps not the prettiest.'

Kamal threw away the entire packet of colour photographs and marriage candidates and wrote Daadi a curt reply: 'None of them are right for me, Daadi. Please do not send any more marriage proposals, and please do not search for anyone else.'

Kamal met Caroline Mitchell in his fourth year at MIT. He first came across her at a birthday party in the home of a mutual friend. He spotted her across the room; there she sat, surrounded by a group of bubbly young ladies – all young and pretty, but she was... different. Amber eyes, jewels that sparkled even from across the room, laughing at someone's story. Relaxed, confident, happy. At ease within herself.

Perhaps she felt his gaze on her. Perhaps she felt, in that gaze, the magic missing in her life. Perhaps it was less magic and more rational: maybe it was simply his *Indianness*. Perhaps his tall, handsome form evoked the image of those princely warriors of her childhood imagination: Arjuna, Karna, Bhishma. Whatever it was, her own gaze caught his. She stopped laughing, and did not let go. She knew.

He did not hesitate. He walked over, held out his hand to her, introduced himself, and then, for the sake of politeness, to all the other young ladies, only to instantly forget all the names but hers. Caroline. With the instinct that aligns with the rules of courtship, her friends melted away. The party melted away; it was as if they were alone in the room. Kamal spent that first evening answering all her avid questions about India.

'I had an Indian nanny!' she said. 'She told me all about India. She told me all the stories of the epics *Mahabharata* and *Ramayana*. I love India so much!'

He only laughed. 'You can't love India until you've known her,' he said. 'Known her in all her riches, but also all her rags.'

'I'd love to,' Caroline answered without hesitation. 'And I will!'

She would be going to India in a year's time, she told Kamal, to do the fieldwork in Tamil family traditions, ancient and modern, necessary for her dissertation. She hoped he could give her some tips, maybe some addresses.

She looked up at him with warm amber eyes that somehow touched him with their cool blend of naivety and intelligence. He could see that that naivety had come from a pre-knowledge of India that was entirely idealistic and totally clichéd, established by a homesick nanny in whose lap she had dreamed her first Indian dreams; but later modified by a thousand books and articles written by Westerners, brimful of Western prejudices and Western condescension. Kamal answered her questions, and shook his head at some of her more questionable views.

On that first evening, they were so thoroughly engaged in discussion that they did not notice the passing of time and had to be gently levered out of their wicker chairs on the wrap-around porch at two in the morning.

Caroline lived with her parents in Cambridge, just a ten-minute walk from the friend's house. Kamal walked her home. They talked all the way. Then Kamal felt her hand in his and stopped speaking in mid-sentence. They walked the next few paces in silence. Caroline said, 'There's my house,' and pointed with her other hand to a beautiful Queen Anne mansion set to the back of a lovely garden in golden autumnal splendour.

Kamal squeezed the hand in his.

'I hope—'

'Kamal, it was—'

They spoke simultaneously; both stopped and looked at each other and laughed. Then Kamal said, 'Go ahead, you first.'

Caroline took his other hand and clasped them both between her smaller ones.

'I just wanted to say, I haven't had such a stimulating evening for... oh, my God. I don't think I've *ever* had such a stimulating evening in my whole life! It was awesome talking with you, Kamal, and I think we're going to be great friends.'

From that first evening Kamal knew that this was the woman he was going to marry. She was so different from him, and not only physically, with her long blonde hair and pale heart-shaped face. She was the stranger he longed to embrace because she represented the half of himself he did not yet know, that missing part of himself that, once united with him, would make him whole.

Caroline was intelligent and warm at the same time; genuinely interested – no, interested was too weak – *enchanted* by India and all things Indian; touchingly ingenuous; sometimes brittle, but the brittleness was only superficial and easy to melt. They could talk for hours, and be silent for hours.

When the first snow fell she drove him out to the countryside and they walked through the whiteness without speaking a single word, arms slung around each other in a silent intimacy overflowing with warmth, and though the bitter cold stung his bare cheeks Kamal felt the winter must melt before them, like the snowflakes melting on his lashes.

He opened his lips and caught the snow on his tongue and laughed out loud. Caroline, her face small and white in the soft maroon shawl wrapped around her head, glowed with inner joy. She pressed an icy-cold, snow-encrusted glove against his cheek and said, 'Kamal Darji, if you don't promise to marry me I swear I'm going to lie down right there in that snowbank and let the snow drift over me and cover me till I look like the Abominable Snowman and just wait there until you do!'

Kamal chuckled and moved her hand from his cheek. He pulled off her glove and flung it away onto the snow and replaced the warm hand on his warm cheek.

'That's more like it. Now, Caroline Mitchell, what do you want me to do? Go down on one knee and propose officially?'

'No. Just say it. Say it. Say you want to marry me. Say you want to be mine forever and ever.'

'You know it already.'

'But I want to hear it. I want you to say it out loud. I can't stand this deep Indian silent communication. Go on, just say it. Tell me you will sweep me off my feet and carry me to India in your strong manly arms.'

'You don't know me properly yet, you know. Wait till I get you back to India. I will turn into the tyrannical Indian patriarch of your worst nightmares! I will ravish you as my wife and keep another four women in my harem just for good measure. I will keep you well under my foot, forbid you to step outside the walls of our marital abode unless you walk four paces behind me. You will occupy yourself with raising five fine sons to follow in my revered footsteps. You will refer to me exclusively as "Father of my Sons" and bow your head, hiding your face in the folds of your sari when I enter the room. You will humbly serve me delicious meals you have cooked with devotion on golden platters and only take food yourself when I and all our sons have been sated. When I die you will—'

'I'll stuff this snow down your damned *throat* if you don't look out!' cried Caroline, then made good on her threat. Kamal wrenched himself out of her grasp and ran stumbling, laughing, through the snow. Caroline bent down and picked up a handful of snow, pressed it into a huge snowball and pelted him with it, screaming, 'You asked for it! You *jerk!*' It hit him square on the back of his head.

'OK, it's WAR!' cried Kamal, and bent over for his own snowball.

They fought fiercely, hysterically, for a good half-hour and then, suddenly, Kamal threw up his arms and said, 'OK, OK, you win. I quit. I surrender unequivocally. I will fulfil each and every one of your commands.'

She flung herself at him so that they both lay in the snow. 'Marry me. That's all I want. Say it out loud.'

'Marry me,' he whispered, and the words came out on a breath like smoke, fading into the crisp cold air.

'Louder. I can't hear you.'

'Marry me, Caroline.'

'Sorry? What was that?'

'I refuse to shout. I'm not going to shout. Come here.' He drew her head close to his, her ear to his lips, and there he spoke the words again, clearly and gently. 'Will you be my wife? To have and to hold, till death us do part?'

She smiled, put her arms around him and rested her cheek on his.

'Yes,' she sighed. 'I will.'

'I don't have a ring for you,' he said. 'That's not an Indian custom. But I do have this. It's an heirloom. It was my mother's; the sapphires are precious, and have quite a history.'

He took a small box out of his pocket, and opened it for her. In it lay a pendant, in the form of a flower, the three blue petals clustered around a central diamond.

'Oh Kamal! It's beautiful! An engagement pendant! I shall always wear it.'

He clasped it behind her neck. She opened her coat and dropped the pendant through the neckline of her blouse, and smiled up at him. He put his arms around her and pulled her close.

'Where I come from,' he said, 'sapphires represent Venus. They represent love, unbreakable love, which will last for all eternity. That's us.'

The path to marriage was, for Kamal and Caroline, rough. Caroline took Kamal to meet her parents and they received him with a civil but icy reserve that caused him to fear the worst.

'You see, they belong to the old Boston aristocracy. Old money, real old. Very Anglo-Saxon, very white, very Protestant. They have a precise idea of the kind of man they want me to marry and – well, Kamal, you just don't fit the cookie-cutter.'

'They haven't even *tried* to get to know me.'

'Getting to know you isn't the issue. *Who* you are doesn't count; it's *what* you are.'

'What I am? Come on, I'm not exactly the plumber! I'm a MIT student, for goodness' sake. All right, I realise a medical or a law student might be more up their street but—'

Caroline cut in. 'That's not the point, Kamal. Even if you were going to be a doctor they'd be against you. It's where you come from, how you look.'

'In other words, they're racist.'

Caroline hung her head. 'I'm sorry, Kamal. That's just the way they are. They can't jump over their shadows. I *warned* you they'd be this way.'

'Look, I don't give a damn about *them*. The question for me is, can *you* jump over their shadows?'

'Oh Kamal, why do you even ask!'

'So you'll go against them? Marry me, even if they don't agree? Come with me to India?'

'Kamal, I've always known I'd end up in India. Ever since I read *The Jungle Book* as a child I've known it – it's a pull I can't explain and for me it's only logical that I should marry an Indian and go there with him and there's nothing in the world my parents can do about it. They can't hold me back. But anyway' – she smiled – 'sooner or later they'll have to give in because they love me. And when they hold my first baby in their arms, they'll be just like grandparents anywhere. They'll go completely gaga.'

Of course, Kamal told Caroline all about his childhood in the golden cage. Caroline was beyond excited.

'So you're a real Indian prince? Wow. I can't believe I'm going to marry a prince! Will that make me a princess? I can't believe it! Kamal, I used to dream of becoming an Indian princess, but no one would believe me, and now it's going to be true. I can't wait to see the palace. Shall we have a big wedding in the palace? Shall I arrive riding on an elephant? Just kidding, don't give me that look... But you know, knowing you're a prince might be just the thing to win over my parents. You should have told me earlier!'

But Kamal frowned, and his eyes clouded over.

'No,' he said. 'You're not a princess, and I am not a prince. I'm not taking you to that palace. I don't want to see Daadi ever again.'

Caroline was persistent. 'But why, Kamal, why? She's your grandmother; your only relative. Surely she'll want to meet your wife, and when we have kids—'

'I don't want to discuss it, Caroline, OK? She wouldn't approve of you anyway, so you can forget about a big royal wedding. It's not going to happen.'

That was the only time they ever came near to a quarrel, and Caroline thought it was wiser to leave well enough alone. She understood: Kamal wanted to be loved for himself, not for his supposedly blue blood. And she did love him for himself.

Kamal got his master's degree in civil engineering, and then he married Caroline at a quiet civil ceremony in Cambridge, Massachusetts. He began the application process for civil engineering jobs in India. Almost immediately, he was offered a job at the Aliyar Reservoir, a hydroelectric dam in the foothills of the Western Ghats, near Coimbatore, in Tamil Nadu. He would work on the Hydel Power Project, a series of dams interconnected by tunnels and canals for harnessing the waters of the local rivers flowing at various elevations for irrigation and power generation. It was a tremendous opportunity for him to work on a major engineering project, which would be of benefit not only to his career, but to the local communities.

Caroline, meanwhile, would write her thesis while living with a real Tamil family, a family which held traditional values but was educated enough to help and advise her as she did her research.

Six months later they boarded a plane, bound for Madras, South India.

FIVE

MADRAS, 1983

Caroline and Kamal stepped out of the Air India plane, down the aircraft stairs, and onto the tarmac at Madras International Airport. Caroline tugged and wiggled the neckline of her blouse to allow the air to circulate.

'Whew!' she said, fanning herself with her free hand. 'It's like walking into hot soup!'

'I suppose summer is the wrong time of year to arrive,' said Kamal. 'Here, let me take that bag.'

He slung her carry-all across his shoulder along with his own. They queued for ages at Immigration and then waited another age to collect their luggage, and then, pushing a trolley piled high with luggage, walked out into the frenzied melee waiting outside the arrivals hall.

It seemed like thousands of Indians were jostling for front space along the metal barriers, holding up signs with names written on them in big bold lettering, shouting out names.

'Wow! This is utter madness!' said Caroline. 'How are we supposed to find—'

'There he is!' cried Kamal, and waved, calling. 'Mr Patel! Here we are!'

A middle-aged man holding high a sign on which was scrawled *Mr and Mrs Darji* pushed through the crowd, grinning broadly. 'Hello, hello, hello! Welcome to India! Pleased to meet you, Mr Darji!'

Escaping the confines of the barriers, Kamal placed his hands together in *namaste*.

'Pleased to meet you Mr Patel, and do call me Kamal. This is my wife, Caroline.'

Mr Patel returned the *namaste* and bowed slightly to Caroline, then wrenched the trolley from Kamal's hands, saying, 'I am Ashok. Pleased to meet you! Very pleased! Happy, happy! Come this way, a taxi is waiting.'

Using the trolley as a battering ram, Ashok barged through the crowd, zigzagged between rows of cars in the parking lot, and led them to their taxi. While the driver took care of their luggage, Mr Patel climbed into the passenger seat and Kamal and Caroline slid onto the back seat.

As they drove out of the airport parking lot and into the main road, Ashok turned around to chat with Kamal and Caroline.

'So happy to meet you at last! I have everything arranged.'

'We're so grateful for all your help, Ashok. I don't know this part of India at all. And I don't speak Tamil.'

'Anything to help a new colleague. It is all arranged nicely. And you won't need to speak Tamil. Everyone speaks English in South India. I mean, most people. Educated people. I even found a nice family for your wife already. Unfortunately, it is four or five hours' drive from the dam. But you can visit her on weekends.'

Caroline, her brow wrinkled with concern, turned to Kamal, wide-eyed in apprehension.

'Kamal! Five hours from the dam? That's not what we...'

'We want to live together, Ashok. Couldn't you find something closer for her?'

'Sadly, it was not possible to find a suitable family who would fulfil your wife's requirements in close vicinity to the dam. I did look for a family there, but in vain. The Iyengars are friends of a distant cousin, and the family is ideal for your requirements.'

He turned to Caroline. 'I understand you're writing a dissertation on Tamil culture and family structure?'

'Yes. It's for my South Asian Studies master's degree.'

'The family lives in a village close to Gingee, in a village called Thenanguddi. It means the Village of Coconut Trees. Gingee itself has a fascinating history, with an ancient fort; the British called it the Troy of the East. You should see the massive stone walls! They stretch for miles and miles. It was ruled by so many dynasties – but Mr Iyengar will tell you the history and show you around. It is entirely suitable. You must also visit some of our ancient temples. Thousands of years old, and perfectly constructed. Gingee is a wonderful base for you.'

'But I don't want to be separated from Kamal!' Caroline cried out, her voice sharp and veering towards rude.

'You'll be perfectly at home with the Iyengars. They are a very hospitable and well-respected couple, and educated. Mr Iyengar is a private-school headmaster and has a history degree. He is also the president of the village panchayat, the village self-governing body – a village leader! Mrs Iyengar has a degree in English but she is now at home raising her children. She already has four or five, one more on the way. A lovely woman. You will be great friends, Mrs Darji.'

'Caroline. Please call me Caroline.' She paused and looked at Kamal, still aghast. 'But Kamal, I don't want to live apart, with strangers.'

Kamal took her hand and squeezed it. His voice was tender, measured, calming.

'It's not forever, Caro! Just for the start. I guess it wasn't easy, finding a family that fits the bill perfectly. Once you've finished your thesis you can join me near the dam. I heard it's a lovely area. We'll be separated for only a few months. At the most, a year. I'm sure it wasn't easy to find exactly the family you need.'

Ashok said, 'It's a pukka job he landed at that hydroelectric dam, Caroline. I've been working there for five years now. It's a very innovative project, absolutely modern. Kamal and I will be first-rate colleagues and you will both be happy. His future is bright. As a foreign-educated and foreign-returned Indian he can get any job anywhere in India later on.'

Kamal said, 'For the time being, though, we have to make do with a weekend relationship.'

Caroline gripped Kamal's hand with her own two hands, shook it for emphasis. Her voice trembled as she spoke. She tried to be valiant, but everything in her pushed against the plan. She tried to tone down her objections, tried to be less emotional about it.

'It's just a bit weird, going to stay with strangers.'

'It's her first time in India, Ashok. First time in a foreign country, first time living with strangers. But I know you, Caroline. You'll be fine. I don't start work for a week and I'll stay with you till then. And I'll come back as often as I can.'

'I'll hold you to that,' said Caroline, and squeezed Kamal's hand as tightly as she could. It was not a terribly auspicious start. This was not the India she'd dreamed of.

The heat, the noise, the jam-packed streets, the dust.

The HEAT!

SIX

GINGEE, TAMIL NADU, 1983

Their taxi drew up outside a bungalow in a leafy garden. Climbing out of the air-conditioned taxi was once again like stepping into a bathtub filled with hot water. Caroline, still pulling at her blouse to allow air – hot air – to circulate, stepped away to allow Kamal to get out, and looked around.

A few small, half-naked children had come running down the dusty road and now stood at some distance, staring at them; at her in particular. She gave them a strained smile, wriggled her fingers at them and turned away.

Mr Patel led them through the gate to the open front door, and there he called out, 'Mrs Iyengar! We are here!'

A woman in her mid-forties came bustling up, smiling enthusiastically. She was heavily pregnant. A naked toddler buried his face in the loose fabric of her sari skirt.

'Welcome, welcome!' she said. 'So happy to meet you! Mrs Darji, Mr Darji...'

'Please call me Kamal. My wife's name is Caroline.'

Caroline greeted her with a polite *namaste* gesture, smiled and said, 'Pleased to meet you, Mrs Iyengar!'

'Do call me Sundari. Come, let me show you to your rooms.

We have a little cottage at the back, where my father-in-law used to live.'

Sundari led the way through the bungalow, down a hallway through the middle of the building, through the kitchen and out the back door into the garden. A small, pretty cottage, white with a red tiled roof, surrounded by bougainvillea bushes in full flower stood waiting in the back garden, its door wide open. Sundari led them into the cottage.

'Please feel at home in our humble abode. My husband will be home at four. He is the principal of the leading private English-medium school. The other children are at school and most of them will be home for lunch.'

'How many children do you have?' asked Caroline.

'Five already! Four boys, one girl. And number six on the way.' She rubbed her belly and gestured. 'Here is the bedroom.'

She led them into a room with a double bed in the centre, taking up most of the space.

'See, there's a cupboard where you can stow your garments. And a desk.'

Leading them out again, she opened other doors.

'This is the kitchen. It has a gas cooker. And here is the bathroom. The bathroom even has a hot-water boiler. There's only the one bedroom, but as you have no children yet it will be adequate. There's even a sofa in the living room.'

Yes, Caroline had noticed the sofa. She sank into its soft cushions, already exhausted.

Sundari said, 'You must be tired after the long flight. Please have a rest or else you can join me for tea and snacks in the front house. Just come over. I am preparing lunch right now for my hungry family, and now you are my family too.'

Caroline stood up, yawned and said, 'I think I'll have a siesta first. Kamal?'

'Yes. Me too.'

'Then I'll leave you to settle in. Have a nice rest and see you later!' Sundari bowed slightly and left.

Caroline turned to Kamal with a deep sigh. 'Oh Kamal! It's so overwhelming. She's so friendly. And yet...'

Kamal took her in his arms. 'Not what you expected?'

Caroline shook her head sadly and wandered around the cottage once more. She felt the mattress, turned on the overhead fan. 'I don't want to complain. But it's all a bit... basic. No air-conditioning! How can I even survive?'

'It's certainly not a palace. Will you be all right? We can buy a table fan. If you want more comfort we can...'

'No, no. Of course not. I don't want to complain like some spoilt rude American. I'll get used to it. It's just... Well, like I said. Basic. I thought... Never mind.'

'You wanted to experience the authentic India, Caroline. This is a good start. It's what it is. OK, it's not what you're used to. But it's scrupulously clean and I bet the food's good. Home-cooked Indian meals!'

'Yummy! Yes, I *am* behaving like a spoilt American brat looking down her nose, aren't I.'

She sighed and yawned, placed her suitcase on the bed and opened it. 'I'm going to get into my PJs, get into bed, sleep for hours. Join me? But first, a shower.' She laughed. 'Just imagine, they have *hot water*!'

'Caroline!'

'And did you see the toilet, Kamal? You have to squat and hover over the hole!'

He smiled and shrugged. 'It's said to be healthy. Better than a Western sitting toilet. But we can install one of those if you prefer.' Caroline shrugged and made a face. She picked up a towel from a heap of folded ones on the bed and walked off to the bathroom. Another shock awaited her. She called out to Kamal.

'Kamal! There's no shower!'

Kamal came to have a look and sighed. No shower indeed, but a tap, a bucket and a scoop.

'Yes,' he said. 'It's called a bucket-bath.'

Caroline sighed and threw up her hands in surrender.

'At least it has hot water.'

That evening she and Kamal met the rest of the family: three boisterous boys, a girl who looked at her with clear, curious eyes, and their father, a bespectacled, studious man in his early forties, who, after a light supper, questioned her intently as to her intended work.

'Call me Vikram,' he said. 'You are most welcome in our humble home.'

'Thank you,' said Caroline. 'You're very kind.'

Kamal laughed. 'I hope my wife doesn't pester you too much with all her questions! She's already peppered holes in me – but I'm not a Tamil, so can't help much.'

Vikram turned to Caroline.

'I like the subject of your thesis, Mrs Darji...'

'Please, call me Caroline.'

Vikram bowed his head slightly in agreement, and continued.

'So, do you have any specific questions? What do you want to focus on? It's an extremely wide subject, you know.'

Caroline's eyes sparkled with enthusiasm.

'I know! I'm trying to narrow it all down. In general, I want to know about the roles and responsibilities within extended family structures. And changes in family dynamics due to twentieth-century modernisation. And the interplay of caste, religion and local governance in shaping village life, and...'

Vikram laughed.

'My goodness! Already there you could write a whole book, never mind a thesis. But yes, I can help. I'll introduce you to the other men in the village panchayat – the elders, governors of the village. I'm the president, but they are closer to the villagers. They can help you further. At least one of them is fluent in English.'

'Oh, great! And I also want to know about marriage itself. Traditional matchmaking customs and rituals. The dowry system and how it affects the poor. Cross-cousin marriages. How love marriages are challenging traditional arranged-marriage norms...'

Vikram gestured to Sundari. 'My wife is the one to help you most there. She loves nothing more than discussing marriage.'

Sundari laughed.

'He's right! Marriage is the building block of society. It's most important to get that right. I will introduce you to all my female friends and they can all tell you their stories. I've already told them you are coming, and they are all keen to meet you. You're the first foreign lady who has come to our village.'

'I'd love that!' Caroline looked from one to the other and couldn't stop smiling. This was exactly what she was looking for. Yes, the accommodation might not be her usual standard, but she could live with that – it was the people that mattered, and these people were all she could ask for. They were gracious, hospitable, intelligent, educated and, above all, helpful.

She took a deep breath. Yes. It would be hard, living apart from Kamal. But he'd promised to come home as often as possible, and perhaps it was even a good thing, to be alone most of the time. She could focus on her work. She could assimilate. She could actually become a member of the village herself, fit herself in without the distraction of a husband.

All was well.

SEVEN

GINGEE, TAMIL NADU, THREE MONTHS LATER

Caroline pulled the page and the carbon from her typewriter, laid them on their respective stacks, patted them into neat piles, stood up, stretched and walked over to the bungalow. She was late, again; she'd wanted to help prepare dinner, but she'd needed to finish that last part of her thesis.

The Iyengar family was already gathered when she walked into the dining room, sitting on cushions on the floor around a straw mat. At least, the males were gathered: Vikram, Sundari's husband was chatting with the boys – Shankar, the eldest at thirteen, Kumar, aged nine and Murugan, six – asking them all about their school day.

Behind the eating area, on a heap of blankets on the floor, slept the baby, Dev. The toddler, Rajan, sat on Vikram's lap, playing with a toy engine.

Caroline took her seat on one of the three vacant cushions and greeted them all. Eleven-year-old Janaki entered and set a steaming cooking pot on the centre of the mat, next to the pile of *thalis*, large stainless-steel plates; she knelt down and began to ladle rice onto the top *thali*. As she handed the *thali* to Caroline their eyes met, and they smiled at each other.

'Thanks, Janaki!' she said, and Janaki nodded in reply. She and Janaki had grown so close over the last few months. Janaki had so much promise, Caroline thought; what a pity her mother's plans for her were so limited.

Sundari came in from the kitchen holding another pot with wads of dishcloths, and she too knelt down, pouring steaming ladles of red-orange sambar onto the piles of rice.

'Sundari, come and sit down and eat!' said Vikram. 'Stop walking around serving. We are all hungry. You too, Janaki.'

Sundari returned to the kitchen while Janaki sat down on a vacant cushion next to Caroline, who smiled at her again.

'So how did the math test go today, Janaki?'

'It was actually quite easy, Caroline Auntie. I think I passed it.'

Vikram said, 'Of course she passed it! I can guarantee it. She is the best mathematics student of her year. We are so proud of you, Janaki-Baby.'

'Thank you, Appa.'

Sundari returned with a large plate of crispy pappadums and a bowl of curd; she took her place next to Vikram, and Rajan immediately moved to her lap.

Vikram chanted a short Sanskrit prayer of thanksgiving. Everyone started to eat, mixing the rice and sambar into bite-sized balls with their hands and popping the balls into their mouths. Only Caroline ate with a spoon. Sundari fed herself and Rajan alternately, with her fingers.

Vikram turned to Caroline. 'And how did you get on today? Did you find the books you wanted in the college library?'

'Sort of. But there's still a lot I need to know and it's not even on the Internet. I might need to go to the university library in Madras.'

'I have to go to Madras soon; I'll take you to the library. But your dissertation is coming along nicely?'

'I've made a good start, I think. But I wish I knew Tamil.

Most of the really great books are in Tamil and they aren't translated.'

'I can give you Tamil lessons.'

'Thank you, Vikram. I'm picking it up slowly. But I'm afraid I'll need advanced skills to get what I want. It's such a complex language.'

Janaki said, 'When is Kamal Uncle coming again, Auntie?'

'Not till next month, I'm afraid. It's quite a long bus trip and he only gets the weekends off.'

'You must miss him a lot,' said Sundari. 'Especially in a foreign country.'

Caroline nodded. 'I do. But it's only temporary. When I finish my work here we will look for a place near to the dam and we can be together.'

'I'm praying that will be soon.'

Janaki said, 'I hope it won't be soon! I love having Caroline Auntie living here, and hearing all about America. And Kamal Uncle, he's so interesting. I want to be an engineer when I grow up, Appa.'

Sundari frowned. 'Don't be silly, Baby. Engineering is for boys.'

'No, it isn't!' said Caroline. 'Girls can be engineers too!'

Janaki nodded. 'That's what Kamal Uncle told me. Lots of girls study engineering in America, he said. And even in India.'

Sundari wasn't pleased. 'And anyway, you should be thinking more about marriage than all this engineering rubbish.'

'I will get married after I get my degree, Amma. Not before. So plenty of time.'

'We will see about that. I am already on the lookout for suitable boys.'

Janaki rolled her eyes. 'Please, Amma, I'm only eleven!'

'Don't you make roll-eye at me! It's never too early to be thinking about marriage. Not this engineer nonsense. Leave that to the boys. Kumar, you want to be an engineer, don't you?'

Kumar nodded. 'Yes, Ma. I want to study aeronautics.'

Sundari looked at Janaki. 'See? We already have an engineer in the family.' She pointed to the other boys. 'And Shankar is going to be a doctor, and Murugan will be a lawyer. Rajan' – she pointed to the toddler – 'can go into business. And that little one' – she indicated the sleeping baby – 'can be a scientist. A professor. If Janaki wants a degree she can study something like English, like I did.'

Janaki chuckled. 'As you can see, Caroline Auntie, Amma has planned out a career for each of us.'

'Janaki has the best brain of all of them,' said Vikram, 'and she should make the most of that blessing.'

He patted Janaki's arm. 'Don't let your mother put you under pressure, Baby. I am so proud of you. Study whatever you want, medicine, engineering, law. And you can marry whenever and whoever you want.'

'Thank you, Appa.'

Caroline turned to Sundari. 'I agree with Vikram, Sundari. She has lots of time. Let her discover what she really wants. It's what I did.'

She and Sundari had formed a really good relationship, almost a friendship, over the last few months, but Sundari was so... so fifties-housewife-ish. Nevertheless, it was possible to discuss such matters with her reasonably, and even though Sundari might disagree and argue, it was all good-natured. Perhaps, Caroline thought, perhaps she could influence Sundari on Janaki's behalf.

Sundari said, 'Yes, I know you went against your parents' wishes. It's not good that you and them are still estranged, Caroline. It's bad karma.'

Right then the baby stirred and started to cry. Sundari handed Rajan back to his father, stood up and picked up the baby. She started to breastfeed.

Caroline said, 'I will reconcile with them one day. It might take a few years. I do love them and I miss them. Especially at times like Thanksgiving.'

She sighed. 'I just wish they'd understand.

'About you and Kamal? It's difficult for parents when their children are so headstrong. We want the best for them, and we do know best when it comes to marriage. Especially girls. That's why I'm looking out for Janaki.'

'You don't need to look out for me, Amma. I'm quite capable. And when I marry it will be for love.'

'Don't you answer back, girl! You know how many love marriages go wrong? Look at the divorce rate in the West!'

Caroline said, 'Well, I agree with Janaki. I married for love and I would never have accepted my parents' choice. They'd have chosen some boring corporate lawyer with slicked-back hair. Not for me! Now I've got Kamal.'

'Well, I agree that you chose well. Kamal's a reliable husband with a good profession. What do your parents have against him?'

'That he's Indian. But I always loved India, since I was a little girl. I used to have an Indian nanny and she would tell me all those wonderful stories of kings and queens. Even then, I wanted to marry an Indian. An Indian prince.'

'Well, we don't have kings and queens in India anymore. The British did away with all that. So, no princes.'

'Oh, but Kamal *is* a prince!'

'Nonsense. All the kings and queens and princes are in the *Mahabharata*.'

'Maybe, but he's from a royal family. You ever heard of the kingdom of Chandrapur? Near Gujarat?'

'No, never. It must be tiny, and certainly not a kingdom anymore.'

'Well, tiny or not, that's where Kamal gets his royal blood. His grandmother is the Rani Abishta. Queen Abishta! He actually grew up in a palace. His parents died when he was a child, and his Daadi raised him and always told him he was of royal blood. He hated it, especially when she tried to marry him off to some rich heiress. That's why he ran away to study in America. And that's where we met.'

'Well, if he's from Indian royalty it's an excellent match. Your parents should be proud.'

'Well, Kamal doesn't want me to tell them. He wants to be accepted for himself.'

'And what did his family feel about you?'

'I don't think he even told his Daadi about me. He doesn't speak to her. But of course, I wouldn't be good enough for her. She wanted an Indian heiress.'

Later, when they were alone, Caroline laughingly told a curious Sundari the story of how Daadi had tried to find a bride for Kamal. Sundari did not laugh; she found it rude of Kamal to reject the potential brides, after Daadi had gone to so much trouble.

'It was his Daadi's *duty*,' she told Caroline sternly. It wasn't a joke. Marriage was an important step; it should not be left to chance meetings. Kamal had been wrong to reject them all out of hand.

'But then,' Sundari said, with a smile of reconciliation, 'he found you and now I have met you and we are such good friends. Everything happens for a reason. Even when we make mistakes, the outcome is what had to happen, what matters. Your marriage had a good outcome, in spite of Kamal's mistake. You and I, we had to meet.'

Sundari was curious about Rani, as Kamal himself never mentioned her, never spoke of his childhood. Caroline herself knew little, but what she knew, she told Sundari.

'He doesn't tell me much either,' she said. 'It's like a taboo subject for him – I've no idea why. He just has issues with her, I guess. She's extremely possessive and domineering, I think, and I guess he just wants to assert his independence. He likes to think of himself as an ordinary person, not a prince. He's so modest. It's what I love about him.'

'It is not good to be estranged from family,' said Sundari. 'Family is everything. It is the foundation of society. One must respect one's elders.'

Caroline shrugged. 'I agree, and I'd love to meet her and go to that palace and meet my grandmother-in-law,' she said. Laughing, she added, 'It's not every American girl that gets to go into a real old Indian palace and meet a real old Indian ex-queen. I wish we could have married there. My parents would have adored it – their daughter, a princess!'

'You should have told them he's a prince, even though he's not really. But blue blood runs in his veins.'

Caroline laid a hand on Sundari's wrist.

'Please don't ever call him a prince, Sundari. Don't tell him I told you that story. He doesn't like it at all. I really shouldn't have told you.'

'I won't say anything. But it's so sad. Poor Daadi. He was wrong to cut himself off completely. Family is family.'

'Well, he did give me this. It's a keepsake from his mother, a sapphire pendant given to her by the Maharani of Jaipur at her wedding.'

She pulled out the sapphire pendant she wore around her neck, and showed it to Sundari. 'One day, it will be my daughter's. If I ever have one.'

EIGHT

GINGEE, TAMIL NADU, ONE MONTH LATER

They hadn't planned to start a family just yet – but just a month later Caroline found she was pregnant.

In excitement, she wrote to Kamal with the good news. He was delighted. 'I'll be home as soon as I can,' he wrote back. 'We have to celebrate!'

He kept his promise. At the Gingee bus station, Caroline made her way through the milling crowd: noise, chaos, people with loads on their heads, people selling bananas, sweets, bottled water. She was used to it by now. She found the right bus stop and waited.

After a long wait, a rickety old bus drew up, and passengers began to pour out of the open door. There was Kamal. She called and waved enthusiastically, and a moment later she fell into his arms. 'I've missed you so much!'

'I missed you more!'

'Oh, Kamal, I can't believe it!'

'Me neither.' He placed a hand on Caroline's belly, rubbed it a bit. Caroline playfully slapped the hand away.

'Not here. No touching in public!'

Kamal laughed and removed his hand. 'Sorry, I forgot.'

'You're the Indian around here. You're supposed to be teaching me the etiquette, not me you.'

'Well, Sundari's teaching you OK.'

Caroline sighed. 'Not really, Kamal. I'm just being polite. I can't wait to have our own place. And with the baby...'

'You think you'll be ready? When the baby comes, I mean. You've still got that thesis to finish.'

'Bloody thesis.'

'Lost interest?'

'Not really. But it's hard being apart from you. This long-distance marriage thing, it's driving me crazy.'

'It won't be forever.'

'A baby kind of puts a spanner in the works, though.'

Kamal looked at her in concern. 'You'll be OK?'

'Sure. And Sundari will help. She knows all about babies. So I'll stay with her for a while after the birth.'

'Good that you two get along so well.'

'She's a bit fifties-housewife-ish but she's great. I'm glad she'll be there in the beginning as I'll need help, and my wonderful husband won't be around.'

She laughed and punched him playfully. He too laughed, skipping aside. He grabbed her by the arm, and, elbows hooked, they waited on the busy street, hailing passing auto-rickshaws in vain. Eventually a rickshaw stopped and they got in.

They made plans. They'd build a nice house in the scenic hills near the Aliyar dam. Caroline already had enough material for her thesis; she only needed to finish writing it. Her supervisor back home, with whom she'd kept in touch all along, had approved and was only waiting for the final package. It was done.

At last, they'd be together. She'd have the baby, they'd find a home, she'd move in with Kamal, at last. They'd be perfect parents.

Who needed the Mitchells of Cambridge? Who needed Kamal's Daadi of Chandrapur? Not Kamal and Caroline Darji.

However, they were forced to delay their plans for a while. There wasn't enough money yet to build a house, and both refused, for obvious reasons, to ask their families for help. Perhaps they'd rent for a while...

Then Kamal received a lucrative offer to go and work on another dam project, the Tehri in Uttarakhand, in the far north. He could work there on a two-year contract. He'd earn well and improve the family finances; they could have their home sooner. It was a magnificent offer.

'That's the benefit of an MIT degree,' he said, laughing. 'It's an offer I can't refuse.'

When the two years were up, he'd come home, get back his old job but with a better salary – his present employers certainly didn't want to lose him – and build their home.

The set-up with the Iyengars was so ideal it would be nonsensical for Caroline to accompany Kamal to Uttarakhand. She was basically happy with her Tamil family; Sundari and she were now close friends, and she was learning Tamil. Moving to the north would mean a new language, a new environment, disruptive for all. Sundari was eager to help and advise Caroline in all matters concerning pregnancy and childbirth; with six children of her own, she was an expert. And Janaki, too, was excited and longed to help out. Yes, it would be foolish for Caroline to move. But once again, reality did not adhere to the plan.

. . .

Caroline sat leaning against the headboard, holding her one-day-old baby, Asha, at her breast. The baby's wails were heartbreaking. Asha refused the nipple, and Caroline wept along with the baby. Sundari knocked, and entered.

'She still won't latch on?'

'No!' Caroline wailed. 'She's just crying and crying. I don't know what to do. It's been a whole day now. She'll starve!'

'No, she won't. Some babies need more time. Try to calm down and be confident. Babies can feel the mummy's agitation and fears.'

'But I can't help it! Of course I'm worried. I want to feed my baby. Maybe I should use the bottle after all. I just don't know what I'm doing wrong.'

'You're not doing anything wrong, but you need to relax.'

But it wasn't possible to relax on command, no matter how much she wanted to. The baby continued to scream and squirm in her arms. Caroline held Asha out to Sundari.

'Take her. Maybe you can calm her down.'

Sundari held out her arms. 'Come here, little Asha.'

She took the baby, cuddled it and smiled down at her. Asha immediately stopped crying and nuzzled against the bulge in Sundari's sari blouse.

Sundari looked up. 'Caroline, I didn't want to mention it before but as it's a whole day, and I've got lots of milk, I wondered...'

'Yes, yes! You feed her. I just want her fed. I didn't want to ask you, but...'

Sundari sat down cross-legged on the floor, took out a breast, offered it to the baby. Asha immediately began to suck, eagerly. Caroline burst into tears, sank down on the bed, buried her head in a pillow.

'See? See? It's me she hates! I'm a terrible mom and she knows it.'

'Don't be silly, Caroline. It's just nerves. You probably

haven't even slept properly. You're exhausted. You need to sleep. Just sleep, and leave her to me. She'll be fine. And when you're rested you can try again. I'm sure it'll be fine. Don't worry.'

'I just wish Kamal was here.'

'He'll be here as soon as he can. He'll help you relax. You're a family now, think of it. Now go to sleep. I'll take care of her and so will Janaki when she comes home. She's so excited to have another girl in the family.'

'Not exactly in *her* family.'

'Of course not. Asha is your family. I meant in the house. Now I'm going to take Asha, and I want you to sleep for a long, long time. And when you wake up, you'll see that everything is fine.'

Sundari rose to her feet, the baby still latched to her breast. She covered Caroline with a sheet, gave her a kiss on the forehead, drew the curtains and left the room with Asha.

And so it continued. Asha refused to drink Caroline's milk and seemed to relish Sundari's. Caroline was slightly jealous, but at the same time, slightly relieved. And Sundari didn't mind at all.

'But can you manage with two babies?' Caroline asked, again and again. 'What about Dev?'

'I have enough milk for both,' Sundari said with a laugh, as she took the squalling Asha confidently from Caroline's arms and laid her at her breast. It was always the same. Asha's lips would close around the nipple; the screaming would stop. And every time, Caroline breathed a sigh of relief and tucked her own breast away. Was it wrong to feel such relief? And such guilt? But no. She was just so happy to see her daughter drinking with such gusto.

Sundari did not just take care of the feeding. She seemed to actually enjoy the more unpleasant aspects of baby-care, like the changing of nappies. Again, Caroline felt guilty.

'Are you sure?' she said, when Sundari sniffed the baby's bottom and took her away for a change. 'Two babies, and a toddler – it's a lot!'

'Janaki's a big help. She loves helping out. Don't you, Janaki?'

Janaki nodded eagerly. She was now thirteen years old, already her mother's right hand in the home. And she loved babies.

'You're my baby, so you'll be a baby-amma!'

Janaki laughed. 'Of course!' she said. 'I'm Asha's baby-amma.'

NINE

GINGEE, TAMIL NADU

Asha was two weeks old before she met her father.

At Madras airport he saw her right away, behind the wall of swarthy Indians waving their signs behind the barrier. Caroline stood aloof, beyond the fray, just as she was in that sacred place where he held her in his mind. She wore sparkling white cotton trousers and a long, soft blouse batiked in various shades of blue. Her blonde hair, cut short now, was like a sleek, polished cap framing a tanned face, gleaming in the midday sunlight; she held one hand as a visor above her eyes as she scanned the line of passengers pushing their trolleys out of the airport building. At the moment of recognition her face lit up, as at the sudden emergence of the sun from behind a cloud; her hand shot upwards, waving furiously. She ran forward and into his arms.

When they separated again Caroline took his hand and led him to a waiting taxi.

'You didn't bring her?' Kamal said, peering into the back window of the taxi. He felt a twinge of disappointment. Time was so short; their minutes together were precious. She should have brought Asha.

'Oh, no, I left her with Janaki,' said Caroline. 'It's a three-hour drive in this hot sun; it would just have been a hassle.'

'So you had to leave her for six hours? Is that all right? I mean – doesn't she have to be fed?'

'Kamal, I told you. I can't breastfeed, and my milk dried up. It happens often with first-time mothers, you know. But thank goodness Sundari has more than enough and so she has been feeding her. It's practically pouring out! Enough for three babies: Rajan, Dev and Asha.'

Kamal's face fell. 'So you haven't been feeding her at all?'

'Oh, sure!' said Caroline. 'Sundari expresses the milk sometimes and puts it into a bottle, so I can feed her. You can too – you'll love it!'

She squeezed his hand and he squeezed hers back.

'Kamal – you're the father of the most beautiful little girl in the world and you don't know it. I can't wait for you to meet her!'

The drive home was interminable. But then they were there, the taxi bouncing slowly down the unpaved street to the big white house at the end, meandering around the potholes. Children swarmed around the car – for motor vehicles were rarities in this village – running backwards before it or skipping along beside it, slapping its bonnet, grinning in through the open window, calling out to Caroline and Kamal. One little boy in ragged blue shorts threw himself across the bonnet and sprawled there waving; another hooked his elbow in through the open window.

Two others jumped onto the back bumper and clung to the hind parts of the car like stick insects glued to a window.

Kamal, with wise prescience, had brought several packets of wrapped sweets. He opened one with his teeth and held it out of the window, emptying the lemon and orange sweets onto the dusty road. Immediately the children dropped away from the car and fell on them, scrambling on the ground and grappling frantically. Kamal looked out of the rear window, then turned to Caroline.

'Some things never change!' he said.

'And some things do,' she replied. 'Look in front of you.'

Kamal turned around. They had arrived at the Iyengar home; the taxi halted. Janaki, who had either heard the commotion or the hum of the car, or been warned of their coming through the swifter-than-light grapevine, stood in front of the door, a broad smile on her lips and a bundle of Asha in her arms. Sundari came out behind her, wiping her hands on a towel and beaming.

A tiny hand waved clumsily above the bundle. Two small legs hung below it. The rest of Asha was concealed by a thin cotton cloth, but now Janaki changed the position of her arms and held the baby upright in the crook of her arms, one hand bracing her, so that the cloth dropped away from the little bare chest and the child sat as in a comfortable chair, facing her father.

Kamal stared, suddenly silent. Slowly he left the car, not bothering to close the door, and crossed the short stretch of sand to approach his daughter, coming to a stop immediately in front of Janaki. He wanted to speak, to reach for the child, but the words caught in his throat and his arms felt crippled – he could not move them. His breath stopped, it seemed, and his mouth was dry, and his ears had lost their hearing for all the world was silent around him. Even his thoughts had raced headlong into a wall and ceased.

But then his eyes were suddenly involuntarily moist, his arms moving upwards to receive the child that Janaki was holding out towards him. He took Asha as if he had held her a thousand times before, clasped her to his chest and covered her with his crossed forearms and moved away, walking towards the fence and away from the others so that no one could see his face – or his tears.

. . .

Kamal came home again for Asha's first Christmas.

Caroline had tried her best to make it special. She had bought a plastic Christmas tree and decorations in Madras. She had arranged cotton wool around the base of the tree for snow and hung the cheap plastic baubles in glaring red and gold along its branches, and draped long strips of glittering tinsel around it, all in an attempt to reproduce the spirit of Christmas as she remembered it.

It didn't work. Not even the fat candle glowing on its polished brass stand could make her believe it was truly Christmas.

There was no avoiding it. Christmas just wasn't the same. Again and again her thoughts drifted back to home. Again her heart lurched away from the place and the present, back to the memories seared into her being.

You couldn't replace home. The blazing fire, flames leaping in the hearth, spreading warmth and well-being around the cosy living room. Dad, in his special armchair next to the fireplace, smoking his pipe, reading the newspaper. Mom, bustling in and out of the kitchen with Christmas cookies and punch or eggnog. She and her brothers on Christmas morning in their pyjamas, tearing off the paper from their presents, squealing in joy, excited voices squealing with pleasure. Granny and Gramp sitting on the sofa at the back, looking on in fond contentment.

It just wasn't the same in Gingee.

'Look at this angel,' she said, handing Kamal a tinny white thing that had fallen from one of the branches. 'Isn't she unbelievably tacky? But I couldn't find anything else. And believe me, I really scoured the stores. I guess Christmas isn't a big thing here.'

'It isn't,' Kamal said. He looked down at Asha, who was wearing a bright red dress, which set off perfectly the jet black of her hair and her sparkling eyes, now fixed on the bright angel. Kamal, as he had done so often, marvelled at the perfect little features.

'Christmas is something we read about in books. I'm sorry.'

'Well, could we at least sing some carols?'

'I'm not so good at carols,' Kamal admitted. 'Remember, I'd never even heard "*Jingle Bells* till I got to America. So I don't know if... Hey, what's the matter? Caro, Caro, why're you crying?'

Caroline wiped away a tear with her bare forearm. 'It's nothing, I guess. Well, no. It's just that... it's just that... that...'

Kamal gently laid Asha on her blanket on the floor and leaned towards his wife. Her face was turned away from him, huge tears rolling down her cheeks. He placed his hand on her chin and gently turned her face up towards him.

'Tell me. Please tell me what's bothering you. You know you can tell me everything. Here.'

He gave her a clean square of cloth, one of several they used for Asha to burp on, and she wiped her cheeks with it. 'Can't you tell me what's the matter?'

'I... I suppose it's just Christmas,' Caroline admitted. 'A bit of homesickness. Nostalgia and all that. I feel so... so sentimental... I sort of miss my parents for the first time. And snow. And church. Santa Claus. All that soppy stuff. Family stuff, I guess. And Christmas dinner. The turkey! Oh, Kamal, what I wouldn't give for turkey. And apple pie. When... when I was a kid I used to be in the church choir and we used to walk around town singing carols and collecting for charity. I had this muff and a red coat with a furry bonnet and it was all so warm and snuggly and I would so love to offer all of that to Asha and I can't. She'll never know Christmas. She'll grow up without snow and Santa!'

But she couldn't speak anymore because her face was buried in Kamal's warm shoulder. Kamal patted her back and held her close. She let the sobs come and they broke from her in stifled, breathless gulps. Finally she moved so that her lips were free and she could speak.

'Oh, Kamal! I don't want to complain because at least Asha is happy and that's all I care about. But *I'm* not, Kamal. I'm not happy. I'm so desperately homesick. And I feel bad because I was the one who was so in love with India and wanted to come. And now I hate India. I long for America. The holidays. Christmas! Winter is my favourite season and I miss it. No snow, just heat and sunshine, no carols, no Santa, no church, no tree, no presents. Asha's first Christmas, and it's a complete wash-out. Just like Thanksgiving. All those sweet American rituals and traditions. She's missing out on all of them. And so am I. I don't like the toilets or the showers, or the crowds or the language. I hate the food. No Thanksgiving turkey. And Asha will become a little Hindu girl!'

'Oh, my darling!' whispered Kamal. 'I'm sorry. I'm so sorry. I guess it was a mistake, bringing you to India. We should have stayed in America. I should never have brought you here. It's all my fault.'

'No, Kamal, no. It's not your fault. It's mine. I was the one who had this unrealistic need to come to India. I was the one who insisted. I forced it. And now... now I'm paying the price.'

She took a deep breath, wiped her cheeks on his shirt, and in her bravest voice said, 'I brought us here. I have to learn to cope. And I will. That's all there is to it.'

She sighed. 'But I do miss Mom and Dad. I miss them so much.'

'Write to them,' said Kamal at once. 'They miss you too. You know the way you feel about Asha? That's what your mom felt about you, when you were small. You must let her know she has a granddaughter. It's time to make amends. You must write to them.'

She bit her bottom lip, and took a deep breath. 'Yes. I will.'

TEN

GINGEE, TAMIL NADU, ONE YEAR LATER

Sundari walked across the main court of the Gingee main temple with Asha, Rajan and Dev. At the Sanctum Sanctorum, the Holiest of Holies, she smeared holy ash on Asha's forehead with three fingers: the mark of Shiva, signifying renunciation. Then, with the third finger of her right hand, she dipped her finger into the vermillion powder and placed a little red dot, a *bindi*, on Asha's forehead. She did the same to all three children, and herself.

Sundari and the children all bowed down at the temple shrine, while Brahmin priests chanted the appropriate Sanskrit verses. She laid flowers and fruit at the altar, placed her palms in *namaste*, bowed again and turned to walk away with the children.

Caroline stood waiting outside the temple; she didn't feel comfortable about attending these Hindu ceremonies, but she could hardly keep Asha away. Asha would scream and fight to go with the others. So Caroline always waited, outside the temple.

Afterwards, Sundari and Caroline walked through the busy market with the children, Caroline holding Rajan's hand.

Sundari carried Asha strapped to her back and Dev on her hip; it all seemed so natural, so effortless, as if they were a part of Sundari.

This was something Caroline could never be, never do. Something lacking, she thought. *Terrible mother, terrible mother.* She couldn't help it. The words were like a mantra, constantly running through her mind.

They bought the needed vegetables, caught an auto-rickshaw, and went home.

Caroline sat once again at her desk, writing a letter.

Now and then she glanced up, through the open window, where she could see Janaki playing with the toddler Asha in the garden.

'*I'm a bad mom, Kamal,*' she typed. '*A terrible mom, and Asha knows it. She hates me, and there's nothing I can do about it.*'

The thought was becoming an obsession. It seemed the more she thought it, the more it came true; as if even the thought wiped confidence from her mind.

Pensively, she watched as Janaki pushed Asha on a swing hanging from a tree. Asha was laughing and looked overjoyed. Caroline looked down at the letter and wrote again, gripping the pen too tightly. She made many mistakes as she wrote, because of the distraction in the garden.

Sundari says it's all in my mind but <u>she</u> can talk – Asha loves her and her first word was Amma – to her, Sundari, not me. She thinks Sundari is her mom! I'm actually jealous, Kamal. I don't know how to deal with this. I'm a hot mess.

She put down her pen, got up and walked outside, joining Janaki in the garden. Janaki was sitting on a log, watching as

Asha, Rajan and Dev played in the sandpit. Caroline squatted down next to her. Janaki looked up.

'Hello, Caroline Auntie. Look at her. She's so cute, I could eat her up!'

Caroline forced a laugh. 'Well, I'm not sure I'd like that!' She held out her arms. 'Asha! Asha, darling! Come give Mommy a kiss!'

Asha ignored her, and laughed with Rajan and Dev as they built sandcastles.

Janaki said, 'She's such a happy child. A darling. And so pretty... what's the matter, Caroline Auntie?'

Caroline burst into tears, sprang to her feet and rushed indoors. Asha looked up but continued to play. Janaki got up, started to follow Caroline into the bungalow, then shrugged and sat down again.

A week later, Caroline was sitting on her bed, reading a book when a knock came on the door. It opened a bit, and Sundari put her head around it.

'Hello, Caroline! A surprise for you!'

She opened the door wide and Kamal walked in, his arms held out for her. Caroline threw aside the book, jumped to her feet and catapulted herself into his arms. She buried her face in his shoulder, crying.

'My darling, I'm sorry. I'm so sorry. It's all my fault.'

'No, it's nobody's fault. If anything, it's my fault. I failed as a mom.'

'No, you haven't. I've let you down. I should have known. I should have stayed with you. I should have—'

'Stop blaming yourself! Maybe it's nobody's fault. Maybe life is just like that.'

'You need a break, Caroline. So listen: I took two weeks off work. You and me, we're going to Madras. We'll stay at a hotel, swim in the pool, get you a good romantic dinner. What d'you say to that?'

'And Asha? We'll take her?'

'No. It's just us. She'll be fine with Sundari. But you: you need to heal. You need to find yourself, as a woman, as a wife, as a person. You're obsessing too much about being a bad mother. We're going to escape for a few days. And I've got some news.'

'What?'

'I'll tell you tonight, at dinner. Candlelight poolside dinner at the Connemara.'

Kamal and Caroline sat at a table, a candle glowing between them. The atmosphere was luxurious and romantic: palm trees swaying gently around the pool, a live band playing Western music, a singer crooning away to 'The Way You Look Tonight'.

On the dance floor, several couples were dancing, while waiters in uniform glided between the tables, bearing trays. A waiter stopped at their table and slid a plate before her.

'Steak! I can't believe it!'

'You need a husband again, a husband who spoils you and shows how much he loves you.'

'Oh Kamal. It's not your fault... it's just...'

'Let's not talk about it, Caroline. Let's just enjoy the evening. Enjoy the food. Just be here, with me, now.'

They ate then, in silence, Caroline relishing every mouthful.

'What was the news you're going to tell me?'

'Later. Just enjoy the food.'

The meal over, their plates empty, Caroline laid her knife and fork together and looked up at Kamal with deep satisfaction.

'So, what's the big news?'

'Listen, Caro. I've made a decision. We can't go on like this.

We are parents and that has to come first. We need to reclaim our daughter. So, I'm quitting my job. My contract was for two years. It expires next year, just before Asha turns two. When that happens we'll return to America. I'll find work there; we'll buy a home. We'll settle down. You'll have all the Thanksgivings and Christmases you need. All the steaks you can eat. Asha will learn to love you because you'll be a brilliant mom and I'll be a brilliant dad. We've made mistakes, but it's not too late to start again. We'll live close to your parents, so they can see Asha.' He leaned across the table, took both her hands in his. 'How'd you like that plan?'

'Oh, Kamal! It sounds perfect...'

'We'll start from scratch. It will all work out. You'll see.'

She squeezed his hands, then let go, leaned across the table and placed her hands on his chin, cupping his face. She gazed into his face, drinking him in.

'You're a darling. And... it sounds perfect, but... but...'

'But what? How can there be a but?'

Caroline said nothing for a few seconds. She closed her eyes and placed her palms together as if in prayer.

'But *Asha*, Kamal. Is it right to tear her away from the family she thinks is hers? The mother she sees as her own? Isn't it the same as taking a child away from its biological mom? All the books say that the bond should not be broken in those early years. She really sees Sundari as her mom, and Sundari loves her like her own children. It's such a tight bond, Kamal, and I don't think we should break it. Yanking her out of a stable home now... it could permanently damage her. It's too soon; even a year from now is too soon.'

'You can't go on sacrificing your own needs for your child!'

'But that's what moms do, Kamal. Real moms. The child's needs come first.'

'But you're so unhappy!'

'Yes, but I'm an adult. I can stick it out a bit longer. I think, long term, we do need to return to America, with Asha. I want her to know all our traditions, go to school there, and do things like sledding and sleepovers. But not yet.'

He shook his head in disagreement.

'Surely...'

Caroline spoke quickly now, as if she had finally convinced herself and had only to convince him. The words tumbled from her lips.

'The first five years, Kamal: they're the formative ones. When she gets older, say six or seven, we can explain it to her and she'll understand, and it will be like a great adventure. We'll show her all the American kids' movies and I bet she'll want to move there. Who wouldn't want to grow up in America? It's a wonderful idea, and thank you for the suggestion. I love you for it. I do.'

Again, she reached out for him. Their hands met across the table.

'...But for the time being, I do think Sundari is the best mom for her. And she has a big sister here, Janaki, and she's so happy. Can you imagine the screams if we were to tear her away? She'd yell the whole flight over! The tantrum to end all tantrums!'

Kamal sighed. 'I guess you're right. But what you just said proves to me that you're wrong: you're not a bad mom, Caroline. You're the best mom in the world, putting your child's needs first, before your own needs. That's what good moms do.' He shrugged. 'You win – for now. But I think we can do it before she's five. We must do it, Caroline. I want *us* to raise our daughter, not the Iyengars.'

'I do too, Kamal. I really do. But we have to choose the right time.'

Kamal could not make it home that Christmas, their third in India. It was just too far, the trip from Uttarakhand.

Another Christmas in a foreign country. Far away from home (her real home), far away from all the things that made Christmas special. Snow. A real tree. Carols. Turkey. And this time, without her husband.

Though there *was* a tree; the only Christmas tree she could find: a small, scrawny fake one. Caroline sighed as she hung the baubles on it, cheap, plastic ones she'd found in a bazaar shop. A few presents lay scattered under the tree.

On Christmas Day, the Iyengar family indulged her; they all gathered around, trying to sing carols, but only she knew the words or the melodies. It was a disaster. The children liked the presents, though – books she'd bought in Madras.

Caroline walked down the aisle of a small supermarket, throwing packets of processed food into her trolley, familiar American labels. She craved these things and had found a small supermarket in Madras that sold them all in this particular aisle, labelled 'Foreign Food'.

She threw package after package in her trolley. She arrived at the *meats* section, her favourite. She'd become so weak and scrawny; she simply longed for a juicy hamburger. Anything, really, just as long as it was meat. That was what she craved above all. Meat. Some people are simply not made to be vegetarians.

She threw tin after tin into the trolley. Frankfurters. Corned beef. Spam. Tinned spaghetti Bolognese.

She picked up a can of tinned ravioli, threw it into the trolley.

Once back at home, she opened the ravioli can, poured the contents into a saucepan, heated it up, ladled it into a bowl. Ate up every scrap of it, licking the bowl with her fingers.

· · ·

Caroline, lying in bed, groaned and grasped her stomach. She got up and rushed to the toilet, bent over the bowl, vomited and retched, and, even when her stomach was completely empty, it continued to growl. The pain was excruciating. She leaned against the wall, holding her stomach, groaning loudly.

She made her way to the cottage door and called, loudly, for Sundari. Then she collapsed to the floor.

Sundari was with her in a trice; helping her to her feet, she half-carried, half-dragged Caroline back to bed.

A doctor came in the morning, the private doctor Caroline had engaged throughout her pregnancy and for the birth. Caroline was unable to talk to him; bent double in bed, it was all she could do to stop from screaming out loud at the pain.

Sundari fished the empty ravioli can out of the trash and showed it to the doctor. He read the label, and, looking up, said, 'This is two years out of date! Look at the dust on it. And the can has a dent, look.' He showed her the can. 'Did anyone else eat this?'

'No, just her.'

'I'm going to send an ambulance for her. She needs to go to hospital in Madras immediately. Food poisoning can be dangerous.'

Caroline felt better at last. She sat up in bed, talking on the phone. It had taken a medical emergency to finally melt the ice between her and her parents. She had done as Kamal had advised, and, weeks ago, had written to them. They had responded, but their letters had been cool and loveless; she had clearly not been forgiven.

But a telegram from Kamal, with the news of Caroline's illness, had finally restored the lost bond. Her mother had put through this call to the hospital, insisting on knowing every detail.

'Yes, Mom. Food poisoning! Pretty serious. The doctor's keeping me here for observation, in case I develop botulism. But... oh, Mom. They did blood tests here and I've got anaemia from lack of iron and I'm just so, just so... weak... and...'

She burst into tears. 'And oh, Mom! It's more than that. It's not just... I shouldn't have... I wish... Oh, Mom. I miss you so much. I miss America so much!' She paused, to listen to her mother. Then said, 'I'd love to come home. Yes, yes. I'd love to. The doctors here are pretty good but... I don't know. I don't know anything... I'm so tired. I feel so bad. I feel terrible. I wish... oh, Mom. I just want to come home.'

It was a long, drawn-out wail. Then she listened, nodding, shaking her head. Then, 'Oh, Mom, if you knew how I long to see you guys again! But... but...' She burst into tears again, then listened once more.

'Yes, yes, I hear you. You're right. Maybe you're right. Maybe I just need to...' She nodded, vigorously. 'Yes, yes, it's true. I'm exhausted. Yes, I do need a bit of... maybe... just for a month, to recover. If you could arrange that... Oh, Mom, that sounds just wonderful!'

ELEVEN

GINGEE, TAMIL NADU

Kamal held the bottle to Asha's lips, but she pushed angrily against it with her little clenched fist. She kicked and wriggled, and twisted around so that her head was bent back. Kamal tried to put his arms around her, hold her in the crook of his arm to try again with the bottle, but she lashed it away again and frowned, squawking in fury.

She twisted around again; she had heard sounds in the kitchen and knew who was making them. Kamal gave up and allowed her to scramble to the floor. Immediately Asha was running at full speed towards the source of the sound. She disappeared into the kitchen. A moment later Sundari appeared in the doorway, Asha in her arms.

'She ran away again,' she said smilingly, and held the child out to her father. Kamal reached for her but Asha kicked his hands away, squirming and screaming and struggling, refusing to be handed over.

Sundari smiled. 'The Terrible Twos, they call it in America. Caroline told me. Besides, she just doesn't know you well enough. It will come.'

'And her mom's gone,' Kamal reminded her.

'Yes, that is true. But to tell you the truth, I don't know if she even noticed that. Caroline has always had problems bonding with her, and it hasn't changed. Asha thinks I am her mother, and Janaki is a close second.'

'I noticed that,' said Kamal.

'Well, what was I to do? Whenever the child cried, Caroline panicked. She gave her to me and Asha was immediately quiet. Should I have refused to take her? And when Dev needed me, Janaki took over Asha's care. And now it's the same thing. She doesn't know you're her father. She won't even let you feed her.'

Sundari bent over and picked up the bottle that was lying on the ground, wiped the teat with a corner of her sari and handed the bottle to Asha, who was already reaching for it, gurgling with anticipation.

'The thing is,' Kamal said slowly, 'I don't know how long Caroline will be gone. You don't mind carrying on as before?'

As soon as he could, Kamal had managed to get a month's unpaid leave for a 'family emergency'. This was serious. He had to bond with Asha, because one day, they'd all be moving to America. But just as Caroline had said, it wasn't easy. Asha was simply too attached to Sundari and Janaki. She was nearly three, now. She still drank at Sundari's breast, but also liked her bottle and cosy cuddles. But not from Kamal.

'Of course not. Nothing will change.' Sundari changed Asha from one arm to the other, away from Kamal. Asha lay luxuriantly in the curve of her arm, sucking at her bottle with eyes half-closed in bliss. She looked as if she belonged there, would always belong there.

'I'll keep on paying you, of course, even though Caroline isn't with you. I'll keep paying as if nothing has changed. Room and board, till she comes back. It's for childcare now.'

'*If* she comes back.'

'What do you mean, if? Of course she'll come back!'

'Well, the way she was carrying on, I actually doubt that.

Your wife hates India, Kamal, hadn't you noticed? Well, I had, even if she tried to hide it. She hates India and she won't be back. Trust me.'

'Well, we planned on moving to America later this year anyway. She's nearly three; after her birthday, we decided.'

'Not with Asha, I assume? You will leave Asha with me.'

'No! The plan is for all three of us to move to America as soon as my contract expires. We told you this, Sundari! Of course we'll take Asha! We want to be a proper family at last.'

Sundari turned her back.

'Well, good luck with that. Of course, you have every right to take Asha. But you understand you will be tearing her life apart? She does not know you at all and she has a very poor relationship with her mother. I don't know how you can even *consider* taking her out of the family she knows and loves. In my eyes that is child abuse.'

'Don't exaggerate, Sundari! She'll get used to us and to life in America. She's so small. Children adapt very quickly and easily.'

'And what do you know about children? Just because you're a big-shot foreign-educated foreign-returned engineer doesn't mean you know *everything*, you know. You should listen to me – I'm a mother. *Her* mother, she thinks. I know this child, and I know you cannot tear her from the family she knows and loves without doing her terrible damage. If you want to take that responsibility, then go ahead. But don't blame me when the damage is done. It's your child.'

Kamal turned and walked away. He had to think. Sundari, of course, was basically right – it was just the *way* she said it that bothered him. So bossy! It was true what they said: that women might have a socially inferior position in Indian society, but in the home they were the undisputed head of everything, the queen of the household, and men were the willing servants.

He'd known it from his own upbringing, of course. Daadi

was the boss. And he saw it here, with Sundari. Sundari's husband submitted to her without a murmur, and now she expected such submission from him, too, even regarding his own child.

He wanted to protest, to argue, to shout, even, and yet he couldn't, because at the heart of it she was right. It was not biology that made a parent, but love, bonding and care. And Asha loved Sundari more than she loved her biological parents; Sundari had cared for her more than her parents had. The bond between the Iyengars and Asha was deep and lasting, whereas the bond between Asha and her parents was loose and weak and one-sided and complicated.

Yes, she was loved with a passion by both parents – but that love had never found expression in everyday life. The last thing he wanted was to cause Asha damage – would he, by taking her away to America in a few months' time? But how could he – they – leave her here? Would Caroline return, once she had fully recovered her health, to help him fight for Asha, to make a renewed effort to win her affection? Somehow, he doubted it.

In the end he returned to Uttarakhand. Sundari had won. Of course, Asha's needs must come first. He couldn't tear her out of her familiar surroundings, her home, away from her Amma and baby-amma.

He wrote to Caroline, who agreed that he had done the right thing and wrote back:

We must do what's right for her. I mean, yes, I do feel guilty about not being a good mother and leaving her behind. But, Kamal, I was truly ill. I had to go. The doctors said my health was terrible and that food poisoning could have killed me. I needed to recover with proper medical care. In America. But even apart from my physical health: my breakdown was simply the last straw. Mentally, I mean. I had to come home. It wasn't just physical. I was suffering from depression and had to get away. I've seen a therapist, who said it was absolutely the right thing to do, and I could do it knowing that Asha is truly happy and well cared for. She couldn't have a better mother than Sundari, and I say that as her real mother.

What I mean to say is, Kamal... I want to stay here and build a life for us all. The life we talked about, remember? It seems that Fate has intervened to move that plan along sooner rather than later. We need to be patient.

One day, hopefully soon, we will all be together. Until then, I am trying to put my life together here in Cambridge, get back on my feet, build a foundation for us all.

What I really need to do, Kamal, is think about my own future, my own career. South Asian Studies: how useless now! I need to do something else, something more relevant. I want to go back to college, get a more practical degree.

I'm torn in two directions. Law would be the sensible thing. My parents are urging me in that direction. But I'm tired of being sensible, and a law degree would take ages. I want to do something I truly love, and I'm really pulled towards the Creative Arts Therapy course at Lesley College. That's something I'd love to do, and the good thing is, I can live with my parents. So that's the direction I'm going in.

I've reconciled completely with Mom and Dad. They are happy to have me stay with them, and even if I don't study law, they'll be happy just to have me here. I don't think they're yet accepting of you, my darling, but we can live with that, can't we? You won't have to see them. They'll adore Asha, and maybe in time, once you're here and we're a proper family, they will learn to reconcile with you as her father. I'll do my best to bring that about. I love all of you and I want us to be one big happy family. I'm sure it will happen eventually.

Reconciled with Caroline's decision – which he agreed with, in principle, though it would mean a delay in the grand plan for them all to come together in America – Kamal returned with renewed vigour to his job in Uttarakhand. It was for the family, for the future. For the time being, he was glad that Caroline was happy. That Asha was happy. Even if the whole situation made him desperately unhappy.

But in the end Caroline became *too* happy. Their phone calls – always difficult because of the time difference – grew more and more rare. Letters grew few and far between.

Yet still, Kamal suspected nothing. He answered her letters and wrote his own in the long gaps between hers. Kamal was not given to open emotionality. He did not, could not, show his feelings in writing. Perhaps his own letters were a little stilted, a little cool, even. Whatever it was, at the end of the year Kamal received a devastating letter. A letter, clothed in the kindest of words, that nevertheless broke his heart and ended his dreams of relocation and a happy family in America.

Dear Kamal.

This is the hardest letter I've ever written in my life, and believe me, the pain of writing it is equal to the pain I know it will cause you. I do apologise for taking so long to reply to your last letters. That I haven't called you in months. The truth is, I didn't know what to say; I had no words. How could I put into a letter all the changes I have been going through in the last six months? It was just too much, and I chose to keep silent until the turbulence calmed down and I could arrive at some sort of a resolution, some sort of a conclusion, a confirmation that I have made the right decision.

Kamal, it truly breaks my heart to tell you this but I have met someone else, someone with whom I am completely comfortable, in all areas of life. His name is Wayne. It is as if all the loose ends of my life are tied up with Wayne. He is an up-and-coming attorney at Dad's firm and... well, we just clicked. These things happen – the chemistry was there from the beginning.

I did try hard to fight the attraction; I did, Kamal. I do take my marriage vows seriously, but the hurdles for the two of us have simply been too high to overcome. The physical separation, the cultural differences, the geographical problems: all of these have contributed to the distance between us.

I need a husband who is at my side, and apart from the honeymoon phase of our marriage this has just not been the case. It's just not working, Kamal. I'm sure you have felt it too? I'm sure you have, but your loyalty and sense of duty – those very Indian qualities that I admire so much – have kept you bound to me.

I think we should both be free, Kamal. Free to explore our lives and to find other, better alternatives for our paths forward. I know you will be hurt by this letter but one day you will see it as a blessing: I am setting you free. Free to find the right future for yourself, a better partner. I am sure there is a beautiful Indian woman out there, near your workplace, someone just perfect for you.

It's not that I don't love you – I do, but in a very quiet, passionless way. It's not enough, Kamal. It's not what I imagine I should feel for my husband. I don't feel the butterflies. It's not good enough for you. You will surely find someone who loves you as much as you deserve. You are such a good man; you are wasted on me. And we will always be bound together because we have Asha.

Asha! My darling Asha. My one consolation is that she is in the best hands possible, in a family that loves her. A child needs a stable family, with both parents, brothers and sisters, a stable home, a nest where she can grow and thrive. We have never offered her that. The Iyengars have. Sundari writes often and sends photographs, and I am confident that we have made the best choice, the unselfish choice: we have chosen what is best for her, and not what we want.

I often felt guilty about not being a good mother, but Sundari is just that. Mothers have such a high status in India – they are next to God, and I could never live up to that. I no longer feel that guilt. Just knowing she is in good hands is enough for me, and that makes me a good mother, comfortable with my decision. There are many ways to be a good mother.

I will always write her letters, send her photos, so she will always know she has a second mother – a third mother, because isn't Janaki her little mother too, her baby-amma! And I will visit her as soon as I can, and hopefully often – once a year. But I cannot tear her away from her home, from the people she regards as her parents, from her family, from her culture.

Not just yet. When she is six or seven, she will understand better and as we said already: maybe she'll be eager to come to America at that age. It will be an adventure. I could even invite Janaki to come with her, as a vacation. That would be fun. And she will love it here and want to stay. Now, it's just too early and it would break her heart.

I'm hoping that you feel the same way, Kamal. That when you find the right woman for you – and you will – you will resist the urge to tear Asha away from the family she regards as her own. You will have other children, as will I, and you will always be her father, but I hope that as a father you will always choose what is best for her and however much you want her, I am hoping you will do the right thing. I can see you coming to live in America one day, so that we'll all be together eventually. Until then, please visit her as often as you can; you are so much closer than I am. Perhaps return to your original workplace.

I'm not asking for a divorce as yet. I have three more years of study and we're not planning to marry before I graduate. We're doing this the proper, traditional way. I guess I was always a daddy's girl at heart and it's good to be back in the heart of my family. I hope you, too, will find peace, and soon.

On that note, Kamal, I embrace you as a sister and friend, not as a wife, and hope you read these words in the right spirit and know that my decision is the right one – for both of us. I know you will be hurt at first but trust me, in time you will know that it is best, for all of us.

All my love, Caroline

Kamal was devastated. He had not been expecting this, not at all. For him, fidelity and trust were at the heart of a marriage, and he had not at all, as Caroline hinted, felt that it wasn't working. The difficulties they faced – well, they were challenges to what was basically a strong marriage, he'd thought, and would make that marriage stronger yet.

Challenges, after all, were at the heart of strength; anything that was too easy just wasn't worth having. Challenges gave muscle to a relationship, because you had to work all the harder to keep it alive: a muscle needed to be worked in order to be strong, for otherwise it would grow slack and useless.

Kamal had worked his own muscle; Caroline, it seemed, hadn't. For how else could she do this thing?

As for Caroline's suggestion, that he find another woman, another wife – it floored him. Did she think a wife was like a shirt that you just changed when you felt the old one didn't suit you anymore? Was this really the woman he had married? Was her outlook so very shallow? Or was this just the American way? Perhaps he really was too Indian for her.

That must be it. It was the only explanation he could think of. And now he had no choice in the matter but must live with Caroline's choice. In his heart he would always be married to her. But one thing was certain: Asha's well-being must come first. And in this one thing Caroline was right: thank goodness for the Iyengars.

But what about *him*? What about the turmoil, the sense of abandonment, the disappointment, the pain, of his loss? He had built his life on the hope of a new beginning with Caroline and Asha, in America. What now? His job seemed futile; and unlike Caroline, he had no one in the world except Asha.

He doubled his efforts to be a good father. Caroline's excuses simply did not add up, for him. Surely it couldn't be so difficult to win the heart of a small child?

Determined to do his best, now that his marriage had fallen apart, Kamal rushed back to Gingee. But Asha did not know him, did not want to know him. She hid behind Sundari's skirts, shrinking away from his open arms, crying when he hugged her, resisting Sundari's gentle coaxing: 'Go to Daddy, Asha, go to Daddy like a good girl!' But Asha obviously didn't care for him.

'You see how she is wary of you,' Sundari said, taking the child into her arms and handing her a bottle of water. 'That is normal at this age; to her you are a stranger. The first three years are most crucial in the life of a child. A child needs stability. Familiar faces. A steady home. She has that here, with us. You cannot just tear a child from one home and put it in another, and now you are not even a married couple.'

'I know that, Sundari. Caroline and I know that. Now that Caroline is in America and building a new life, I have to get her used to me as a father, separately. I'll visit as often as I can to get her used to me. I think as she grows older it will be easier.'

Sundari nodded. 'That's true. Still the child will need a mother. You realise that, don't you?'

Kamal nodded. 'I know I can never be father *and* mother to her.'

'So you will have to marry again, once Caroline and you are divorced. Very quickly.'

Kamal shook his head vigorously. 'No. I won't marry again. Caroline was the love of my life. I can never replace her.'

Sundari smiled knowingly. Asha smiled too, gazing up at Sundari and hooking her forefinger into the woman's bottom lip. She threw her empty bottle to the ground, where it rolled into a corner. Asha twisted around in Sundari's arms, saw the bottle and struggled to be put down. Sundari placed her on the floor, and she darted off to retrieve the bottle.

'Ah, that's what you say now. However, once the sadness has faded, you will start searching once more – you will try to fill the emptiness. You must start looking for a new bride. A new mother for Asha. Why not ask that grandmother of yours, that woman who thinks she is a queen? I'm sure she would be eager to find a good match for you. Or if you like, I will help. My husband has some excellent connections, you know. It is always better to have a go-between in these marriage matters.'

'So Caroline told you that stupid story about my grandmother,' said Kamal. 'I knew she couldn't keep it to herself.' He shook his head, held out his open palm as if to repel the very suggestion. 'But, no. You're wrong. I won't remarry. I'm certain of that.'

'How will you look after Asha, then, when Asha is older

and you take her away? It's not as if you have a mother who would help out.'

'Other men have raised children alone.'

'Maybe in those foreign countries. Not here, not in India. Here she has two mothers, Janaki and me. We'll be happy to have her for as long as possible. In fact, Janaki would be heart-broken if you took Asha away. She already feels all the love of a mother for her, even though she is so young.'

Asha, meanwhile, had clenched the rubber teat expertly between four tiny teeth and, the bottle swinging gaily before her, returned to Sundari's feet where she pulled herself upright and made the appropriate noises. Sundari bent over and picked her up. Asha pulled the *pallu* of Sundari's sari over her face and tried to engage her in a game of hide-and-seek. She ignored Kamal completely.

Kamal felt despair wash over him like a cold and final wave. He still reeled at the thought of Caroline's betrayal; he felt inca-pable of making a single decision. He wanted Caroline. He ached for her. Where she had been there was a huge black gaping hole inside him, and he stood precariously at its edge, tottering, bracing himself against a fall. Asha was his only anchor, his only consolation.

He looked at the child in Sundari's arms in despair; Asha was now twirling a curl of her thick mop of silky hair around a fat finger, gazing up adoringly at the woman she called Amma.

Kamal knew he had rights. There had never been a proper contract made between them and the Iyengar family. No court in the world would remove his and Caroline's parental rights. He could fight this in court, and win, and take Asha with him to Uttarakhand.

She will never call me Daddy, Kamal thought, even though I can love her enough for that love to fill the emptiness in me. She is all I have in the world now. But where do I begin? What can I do? To provide for her is my greatest duty. But she must be cared for, mothered. I cannot do both. To take her away from Sundari would be heartless, egoistic; it would be serving my own purpose, using her. She is happiest here. Caroline and Sundari are right. Her happiness must come first. I must love her enough to lose her. True love is letting go. I can love her with a love not bound by time or space.

Two days later Kamal left Gingee. Reconciled to Asha's place as a daughter of the Iyengar household, he went back to work a week earlier than planned, after making arrangements with the Iyengars for the continued payments for Asha's maintenance. He plunged into his work, and that became the focus of his life.

He would save every penny for when Asha grew up and became an independent woman. He lived a quiet, simple life. He was an introvert, a recluse, doing his job well but with no social life to speak of.

He was doing it all for Asha. He would save up for her, so that one day the world would be open to her. And so the years flipped past, turning like the pages of a book.

TWELVE
GINGEE, TAMIL NADU, 1990

Janaki

Janaki finally persuaded her mother that she was not yet ready for marriage. Sundari, who had been keeping her eyes open for a suitable groom since Janaki was a child, was sorely disappointed, as she was keen to send out feelers to the parents of several eligible bachelors. But Janaki was adamant. She wanted to continue her education.

'There are so many fish in the sea,' she said, 'and I will meet so many nice boys when I am a student. I am sure these boys you found for me will find nice brides. Don't worry about it, Amma. I am only eighteen and, if I meet someone I like I will let you know, and you can have great fun chatting to his amma about marriage. Just a few years more.'

And so Sundari, trying to be modern and liberal, had agreed. Appa, being compliant to all of Sundari's decisions, and anyway in favour of women's education, also agreed; he was willing to maintain his daughter for a further four years, and so Janaki went off to Madras. Asha, now six years old, wept bitterly when Janaki left. Janaki embraced her and comforted her.

'See, little sweetheart, I am not far away. Just a few hours. I will come as often as I can and visit you. And when you are a bit bigger you can visit me too. I will show you Madras. I will show you the sea! I will take you to Higginbotham's Bookstore and buy you lots of English books. You'd like that, wouldn't you?'

Asha was an avid reader and that last suggestion comforted her somewhat, because Gingee did not have an English language bookshop, and she loved the stories of English children eating strawberries and cream and drinking ginger beer, and looking for treasure or going off to boarding school. Still, though, she was not satisfied.

'Why you have to go, Janaki? Why you have to leave me?'

'I am going to learn all about computers,' Janaki said. 'I am going to study at the Indian Institute of Technology in Madras. It's a great honour to study there and I am so happy I got a place. And if you work hard at school, you too can study there or somewhere else in Madras or Bangalore, or even in Bombay or Delhi.'

'The Indian Institute of Technology,' repeated Asha slowly. 'It sounds scary!'

'It's not at all scary, Baby.' Janaki laughed. 'It's one of the best technology universities in all of India. I'm going to study something called Information Technology. It's a wonderful opportunity, especially for a girl. Now come on, give me a nice long hug and a kiss and let me go – I have to finish packing. Run along now and remember Higginbotham's! So many books. You will be in paradise!'

Asha had to be content with that. Janaki would go off into the big wide world, and one day she, Asha, would follow. They would talk every day on the phone, Janaki promised, but it wasn't a promise she was able to keep because the hostel didn't have a phone. And anyway, there were only so many hours in the day and they were both so busy.

Janaki did keep her promise to come home as often as she could – after all, Madras, which they were now supposed to call Chennai, wasn't that far away from Gingee. Just a three-hour bus ride. And one day she kept another promise and took Asha to see the sea. Asha frolicked in delight in the surf and went back home having made the firm decision that one day she, too, would go to Madras to study. Janaki showed her the Indian Institute of Technology and the little room where she lived in a hostel for female students, which she shared with a girl called Nadiya.

'It's just a small room but it's my home, and I love it!' Janaki told her.

Nadiya became Janaki's best friend. And just as she had predicted, Janaki met some nice young men and it wasn't long before she met someone she could love. He was an aeronautical engineering student at the same university, and his name was Giridhar. Their parents wrote to each other and eventually the marriage was arranged, to take place a year after Janaki's gradu-ation. Sundari was appeased – Giridhar was an excellent match. His father was a surgeon. It was all nicely settled.

Gingee, 1994

For Asha's tenth birthday, which fell on a Saturday, Janaki came home with a huge cardboard box.

'Guess what's in here, Baby!' she said with twinkling eyes. But Asha could not even begin to guess.

'Just let me open it,' she begged, dancing around the box in excitement. So Janaki gave her a pair of scissors and Asha cut through the tape holding the cardboard flaps together and opened the box. There was a lot of paper padding, but underneath that there was...

'Oh! A television! My very own television!'

'No, sweetheart, it's not a TV set. It's something else that looks like a TV. It's a computer! Look, let me lift it out, carefully. See, there you go. And there are some more parts to it. This is the hard drive, and this is the keyboard, see? And this little thing is called a mouse. See?' She placed a small object in Asha's hand. It fit perfectly in her palm.

'A mouse? That's funny!' Asha turned it over and around, inspecting it. She laughed, holding up a length of cable. 'It's got such a long, thin tail! But it's not a real mouse.'

'No, thank heavens! We don't want a real mouse in the house. But let me set it up for you. It's not a new computer, darling, but it's not very old either. You remember my friend Nadiya? You met her when you came to Madras. Well, her family is terribly rich, and her daddy bought her a brand-new computer, the very latest model called Apple Mac, and so she gave me her old one. She just gave it to me, like that! Because she's my friend. But I thought I'd give it to you, because after all, I can use the university computers. Nadiya didn't mind.'

Asha walked all around the object, pushing buttons on a flat thing Janaki said was a keyboard.

'It's like a typewriter, isn't it? Like Mom's typewriter. But no words are coming out. What's it *for*, Janaki? What can I do with it? Can I watch TV on it?'

'No, Asha, it's not for TV-watching. It's for something special and amazing, called email. I will show you how to use email. When you have email you can write to me every day and tell me what you are doing and I get your messages that very same day, imagine! Now that you can read and write so well you must write to me every single day. Then you won't miss me so much.'

And Janaki set up the computer for Asha in a corner of the

living room, and connected it to the telephone line, and set up an email address, which was ashadarji@yahoo.in.

'So, now let me show you how to send an email. It's very simple. See, you just put in my address – mine is jiyeng@yahoo.in – and then you write something right here. Go on, write something!'

'What shall I write?'

'Anything at all. Just a simple message.'

So Asha wrote, '*I love you, Janaki!*'

Janaki laughed, and kissed Asha on the cheek. 'Thank you, dear, and I love you too. Now let me connect it to the Internet, which is an amazing thing, just like an invisible spiderweb in space.'

Janaki pressed some buttons and the computer began to buzz wildly, and then Janaki said: 'So now it's connected through our phone line. See that little sign? That means it's in the World Wide Web. The Internet. Now all you have to do is press this button on the keyboard – *Enter* – and see! It's gone, and it will be in my account and I can read it. If I were in Madras right now, I could read it immediately, and here I can read it too, I just have to go out of your account and into mine, and hey presto!'

'It's like magic!' said Asha. 'So, no more letters?'

'You can still write me letters, of course you can. But it's such fun to send emails. And quicker!'

'I'll send you an email every day. I promise!'

'We can promise that. And now you can write to your parents every day, too!'

'Why would I write to Amma and Appa every day, when I see them every day anyway? And they don't have a computer. They would have to use mine.'

'I don't mean Amma and Appa, Baby. I mean your real parents. Your mom, Caroline, in America, and your daddy, Kamal, in Dubai.'

For Kamal now had a job in the United Arab Emirates, working on ways to create water in the desert. Caroline, meanwhile, had finished her studies and started working as a therapist, building up a client base back in Cambridge. She still lived with her parents. She'd never married Wayne.

'I'm not really meant to be that corporate wife he wants and needs,' she'd written to Kamal at the time. They had remained friends. It was a very amicable separation. 'So really, I'm just treading water until Asha is ready to join me over here. And then maybe you can come and live nearby. Lots of marriages are like this in America, Kamal. We'll share her.'

But it hadn't worked out that way. Caroline had gone to visit Asha three times: when she was five, when she was seven, and again when she was nine. Every two years. She'd brought all kinds of wonderful gifts from America, including a video player, and Walt Disney movies on cassettes – all the ones she herself had known and loved. Brought her books, and lovely dresses, and toys, and tried to lure her away, back to America with her. But the more she lured, the more Asha rejected her. Asha, in fact, seemed slightly scared of Caroline, worried that she'd be taken away from the people and places she held dear. She was a child who loved home above all. Just like her mother.

'Typical Cancer!' Caroline had sighed every time. 'Attached to family and home, and that's all in Gingee. But one day she'll come. I know it.'

Now, Asha frowned and put on what Janaki always called her Gremlin Face: a sulky, eyebrows-lowered, nose-puckered look to show she disapproved of something.

'Caroline Aunty and Kamal Uncle are *not* my Amma and Appa!' she said. 'Not my real parents! They only want to take me away!'

'They *are* your real parents,' said Janaki quietly. She did not want this battle again. 'And you must stop calling them Aunty and Uncle. That's what I call them. They are Mom and Daddy to you. You must call them that. And one day, you'll go to America.'

'I'll only go with you!' she said and ran away. Talk of Mom and Daddy and America always upset her.

Janaki sighed, shut down the computer and went to find and comfort her.

The years flew past. Janaki and Asha kept in touch via email, though after the initial wonder wore off Asha tended not to write every day anymore, but maybe just once a week, and Janaki would write back and tell her what she was up to. She enjoyed her studies, she said, and was doing very well, and she had ideas and plans. Those plans eventually evolved to an extra year of studies, in which she specialised in cyber security. Sundari, already in wedding-planning mood, fretted, but there was nothing she could do. Janaki had a mind of her own.

In her final year of university, Janaki applied for and won a paid internship at a big company called Grant Reed IT in Silicon Valley, in California, and in great excitement she packed her bags and flew off to America. Asha was devastated.

'But it doesn't matter, Baby. I won't see you for a year, but we have email, don't we? We're never very far away from each other. This is a great opportunity for me. America! Who knows? Perhaps Giridhar and I will move to America later, when we are married, and you can come and live with us then – you will be near your mom!'

Asha, now twelve, cried bitterly when Janaki left, but there was nothing she could do about it. It had to be.

And so it happened that Janaki was in America when the terrible thing happened that destroyed Asha's life.

THIRTEEN

GINGEE, TAMIL NADU, 1997

Asha

Sundari and Vikram sat in the back seat of a packed-full taxi, returning from the Deepam festival in Tiruvannamalai, which they attended every year. The older brothers, Shankar, Kumar and Murugan, had all come home to Gingee to look after the younger children, who, after all, were not so young anymore, with Asha, the youngest, now thirteen, and quite independent herself.

It was a dark night; no streetlamps lit the way. Everyone in the car, and the car itself, was decorated for the festivities: marigold and jasmine garlands, foreheads covered in sacred ash. They were all filled with happiness.

Suddenly a lorry appeared in the headlights, racing straight towards them, without its own headlamps on, as was so often the case on country roads. A blare of horns, shouts and screams sounded within the taxi. The driver flung the steering wheel to the right, but it was too late. The lorry slammed into the left side of the taxi and raced away.

The taxi flipped over into a ditch, like a toy car.

The screaming stopped. The blare of horns stopped. Eventually, a dazed and whimpering man staggered out of the car's back seat. It was half an hour before another car passed by. He flagged it down, and eventually, the police arrived.

It was Asha who heard the knocking and shouting outside, who woke up, stumbled to the entrance and opened the front door to the policeman. It was still dark outside. Long before sunrise, yet somehow silvery. A full moon floated in the sky. She would always remember that. The full moon, on the day her world ended.

'Hello, chellam,' he said. 'I would like to speak to an adult. Who is staying with you?'

'My Amma and Appa,' said Asha. 'I will go and wake them.'

She turned as if to scamper off, but the policeman called her back.

'No, no, not your Amma and Appa. Some other adult. Some big person.' He patted her on the head. 'Which adult is in the house, looking after you? Maybe an auntie?'

'My big brother,' she said. 'Shankar.'

'Please go and fetch him. I need to talk to him.'

She bobbed her head and ran off. The policeman waited in the doorway. She called in great excitement: 'Shankar! Shankar: the police came! The police!'

Never had the police come to their house before. So she didn't just wake up Shankar. She woke Kumar, Murugan, Rajan and Dev, so they wouldn't miss the drama. All the boys gathered around the open door, rubbing their eyes, half drunk with sleep.

'Just one,' said the policeman. He pointed to Shankar. 'You, boy. Come with me.'

He placed a hand on Shankar's shoulder and gently pushed him out into the garden, where they whispered together.

A second later, Shankar shouted so loud Asha thought even on the moon they must hear it.

A few moments later they were all shouting and wailing, and then all the neighbours had gathered and everyone was wailing. Asha had never felt so alone in the world. It was as if the very earth had opened up and she had fallen into a deep dark hole.

The following day Vikram's brother, Paruthy Uncle, who lived in the next town, arrived in the Iyengar home to take charge of the situation. It was a bad day for Asha. The very worst.

'Too many mouths to feed,' complained Paruthy Uncle when he arrived to take an overview of the situation. The older boys had left home by now – they were at university or working in Bangalore – so there was just Rajan, Dev and Asha living at home. But Paruthy Uncle had a wife and three daughters himself and those mouths had to be fed first.

A week later, Paruthy Uncle took Asha on a bus to Madras. She didn't remember much of the bus drive because she was so terrified about leaving her brothers, and of course her home, which, Paruthy Uncle explained, was now his home, and his wife's.

It had been terrible enough, knowing that Amma and Appa were both dead and never coming home. Broken by grief, she had sent panicked emails to Janaki. Janaki, devastated herself, had promised to come as soon as possible, but she couldn't leave for another week because she didn't have the money, and Paruthy Uncle refused to send any. She'd have to raise it somehow. In the end, Nadiya sent her money for the flight.

But even then, Janaki wrote, it would be a long flight home and there were no seats available for a week. Amma and Appa's bodies were cremated long before Janaki could arrive. Only Asha's brothers attended the funeral, even the youngest ones. Janaki didn't come after all, which pleased Paruthy Uncle.

Asha wasn't allowed to attend the funeral, because she was only a girl and not even a real daughter. 'Just a useless mouth to feed,' said Paruthy Uncle and his wife, Sasna Aunty, and took her to Madras.

Asha cried all the way to Madras, which was why she didn't look out of the window much, and when Paruthy Uncle slapped her she cried all the more.

Janaki! cried a forlorn voice inside her. *Janaki! Help!*

And of course she prayed. She prayed and prayed as Amma had taught her. Prayer was like a lifebuoy, those rings people threw to you if you were drowning, keeping you afloat. And perhaps she would have drowned without it, but it certainly didn't change the situation itself. Staying afloat was all she could manage.

She felt utterly desolate and alone as they drove to Madras, which she was now supposed to call Chennai, but she always forgot. Usually, she enjoyed going there. She used to think of the Big City as a kind of paradise, where you could see and do and get everything, and swim in the sea. And if somebody had been to Madras it was a very special thing.

But now? The thought of going to Madras with Paruthy Uncle terrified her, and all of her crying to Janaki in her mind did not help because Janaki was far, far away, in America.

Paruthy Uncle took Asha to a big grand house somewhere in Madras. It seemed to Asha to be a palace. The car stopped in the driveway, and Paruthy Uncle, his grip tight around her wrist, pushed and pulled her up to the front door.

A woman opened the door. That was the first time Asha saw Mrs Pandian. Later, she met Mr Pandian.

Paruthy Uncle left Asha with Mr and Mrs Pandian.

'You must work for your living!' he said as a parting shot.

'You are now a servant. Work hard, and all will be well. God rewards those who work hard. Be a good servant.'

And with those words he walked away.

Asha was not a servant. She was a slave. She was living in this grand house and so it wasn't so bad, she kept telling herself. But even if you live in the grandest of places, if you are treated like a beast of burden the pain is unbearable. That lady, that Mrs Pandian, beat her for the slightest misdemeanour, or what in her eyes was a misdemeanour.

For instance, if Asha polished a mirror, and *she* found one fingerprint on it, she would beat her with the leather belt she kept hanging on a hook especially for this purpose. The house was certainly magnificent and well furnished – they had real tables and chairs, Western-style; it was the first time Asha had ever seen a home furnished this way. And carpets everywhere, and beds, and several electrical machines.

Asha didn't know how to operate these machines at first; as a matter of fact, they terrified her; all those buttons to push, and you had to get the right one. That mixer, for instance. The first time Asha used it Mrs Pandian had given her a bowl with some kind of mixture in it and only told her to place the bowl under the beaters of the mixer and switch on the button. But when Asha did so the bowl woke up and started dancing in wild circles, and when she grabbed it in a panic the yellow slop inside started to dance too and flew out all over the kitchen.

Mrs Pandian whipped her for that, of course.

The vacuum cleaner wasn't much better; it was much stronger than Asha and pulled her in several directions at once, it seemed. There was even a machine that made coffee for you, and one called Teasmade, that made tea automatically, but still needed attention by a maid.

The only machine Asha understood, and potentially liked,

was the computer in Mr Pandian's office, but she was not allowed to touch it, ever. Not even to wipe down the monitor. Still, she tried not to complain about the machines – they couldn't help being what they were; they did not have a soul and they were not trying deliberately to hurt her.

Not like *her*. Mrs Pandian.

There were marks on her upper thighs, horizontal scars, like the rungs of a ladder marching up and down. Those marks were made by *her*. When Asha did something wrong – it was always little things, too little to remember afterwards – *she* would stick a fork into the flame on the gas stove, leave it there till the prongs were red hot. And then she would lift the hem of Asha's skirt and press them against her thigh. And the more Asha screamed, the more prongs she got.

Asha was locked up in that house. She was not allowed to leave. They had other servants: a cook, and a man who went shopping and came back from the market with bags of food that he gave to the cook, and a gardener, and a *dhobi* who took care of the laundry, picking up dirty bundles twice a week and bringing it back in clean, ironed, neatly folded stacks. But Asha was the only maid, and she was not allowed to leave the house, not even for a moment.

With *her* Asha had to do all sorts of things in a different way than Amma had done at home, and she learned a lot about Western ways, though of course they were all Indian. But they said Western ways were better, and she had to do things *so* and not *so*.

Then there were the children. Mrs Pandian had two, and though Asha had always loved small children, she found those two hard to love, for they were as nasty as their parents. They took such great pleasure in hurting her whenever they could, but in sneaky sly ways, especially that little girl. She would walk behind Asha quite innocently, but in passing kick her from behind, or pull her hair, or pinch her. Little things, to be sure, but still they hurt.

The man hurt in a different way. It started soon after she came to live with them, and it always happened when *she* was not at home. Perhaps she had taken her children to her sister's or some such thing; she went visiting often, leaving Asha at home, locked up in the house, which had heavy padlocks at the doors and bars at all the windows.

That man would come out of his office sometimes and touch her here and there. That's when she learned about the demon that lives in every man.

The woman spoke only Tamil but the man spoke to Asha in English, and he tried to force her to speak back to him in English. But she would not speak at all, and he could not force her. Not speaking was the one power she had. Sometimes he got angry when she did not speak and threatened to beat her, but he never actually did. Silence, she found, was her only weapon.

Then came the day when they put creams and colours on her face and made her look like a movie star, wrapped her in a red silk sari, and took photos of her.

That was the day her troubles *really* began.

FOURTEEN

Caroline

*Dear Kamal, thanks so much for sending me your email address.
It will make communicating a lot easier. Because, no matter
what, we are still Asha's parents and nothing can change that.
It's a bond that will remain forever, and I'm so glad we were able
to remain friends – well, pen-pals, I guess.*

*Kamal, I'm writing today because I'm so very worried about
Asha, and I wondered – have you heard from Sundari at all in
the last two months? Because I haven't.*

*You know that I send Sundari money to buy a birthday present
for Asha every year. I kept my HSBC account in India open, and
I just wire money into that account and from there to Sundari's –
Internet banking is a godsend, isn't it? Whatever did we do
before?*

*Anyway, after Asha's birthday, she always writes me a short
thank-you letter. I'm sure Sundari forces her to write it but at*

least it's her own handwriting. Those letters are so precious to me. And Sundari sends a photo so I can see how much she's grown in the past year.

These are always studio photos, so a bit stiff and serious – I understand that the Iyengars don't have a camera, but I long for a photo of her at play, natural, laughing! – I treasure them. I also send photos of myself regularly, so she won't forget what I look like. She hasn't seen me since she was nine. She was just as stubborn as ever then, still flat-out refusing to come back with me to America. I persuaded her to go on vacation with me to Sri Lanka, and we had fun on the beach and I got to know her a little – but still. We've never gotten to be mother and daughter the way I know it. There's this distance, and it's hurtful. I know that she's the same with you. Who would have thought it would turn out like this?

But this year, nothing. I wrote Sundari to ask if everything is OK: no reply. It's been weeks now since her thirteenth birthday. I called the house and a strange woman answered the phone, and she didn't speak English. I sent a telegram last week asking for confirmation that all is well, and again – no response.

I am so worried that I have decided to close down my therapy practice for a month and go to India. It's going to be a huge hassle and my patients are terribly upset but I don't care – I have to do it.

I'm telling you this because my one hope is that for some reason it's just me – that for you contact is as usual, that you got a thank-you for your birthday money, etc.

If not, I expect you are as worried as I am. I'm wondering if it would be possible for you too to take leave and we can meet in

Madras – sorry, Chennai – and travel up to Gingee together? I do feel such a stranger in India, and it would be great to have you at my side as co-parent and to help me out if there is truly some problem. Of course, I don't know how easy it is for you to get leave at such short notice but my fingers are crossed. I haven't booked a flight yet, but I'd like to travel ASAP – next week hopefully. How about you? If you can come, we should coordinate our bookings.

By the way, do you have Janaki's email address? She's sure to have one as an IT student. Last year Sundari told me she was coming to California on an internship and hoping we'd meet – she didn't realise just how enormous America is, and that Cambridge is on the opposite coast to California! But Janaki would know more, if only we could get in touch. I wish now I had asked Sundari for Janaki's email – I just didn't think of it at the time.

So this turned out to be a very long email – hope to hear from you soon.

Caroline

Kamal's head hurt. He'd been planning on writing to Caroline himself – had she heard from Sundari? It wasn't like her not to respond to letters, not to send a thank-you letter from Asha after her birthday gift arrived. That is, the money for her birthday gift – not knowing what Asha liked, he always sent extra money and Sundari chose the gift: usually books, which Janaki would buy in Madras and either send or bring for Asha. Asha, he knew, devoured children's detective stories by Enid Blyton; ever since Janaki had given her the first she had craved more and more, and luckily Janaki had been able to supply them.

Though that was likely to have changed – in her last letter, about six months ago, Sundari had said that Janaki was now in America, working as an intern at an IT company. Janaki would know what the problem was – but how to contact her?

Caroline was right – he was worried, very worried. The worry was compounded by guilt. He hadn't seen his daughter since she was eight years old, and she had been so non-communicative then that he had lost all confidence in himself and his role as father. All he could do was send money, transferred from his Indian Overseas Bank account to Sundari's. He knew very well that money wasn't enough. He knew very well he was a bad father. *Bad father, bad father* went the mantra in his head, impossible to silence by positive thinking. Because it was true.

And because he knew it was true, and because the worry had escalated to a nebulous panic, he knew he had to do something, something drastic. It was time to be a good father. Good fathers acted. They didn't just sit back, hoping and praying. Good fathers were on the front line for their children. His return mail to Caroline, unlike hers, was succinct:

I haven't heard from Sundari either. I've been very worried. I'm not taking leave – I quit my job. I've got so much overtime due I can actually leave immediately, without notice, which is good. I've booked a flight to India next week, so great minds do think alike. I arrive in Madras next Tuesday, so book to arrive then. I'll meet you there.

FIFTEEN

Asha

It was long past midnight, a few hours before dawn. Only a few lights were on downstairs. Asha, mopping the hall floor, wore an old, frumpy *shalwar kameez*. She walked up the front hallway, dipping the mop into the soapy water, wringing it out, swishing the mop back and forth, her bare feet padding behind it.

She glanced through the open office door. There, too, a light was on. She glimpsed Mr Pandian working at the desktop computer. She wasn't allowed in there, so she walked past and continued her slow journey down the hall.

Suddenly, she started: the dogs broke into furious barking. And someone was shouting outside in the front yard. The chain on the garden gate rattled.

Mr Pandian dashed out of the office and sprinted along the just-mopped hall, his bare feet slipping on the wet tiles, stumbling but catching himself and running upstairs, calling in alarm to his wife. Asha ran to the barred window and looked out into the night. In the ghostly light of the yard lamp, she saw a police car crouched on the road outside the fence, men in uniform rattling at the gate chains, shouting through a megaphone.

'Open up! Police!'

Glancing up, Asha saw Mr and Mrs Pandian on the top landing, whispering in panic. Their daughter ran out of her room, crying, and ran into her mother's arms. Asha quickly slipped into the living room, and from the front window, hidden in darkness, she watched as a policeman cut through the chain and three officers swarmed up the garden path to the front door, still shouting.

The dogs leapt at the intruders, barking and snarling furiously, but in vain; they leapt against the chains that bound them to their kennels, snarling and baring their teeth even as collars strained against their necks. One of the policemen took aim. Gunshots blasted the air. The barking stopped.

Terrified by the commotion, Asha ran into the kitchen and hid in the mop cupboard. She cowered in darkness, hugging her legs, her head buried between her knees. Outside, in the hallway, the furious shouting terrified her: the Pandians yelling at the police, the children screaming, the thunderous hammering on the front door. And then a loud crack as the police officers broke down the door. The pounding of heavy footsteps as men swarmed through the house, through all the rooms, then up the stairs, leaving all the doors open. There was a clear view from the kitchen into the hallway, and peeping through the slats in the cupboard door, Asha watched as the police led Mr and Mrs Pandian down the stairs, along the hall, to the open front door. The children screamed for dear life, hanging on to their mother's nightdress, their father's lungi. The Pandians were shouting something about lawyers and injustice. Then they were all gone. Noises drifted in from outside, car doors slamming, more shouting. And then silence.

Asha waited for a while, to be sure she was quite alone. The silence in the house, after all the commotion, seemed suspicious.

She waited and waited, and then once she was quite certain, emerged warily from the cupboard. She walked through the house, checking carefully, just to make sure.

She entered the office. The computer sat there, dark, silent, inviting. She touched the keyboard.

The monitor woke up with the familiar sound she knew so well. The screen filled with light and colour. For the first time in weeks, her heart lifted.

SIXTEEN

Caroline

As Caroline stepped off the plane at Chennai International into what felt like a soup of sweat, she remembered her first arrival, exactly fifteen years previously. So much had changed since then, but not the heat and humidity, the closeness of climate that clasped you the moment you set foot in India.

And then the endless waiting in an endless queue while they checked her passport and visa. And then another endless wait for her suitcase among a milling crowd of Indians and Westerners, all pushing themselves forward to be near the luggage carousel once it chugged into action.

Remembering how long it usually took before the luggage started to be disgorged, she went to the State Bank of India counter to change her dollars into rupees. That done, she returned to luggage claim and was relieved to see movement: people, mostly Indians, grabbing suitcases and lugging them away, piling them onto rusty creaking trolleys.

Some people seemed to have mountains of luggage, piles of

suitcases and boxes. Caroline had only one suitcase. She knew the value of travelling light, especially in India. And after all, what would she need? She wouldn't be doing any sightseeing or going on any pleasure outings where she would need nice new clothes. She was looking for Asha. She had brought practical things: light cotton trousers, T-shirts and loose blouses: comfortable clothes, suitable for the heat, but nothing armless or skimpy – a concession to Indian modesty.

There it was, her small green suitcase leaning against a huge one wrapped up in pale cotton and tied with several bands of rope, an address scrawled in large letters across one side of it. A burly man barged forward, grabbed the large suitcase and lugged it off the carousel and, by the time he had dragged it away, Caroline's suitcase was several metres away, chugging around the bend in the carousel and making its way back to the bowels of the airport. There was no way to push her way through the crowds to grab it; she would have to wait till it came around again.

At last, suitcase on a wobbly-wheeled trolley, she was ready to exit the airport. Two uniformed agents checked her documents, wrote something in chalk on her case, and then she was walking along a corridor outside the airport with a metal barrier to her right and crowds and crowds of Indians behind it, many of them waving signs with names on them, names of passengers or hotels or companies, leaning forward over the railing, scanning the emerging passengers for the one they had come to meet. No matter how often she came to India – this never changed.

Oh, it was all so familiar! India opening its arms and folding them around her, possessively, stealthily and yet blatantly, brazenly. Two-faced India, gentle and brutal, gloriously beautiful and hideously ugly. The India that kissed you on one cheek and slapped you on the other. The India that soothed your soul one day and ripped it to shreds the next. The India that nourished your senses and starved your ego, kicking it into the ground.

The India she had embraced so eagerly the first time she had walked this very path, emerging from the sanctuary of the airport into the heart and the bowels of a culture she would never understand. That first time, so many years ago, her beloved Kamal had been at her side, and she had been in love not only with him but with his country, sight unseen. India. The India she had rejected so thoroughly, fled from in the throes of a debilitating illness, and then reluctantly returned to, again and again, to see her daughter and coax her away.

But Asha loved India as much as Caroline loved America, and that was the problem. Asha wasn't willing to even try America. Caroline had tried. Oh, how she had tried, to persuade her. She'd been back so many times, and every time, Asha seemed to have distanced herself a little further. Become more Indian, just as Caroline became more American, and not in the least tempted to join her mother in the Land of Opportunities. Not even the books and videos Caroline brought could tempt her. Not even the tales of Disneyland, and shopping malls, and Toys R Us. Not even when Caroline suggested that Janaki come too, for a holiday. Janaki had been keen. But Asha had even then refused.

The Iyengars had television now and a video player, and Caroline brought old and new videos for Asha and the children: *Lady and the Tramp*, 101 *Dalmatians*, *Honey I Shrunk the Kids*. Asha liked the movies, but they did not tempt her in the least to return with Caroline. It was so depressing.

Now, back for the third time, it was different. This time, close to senseless with worry. This time, a piece of her heart was missing. This time it was to find her daughter and secure her well-being. This time, too, to meet Kamal again.

And there he was. Kamal. Waiting for her at the very end of the walkway. She hadn't seen him for ten years; of course he had changed. Still tall, still handsome and smartly dressed, this was an older, more mature, more worldly-wise Kamal. A different, older Kamal. She couldn't help it: her heart pinged. And it wasn't just because it was him; the man she'd once thought was the love of her life. Yes it was him, unmistakeably; but this time, something was different. And seeing him, it all gushed out.

She had been holding back the emotions so bravely for the last few weeks – the mounting fears, all the worries and the guilt; now, on seeing him, the relief burst forth and she flung herself into his open arms. They closed around her, like the wings of an angel, and for a whole minute she just stood there, in his arms, weeping silently. He held her, strong and protective, just the way he'd always been. Oh, how she'd missed those arms around her! Missed them, without even knowing it. Now, it was a raw, naked sense of comfort, enfolded in those arms.

It was Kamal who broke the spell. He pulled away, smiled kindly down at her, and said, 'Come, Caroline. We'll talk later.'

He gestured to a man standing behind him and then she was once again in the reality of India.

Kamal's taxi driver grabbed hold of the trolley and she pulled away and smiled at him with trembling lips. Suddenly, she felt shy. Kamal's welcome had been – well, not as warm as hers. He had embraced her, yes – he could hardly not embrace her, seeing as she had flung herself at him, sobbing. He had been forced to open his arms to receive her. But had she just imagined they were angel's wings? Was his embrace actually... cold? Was she the only one to have felt such a waterfall of emotion?

And now he walked beside her, not touching her – really, they could have held hands, thought Caroline. They were still friends, after all – what was wrong with a perfectly platonic holding of hands, between two people who had once loved each other? But perhaps, as an Indian, Kamal was inhibited about touching her, a female, even if she was, technically, his wife?

She could, of course, take his hand. She was a modern woman who didn't wait for the man to make the first move. But she had her pride.

SEVENTEEN

Asha

Asha sat at the keyboard before the live monitor. She pressed a key, tentatively. Was it really true? Was the world now open to her? Her heart lifted at the familiar buzzing sound as the machine connected to dial-up Internet. She was in. She typed a few letters. Yes! Her email account asking for a password. She entered it. And there, waiting for her, as if by magic, a list of several unread mails from Janaki.

She started to read, from the bottom up:

Asha Baby, where are you? I am worried out of my mind! We all are. Please reply ASAP and let me know where you are. Paruthy Uncle refuses to tell me!

All the other emails said basically the same thing. She read them all, and then typed her reply:

Dear Janaki, Paruthy Uncle is a very bad man. First he sold my computer, and then he sent me away to Madras to work for some

*bad people and I have been working as a maid for a long time
and they beat me. But the police came and took them away, and
now I am alone in the house so I am using the computer. Janaki,
I don't know what to do. You are so far away in California!*

She sent the email, and then sat at the desk, waiting for
Janaki to reply. She had a new thought. She looked at the desk
telephone, picked up the receiver, dialled 999. She knew that
was the emergency number. No reply except for a recorded
voice in Tamil thanking her for the call and asking her to hold
on. She replaced the receiver so as to leave the telephone line
open for Janaki's email.

While waiting she opened desk drawers, looked through
various papers. In a bottom drawer, she found several slim
photo albums. She picked up the first one, looked through it. It
was full of photos of girls in ornate red saris. Her own photo
among them, wearing that dreadful red sari, her face caked in
make-up so that she looked thirty years instead of thirteen. She
remembered that day with a shudder. She slammed the album
shut and picked up another, opening it. She uttered a cry of
shock.

This new album was also full of girls, girls around her own
age, or younger. But all of them were naked. She quickly
slammed that, too, shut. Enough of photos.

She picked up a notebook and looked through it. Closed it
again. It seemed to be full of telephone numbers. There was a
piece of paper, hidden beneath the desk pad. On it was a hand-
written list of random words, names, mixed with numbers,
some of which looked like birthdates, with little notes beside
each one. All except the bottom one crossed out. It looked like
the list she kept at home; her list of passwords, and what they
were for. She checked her mail account again. Nothing. Dialled
999 again. This time she waited. And waited. But it kept
ringing and nobody picked up. It was still very early in the

morning. She checked the time. Five a.m. Amma used to get up at that time so it wasn't *that* late. Especially not for an emergency.

Irritated and impatient, she got up and walked into the kitchen. She opened the fridge. It was packed full of food. She took out various covered containers, looked inside them. She realised she was hungry from the emptiness of many weeks. She sat at the table with the containers and started to eat.

She ate everything. Old *idlis*, *sambar*, rice. Eggs. Bread. She made scrambled eggs on the electric hob, with butter. Ate it with toast, from the toaster, which she had learned how to operate. Made herself a cheese sandwich. Gobbled down some old rice. Poured cereal into a bowl, added milk, ate it up. Ate half a banana, and a slice of mango. She hadn't eaten a mango for – well, it seemed like years.

Sated, she washed up, put away the dishes and returned to the office. Connected to dial-up, and checked her email again. No reply yet from Janaki.

She then wandered around the house. Climbed the stairs. She entered the bathroom, took off her ragged clothes – a cotton *shalwar kameez*, so old and faded the colour was no more than a washed-out grey – and had a long hot shower. She washed her hair, using *her* expensive shampoo. She dried herself with a fluffy towel, and wrapped another towel around her head.

Towels wrapped around her body and head, she walked to the master suite, entered the walk-in wardrobe, opened the closet, inspected the expensive saris, held them against her body. All much too big for her.

Also hanging in the closet, a *shalwar kameez*, closer to her size, though still too big. So different from the ragged one she wore! It was of pure silk, exquisite in swirling colours in a pattern she recognised as from Jaipur. She slipped the soft tunic over her head. It felt wonderful. She stepped into the wide loose trousers, pulled the waistband tight and turned up the cuffs.

But it was sadly much, much too big. Mrs Pandian was not a slim woman, and the voluminous *kameez* hung down to halfway down her calves and the wide slippery *salwar* legs did not stay cuffed as she walked back and forth in front of the mirror. And anyway, it was wrong to steal. Asha sighed, removed the suit, put her old clothes back on. She wandered back downstairs and returned to the office, the towel still wrapped around her wet hair.

She connected to dial-up again and checked into her mail account without much hope. But this time, there was a new mail from Janaki.

At last! Asha, I've been frantic with worry. You must now go to my friend Nadiya. She's the one who gave you your computer. You can trust her. I've already told her to look out for you. Here's her contact number and address below. Call her asap! Do you have money for a rickshaw? If not search the house. I'm sure you'll find a few rupees in a drawer or a jar, just like Amma used to do. Do not speak to anyone else. Don't trust anyone, except the police. If you can't find money, still go. Nadiya will pay the driver. Don't waste any time. Just go! Maybe they were arrested but who knows, maybe they will be let go. Get out of that house asap!

I am trying to find your mom and daddy, because now you will have to go to them. You know that, right?

Asha typed a reply.

I know I have to go to Mom and Daddy. I'm just scared because they must hate me now because I was so rude to them. I was so mean! Even when they were kind and generous!

Janaki replied:

Oh, of course they don't hate you, darling! They love you with all their hearts and as soon as they know where you are they will come and get you.

Asha wrote:

I hope you are right about Mom and Daddy. But oh, Janaki! These people are so disgusting. I'm so glad they got arrested. You know what I found? Photo albums of girls all in red saris and lots of make-up, but also naked photos of girls. It is so horrible. Now I will call Nadiya.

She picked up the phone, dialled the number Janaki gave her, but there was no reply. She dialled 999 again, again no reply. She wrote to Janaki:

Janaki, Nadiya is not answering her phone and I didn't find any money. And also no reply on 999. And this is a quiet street, there are no rickshaws here at this time of night. I don't know what to do. I wish Mom and Daddy would come!

Janaki seemed to be online right now, because the reply was immediate:

Just keep trying. Nadiya will wake up soon. Maybe she didn't hear the phone or switches it off at night. But I was thinking, Asha. Is that man's mailbox still signed in?

Asha checked:

Yes.

Janaki replied:

Could you forward all his last mails to me? I want to know what he's up to.

She worked on the computer, forwarded several of Mr Pandian's last mails to Janaki.

Janaki:

OK, thanks. Listen, Asha, can you do this for me? I noticed that there's a group mail there where they all talk to each other. About twenty of them. I think they are doing something really bad. Maybe we can catch them and help other girls. What I want you to do is this: look through the inbox and look for a sender called Rajagopal. And then send all of those particular mails to me here. OK? Also the ones sent to Rajagopal.

Just do that and wait till I reply. Also see if you can find the street address of the house where you are now. Maybe some letters, envelopes. Any business files. It must be there somewhere. I will get Nadiya to come and pick you up. You will soon be rescued, darling! Don't worry at all. I am sure your mom and daddy will come soon to rescue you. You must pray for them to come.

Asha typed furiously on the keyboard, looking up occasionally to the monitor:

I did it, Janaki! I forwarded all the Rajagopal mails. And I am praying for Mom and Daddy to come.

Good. One more thing. Can you look for that man's email password? He might have written it down somewhere around the desk. Have a quick look.

When I was looking through the desk earlier I found a paper poking out under the desk mat with a list of random words on it, and numbers, all crossed out except the bottom one. It looked like a password list. At least, that's what I thought.

Send me it. The last word, the one not crossed out.

While Asha typed, she heard background noises. Male voices. Sound of footsteps in the corridor.

Janaki, there's someone at the door! Someone in the house!

Hide, Asha! Hide quickly!

EIGHTEEN

Janaki

Nadiya love, have you heard from Asha? I'm a bit worried as we were chatting on email and suddenly it stopped. She does have your address and phone number. I told her to ring you or try to get to your place. I couldn't sleep a wink all night, kept checking my email and as I haven't heard from either of you I'm terribly worried. Did she come? It's 6 a.m. over here, so must be late afternoon in Madras. Please tell me she's safe and sound with you!

Janaki had waited and waited for news: another mail from Asha or a mail from Nadiya confirming that Asha had safely contacted her by phone. Nothing. She paced her room. Had something happened before Asha could escape? What a fool she had been, to waste Asha's time looking for a stupid password! The important thing would have been for Asha to escape ASAP. What if they had come back and found her? What if her captor had somehow bribed the police and returned home? Everything was possible in India.

The last thing she had received from Asha was the pass-

word of her captor's mail address. And an idea popped unin-
vited into her head. She wasn't sure if it was a brilliant one or a
terrible one or just a very stupid one, but it couldn't hurt. So, to
fill the time, Janaki logged in to Pandian's account.

There were hundreds of mails waiting to be researched,
but she hadn't time for that now, nervous as she was and
waiting for Nadiya's reply. She didn't care about the past mails;
those she could read later. She only cared about the present, an
answer to the question: *where is Asha?* It was while checking
the recipients of the mails that she had her brilliant, or stupid,
idea. The mails, it seemed, were sent to several recipients.
Eleven in all. Many of the replies in the email exchange were a
simple: *Great,* or *How many? Or Maybe K should go?* Or, *I
agree with Kapoor.*

The arrest had not yet been mentioned. That meant the
other group members possibly did not know that one of them,
Pandian, had been arrested. Once they knew, they'd probably
remove his address from the cc list. So Janaki did something
very naughty. She replied to the last mail with an innocuous
question, *Are you sure about that?* and added her own throw-
away email address, one she'd just created: jiyeng@yahoo.in, to
the bcc recipients. They won't notice, she told herself. They
won't even check. And if they don't check, they won't know
who I am or who added me. But I will get all their future mails.
It was a risk worth taking, and could do no harm. So she did
that, and since time hung heavy on her hands, she began to
scour Rajagopal's old emails, until finally a reply came in from
Nadiya:

*Well I stayed home all morning expecting to hear from Asha but
not a word. Do you have an address? If I knew where the house
was I could go and take a look.*

Janaki responded immediately:

No, I don't have an address. I do have the mail account details of the asshole who was keeping her captive in Madras. I've been reading all his mails and, you know what? He's not just an asshole – he's a big-time criminal. From what I gather from his mails he's involved in trafficking a ring of young girls. All stolen from their homes. He's in charge of the Madras branch. It seems to be an India-wide ring. I've no doubt that was the plan for Asha too, until he was arrested yesterday and the plan fell apart. I can't imagine what happened after that. Asha and I emailed a few times back and forth but then silence. I'm desperate with worry. There was no clue in the emails as to where the house is so no help there. I'm thinking you should just go to the police and ask. Open a FIR case. They might know something. It's terrible being so far away. If I don't hear back from Asha today, I'm going to have to come myself. I'm desperately looking for her parents; they need to be informed so they can help. Let me know if you hear anything and thank you SO MUCH for your help! XXX

Email from Nadiya to Janaki:

Anything for you, my love! I remember Asha from when you brought her that time, such a sweet little girl! I can't bear to think of what she must have gone through and I'm praying that she's still safe. Anything more I can do, just say the word. If you do come you know I'm here for you.

Email from Janaki to Nadiya:

No word at all from Asha. It's now 24 hours since I last heard from her, and I just KNOW she's in danger. I'm trying to contact her biological parents, but I have no idea how to find them. Paruthy Uncle will never tell me. I can't believe this is happening! Poor Asha. She's the last person this should happen to, such a sensitive girl! Not that it should happen to anyone but you know what I mean. I'm going to move heaven and earth to find her. But I need to find her parents. They have to know.

Janaki bent over her desk, her head in her hands, trapping her skull with her fingers, which was what she did when she needed to concentrate. *Think, Janaki, think.* How can you contact Kamal Uncle and Caroline Aunty?

Caroline Aunty was in Cambridge, Massachusetts. She remembered Amma had sent a letter with her address and telephone number, but she, Janaki, hadn't bothered to write at the time – who wrote letters these days anyway? She had lost touch with Caroline over the years, so she hadn't rung her, either. Had she written it in her address book? She checked. No. Damn it! Had she kept the letter from Amma? Probably not. Her apartment was so tiny, Janaki didn't keep paperwork she didn't need. She hadn't thought she'd ever need to visit Caroline Aunty in Cambridge or contact her. So she hadn't bothered to keep those details. Damn.

As for Kamal Uncle – Janaki had been fourteen when she had last seen him on one of his short, sporadic visits. He had been friendly enough and obviously pleased that Asha and she were so close, but after all he was an adult, living in his important engineer world, foreign-educated besides, and Janaki had been in awe of him. She thought he had moved to Dubai – hadn't Amma said he had a big-shot job there?

Think, Janaki, think.

All the information would be in the Gingee house.

Finally, she shot off an email to her eldest brother, Shankar:

...you need to find a way to search all their papers. I know that Caroline Aunty and Kamal Uncle used to write to Appa and Amma regularly. The letters must be there somewhere. I need their addresses, contact details. Preferably email address and

phone numbers. See if you can find Appa's old phone book, the numbers must be in there.

Email from Shankar to Janaki:

They were both out yesterday and I searched the office. Not a single letter from Aunty and Uncle. And that old phone book of Appa's? You mean the one with the black cover that was falling apart? They threw it out long ago. They have a shiny new phone book. I once saw a letter with an American stamp on it in the wastepaper basket, unopened. And later that day Sasna Aunty burnt all the paper in the yard. I think that's probably what she does with all their letters: burn them. Sorry I can't help. If I can do anything else let me know. When you find Asha give her a hug for me.

Damn it. Typical. There was only one option left for Janaki. She had to go there herself. Back to India. Somehow pick up Asha's trail. She had just one hope remaining, and that lay in the email trail left by Asha's captors. She'd have to read those mails, one by one; some, the ones in Hindi, she'd have to get translated. There must be a clue in there, somewhere.

If there was a clue she'd have to follow it. She had to be present. But she had another idea too. Quite a brilliant one, in fact. Amma had been so impressed because Kamal Uncle was really a prince. And he came from some former kingdom called Chandrapur. The name of the kingdom had stuck. There, he would have relatives. There, she would track him down.

Email from Janaki to Nadiya:

Just about to leave for the airport, see you soon; flying to Bombay. I'm going to look for her father's family. Kamal Uncle's. Amma used to tell us that Kamal Uncle is really a prince from this old kingdom called Chandrapur. The kingdom no longer exists but the palace does – it's where Kamal Uncle grew up. He's bound to have family there and they will know where to find him. He needs to know that Asha is missing. The more people looking for her the better. We will probably need money too and hopefully he has some, because I am dirt poor. Used every bit of my savings and sold my beloved PC to buy my plane ticket home.

Email from Nadiya to Janaki:

By the time you get this you'll probably be here in India already but just wanted to say don't worry about money. I have enough to help as much as I can. You didn't have to sell your PC! But no worries, I'll buy you a new one.

NINETEEN

Rani pulled impatiently at the bell-rope. The big brass bell swung back and forth several times, clanging out an impatient summons.

Seconds later a servant clad in a long, gathered skirt and matching blouse of evidently the finest silk hurried through the velvet curtain that separated the Surya Hall from the Corridor of Mirrors.

'Your Majesty?' she said, placing her palms together, lowering her eyes and bending forward from the waist. She had to speak loudly to be heard above the music.

Rani's finger traced a languid bow and pointed upwards to one of the two monitors fitted into the ornate woodwork arch at the entrance to her cubicle. One of the screens was a regular TV screen. Across it flickered the coloured pictures of a new video film that Lakshmi, her lady-in-waiting, had brought the day before. Rani pressed the mute button on the remote control. A ravishing apple-cheeked heroine in a bright green sari mouthed the words to a soundless song as she danced around a tree.

The other screen was a black-and-white CCTV screen, and it was to this screen that Rani now pointed. The girl's gaze followed the finger. She looked up at the screen. It showed the closed front gate and a lone figure standing outside it.

'There is a stranger at the gate,' said Rani. She took a long, deep drag on the hookah pipe beside her. 'A female. Find out who it is. And summon Lakshmi.'

Rani's hand sank to the carved sandalwood table at her side, and her fingers closed around the remote control. She pressed a button, and with a thwack the television screen turned blank. The servant frowned; Rani hardly ever turned off the video. From dawn till dusk the moving pictures flickered. Occasionally, during conversation or to issue a command, the film was muted for a short space of time, after which Rani would press the rewind button to replay what she had missed. Two or three times a week Lakshmi would sally forth into the town to Bisheswar Video Rentals and return with a bagful of new films, which Rani would consume without a break over the next several days.

Breathless and flustered as she plunged through the bead curtain, Lakshmi approached Rani, gliding up with folded palms and a winning smile.

'You called, Majesty? Shall I change the film? Did you not like that one?'

'I want to know – who is that female visitor? What does she want?'

'She wants an audience with you, Majesty. I tried to find out what her quest is, but she said it is private. She wants to speak to the head of the household but when questioned she knew nothing. She does not even know that it is just you here. She asked to see the family.'

'Bring her,' said Rani, and a few minutes later Janaki was ushered into her presence.

Lakshmi said to Rani: 'Janaki Iyengar, Majesty. She says that is her name. She is from a place called Gingee in Tamil Nadu. Please take a seat, Miss Iyengar.' Lakshmi gestured to a low, ornately embroidered pouf opposite the grand dame, and Janaki carefully lowered herself onto it.

Rani rolled herself a leaf of *paan*, her eyes fixed on the young woman before her, not saying a word. Under that unnerving gaze, Janaki fidgeted, adjusting and readjusting her legs beneath her. She was unaccustomed to sitting so close to the floor after several months in the States; the pouf was neither up nor down, and she sat awkwardly hunched, knees hovering in the air, ankles crossed.

Lakshmi moved a small low table into reachable distance and a serving girl placed a jug of clouded liquid and a bowl of mixed sweets on it.

'*Nimbu pani*,' said Lakshmi, pouring her a glass. 'Very cold, very refreshing. And do have some nice sweets. Those *laddus* are delicious.'

Grateful for the distraction, Janaki reached for a *laddu* and bit into it; it was indeed melt-in-the-mouth delicious. She picked up the glass and sipped at the lime juice, trying to avoid Rani's gaze, which was fixed unwaveringly on her.

'Well, Miss Iyengar, what brings you to me? You know I am a busy woman.'

Janaki cleared her throat, coughed, and began to speak.

'I am looking for the relatives of Kamal Darji.'

Rani did not so much as blink. She kept her eyes on Janaki and took another deep drag on the hookah. Water gurgled, loud in the silence of the room. Outside in the garden a songbird warbled, a peacock wailed, and far away a dog barked, but Rani only sat there gazing at Janaki. Those who knew her well, however, might have perceived a slight raising of the eyebrows, a very slightly heightened pulsing of a blood vessel near her ear.

'So,' said Rani at last, 'and how are you acquainted with the person you mentioned?'

Janaki, so encouraged out of her discomfiture, stumbled over the words in her eagerness to explain.

'Well, you see, Mr Darji, he has a daughter, she's thirteen now, and my mother, well, my late mother, I mean, she died a while ago, she was looking after the girl. Since birth. And I am like a big sister to her – I looked after her when she was small and we are very close. And now she is missing. Lost. I am trying to find her. And I need to inform Mr Darji that his daughter is lost, as possibly he does not know. And I do not have his address so I was wondering, I was hoping, his family could contact him or help me find him. It's urgent, you see. I think Asha – that's the girl's name – is in danger, and we have to find her quickly, and—'

'Stop! Stop, stop, stop. That is enough. Did you know, young lady, that this Mr Darji broke off contact with me many years ago? How many years ago was it, Lakshmi?'

'Twenty years, Your Majesty. And three months.'

'Twenty years and three months. Not a letter, not a card, not a phone call. That is the gratitude I have earned from my grandson. My only grandson.'

Janaki's heart clouded over.

'Oh! You mean—'

'I mean he has broken contact. Doesn't want anything to do with me. I, on the other hand...' She smiled and leaned forward, and lowered her voice. 'I, on the other hand, know all about him. I have kept track. I have my methods. I have my spies. I know the date he married and the name of the white foreigner he married. I know the date the two of them flew out of America and landed in Madras. I know the name of the family they put up with in Gingee – you are correct, it is Iyengar. I know that he first worked at the Aliyar dam at Coimbatore and then at the Tehri in Uttarakhand. I know the date of his daughter's birth and the date his wife flew back to America. I know the name of the company in Dubai who employ him. And I have his phone number at that office. Why don't you just phone him and tell him what you told me. Lakshmi, bring the phone and dial Kamal's number for me. It seems it is time we used it.'

And a minute later Janaki was holding the phone to her ear and it was ringing, somewhere in Dubai.

Somebody answered, spoke in a foreign language, presumably Arabic. Janaki placed her hand over the phone and with wide-open eyes mouthed to Rani, 'I don't understand!'

'Just ask for Kamal,' said Rani.

Removing her hand, Janaki said, in English, 'May I speak to Mr Darji, please.'

In perfect BBC English, the voice said, 'Mr Darji is unfortunately abroad. Can I help you?'

'Oh, um, no – when will he return?'

'I'm afraid I can't help you with that. Shall I take a message?'

'No – but can you please ask him to ring me when he returns. It's urgent.'

'Certainly – but may I know who's calling?'

'Oh – oh sorry. Yes, of course – my name is Janaki Iyengar. My number is – hold on a moment...'

Janaki fumbled in her handbag for her address book, flipped the pages until she found Nadiya's number. She spoke it into the receiver.

'Will he be back soon? Like, in a day or two? Or has he gone away for longer?'

'I'm sorry I can't tell you that, ma'am,' said the soothing, polite voice on the other end. 'However, we certainly don't expect him back this week.'

'Oh! Well, it's very urgent, a personal matter. Do you have an email address for him? Any way I can contact him urgently?'

'I'm sorry, ma'am, I cannot give out his private email address. I can gladly let you have his business address. You can write to him there.'

'Yes, but will he be checking his business email in the near future? It's really terribly important. An emergency. A private emergency!'

'Ma'am, unfortunately I can't tell you if or when Mr Darji will be checking his business email. Can I help you further? If not perhaps you'd like to write it down. Do you have a pencil to hand?'

'Just a minute.'

Janaki made frantic writing-in-the-air signs. Instantly Lakshmi handed her a ballpoint pen and a notebook, and she scribbled down the address dictated by the voice.

'Is that all, ma'am?'

'Yes – no. Just, if he calls, tell him it's very urgent.'

'I will, ma'am. Thank you for calling. Goodbye, and have a nice day.'

The voice clicked off; the line began its empty buzz. Janaki handed the phone back to Lakshmi and turned to Rani.

'He's gone – he's not there! Seems whoever you have stalking him isn't quite up to date.'

Rani chuckled and held out her hand for the phone. She punched it a few times and then spoke in a language Janaki did not recognise – possibly Gujarati.

'I'll have that information within the hour,' she said. 'In the meantime, shall we have a little chat?'

The words, though framed as a question, were spoken as a command, and Janaki, who did not feel in the least like chatting, found herself in the middle of an interrogation. At many points, she wanted to say, 'None of your bloody business,' but couldn't. Meekly she answered Rani's questions; it was as if she were under a spell and could no more resist than she could resist eating when hungry or drinking when thirsty.

'You are very beautiful – how old are you?'

'Twenty-three, ma'am.'

'I prefer to be addressed as Your Majesty. Are you married?'

'No, ma'am – um...' Janaki coughed. She couldn't bring herself to say Your Majesty. She decided to omit all terms of address.

'You are very old to be still single.'

'That is because I want to finish my education before I marry. And actually, I am engaged to be married.'

'Where is your fiancé at this time? Did he allow you to come here on your own?'

'My fiancé is working in Delhi, and he is a modern man – he does not control me.'

'Aha. So you are a modern couple? Arranged marriage or love marriage?'

'It's a love marriage.'

'So not binding I assume. No contract between the parents? Your parents would not be angry if you broke it off?'

'My parents are dead. Surely you know that, the way you keep tabs on Kamal Uncle's life.'

'Don't be rude, just answer my questions. I am asking you all this for a purpose. Why is your fiancé in Delhi and you are here?'

'Because I am trying to find my little sister. She's important to me.'

'Kamal's daughter?'

'Yes.'

'So not your real sister. But you are also trying to find Kamal, is that not true? That's why you came here?'

'That is true. Because Kamal Uncle needs to know—'

'Could it be that secretly you are planning to seduce my grandson? A beautiful young woman like you?'

Janaki jumped to her feet, hot with anger.

'What a preposterous thing to say! Of course not! How dare you insinuate—'

Rani threw back her head and laughed. She waved at Janaki, downward movements with both hands.

'Sit down, sit down, girl, and don't act so offended. You foreign-returned ladies are all the same – always taking offence. Listen to what I have to say.'

As if again under a spell, some power she could not resist, Janaki fell back onto her pouf. Rani continued, in a soft, soothing voice:

'There's nothing wrong with a beautiful woman trying to seduce a man. That has happened for centuries. It is the way. Men are weak when it comes to women, beautiful women. Most men, that is. Unfortunately not my Kamal. I tried my best with so many beautiful women. Tried to arrange his marriage with the most exquisite maidens – any man would have fallen for those girls. Instead, he got angry. Finally, he wrote me a rude letter and cut the connection to me. Then he married that blonde *ferengi*, that foreigner. I would never have allowed it but what say did I have? Luckily, she left him.

'So Kamal is ripe for the plucking. I need a great-grandson – I need Kamal to divorce her and remarry. Unfortunately, it seems he has taken a vow of celibacy and is hard to pluck. He lives like a monk, blind to the charms of women. So my private detective tells me. But I will crack him yet. Every man has his weak spot. Your fiancé doesn't sound very attached to you. Why don't you try to marry Kamal, once you find him? All this will be his one day. He is a very good catch, if you can catch him.'

She spread her arms and waved them around, to demonstrate what 'all this' was.

Janaki, reeling from the effects of that outrageous, rambling discourse, jumped up indignantly.

'That's just – that's just – it's ridiculous! Just crazy! I'm engaged! I adore my fiancé! And Kamal Uncle – he's *old*! Why would I even – I never once thought – that's just crazy!'

'Not so crazy, not so old. Only fifteen years older. That's perfectly reasonable. My husband was twenty years older than me and we were perfectly happy. The younger you are, the more likely you are to succeed. Older men like younger women. It's in their blood – it's biology. Young women to carry their seeds. They can't help it. A young, beautiful woman to wake up Kamal from this half-monk nonsense. He married once, he can marry again. It's my duty to facilitate a marriage but he is not communicating with me. But if you can find him it might work, if you don't mention that I sent you. Of course, you would have to be subtle about it, use your feminine wiles. All you have to do is act helpless and sweet, bat your eyelashes a bit at him. How could he resist? I need an heir for my business. You would be the perfect mother. What do you say? All this would be yours.'

She made a sweeping gesture, indicating the palace and the grounds.

Janaki bent down to pick up her handbag. With her absurd proposition Rani had broken the spell. The woman was out of her mind, Janaki realised, living under an obsession, an illusion, and trying to make her party to that fixation. She would have none of it. Ignoring the last preposterous suggestion, she said, 'Thank you for your information, for letting me use the phone. It was very helpful. Hopefully Kamal will contact me through my friend. Hopefully I can make some headway and find Asha. Goodbye, Mrs Darji.'

She turned away. Lakshmi leaned towards her ear. 'Your Majesty,' she whispered. 'You must address her as Your Majesty.'

'Well, I won't,' Janaki spat back, but under her breath. 'She's just a crazy old lady.'

'Ha! I heard that!' Rani laughed. 'We will see. Goodbye, young lady, and good luck with Kamal. In *every* respect.

'Kamal Uncle? Ha! Very funny.'

Out in the Corridor of Mirrors, Janaki turned to Lakshmi.

'Do you think... I mean, it might sound rude after what I just said to her, but I desperately need to check my email. Do you have...?'

'Oh, yes, yes of course. I will take you to the office – come with me.'

TWENTY

Asha

Asha hid behind a curtain as footsteps marched through the house. She peeped from behind the curtain and saw two uniformed police officers lifting the computer's hard drive from the desk. She stepped out from behind the curtain, walked up to one of the officers and said, 'Please help me, sir.'

The officer, startled, looked down at this girl with the towel wrapped around her head and the too-big amber eyes and the ragged clothes. In Tamil, he asked, 'Who are you, girl?'

'My name is Asha, sir.'

The second officer walked up and frowned.

'What are you doing here?'

'I live here, sir. They were keeping me, sir. I'm a servant. But it's not my home. I want to go to Nadiya. My sister's friend.'

The officers conversed quietly.

Officer One said to Officer Two, in Tamil, 'Think she's involved?'

'We better take her to the station. Interrogate her there.'

He removed a pair of handcuffs from his pocket and

stepped towards Asha to grab her wrist. Asha cried out and jumped away. He grabbed her again.

Officer One shot his arm out between them, and said in consternation:

'What're you doing? She's just a maid. You don't need cuffs.'

Asha cried out, in English: 'I didn't do anything! They're bad people! I'm only the maid, please don't arrest me, I want my mom and daddy!'

She burst into tears. It was so confusing. Why had they tried to handcuff her? Well, one of them had. The other one – she couldn't tell. What was going on?

Officer Two asked, quite kindly this time, and in English, 'Where are your parents?'

'My Indian parents died. My other mom – the foreign one – she's in America, and Daddy... I don't know where he is. Dubai, maybe.'

Officer Two turned to Officer One and said, 'You're right. She's just the maid. She doesn't know anything. You know what, I'll take care of this. Let's get the computer and take her back to the station.'

That sounded helpful. At the police station she could ask for help. Asha put her hand in her pocket and withdrew a slip of paper with writing on it. She handed it to Officer One.

'This is where my sister's friend lives. I'm supposed to go there. That's where I have to go.'

The two officers looked at each other and nodded. Asha, meanwhile, was on the verge of tears. Weren't the police supposed to be helpful, friendly? These two – they didn't feel or sound like that. They were treating her as if she had done something wrong. She wished with all her heart she had stayed hidden. Not trusted them. Escaped from the house once they were gone – it seemed they'd only come for the computer – and then escaped, run away, looked for a rickshaw. It was morning outside; she'd have found one quickly enough. Why had she trusted these two? Everything in her instinct screamed danger.

Officer Two said to Asha, in English, 'Your sister's friend, huh? Don't worry, little one, we'll get you safe. Come with me.' He turned to his colleague.

'Leave this to me. You can take the computer; I'll take the girl.'

They both headed back to the car, Officer Two grasping Asha's arm firmly, the other one carrying the computer and its paraphernalia. They all got into the car, Asha in the back seat. Relief flooded through her.

At last, she thought. We're going to Nadiya. I will be safe.

TWENTY-ONE
CHENNAI, 2004

Caroline

As the taxi pushed its way through heavy traffic from the airport into the city centre, Caroline's mind buzzed as if a thousand bees had been let loose within it, and not just from the lack of sleep and disruption of her inner clock from the flight to the other side of the world, stopping here and there with never a proper rest.

To dispel her nervous exhaustion and anxiety, Caroline chattered away to Kamal during the drive. Talking helped to release that pent-up emotion. Just talking about anything, anything at all, looking at him as she talked. But apart from a few glances her way, and a nodding of his head as if he were listening, Caroline felt isolated.

She remembered that Kamal had never engaged in small talk – was she being pesky with her chatter? Or was he being rude? Or perhaps he felt it was inappropriate to talk about aeroplane meals and delays in Frankfurt and screaming babies on the plane when such a huge problem lay in both their hearts. But there was time enough to discuss Asha in the coming days.

She couldn't, just couldn't, plunge into that heartache right now. So what were they supposed to talk about? Or should they just sit in silence on the back seat? He hadn't even asked her how her trip had been. Caroline just told him, without invitation, as if to bridge the yawning gap.

It was now close to midnight in Boston; she'd lost not only a whole day, but her whole life. And here she was, back where it had all started.

Back in India. Back in the chaos. The monster she had fled. But that was the price she had to pay. Greater than all the monsters in the world was her love for Asha, and that was what drove her, fired her, gave her strength.

The taxi turned into the curved hotel forecourt, and she relaxed a little. It slid up to the entrance. A porter in ornate livery opened the door and Caroline stepped out from the air-conditioned back seat. The mid-morning heat wrapped itself in a tight cloak around her; stifling, suffocating heat. She could hardly breathe. *This*, she thought, *is why I dislike India so much. This, and the crowds and the noise and the stench. Why I had to leave.*

More porters stood back, greeted her, smiled as they once again walked through the entrance portal to the hotel doors, evoking memories of their last visit, so many years ago. Just like then, the cool luxury of the hotel lobby slid around her like a fresh ocean breeze. This was why she loved the Connemara. There were no crowds and no noise and no stench and no heat; only cool aristocratic luxury. It was like walking into a bygone age; the Connemara style reflected past glories of an older, more sedate India, and Caroline once again felt right at home in its serene opulence. The other face of India. The India of those childhood fables. Kamal had done well to bring her here, back then, and now she relaxed just a little.

A porter gestured towards the reception desk. They walked over.

'Just one night, so you can settle down,' said Kamal at her side. 'Tomorrow we leave early in the morning for Gingee. Do you think you can make it for 6 a.m.?'

'Of course!' said Caroline, affronted. 'Earlier, even! I *know* how urgent it is. I could make it right away, I don't have to settle down.'

But she knew it was a lie. Already the internal buzzing had started up again. The inner ache, the inner mantra: *Asha. Asha. Asha. Where is Asha?*

They arrived at the reception desk.

'Mrs Caroline Mitchell,' said Kamal to the receptionist. Caroline had taken back her maiden surname years ago. 'There's a room booked.'

The receptionist beamed an effusive welcome, booked her in, and handed Kamal a key card, which he passed to Caroline. 'Room 212,' he said. 'A porter will bring up your luggage. I imagine you need a long rest.'

Caroline took the key and smiled at him. 'Yeah, I could do with a long, long nap. But we could meet up later – which is your room? When shall we meet?'

'Oh, I'm not staying in this hotel,' said Kamal. 'I'm at Broadlands Lodge. But I'll come around this evening and we can talk strategy. So, here's your porter with your luggage. I'll be off.'

'Oh, but – we could have a drink first. Relax a bit before I go for my nap? There's so much to catch up on.'

'No – no. I think I'll let you rest, Caroline. See you later. I'll drop in at supper time.'

And he was gone. Caroline stared after him, disappointed and, yes, hurt. Kamal had been nothing but polite and friendly, the perfect hospitable Indian host, picking her up at the airport and escorting her to this wonderful hotel, an icon of Madras, full of history and tradition, reeking of Empire and the Raj. An oasis in the midst of madness. He'd been so kind, enquiring into her well-being, solicitous; gallant, even. There was nothing at all she could fault him on. Except for the distance of his demeanour. Coldness, even.

It seemed as if the cultural divide had opened so wide in the intervening years that there was nothing left between them, nothing at all. How could that be?

How could two people who had once loved each other, who had shared all their thoughts and feelings, who had laughed and cried together and become parents together and fallen in love with a baby together, become strangers, just because – well, Caroline conceded, it was true that she had hurt Kamal deeply. Probably more than she could even guess – he had never really told her just how much the break-up had affected him. He had retreated into himself, and though they had corresponded – she had insisted that they remain friends, not only because of Asha – he had never spoken of his feelings.

Caroline had thought that it was because he didn't like writing. She'd believed that seeing her again would bring back the old funny, relaxed, warm, caring Kamal she had once known. That they would fall into each other's arms and be the close friends they were meant to be. Instead, she had this: a stranger.

Could it be that to this day he had not forgiven her for leaving him? Not even after so much time? But he had to see how incompatible they were. And surely it wasn't *her* fault that he had not moved on, found a new life, a new wife, started a new family. It wasn't her fault at all.

There was so much she wanted to tell him. She had thought that, behind it all, they could now be friends: close friends even. That was the impression he had given her in his last email. Sure, it had been succinct, but she had divined a warmth beyond the words. She had so looked forward to meeting him again in person and establishing a new relationship, one that centred on Asha, and their love and concern for her. All that chatter in the taxi – it was supposed to break the ice. But maybe he had found it boring? Found her shallow? Now, finally alone in her room, she blushed. She felt a fool. Something was wrong between her and Kamal, and she hadn't noticed it. Kamal had changed.

Well, she reasoned, of course he's changed! For a start, I dumped him as a husband. And for another start, I haven't seen him for over ten years. We've both changed in that time. I've become more American – or, I've become American again after trying, and failing, to be Indian. And he is back to being the Indian he always was, without having to make concessions to me, an American wife. Maybe we were never well matched. Maybe mixed marriages – at least, marriages of such extremes – just don't work.

But we have Asha. We have a quest to find out what's going on and secure her well-being. Christ, I hope she's all right. I hope there's a plausible explanation for Sundari's silence – that maybe she's sick or something and can't write, or maybe they moved house. But then, surely she would have, should have, informed her and Kamal?

The nagging worry that something really serious was wrong clawed at her, again. That lurking beast she could not shake off. Something bad, really bad. But she couldn't give in to negative thoughts. She was a therapist herself, for Christ's sake. She took several deep breaths to calm her mind and closed her eyes. She would NOT give in to those lurking fears!

She took off all her clothes, had a quick shower and threw herself into the luxury of a soft sweet-scented bed. She slept for six hours straight.

As promised, Kamal returned at 6 p.m. They had supper by the poolside: curried fish for Caroline, and an omelette for Kamal. This time, Caroline decided, she'd be cautious with her speech; she would not chatter away but let him lead. And this time he did, at first. But again, he spoke of nothing personal. He seemed uninterested in her life, and her feelings; he spoke only of Asha, and their movements the next day.

'I've ordered a taxi for five thirty,' he said, 'I'll pick you up outside. We should arrive at Gingee before Vikram and the kids go off to college and school. The more of the family we can meet, the better.'

'I just don't understand it,' said Caroline for the hundredth time. She shook her head slowly. 'Sundari has always been so reliable.'

'But surely Janaki would have contacted us if anything was wrong.'

'Yes, she would. But still. I wish I knew! I so wish I'd made a note of her phone number when Sundari wrote to me last year. But I knew I wouldn't be visiting her in California and who writes letters these days? If she'd sent her email address it'd have been a different story – I'd have fired off a quick greeting and welcome note. Sundari seemed to think we'd be living around the corner from each other.'

'You could have called her, Caroline.' There was an accusation in his tone, which put her back up.

Her voice took on a sharper, more aggressive tone. Bad enough to feel guilty about not welcoming Janaki to America; to link it somehow to their present predicament was unfair. As if Kamal was blaming *her* for the problem.

'Well, Janaki and I were never actual friends; I was an adult, a mentor, really, and she was just a kid. A mature kid, it's true, the way she looked after Asha, but really, it never occurred to me to call her. What would we talk about? All we ever spoke of was Asha.'

She sighed, reached out and took his hand. In a way, he was right. She had to acknowledge it. She'd been so carried away by her flourishing career she had forgotten the societal niceties. She took a deep breath, and admitted it.

'I suppose, though, I should have called to welcome her to

America, asked about her work, maybe even invited her to visit me in Cambridge. Maybe she expected that? Oh, Lord... Kamal, I feel like such an idiot now. Yes, I guess it was rude of me to ignore Janaki in America, but you know how it is – one is so wrapped up in the daily grind, my work, my clients, my career, that all those little niceties tend to be neglected. It's all my fault I didn't keep in touch.'

'But surely Janaki would have also had your address and number and would have contacted you if something was wrong?'

'Yes – surely Sundari gave her my contact details. And Janaki would certainly get in touch with me if there was a problem. So I'm hoping no news is good news. The only explanation I can think of is that they moved house, and our letters and telegrams never arrived. But that doesn't explain why Sundari hasn't sent the birthday photo.'

'Perhaps they were moving just around that time, and she forgot or couldn't find the time.'

They had gone through the same questions and possible explanations again and again and again and it always ended up this way.

'Well, we'll find out tomorrow. No point in speculating,' said Caroline.

Talking about tomorrow's plans helped to relax Caroline. She couldn't help it – she could not maintain her reserved stance. Talking was the only thing that calmed her, that distracted her from the frantic beast worrying away inside her. Talking about anything.

So Caroline told Kamal all about her career as a creative arts therapist; what she did and how many clients she had, and how she particularly enjoyed working with children and hoped to perhaps work only with children in future. That led to even more personal admissions.

'As for other stuff, personal stuff; you know. Dating and so on. I just haven't got the time. Or the interest.'

When Kamal said nothing, she took it as a sign to continue. She sighed.

'Since Wayne and I broke up – well. I haven't found anyone new. So glad I realised in time that I can't be a corporate wife. I wish I had done things differently, but I felt such guilt. And shame. You're a good man, Kamal, and I treated you despicably. I think you're the only one who ever understood me. I'm sorry.'

He nodded, as if accepting the apology, but still said nothing. After a pause, which he did not fill, she continued.

'And you? Did you find someone, like I told you to so many years ago? You're such a dark horse, Kamal.'

'No, still the old bachelor, growing old on his own.'

'But you can't really call yourself a bachelor. We're still married, remember?'

'I know. I haven't forgotten.'

She chuckled, a nervous chuckle. What did that even mean? Something just wasn't right between her and Kamal, and she couldn't put her finger on it. He just wasn't responding the way a good conversationalist should. The way an American would, a girlfriend. At such intimate revelations – well, there was surely a right way to respond and Kamal wasn't doing it.

Not that he was rude – by looking bored, for instance. No, not at all. He listened attentively, smiled and nodded in all the right places. She couldn't fault him in any way. And yet...

It was as if an aura surrounded him. Yes, that was it. Something impenetrable, something she didn't understand. His quietness, for instance. Caroline was OK with being quiet; quiet was good. But Kamal's quietness now was – *weird* was the word that came to mind. Not weird in a bad way. No, not that. Weird in an uncanny way. It was as if her words bounced off him, echoed off him, and created more words, and the more words she spoke the emptier they felt, and the more a sense of frustration grew within her. This wasn't the Kamal she knew.

She needed to know him better, so changed tack, using her own methods. Asked him questions about himself, to get him talking, to draw him out. She asked about his job, what it was like in Dubai, what he did in his free time, his friends and so on. And indeed, she did manage to get him talking in more than monosyllables. She nodded enthusiastically as he spoke of his life in Dubai.

And yet, when he left her for his own hotel, she was no nearer to knowing him than she'd been at the start. She shrugged and went to bed, and, lacking further distraction, the worry about Asha snatched her back into its claws. But jetlag was stronger, and she fell asleep again the moment her head touched the pillow.

She was ready and waiting when the taxi arrived; though it was so early, her inner clock was still in turmoil and she'd been awake even before the alarm went off – worrying, as usual, about Asha.

She slid into the back seat. Kamal sat in front, in the passenger seat, and swivelled around to greet her.

A thought had occurred to her in the shower this morning: *What if he's still in love with me? What if he never got over me, can't get over me, and that's why I can't seem to connect with him? What if he's wearing armour around his heart, so as not to feel pain?*

An interesting thought, one she would have loved to pursue had it not been for the situation with Asha. But hopefully they'd solve that today. As usual, she pushed away all her worry, all her dread, with positive thoughts.

Asha is fine. Everything is fine. Everything is going to be OK. There's an explanation; I just don't know it yet. Today I'm going

*to see my darling daughter. Hold her, kiss her, tell her how much
I love her.*

Once they'd found Asha, she'd tackle the Kamal problem.
Find out if she was right. If Kamal's weirdness was simply due
to him not being able to get over her, get over losing her. If that
was the case, well, she'd get to the bottom of it. That was her
job, after all, her profession as a therapist.

Maybe the three of them, she, Kamal and Asha, could go off
somewhere for a vacation. They needn't even mention America.
Asha was thirteen now; surely she'd be eager to go somewhere
nice. Somewhere by the seaside. Goa, or Sri Lanka again. Or a
luxury vacation in the Maldives. She could get to know them
all. She wondered about Asha's school vacations – when were
they? Could she simply take time off to go off with her parents?

They should have done this long ago. *She* should have done
this, with or without Kamal. Made more time for Asha, come to
India more often, not given up, not be put off by Asha's rejection. But yes, a vacation was necessary.

They arrived at Gingee. The taxi made its slow, horn-
blaring way through the crowded streets: bicycles, two-wheel-
ers, lorries, cars, pedestrians, cows, dogs, bullock carts, and, of
course, the ubiquitous auto-rickshaws with their raucous
klaxons all contributed to the congestion, all moving haphaz-
ardly in this direction or that so that it was a wonder that the
taxi made any kind of progress at all. Through the town to the
quiet outskirts, to the village of Thenanguddi.

Caroline couldn't help it: a sense of fondness, or nostalgia,
settled within her. This was the place she had come to with
such love, such enthusiasm, so many years previously and, like it
or not, it had won a little corner of her heart. And it was Asha's
home.

Asha! If all went well, in a few minutes she'd be holding
Asha in her arms. It was possible to manifest a good outcome to
any problem. Caroline had made every effort to maintain a posi-

tive attitude throughout everything. That's how you made good things happen. So she'd clung to the belief that all's well that ends well; that the lack of news about Asha, the lack of correspondence, had a plausible reason and Asha would be right now – she looked at her watch –right now happily sitting in class.

Hmmm. That meant she might not be at home. Very well, then; if so, they'd drive straight on to the school and take her out of class for the day. The school principal would understand. She smiled. The school principal – that was Vikram, Sundari's husband, Asha's foster-father! Of course he'd allow it.

They'd take her out of school and do something nice with her – a day trip somewhere. And at last, she would connect with Asha. All the worry about her, the suppressed panic, had forged invisible bonds that cut through every last bit of estrangement. Asha was her daughter, her beloved, and she had finally found the deep and lasting love that had been so absent when she was a baby. All would be well.

And so, Caroline was wallowing deep in positive, loving, manifesting thoughts as the taxi drove up to the Iyengar abode.

Kamal and Caroline stepped out of the cool air-conditioned taxi interior and into the heat that already felt like an oven warming up, though it was not yet mid-morning. Caroline removed the light cotton shawl she had been wearing to ward off the chill of the car's interior, but then remembered that the spaghetti straps of her summer dress might count as disrespectful, and so draped it once again across her shoulders.

They walked through the gate and approached the front door. Everything seemed the same as it had ever been. Nothing had changed. They had worried for nothing. Caroline talked the hammering of her heart into calmness.

Somewhere within her fear still lurked; fear, the uncontrollable enemy that fought for supremacy. The enemy she forced into retreat again and again and again, tirelessly. She would beat it. She would.

They heard footsteps, behind the door. Sundari was coming to open it. They would fall into each other's arms, weeping, and all would be well.

But the door opened and a strange woman stood there. Not Sundari. The woman looked them both up and down without speaking.

Kamal spoke.

'Is Mrs Iyengar at home?'

The woman shrugged. 'No Eengleesh,' she said.

'Mrs Iyengar – Sundari!' said Kamal, louder now, as if *No English* translated to Deaf.

'Sundari, Sundari!' said Caroline, brightly, smiling, trying to peer into the dark interior of the house as if Sundari might be lurking there, right behind this strange woman with the shiny green nylon sari and rattling bangles on both wrists.

The woman said something in Tamil.

'What do you mean?' said Caroline, her voice far too loud. She had learned a bit of Tamil during her stay, but all was now forgotten. She had wanted to learn more, but then, why bother? Everyone of consequence spoke English.

Everyone except this woman here, who seemed to be – temporarily – of consequence.

'Do you speak Hindi?' said Kamal in that language. The woman shrugged again and made as if to shut the door in their faces. Kamal pushed it back.

'Sundari...' The woman lolled her head to one side, tongue hanging out, eyes rolled back.

An unmistakable mime for a terrifying possibility.

'Where's Asha? Where's Vikram?' Caroline tried to keep her voice low, calm, rational, but panic had already closed its cold fingers around her heart and was pressing down, and the words emerged shrill, alarmed.

The woman's gesture was unambiguous. It meant *dead*.

Split-second emotions shot through Caroline, darts of conflicting reactions.

First, panic gave way to joy. Because *Sundari dead* was exactly the kind of plausible explanation she needed for Sundari's silence. Then joy gave way to shame – shame that she should feel joy, not grief, or shock, on learning of Sundari's death. What kind of a woman, what kind of a friend was she, not to first be shocked about Sundari; to wonder how she'd died?

Then the assertion: *I'm a mother, that's who I am. Asha's well-being comes first.* Then, again, worry. If Sundari was dead, where was Asha? Who looked after her? Who was this stranger at the door? This last emotion emerged as prominent. She had to know.

'Where is Asha? Who looks after her?'

'No Eengleesh,' said the woman again and this time succeeded in slamming the door in their faces.

Caroline and Kamal stared at each other in confusion. Then Kamal said the only sensible thing in the circumstances.

'Let's go to Vikram's school. Ask Vikram what happened. And Asha'll be there too, at school. It all makes sense now. Sundari died. There was no one to reply to our letters, send the birthday photographs. Vikram must have forgotten about us, or didn't even know about our correspondence. We'll go to him.'

'Oh – right!' said Caroline, cheering up immediately. 'That must be what happened. But poor Sundari! I wonder how she died. She never mentioned any illness. Poor Vikram. And the children, half-orphaned! I wonder if that woman is Vikram's new wife?'

They were back in the car by now. Kamal shook his head. 'Probably just a housekeeper. She's uneducated. Vikram wouldn't marry someone who doesn't speak English. Trust me on that.'

Quite relaxed now, Caroline chuckled. 'You're right about

that. If ever there was an Indian Anglophile, it's Vikram. He'd marry an English-speaking woman. They'd speak English at home.'

Then she remembered again that Sundari was dead and adjusted her voice and her conversation accordingly. *How callous and cold I am, to laugh like that! Sundari is dead. I must grieve. I must be more caring.*

'Poor, poor Sundari. Poor Vikram, poor children. It must have been devastating for them. No wonder we didn't get any news about Asha. Vikram probably didn't even think of contacting us in his grief. Asha must be devastated.'

'Yes, that explains why Vikram didn't inform us right away. It would have been the last thing on his mind. It probably didn't even occur to him that we'd need to know, and to reconsider leaving Asha with him. And with that strange woman.'

Caroline shuddered. 'I didn't like her at all. She's definitely not a fitting foster-mother for Asha. We'll have to take her away immediately. Oh, Kamal!'

They looked at each other and smiled, both knowing what the other was thinking. With Sundari's passing, Asha would be theirs. No reason anymore to leave her in India. Caroline reached out, took Kamal's hand and squeezed it. She left it there, because his hand was cold. Kamal had never liked air-conditioning he always froze.

She smiled, took a deep breath and closed her eyes, her head slightly thrown back against the backseat upholstery. She knew it! That was the logical explanation that had been missing. Sundari had died, and no one had thought to inform them. Asha was so much a part of the Iyengar family that Vikram, absent-minded as he was about domestic affairs, had probably forgotten completely that Asha had biological parents who'd need to be informed.

She began to dream. This meant that there was no reason on earth to leave Asha with the Iyengars any longer. Not even

Janaki was still here. Sure, this was Asha's home and no doubt she loved it, loved Vikram, but Caroline was in no doubt whatsoever that Asha, now thirteen, would be mature enough to understand the chance now offered to her. She would go to America. Yes, Asha had always refused, but now, she had no choice.

She, Caroline, would pluck Asha out of India, whisk her off to Cambridge and show her a life she could until now have only dreamed about.

Of course, there was the question of Kamal, who, as her father, would also perhaps want a piece of Asha. But Kamal was a single man, a single working man. In Dubai. He could not offer her a home. She could, with her parents' help, her parents' money. They would find a way. Kamal could come and work in America, to be near Asha. They would work something out...

TWENTY-TWO

Caroline

'Here we are!' said Kamal, jolting Caroline out of her daydream. She had been visualising Asha in America, starting high school. Making new friends, pyjama parties, swimming pool parties. Christmas and Thanksgiving and Halloween – what a life waited for her! But first of all, a vacation. They all needed that.

The school was a little way outside of town, a large, functional two-storey building. The taxi drove into the grounds under an arched entrance gate and parked in front of a sign that read *Mahatma Gandhi English Medium Academy. Secondary Co-Education.*

Once more, they stepped out into the broiling heat. Caroline was sure she'd catch a cold with all this back-and-forth between the extremes of hot and cold. They entered through the main door. The place was quiet, not a soul to be seen. Obviously everyone was at lessons; all the teachers, all the pupils. They found themselves in an open hallway with a broad staircase leading up, and a corridor leading off. A sign pointed towards the corridor that read, among other things, *Principal's Office.*

Kamal gestured and they both turned down that corridor.

There was the door. Kamal rapped on it.

'Come in!' said a voice from within, and Kamal opened the door and they both walked in, smiling in preparation for meeting Vikram again.

The smile did not last long, because sitting behind the dark wood desk was a stranger.

'Oh!' said Caroline, stopping in her tracks. 'Excuse me, but...'

'Mr Iyengar? Where is Mr Iyengar?' Kamal asked.

The man at the desk half-rose, looked from one to the other. His initial smile of welcome morphed into a more appropriate expression of solemnity.

'I am sorry to inform you that Mr Iyengar has passed away.'

Caroline's eyes opened wide. 'Vikram – dead too? But... when? How? He and his wife... both dead?'

The room was not air-conditioned and the overhead fan did little more than move the hot air around, but Caroline felt suddenly cold. All over.

The man was speaking again.

'I am the new principal – Mudaliar is my name, Gopal Mudaliar. My name is actually on the wall outside the door. Are you friends of Mr Iyengar? I am so sorry to break the news to you; it must be such a bad shock. He and his wife were involved in a tragic accident two months ago and neither survived.'

'Oh my God! *Both* of them! I can't – I just can't...'

So not just Sundari – Vikram was also dead. Caroline grabbed Kamal's arm for support. She felt faint; she swayed, and Kamal placed his arm around her for support.

'Yes. It was extremely sad, especially for the children of course. Terrible accident. Just terrible.'

'But – Asha? Asha Darji? Our daughter? We need to see her. She is a pupil at this school.'

'Oh! Asha! Delightful little girl – but she is no longer with us. She was taken out of school about four weeks ago.'

'Asha – not here? B-but... the other children? The other Iyengar children? What happened? We are her parents – we need to know!'

'I think, Mr and Mrs Darji, you should take a seat. We need to talk. Can I get you a glass of water? Coffee? Tea?'

Caroline did not bother to correct him regarding their names; he was technically correct. She was still cold, numb inside. She needed something to shake off that numbness. 'Coffee, please,' she said as she took a seat across the desk from Mr Mudaliar.

Kamal nodded. 'Yes. I'll have coffee too.'

Mr Mudaliar picked up a phone on his desk, punched a button and spoke into the receiver. 'Two coffees, please.' He then turned back to his visitors, shoved some papers to one side, linked his fingers on the desk in front of him, leaned forward a little and said in what was obviously meant to be a soothing voice, 'Mr and Mrs Darji—'

Kamal interrupted. 'I am Mr Darji. She is Ms Mitchell. We are separated. We came to Gingee to find Asha because we have had no news of her for all this time   usually we hear from Mrs Iyengar punctually on her birthday and this year there was only silence. No one told us the Iyengars were dead, no one told us Asha was removed from school. Who took her out of school? Where is she now?' Righteous anger was in his voice now, and Caroline laid a calming hand on his arm. 'We do need an explanation, Mr Mudaliar. Who removed her from school?'

Mr Mudaliar coughed. 'Well, it was another Mr Iyengar, I believe a younger brother to the deceased. It seems he took over the care of the children and moved into the house. He came some time ago and said she would no longer attend the school. It happened very suddenly. He took all the Iyengar children out of school.'

'Where did she go to? Which school? This is ridiculous! We are paying fees for this school!'

'Well, perhaps he sent her to another school in Gingee, a free state school? I wouldn't know, I'm afraid.'

'But we pay fees! He has no right!'

Kamal looked at Caroline. 'That woman at the house must be his wife.'

He turned back to Mr Mudaliar. 'You say he took all the children out? So all the boys have gone too?'

'Yes. The eldest boy of course has left secondary school anyway – he attended the engineering college, I believe. Probably already graduated. The daughter, Janaki, is studying in Madras, I believe; probably married by now. The youngest boys were all taken out of school. I assume that the younger Mr Iyengar could not afford school fees. Although his two daughters are now pupils here – strange indeed!'

'And you don't know which school they are going to?' asked Kamal. Mr Mudaliar shook his head.

'I'm sorry, no, I don't. There are two or three state secondary schools in Gingee.' His face brightened. 'But we could ask one of his daughters. She would know.'

At that moment a woman knocked and entered the room bearing a tray with two mugs. She placed the tray on the desk and handed Caroline and Kamal a mug each. The coffee, of course, was already milked and sugared. Caroline had forgotten that that was the way coffee was served in South India. She liked hers black and no sugar. She sipped at the milky liquid, then put down the cup; it was horrible, much too sweet.

'Miss Pillai, please ask Miss Sohini Iyengar to come here at once. She is in fourth standard.'

An awkward silence descended on the room once Miss Pillai had left. Kamal sipped at his coffee, and Caroline decided to give hers a second chance, simply so that she'd have something to do. Mr Mudaliar spoke of the heat and the drought and obviously wished them gone.

Sohini Iyengar rapped on the door, Mr Mudaliar called 'Enter!' and she did, standing before the desk with hanging head.

Mr Mudaliar spoke to her in Tamil, and then explained,

'She and her sister don't know a word of English yet. It's hard for them at an English Medium school – they struggle. I just asked her which school her cousins and Asha attend.'

He turned back to the girl and gave her a sign to reply.

She said something in Tamil. He asked more questions; she gave more answers. Mr Mudaliar said, 'She says she doesn't know what school the boys attend. And Asha has gone.'

Caroline and Kamal stared. Kamal spoke: 'Asha, gone? Gone where?'

More conversation in Tamil. Mr Mudaliar raised his voice and the girl seemed to visibly shrink. He then sent her away; she shuffled to the door and disappeared.

'I'm sorry – she doesn't know much. She just says that Asha was bad. She doesn't know any more than that. The family is living in her deceased uncle's house. She just says that Asha is a bad girl and is gone. She won't say more than that.'

Kamal stood up, his face like stone.

'Thank you for your time and your help, Mr Mudaliar. I think we must have a little talk with the police. Come, Caroline.'

Caroline nodded her thanks, turned and walked to the door, coffee unfinished.

TWENTY-THREE

Asha

The car, which was just an ordinary Tata and not a police car at all, drove off, Officer One at the wheel. At the police station, Officer One got out. He bent over and smiled at Asha through the open back-seat window.

'My colleague will take you to your sister's friend,' he said, not unkindly. He picked up the computer and walked away, into the station.

The car drove off again, Officer Two at the wheel this time. As he steered with one hand, he talked on a huge mobile phone, in Tamil, nodding all the time.

After about an hour, they arrived at a tall, narrow house, like an upended shoebox, painted in gaudy colours.

This must be Nadiya's house, Asha thought. Though her memory of Nadiya's home was different: a student boarding house. Not this town house. Maybe she lives with her parents now, she thought.

A woman in a blue sari and flowers in her hair came out of the front door, walked over to the car. Nadiya's Amma, Asha thought. After speaking a few words to Officer Two through the open window, she opened the back-seat door, grabbed Asha's hand and yanked her out of the car.

'Come with me, girl.'

'Ow! Let me go!' cried Asha, but the woman ignored her pleas and pushed her into the house. It was definitely not Nadiya's house. Not Nadiya's Amma.

'You can call me Aunty,' she said to Asha.

Later that afternoon, Asha and Aunty arrived at Madras train station and merged into the immense crowds. Aunty led Asha through the chaos, an iron grip on her wrist. She turned onto a platform that said Mumbai, in three different scripts, pushing through the crowds and the chaos.

On the platform, Aunty consulted her ticket, checked the carriage number, pushed Asha into the train and got in behind her. She shoved Asha into a compartment where several other women were also settling in, pushing bundles under the seat and onto the luggage rack. They both sat down, Asha squashed between her escort and a stranger.

The train chugged off, hurtling through the Indian countryside.

It stopped at a station. On the platform outside, small traders with baskets passed by. Aunty bought snacks through the window, offered them to Asha, who simply stared into space, and ignored the snack.

The hours ticked by. Lulled by the rhythmic chugging of the engine, the swaying of the carriage and the chatter of the women, Asha fell asleep, leaning against the wall. She woke up, whispered quietly to Aunty, her one and only attempt at speech since leaving the police car. If that was what it was. Aunty stood up, pushed Asha into the corridor and along to the toilet. Shoved her in. When Asha emerged a few minutes later she was still standing outside, waiting.

As night fell, staff arrived with sheets, pillows and blankets, and converted the seats into bunks. The women in the compartment – who had now all become friends – rearranged themselves, climbing into the three tiers of bunks. Aunty and Asha got into the same bunk, head to feet, with Asha squeezed against the wall.

After another day and another night, the train arrived at Mumbai. Aunty, still gripping Asha's wrist, descended to the platform, pulling Asha behind her. She pushed through the crowd to a taxi, shoved Asha into the back seat and got in beside her, before barking instructions to the driver. They drove off, into the throbbing, pulsing pandemonium of Mumbai's streets.

TWENTY-FOUR

Caroline

Kamal and Caroline slid back into the taxi's back seat. The driver, who had been sleeping behind the steering wheel, leaning against the door, sprang back into life, turning to ask for further directions.

'Let's try to get some more information first,' said Kamal. 'So that we have actual evidence for the police. You know how police bureaucracy works. We need concrete proof. I have an idea. Since that woman doesn't speak English let's get an interpreter.'

Caroline, sitting glumly next to him, nodded, glad to see that Kamal was taking charge. She was incapable of thinking. Numb with terror.

'Good idea,' she said. She thought for a bit, and remembered a woman she had once befriended, a friend of Sundari's who spoke tolerable English as well as Tamil.

'Vasanthi! Let's go to Vasanthi. She can translate for us. And explain what happened. I hope she's home.'

She leaned forward and told the driver which way to drive. It all came back to her, the twists and turns through the town.

'Kamal, I'm scared,' she admitted. 'What's going on? Why did no one tell us that Sundari and Vikram were both dead? Why did they take Asha out of school?'

'I don't know but we'll find her. Vikram's brother has a lot to answer for. We're paying school fees for Asha, and she should have been left in the school, no matter what the circumstances. And we should have been informed.'

She reached into her backpack for her water bottle. The water was now lukewarm. It didn't matter: her throat was parched. Her body was parched. She finished it off.

'Kamal – look! I'm shaking. I can't help it. I'm shaking.'

She held out both quivering hands. Though it wasn't yet cold in the car, Caroline's teeth began to chatter involuntarily.

'I'm so scared, Kamal. Where's our daughter? I want my daughter!'

She began to whimper. She placed her hands under her armpits and curled up on the back seat, into a ball. Kamal placed a comforting arm around her. She leaned against him, for courage.

'She'll be fine. Vikram's brother will tell us which school she now attends. We'll drive right there, pick her up, and on to Madras. Don't worry. She'll be fine.'

Think positive. Uncurling, Caroline stretched out her legs again.

But in spite of his confident words Kamal, too, could not shake off the sense of dread that gnawed at his bowels, and he too felt the cold that comes from inside and freezes the very blood. He tapped the driver on the shoulder.

'No AC,' he said, and the driver turned off the cold and they opened the windows so that the warmth from outside entered the car, but it did not help, for the ice of fear had them both in its grip.

'I just hope Vasanthi's at home,' said Caroline again.

She was. Vasanthi burst into smiles when she saw Caroline, but then her smile vanished, for Caroline was crying now, tears of fear and frustration – and relief; Vasanthi would surely know more?

'Cold hands!' said Vasanthi as she gripped Caroline's hands in her own. 'Come in, come in.'

She led them both into the cool dark interior of her home, and bid them take a seat, gesturing to a pile of cushions in the corner. Caroline and Kamal took a cushion each and sat down in front of a low wooden table. A small naked child was crawling on the tiled floor; Vasanthi scooped him up and in a fluid motion set him on her hip, one arm around the little bare back. The child smiled at the newcomers and waved. Caroline and Kamal waved back, but unsmilingly, and the child too stopped smiling and reached out with both hands to be put down, grunting in impatience. Vasanthi returned him to the floor, where he quickly scooted off through a doorway. Vasanthi lifted the hem of her sari and sat down cross-legged on the bare floor opposite her guests.

'Tell us what happened,' said Caroline, and Vasanthi did.

'Sundari and Vikram, both accident on street, car hitting, both dead. Vikram, he live three days then dead. Vikram brother family move into house.'

'What happened to the children, Vasanthi? What happened to Asha?'

Vasanthi shrugged.

'Children, they go another school, secondary school in town, but not Asha. My children tell me.'

'Vasanthi, we want you to come with us to help us speak to Vikram's brother's wife. She speaks no English – could you translate for us?'

Vasanthi shook her head.

'Don't want speak with that woman,' she said. 'She bad woman.'

'Please, Vasanthi! Please come.'

'We need to speak to her husband too,' said Kamal. 'I think he's the one we really need to blame for this. He's stealing our money, literally! Fees for that school are high, by Indian standards. He's taken Asha out but is still pocketing the money we sent, as well as the money for her maintenance, her pocket money. That's theft.'

'Paruthy bad man. Beat children.' Vasanthi held out her palm and clapped it with her other hand to demonstrate.

'I'll be after him,' said Kamal. 'But we have to go, Vasanthi, to find out where Asha is. And to talk to that man. We need you, Vasanthi, please! Come with us.'

'Please, Vasanthi! I'm so – so...' Caroline didn't know what she was anymore: fearful, confused, desperate, guilty (because this was all her fault); yet full of hope because, after all, they were going to get Asha and nobody would ever take her away again, and she would make good for all the years of neglect.

Asha, you will be first in my life. From now on, you come first.

Vasanthi, seeing the tears in Caroline's eyes, reached out and pulled her to her bosom, placing her arms around her.

'I will come,' she said. 'I am mother too. I will come. I will help. One minute please.'

Vasanthi needed ten minutes to dress her child and make herself presentable, and then they all got into the taxi, Vasanthi in the front seat with her child on her lap, where he kneeled, both hands on the open windowsill. Vasanthi laughed.

'He never been in car before!' she said.

Caroline had an idea.

'Shall we just go and pick up Asha and not bother with going back to that house? Why should we even talk to those people? What can they tell us? I think we should just get a

Tamil lawyer and sue the skin off them. How dare they not inform us of Sundari's death! How dare they take Asha out of school!' Her eyes blazed with indignation. Now that Vasanthi was with them she felt emboldened. 'All I want is Asha. Let's just go to the school and get her. We're her parents. We have the right.'

'Definitely a lawyer,' said Kamal. 'But we don't know which new school Asha attends. And I need to speak to those people myself, look them in the eye. Besides, we need to pick up Asha's papers. Her passport, at least. They'll have that in the house.'

The same woman opened the door when they knocked, but this time she called into the interior, and a moment later a man, her husband no doubt, replaced her in the doorway. A man with a sickening false smile plastered across his face, his gaze wandering nervously between Caroline and Kamal.

'Tell him we want to know where Asha is and why he took her out of school,' Kamal said.

A long exchange in Tamil took place between Vasanthi and Paruthy; they seemed to be arguing.

'What's he saying?' Caroline interrupted. Vasanthi turned to her and switched language.

'He say Asha naughty girl, not good behave in school when Vikram and Sundari dead, bad girl, school make her leave.'

'You mean, expelled her? That's a lie. Tell him we just came from the school and we know that he took her out and all Sundari's other children and replaced them with his own. Tell him we met his daughter. Go on, tell him.'

Caught out in the lie, Paruthy didn't even have the grace to look embarrassed. He launched into a new endless speech.

'What's he saying?' said Kamal to Vasanthi.

'He said Asha bad behave at home. Not helping in house. Rude to his wife and always fighting his daughters. Therefore he had to remove her.'

'Remove her from – where?'

'From the house, Caroline. He remove her from the house.'

'I don't understand. Remove her? She doesn't live here anymore?'

'No. She gone, Caroline. He send her to Madras. Wife cousin was looking for maid and he send her there to work.'

White-hot rage consumed Caroline. She sprang at the man, at his face, fingers spread, screaming, 'I'll kill him, I will! Lies, lies, lies! Where's my daughter?'

The man gave her a hard shove so that she tumbled backwards to the dusty ground. The front door slammed in their faces. Kamal helped Caroline to her feet, dusted her off, put a calming arm around her. Caroline tried to fling herself at the closed door but Kamal held her back and turned to Vasanthi.

'Is it true? Is that what he said? That he sent Asha to Madras to be a maid?'

Vasanthi nodded. 'I not know. My son say Asha not in school for long time, but I not know she in Madras. That man just now telling.'

'But – but... how could he?'

Vasanthi shrugged and said nothing.

Kamal thought for a while. Then he said, 'Janaki. We need to talk to Janaki. Do you have her address, Vasanthi?'

'Janaki not here, gone America long time ago. Don't know where.'

'Her brothers will know her address, surely. One of the elder boys. They'll be at school now, surely.'

'The eldest, Shankar, is at engineering college in Madras. Sundari told me that a while ago. The others must be living at home still. With those people. How could they *do* this, Kamal? How can people be so horrible? So mean? Poor little Asha. How scared she must be. Kamal, I want her back! I want my daughter back. *It hurts so much...*'

The last words came out as a wail. They were still standing outside the Iyengar house; Caroline flung herself against the door and pummelled it with all her might, wailing and sobbing. Kamal quietly drew her away and to himself, in an embrace that helped to quieten her; her sobbing relaxed into a silent heaving of the shoulders.

'They're obviously not going to help without pressure,' said Kamal, though Caroline wasn't listening. 'We need a lawyer. And, like I said, police.'

Vasanthi nodded. 'Police!' she said. 'Bad people. Police help find Asha.'

'Right. Come on. The law it is. We'll find her, Caroline, I promise. We'll find her. Wherever she is. We'll squeeze the truth out of those people. They chose the wrong victim this time.'

An arm around a weeping Caroline, he led the way back to the car.

There followed hours and hours of the debilitating, exhausting, mind-draining bureaucracy that Caroline so hated about India. Sitting in a waiting room filled with rows of plastic chairs under a slow-rotating ceiling fan, while a police officer deigned to listen to their story and file a report.

Another waiting room; this time a lawyer's, this time on a wooden bench, where Caroline sat squeezed between several Indian women while Kamal stood in the hallway swatting away flies.

Vasanthi had long gone home, not without inviting them to lunch; she had waited to file the police report in case no one spoke English. But neither of them was hungry, and the hot midday hours slipped by with hardly an inch of progress made.

The lawyer proved far more helpful than the police, and once he understood what had happened – and that these were clients who would pay well for his services – he sprang into action. He picked up a phone and spoke a Tamil diatribe into the receiver.

'Police!' he explained, as he replaced the receiver and stood up, tucking his shirt into his belt, which hung beneath a small paunch. This man did not waste time, Caroline was happy to see. He unceremoniously shooed his other waiting clients away, marched her and Kamal down to the taxi and gave sharp instructions to the driver.

Back to the Iyengar house. They arrived simultaneously with two policemen on a motorbike.

'He must have offered a bribe,' Kamal whispered to Caroline, and she nodded. This lawyer meant business, and for the first time for hours hope swelled in her heart. This was action. Better than all her positive manifestations.

Reinforced with the law, it was easy to gain entry to the Iyengar house. Much talking, some shouting took place, of which she understood only the occasional word. *Asha*, and *Madras*, and *school*, and *rupees*, and *foreigners*. Paruthy, belligerent at first, turned into a cowering mass of fear in the presence of the police and finally produced a flimsy-paged notebook, which he leafed through until he found what he was looking for. He passed the notebook to the lawyer, who smiled up at Caroline.

'It is Asha's address in Madras,' he said. 'She is working as a maid for this man's wife's cousin.'

'How dare he! How *dare* he!' Caroline quivered with rage and would have flung herself, nails bared, at the man again had not Kamal held her back.

'He will face the full force of the law,' said the lawyer. 'There will be a charge of abduction as well as other charges. Theft of school and maintenance money. He did not fully understand who he was dealing with. Seemed to think she was just some abandoned girl he could exploit to the maximum.'

'Well, he's in deep shit now!'

He chuckled, and Caroline too nodded and grinned at the choice of words, so unusual coming from Kamal, usually so polite.

'I hope he drowns in it,' she said. 'He deserves it.'

The lawyer finished copying the address into his own note-book, tore out a page and handed it to Caroline.

'This is the place where your daughter is staying,' he said. 'You can go there now and hold her in your arms. She is waiting for you.'

Caroline wanted to jump at him and hug him, but knew it was inappropriate in India, and maybe even in America. Instead, she hugged Kamal, who hugged her back, and as they walked towards the waiting taxi – leaving the police to deal with Paruthy – she whirled him around and laughed out loud, her body loosened by the elixir of relief.

'Back to Madras!' she sang. 'Straight to that place to pick up Asha!'

Just as they reached the car, a boy in school uniform rushed up to them.

'Kamal Uncle! Caroline Aunty! I am so glad to see you!'

'Dev!' cried Caroline. Indeed, it was Sundari's youngest son, now a handsome teenager taller than herself. She had always liked Dev; he was bright and friendly and had loved her stories about life in America.

'I will go there when I am big!' he had always said, and Caroline had always promised, 'I will help you. When you apply for studies there you must ask me. I can help.'

Now here he was again, twice the size and grinning in delight at seeing her.

But then the grin faded from his face.

'Oh, Aunty, Uncle... Janaki is trying to get hold of you. I have been looking for your address but could not find it. You must email her straight away. Asha is missing.'

'Yes, we know that. She's working as a maid in Madras. We

have the address.' Caroline waved the notebook page at him. But Dev shook his head.

'No, Aunty, she's not there anymore. Janaki said she's gone. Disappeared. Janaki thinks she's been abducted...' – he paused, looked from one to the other, his eyes tiny mirrors reflecting the same fear growing in her heart with every word he spoke – 'by child traffickers.'

The fear immediately morphed into sheer terror.

TWENTY-FIVE

Asha

After an endless drive through the teeming city streets, they arrived in front of a grand mansion in an exclusive area of Mumbai. Aunty led Asha to the front door.

A well-dressed middle-aged woman in an expensive sari opened the front door. She stood on the threshold, frowning as she looked Asha up and down. Asha was aware of how bizarre she must look in her old and faded clothes, her hair hanging in scrawny rattails over her shoulders. Somewhere between leaving the Pandians' home and arriving here she had lost the towel she had appropriated from Mrs Pandian's luxurious bathroom, and there had been no chance to brush it, not even with her fingers, or plait it into decency. She felt herself shrink all the more under the woman's critical gaze.

'You are late,' she said to Asha's escort.

'Sorry, Madame. Traffic was terrible.'

The woman at the door grasped Asha by the wrist.

'Come inside.'

To Aunty, she said, 'You can go now. Leave her with me.' The other woman nodded and walked away.

She turned to Asha. Her voice was harsh, the Tamil syllables sharp as knives.

'I am Devaki Aunty. I will look after you from now on. You are in good hands.'

But her actions contradicted her words. She closed the front door, grabbed Asha's wrists and yanked her over the threshold and into a dark hallway.

'You are a very lucky girl. Mr Chaudhuri is very particular and he has chosen you. You'd better behave yourself.'

Asha said nothing but allowed herself to be dragged along a corridor into the interior of the house.

'You've lost your tongue? You need to answer when I talk to you. Mr Chaudhuri expects you to speak.'

Asha stayed silent. She looked to the ground. Devaki led her upstairs and opened the door to a small bedroom.

'You will stay here. It's very comfortable. But first we need to get you cleaned up. You are filthy and you stink. You need a bath, and you are no doubt covered in lice. I will send a girl to bathe and dress you. Go in.'

Asha wanted to say she did not stink, that she had had a luxurious shower and washed her hair with expensive shampoo. It was the old clothes that stank, not her body. But the words stuck in her throat. She couldn't manage even a croak.

Devaki shoved Asha into the room, closed the door. Asha heard the key turn in the lock.

Devaki, sitting on a couch reading a fashion magazine, looked up as the door opened and Asha, escorted by the girl who had helped her bathe and dress and done her hair, entered. She wore a new *shalwar kameez*, and looked clean and fresh, her hair nicely plaited and decorated with marigolds. Devaki smiled.

'That's much better. You finally look human. Come sit down next to me.' To the girl, she said, 'Bring her here.'

She patted the seat next to herself. The girl led Asha over to the couch. Asha sat down next to Devaki. Devaki lifted her chin up and inspected her face.

'Quite lovely. Your golden eyes. Perfect lips. Mr Chaudhuri will be very pleased. You are such a lucky girl. Your name is Asha?'

Asha said nothing. She looked at the ornate, and probably expensive, carpet.

Devaki's voice was sharp, annoyed. 'Still not talking? You need to answer when I talk to you. And look at me. Anyway, I'm giving you a new name. Your name from now on will be Kamini.'

Asha continued to look down in silence.

'So rude. Well, we'll see about that, young lady. That's why you're with me. I'm going to teach you good manners and how to be nice to Mr Chaudhuri. You are a very lucky girl, because Mr Chaudhuri is a wealthy man, and he is looking for class. He doesn't want some cheap girl from the streets. He chose you. As a companion, long term. Lucky girl.'

She paused, waiting for Asha to reply, or even to nod. No reply came.

'I will have to get you talking in the next few days. Otherwise it's to the streets for you. Or even the cages. You ever heard the word Kamathipura? It's your choice. But I think you are just a little shy. You do understand English, don't you? They say you speak English and Tamil. Well, I don't speak Tamil and neither does Mr Chaudhuri. He's a Bengali millionaire. He speaks Bengali and Hindi and English. Such a lucky girl, to speak English. He will like that because it shows high class. Education. You will stay with me for a few days so I can prepare you and teach you how to be nice to Mr Chaudhuri. If you are good to him, you will have a pleasant life. Like a second wife. You will have a very comfortable life.'

Asha did not react. She continued to stare at the carpet.

TWENTY-SIX

Janaki

There was only one thing left to do; she'd do it reluctantly, for she hated to beg, but she'd do it for Asha. Rani was Asha's great-grandmother. She would help.

And so Janaki returned to Rani and told her the new developments, confessed her fears to her.

'I need to find her,' she said. 'She's there somewhere, in danger; maybe a prisoner again. I don't know. I came to you to find Kamal but only so that I can find Asha. Help me, please!'

Rani listened with great interest. Then she said, 'Kamal has left Dubai. After your telephone call to him I put my private investigator back on the job. It is my suspicion that he, too, is looking for Asha. She is the bait. Find her, and you will find Kamal. Find Kamal, and you will find her. You must go back to Madras. I will tell Lakshmi to give you the money. Stay the night and fly there tomorrow. Lakshmi will book the first flight out for you.'

And so Janaki stayed the night, and to pass the time she

returned to the computer and continued her research of Asha's captor's emails.

She dug deep into them and what she found there disgusted her to the core. *How can men do this?* she screamed to herself. *How can they be so depraved, so utterly debauched? So cruel? These are young girls they are talking about – children!*

And so she spent the night digging through the emails, starting as far back as possible. The first emails were in Hindi, which she couldn't read. Then suddenly they switched to English; as if a non-Hindi speaker had joined the group. Sometimes broken English, sometimes fluent. The occasional Hindi, once Tamil, thoroughly protested by the others. They finally settled on English, with occasional Hindi messages.

The subject was girls. Girls were spoken of as if they were cattle being assessed and sent to market. Shunted here and there, priced at such-and-such. This customer would like this, and that customer would like that. Now and again there were attachments, images of young girls, dressed up like adult women in opulent red saris and fake jewels, their unsmiling faces giving the lie to the lavishness of their attire. Such despair, such abject hopelessness in those opaque eyes. Now and then the word Kamathipura fell, sometimes abbreviated to 'K', but that hell-hole was a world away from Madras. Thank goodness.

There was no mention of Asha. And then, in a recent mail:

I have a new girl, very fair-skinned, thirteen years old. Speaks English but not yet ready for trade. Virgin: I had it checked. Contact Rajagopal; this is one for Chaudhuri. I am keeping her as a maid in my home for the time being until we hear from Rajagopal. He's got a customer looking for such a girl. Problem is she does not speak at all. He likes them relaxed and chatty in English, so we have to work on her. Will take photo soon and send; this one is superior, will bring a good price. She is wasted here in Madras.

That could only be a reference to Asha: fair-skinned; a maid in Madras; speaks English. It had to be her.

Janaki's skin crawled. Nausea rose in her, and a creeping coldness that started in her stomach and spread everywhere, down to her fingertips. Everything churned within her.

Why oh why had she asked Asha to search for information, for the password? That had cost Asha precious time. *Get out Asha; run. Leave that place and run. Go to Nadiya. Get out.* That's what she should have said. Because Asha's silence now could only mean trouble. Perhaps someone came back for her; obviously there was a gang involved and the very minute her captor was arrested Asha had been in jeopardy. She was '*superior quality, would bring a good price*'.

Someone must have gone back for her, and poor little Asha had been trapped while she was at the computer looking for a bloody password. And it was all her, Janaki's, fault.

Where are you, Asha, where are you? Call out to me and I will find you, I promise!

Janaki read on. There had been several new emails since that one, all cc'd to her due to Asha's intervention, but apart from all-round approval by the other recipients no further reference was made to 'the maid in Madras'. Other girls were discussed; sometimes photos were attached.

Then, soon after the reference to Asha, a flurry of anxious exchanges:

URGENT. Balram arrested this morning in raid. Tried to defraud Mr K. and Mr K. of course is the wrong one to vex. Idiot. Got the police to go after him.

Damn! What about the computer? The girl?

Don't think they got those. My source didn't mention them.

Need to get them. Too many big names on the computer. And the girl too valuable to lose.

Don't worry, got someone dealing with it. Can get the computer def., most probably the girl ran away after the arrest.

Damn!

After that last *Damn!* the language reverted to Hindi, to Janaki's frustration. But, she thought, I can get Lakshmi to translate. Just when they began to talk about Asha. Damn, indeed!

Half an hour later it was over. She knew the worst and it was worse than her worst nightmare.

'They are sending her to Mumbai,' said Lakshmi. 'She is to be sold as a child prostitute to the highest bidder. At the moment it is a man called Chaudhuri.'

Asha was no longer in Madras. Asha was in Mumbai. In Kamathipura. Perhaps, even, in one of those dreaded cages.

And then, one last mail, in both Hindi and English:

Who is jiyeng@yahoo.in?

And then silence. Janaki, cold enough before with the tension of it all, now felt her blood turn to ice. She had been exposed, discovered, and even though the discovery was all in virtual space, in the ether, it was as if she stood there naked before a host of leering criminals. And after that, silence.

'They've found me out,' she said. 'No more emails.'

'I'm so sorry,' Lakshmi said.

'I have to go to Mumbai.' Janaki said.

'Talk to Rani,' said Lakshmi. 'She can help. It's her great-granddaughter, after all. She has detectives working for her; that's how she tracks Kamal. And she has money. She will help. She will. She may appear hard but her heart is soft. She can help find Asha and Kamal and she will finance it. I know her, I am her closest confidante. You need her.'

'Yes,' said Janaki. 'I'll do that. This is too big for me alone. Thanks, Lakshmi.'

Another email was in Janaki's inbox. It was from her fiancé, Giridhar. She smiled fondly, opened it, read it. The smile faded from her lips.

'Men!' She boxed her own head with some vigour, as if to expel Giridhar from her brain. 'No balls.' She deleted the email.

TWENTY-SEVEN

Janaki

And now here she was. Bombay. City of gold, they called it; or city of dreams, dreams that came true or were extinguished in a puff of breath. Mumbai, she was supposed to call it now, but the word stuck in her throat.

You either love it or hate it, a friend had once told her. The friend had grown up there, and therefore loved it, but Janaki knew from the start that she would hate it. Somewhere among these twenty million people rushing here and there, living in luxury or scraping a living from the pavement, was Asha. A grain of sand on an endless beach. How would she ever find that single grain?

Bombay was the enemy. She arrived prepared to do battle, prepared to wrest from its bowels that precious jewel, her Asha. But first she had to find that jewel. Find the hiding place. She would encounter Bombay – as she would always call it – at its ugliest. Let herself be sucked into its underbelly, dig down to its deepest abyss of depravity.

Janaki looked up, gazing into the distance, spiral notebook in hand.

She absent-mindedly clicked the nib of her ballpoint pen in and out, biting her lip, searching for a starting point.

She had arrived by train from Baroda just the day before. She had found a reasonably priced hotel – though she soon discovered that 'reasonably priced' was relative, for even the cheapest Bombay hotels seemed as expensive as the best of Madras – and immediately made her way to the hellhole of Kamathipura.

She had first found mention of that place buried deep in the emails she had trawled through, seeking a clue as to where Asha might be. She had dismissed those mentions at first – they had nothing to do with Asha, obviously – she had assumed Asha was safely in Madras. Though again, 'safely' was a relative term; relative to this monster city-within-a-city whose jaws she had voluntarily entered.

And then, in a more recent email, the chilling words:

This latest one is useless. We'll send her to Kamathipura.

She had heard of Kamathipura before, of course. Which educated Indian hadn't? Fascinating and horrifying at once, its notoriety was known to anyone who read the newspapers. Bombay's red-light district, the place where men went to satisfy their basest urges. Where women lived like sardines in dirty, rat-infested holes, or even in cages overlooking the street, beckoning in their customers in the red glow of streetlamps. Kamathipura was a city of the night, for women of the night.

Now, in daylight, as she walked through the narrow lanes she felt a mounting panic, for the atmosphere seeped deeper into her consciousness like glue: clammy, sordid, vile, clinging to her like a hungry leech. And, she realised, these are only the *streets*. I am only an onlooker; I am safe. Behind the crumbling, grey facades that lined those streets – *there* the horror took place. Day after day after day. Night after night. A thousand wretched voices silently cried out to her: she heard them. And somewhere in the cacophony of woe she could make out a single anguished strain – Asha's voice of innocence, calling out in vain. *Mom! Daddy! Janaki!*

In frustration, she returned to her hotel. Did some more investigation from a nearby Internet shop. Slow, frustrating, mind-numbing research. After many hours, she couldn't stop yawning, and found herself nodding off. It was time for bed.

She was just about to shut down the computer when a new mail popped into her in-box.

She stared, numb, at the sender before moving a shaking finger to open it.

From: Kamal Darji.

Where are you, Janaki? Dev says you came back to India to look for Asha. Have you found her? Do you have any news at all? Caroline and I are both here in Madras and the place she was staying, it is empty, seems it was raided by police. But the police know nothing about her. Desperate to find her. Fingers crossed she's safely with you! Uncle Kamal

Janaki's fingers flitted over the keyboard.

No, she's not with me. Come to Bombay immediately. I'll meet you here.

TWENTY-EIGHT

Janaki

The sign on the gate read *Tulasa Nilayam* in washed-out red paint. It was a crumbling grey building a stone's throw from the sea, protected from the street by a man-high hibiscus hedge. A forbidding metal gate, bars pointing skywards in rusty spikes, delayed her entry by some five minutes as a thick chain bound the two wings together, tied in a complex knot that had to be unravelled. Janaki undid the chain, swung open the gate. She entered.

A few yards down the drive a man stepped into her path. He wore a khaki uniform.

'Good morning,' Janaki said. 'I have an appointment with Dr Nath.' She repeated the words in broken Hindi; she knew barely enough to get by.

Several emails from Kamal had awaited her in the Internet shop she had found last night, but the news was bleak, and Kamal could offer little support at present. He and Caroline could not arrive until the following day, he said. They'd come on the earliest available flight from Madras to Bombay.

After checking her mail Janaki, with nothing left to do, took to Yahoo to find out all she could about the industry that had trapped her little sister here in the city. Her search had led her to this Dr Nath, who, apparently, ran an NGO, the Bombay Safe Haven, whose main focus was under-aged prostitutes in the city.

She had emailed Dr Nath, who replied immediately; he would help. She was to come to this place, this Tulasa House.

'I'll meet you there when I have time,' he'd said, and that was the last she heard from him. He was her only contact in this behemoth of a city; a starting-point through a dark labyrinth that terrified her, the very thought of which caused her to shiver with anxiety for Asha, caused her mouth to dry up and her stomach to churn. This Dr Nath, though – he would help.

So here she was. The guard shrugged and replied in rapid Hindi.

'Dr Nath.' Janaki spoke louder this time, as if it was volume that prevented the guard from understanding.

He frowned, looked threateningly at her and said something that she interpreted as 'Stay here, don't move, or I'll shoot.' He turned away, walked up the steps leading to the front door and disappeared.

Taking his warning literally, Janaki waited, using the time to inspect her surroundings. The house before her was more in the category of villa – large and rambling, built of stone that must once have been red, since this was the colour that here and there showed through the layer of black mould growing up the walls, enclosing the building in a patina of neglect and dereliction. Wooden shutters hung from all the windows, awry where a hinge was broken, the paint peeling away, all with one or more slats missing. Looking up, Janaki thought she saw a face at one of the windows, but she couldn't be sure. Just a dark shadow, that immediately vanished. Perhaps her imagination. Again, she shivered, as if from cold – but the sun was shining brightly up above. The chill was within.

The guard's voice broke the frosty edge of fear. He was standing at the top of the entrance stairs, gesturing for her to come. She did so, stepping up the wide, crumbling stone staircase. The guard stood in an open doorway, speaking again in Hindi and emphasising his words with gestures.

Janaki followed him into the house, stepping over a threshold, a line across the floorboards where darkness sliced through the sunlight. A cloak of musty gloom closed in and wrapped itself around her, cool and dismal. After the glare she could see only blackness. As her eyes adjusted she made out a wooden staircase against the wall of a long, narrow lobby. Several doors left and right suggested that the lobby cut the house into two halves. The doors, the walls, the staircase, the floor, all unadorned wood. The paint on the walls was so old it peeled. A faint background smell, pungent and familiar, told Janaki that somewhere termites were at work, building their underground tunnels, hollowing out the boards. Neglect hung in the air.

She followed the guard along the corridor to the last door on the right. He knocked curtly, called something and gestured to her to follow, all simultaneously.

It was a large kitchen, sparsely equipped. A two-burner kerosene stove stood on a stone counter along one side, and an old green refrigerator, patched with rust in the shape of a giraffe, rattled noisily beside a dirty-paned window.

In the middle of the kitchen stood an oblong table with two straight-backed chairs. Against another wall, a *charpai*, a simple wooden bed-frame; but instead of a corded surface, this one was planked and served as a long, low table. At the foot of it sat a woman, cross-legged and stringing beans. She looked up as they entered, and smiled. At the other end of the bed-frame lay a heap of sundry articles: a pile of folded towels, a basket of onions, two coconuts, several chilli peppers and, somewhat incongruously, a battered alarm clock and a rusty machete.

The woman was stout, in her mid-forties. She wore a faded, threadbare red sari, and under it a blouse, which looked painfully tight, pinched in at the waist and at the sleeves, where tyres of fat bulged out. Her smile was warm, welcoming, echoed by her eyes. She spoke, but in rapid Hindi, too advanced for Janaki. She shrugged and spread her hands, showing that she didn't understand. 'Do you speak English?' she asked. The woman shrugged.

'I want to see Dr Nath,' Janaki said. This was ridiculous. What would she even say to this Dr Nath, should she be fortunate enough to meet him? She felt a fraud.

'Dr Nath?' she repeated and made a questioning gesture.

The woman seemed to understand. She spoke several words, gesturing and pointing outside the house. She repeated some of the words, and Janaki guessed at their meaning.

'He's not at home?'

But the woman did not understand. Janaki could only surmise that indeed, Dr Nath was out; but when or if he would be back could not be ascertained. The woman laid down her knife beside the heap of unstrung beans and, with some effort and deep breathing, rose from the bed-frame, talking all the while.

The woman pulled out one of the chairs, dusted some crumbs from its seat with the end of her sari, rattled it, verified that one of the legs was loose and would fall off at the slightest weight. She shook her head as if shocked, then cleared a place at the other end of the bed-frame. With a damp rag she wiped once over the bare planks, dried the area with the end of her sari and gestured with her open palm for Janaki to take a seat. She did so.

All this time the guard had been standing in the doorway, picking his teeth with his fingernail and watching silently. Now, hospitality established, the woman spoke brusquely to him and shooed him away. The man shrugged, stepped backwards into the lobby and closed the door.

The woman was still on her feet. She stood in the middle of the room, looking inordinately pleased with herself. She patted herself on her voluminous breast and said, 'Subhadai, Subhadai.' Janaki pointed to herself, saying 'Janaki'.

'Leetle English,' the woman explained. 'Koppee?'

She held up a jar with brown powder in it and a faded Nescafé label.

Janaki nodded and smiled. The woman busied herself with boiling water for instant coffee, which she served in a mug on a saucer with three biscuits on the side. Only then did she return to stringing beans. And all the while she talked. Janaki did not understand a word, but that clearly did not matter.

After an hour Subhadai had finished stringing beans, chopping onions and tomatoes, and grinding spices. Preparations for lunch, obviously. Janaki, itchy with impatience, could only hope it was in expectation of Dr Nath's imminent arrival. Hopefully. If Dr Nath did not come soon she might as well return to crawling the streets, as useless as that might seem. At least it was *doing* something, as opposed to sitting here listening to chatter which was as good as gibberish to her.

Subhadai suddenly stopped talking. She placed a finger over her lips and cocked her head, gazing into space. Janaki, too, listened, and she heard. The sound was unmistakable; somewhere in the bowels of the house somebody was crying. Subhadai nodded and stood up. At the doorway she hesitated, as if making a decision, and then she gestured for Janaki to follow her. She led her into the lobby and up the creaking stairs. The crying was louder in the lobby, and grew louder still as they walked upstairs: the forlorn lament of a soul that had lost all hope of solace and every right to happiness.

On the second floor there was another lobby, less gloomy

than the one below for it was lit by a large window at one end. Subhadai opened a door and entered a room. Janaki followed.

The crier was a girl, sitting on another *charpai*, leaning against the wall with knees drawn up. She might have been twelve years old, or a year or two older or younger – it was hard to tell, for her body was tiny and emaciated, the body of a young child, whereas the expression on her face was ancient. Her hands lay limp, palm-up, on the mattress; her uptilted chin was half turned to one side, her lips trembled as she wept, her eyes were vacant. She sat immobile, weeping apparently not because of any specific cause but because that was all there was left to do in all the world and in all of life. She did not so much as turn her face to look at the newcomers.

Janaki felt like an intruder into some intensely intimate experience, unwelcome and inopportune. She backed towards the open doorway, but Subhadai took hold of her upper arm and stopped her.

Subhadai walked over to the *charpai*, taking Janaki with her. She was speaking to the girl, and though the words were unknown Janaki could tell they were words of comfort. The girl did not react.

Letting go of Janaki, Subhadai sat on the edge of the *charpai* in front of the girl and reached over to stroke her cheek. The girl showed no reaction, did not look at Subhadai, did not pause in her weeping. Janaki stood awkwardly watching, the urge to flee struggling with compassion and curiosity. She stayed.

She stood before an abyss of misery so deep and dark it filled every space in that child's soul. Janaki needed no explanation – she knew it. The blankness in those dull black eyes, the downward pull of the trembling lips, the wretched whimpers: all spoke of unimaginable woe, too awful for words. This child was lost.

Is grief contagious? It had to be, for an involuntary trembling took hold of Janaki. She tried to control it, but couldn't;

her hands shook, her heart raced, a feeling of dread spread through her entire being, the fear of being drowned and destroyed by whatever agony possessed this child. Again, the desire to flee – to turn her back and never return to this terrible place – took hold of her, to be immediately superseded by its opposite: compassion, love even, the need to enter into the jaws of despair, defy its power, deny its existence. The trembling stopped as suddenly as it had set in.

Subhadai stood up and gestured to Janaki, who sat down on the *charpai*, directly before the girl, and took the trembling hands in hers.

'Ratna,' Subhadai said, pointing to the girl.

Janaki looked into eyes that saw nothing. Not even a flicker of acknowledgement. It did not matter. She leaned forward. She placed both hands on the girl's shoulders, drew her away from the wall. The child did not resist. She was passive, a rag doll. There seemed not a remnant of human will left in her. Janaki spoke to her in English, knowing she would not be understood, but it did not matter.

'Hello, Ratna. I'm Janaki,' she said. 'I'm from Tamil Nadu and I came to look for my sister. My sister is the same age as you. I hope I can find her. Her name is Asha and I've lost her. I think she too is sad. I think she too is crying. I really want to find her.'

She instinctively lowered her voice, softened its edges; knowing the words themselves could not be understood she filled them with feeling, with heart, knowing that somewhere, deep inside this child's being, was someone who would receive that feeling and understand it. She spoke on a level of communication beyond thought, beyond speech, and superior to both.

The girl, or whatever was still alive in the girl, would understand. She brushed a strand of hair away from the little face, held the little head in both her hands, centred it so that the eyes were directly in front of her. The child wept on. The eyes stared, not seeing. Empty. Dead.

She is dead, Janaki thought. Dead inside. But no. She can't be. If she were dead, she would not cry. Somewhere, deep inside, there is a last spark of life. She has heard, she has understood.

Suddenly a door flew open; not the door into the corridor, which still stood open, but a second, leading to the next room. Looking up, Janaki saw another girl, this time older, perhaps fifteen or sixteen, standing on the threshold.

This new girl was entirely different. She looked first at Janaki, then at Ratna, then at Subhadai. A short exchange of words took place between her and Subhadai, and then her gaze returned to Janaki and she acknowledged her with a curt nod. She walked to the window and stood there for a while looking out before turning swiftly, walking to the connecting door and leaving the room without speaking another word, slamming the door behind her.

This girl was angry.

Ratna had looked up at the newcomer, and then slumped back against the wall, and so she remained, her whimpering the only sign of life.

Janaki stood up, and gestured that she wanted to go. She could not bear it.

Meeting the girls upstairs had at the same time given her hope and plunged her into a morass of despair. It seemed fairly obvious, now, what this house was about. A sort of refuge, a safe house. The girls upstairs had been rescued from some kind of terrible fate; they were being provided for, supported. This Dr Nath was involved and might, somehow, be able to help in the search for Asha.

But where was he? When would he come?

TWENTY-NINE

Janaki

When Janaki again heard the chain it was nearly two, long after lunch, and she had given up any expectation of ever meeting Dr Nath.

She glanced out of the window more from boredom than for any other reason, for she had read *India Today* and the *Times of India* from beginning to end, and had started on a local paper, *Bombay Drums*.

A few minutes later the door opened and Dr Nath entered. A tall, lanky Indian, early thirties, perhaps, with a neatly trimmed beard, he was a prepossessing figure, and Janaki felt authority radiating from him. She stood up and greeted him with a *pranaam*: hands together at her chest.

'*Namaste*,' she said. 'I'm—'

'Janaki,' said Dr Nath. 'Yes, I was expecting you. Sorry I'm late, my time is unfortunately not my own.'

Dr Nath walked across the room and filled a kettle with water; lighting the kerosene stove, he put the kettle on the flame.

'Coffee?' he asked. She nodded, and then began.

'As I told you, it's about my little sister—'

'Little Asha,' he finished. 'You've been able to follow her tracks to Bombay? To Kamathipura?'

'Yes,' she said. 'But I'm not quite sure – I've been walking about in Kamathipura, but it seems to me...'

'A needle in a haystack,' said Dr Nath, nodding. He placed a coffee filter on a jug, filled it with ground coffee and waited for the water to boil. Subhadai, in the meantime, had stood up and was busy dishing out a plate of food from the pots on the stove. She gestured to him to sit down, indicating that she would finish the coffee, and placed the plate on the table. Dr Nath sat down and began to eat; hungrily, hastily, as if eating were a waste of time. Between mouthfuls he spoke to Janaki.

'You met the girls upstairs, I presume. Ratna? And Sita? Two rescued girls out of so many still in hell. I can't make any promises. I don't know if we can find your Asha, if we can save her, but I'm happy to try. I'm always happy to try. One at a time we find these girls, and one at a time we save them, bring them here.'

Janaki nodded. Dr Nath's words tore at her. Asha, lost forever? In Kamathipura? It could not be!

'I have to find her!' she said. 'If you can help...'

'I can help, but as I said, I can't make any promises. This place is a refuge; I do my best, but sometimes I feel it's like water on a red-hot stone.'

'I know,' said Janaki, her voice trembling with the despair she felt. 'I can't imagine... I can't even begin to imagine—'

'How a place like this can exist in a modern city like Bombay,' Dr Nath finished. 'How men can do this thing to young girls, to children. Ratna is still a child. Men have ravished her. Not men, but animals. I've been doing this work for many years now, and I still don't understand how a human can lower himself to such depravity. I still don't understand it.'

'What are our chances of finding Asha?'

He shrugged. 'You expect me to put a number on it? To find one girl, and pluck her out of there? I'm sorry, but I need to be blunt, and you need to be realistic. There are about thirty thousand prostitutes in Kamathipura. Ten per cent are minors, children; and you can be sure the minors are kept hidden away, because they're illegal. Do you know what that world's like? It's an anthill – teeming with people. Brothels on top of brothels and behind brothels; stinking hellholes where you wouldn't even keep a dog. And you are looking for one single little soul in all of that. You can figure out your chances yourself.'

'But,' said Janaki, determined not to be discouraged by numbers, 'we do have clues. I've been investigating; I was able to find some information.'

She told Dr Nath about the emails, about the names and the hints she had been able to glean. She rummaged in her bag and brought forth the little notebook in which she had written down those names, as well as the photo of Asha she had printed out.

'Interesting,' said Dr Nath, 'but still – don't think you can just walk in there with a few names and find a single girl. I'm sorry to throw cold water on your hopes. I'll do all I can to help, but one girl among thirty thousand, well... you can figure out the odds. However, miracles do happen. You're passionate about this one particular girl, and it's always good to have passion. Passion helps. And so does faith; faith can sometimes move mountains.'

Janaki nodded. 'That's what I believe too,' she said. 'And there are three of us. Kamal is coming tomorrow – that's her father – and Caroline, her mother.'

'That's good. So your father is going to be helping to look for her too? That's encouraging. You understand, in that trade especially it's better to have a man investigating. As a young woman, you—'

Janaki raised her hand in a *stop* signal. 'Kamal isn't my father,' she said.

Dr Nath looked up from his food and raised his eyebrows. 'But Asha is your sister, and his daughter – I thought...'

'Foster-sister. It's a long story. She's my cousin-sister. We aren't related. My mother was her foster-mother. Kamal is her biological father. He's coming with Asha's mother, Caroline, his wife – ex-wife. She's American.'

'Ah, that's why she's so fair!' said Dr Nath. 'Fair girls like her are luxury products...'

Janaki winced.

He continued. '...I know it hurts for her to be described as a *product* but that's the reality. That's how she's seen in the trade; "superior quality", she'll be labelled, like a carpet, or a patola-silk sari. And in a way it's a good thing, from your point of view. Luxury products are treated with more care. They can't be blemished or ruined. They are kept apart, for customers with high demands. Especially if they are virgins. Some men believe that virgins can cure AIDS. So a fair-skinned virgin might have a good chance of being kept with more care.'

'But just now you said she was just one out of thirty thousand,' said Janaki.

'Yes, and she is. And I'll help you as much as possible and share my knowledge with you, but to me every one of those thirty thousand girls is worth saving. For a few days I will devote myself to this one. But those two girls upstairs, and thousands like them still out there,' – he gestured out of the window – 'they are all equally precious. Every human life is precious. And I will save them, one at a time. Try to save them. Perhaps it is your Asha's turn to be saved. I won't take that hope from you.'

Janaki, lost for words, said nothing. Dr Nath shovelled the last mouthful of food into his mouth, chewed, swallowed and then said,

'Asha is lucky. She is privileged. She has family looking for her, family with the means to stop their normal lives, come to Bombay, and spend time and money looking for her. Other girls are not so lucky. They have no one looking for them. Their parents back in the villages can't come here to look for them. Yet each one is as precious as the next. I'll help you look for Asha, but only because out of the thousands of such girls, she has the luck to have you here working with me.

'See those girls upstairs? We were able to save them but what can we do with them now? Where can we put them? They can't tell us where they came from, and even if they could, it's more than likely we can't send them back. Their parents might love them but they can't go back after Kamathipura, for their villages will reject them. There's no going back after Kamathipura.

'They will carry that shame all their lives, through no fault of their own. They have lost their homes, their parents, their lives. They've been destroyed. We are working against the greatest evil. To abuse a child is the crime to end all crimes; to destroy a young girl's life – it beggars belief. And that is the only reason I can devote some time to one particular girl, this Asha: because there is hope for her after Kamathipura. That is rare. Still, don't hope too much. It will take nothing short of a miracle.'

Subhadai placed a bowl of some *payasam*, semolina, before him, and his eyes lit up. 'Did you try this *payasam*?' he asked Janaki. 'Subhadai makes the best *payasam* in the world. It is the one enjoyment in my life. I look forward to it all morning. Let me eat now in silence.'

He stopped talking as he dipped his spoon into the soft white pudding, and closed his eyes to emphasise his delight.

'Delicious!' he said. 'Simply delicious!'

Janaki still said nothing; she found his ability to speak of the abomination of Kamathipura in one sentence, and the next to fall into ecstasy at the taste of *payasam*, extraordinary, callous, even. She couldn't even think of enjoying a pudding, ever again, as long as Asha remained lost. She supposed that years of work in the field would force a person to grow a scab, a skin so thick the horror remained underground, allowing one to continue with a shallow enjoyment of life. For her, impossible. She felt as sensitive as a mimosa, the sleepy plant whose leaves closed at the slightest touch. Every inch of her soul ached and longed to withdraw, yet couldn't as long as Asha was out there, lost.

Dr Nath's glance fell on the *Bombay Drums* local newspaper Janaki had laid on the table. The paper was folded back on the page 'Bombay News'. She could tell by the movement of his eyes that he was scanning the news, interest in the delightful *payasam* already faded. Suddenly he stiffened, his gaze held in place. An instant later he sprang to his feet, his pudding half eaten.

'Come,' is all he said, gesturing to Janaki. 'Maybe it's a miracle. Read that.' He thrust the newspaper into Janaki's hands and strode to the door. Janaki sprang up and, infected by his sudden vigour, hurried behind him.

Out of the house, out of the gate, a black car waited in the street outside, a driver asleep at the wheel. Dr Nath practically leapt into the passenger seat, gestured for Janaki to get into the back. The driver awoke with a start and, as the doctor fired off a few words to him, turned the ignition key. The car drove off. Dr Nath seemed to have forgotten her; he was talking to the driver now, in a rapid flow of Hindi.

She still clutched the newspaper, so opened it. What had so galvanised Dr Nath that he had left behind his beloved *payasam*? She scanned the headlines. Impatiently, she let her gaze wander from headline to headline, rejecting, rejecting, rejecting. And then a word in a headline, two words, jumped out at her.

She read the article, and read it again – a small item, tucked away in the bottom left-hand corner.

Child Prostitute Admitted to Hospital.

A twelve-year-old prostitute was admitted to B. K. Shivnandan Hospital with several knife wounds and a broken arm, sustained during a fight between a pimp and a drunken customer in Kamathipura. The girl was in a state of extreme shock yesterday and unable to speak to investigators. However, other prostitutes from the same brothel revealed that she had been kidnapped in Madras and sold into prostitution about a month ago. She was brought to the hospital bleeding from the knife wounds by a health worker from an NGO, who later filed a charge of trafficking with minors...

The article made Janaki sick and hopeful simultaneously. Could this be Asha? The timescale was wrong. Asha had supposedly been in Bombay not a month, but a week, ten days at the most. But people's memories were faulty; a week could very well seem like a month. But twelve years old, and from Madras... Asha was thirteen, so close enough.

The idea of Asha as a prostitute dismayed Janaki to the core. She had lurked around that word for days now, not wanting to even think of it in connection with Asha, instead refusing to admit the likelihood, the probability, of Asha's fate. She had clung to the idea that no, it hadn't happened yet. She had come in time. She would save Asha. She would. She would. There was still time. Asha had not yet been... she couldn't say that word either. Or even think that word.

Because to think it was to imagine it, and she refused to imagine it. But her body knew which thought she was rejecting. Her body revolted. The nausea was too much to bear.

'Stop the car!' Janaki was able to yell, and luckily they were driving not in the middle of a gush of traffic but at the edge, so once Dr Nath had translated, the driver obeyed and came to a screeching halt next to the kerb amid a clamour of enraged car horns and claxons, and Janaki flung open the door and leaned out. The vomit erupted from deep inside in a foul, stinking gush. Her stomach heaved, again and again, even when nothing more came but a clear but putrid slime. Still clinging to the car door for support, her upper body hanging over the road, she retched and retched until, her body now scraped clean of every last scrap of foulness, she wiped her mouth with the back of her hand, sat up on the back seat and shut the car door.

'Sorry,' she said.

'It's all right,' said Dr Nath. 'We're dealing with sickness. Your body understands well.'

The door to the ward stood open. Inside, a number of simple cots, about twenty in all, lined the two sides of a long room. The patients were all girls and women, plainly of low income judging by the simplicity of the beds and the worn-out state of the sheets and pillowcases. All of the cots were occupied; the patients lay in various conditions of apathy or illness, some alone, others surrounded by family members; some slept or sat up in bed talking with relatives, or ate from tiffin boxes, or simply wept.

An elderly woman was being hand-fed by a younger woman; a middle-aged woman with oily, uncombed hair cried, alone, into a corner of her sheet. The ward, sparse and drab in its appointments, smelt of stale urine mixed with medicine and antiseptic. A slowly rotating overhead fan did little to dilute the smell with fresh air from the open window. Nausea again rose up in Janaki, but there was nothing left to puke.

There was only one girl of even nearly the right age.

But the girl was not Asha. Nothing like her; for a start, she was much younger, ten at the most. She lay there, curled on the sheet, her face half-hidden in the crook of her left arm, which was encased in fresh plaster of paris. Her left shoulder was thick with the padding of an elaborate bandage, which could be seen at the short sleeve and the neck of her white hospital nightdress. A threadbare sheet covered the embryo-like curl of her body.

Her terrified eyes clung to Janaki's face. When Dr Nath leaned over her she shrank away, petrified, and he stepped back, nodding.

'She's afraid of men,' he said. 'And no wonder. I'll bring a female colleague. My sister Pratima also works here, as a doctor. And Gita.' He turned and left the room.

It was such a sad place, and all Janaki could do was try to relieve the sadness a little by sitting on the girl's bed holding her hand. She spoke, as she had done to Ratna before, just for the sake of speaking, this time in Tamil; the girl, after all, was from Madras, according to *Bombay Drums*.

Janaki smiled at her, brushed the hair off her face, pulled her slightly up so that she leaned against Janaki's side with Janaki's arm around her. Janaki adjusted herself into a more comfortable position and continued to talk.

Before long, a young woman in her mid-twenties approached, wearing, rather than the usual sari or *shalwar kameez*, jeans and a T-shirt. She was light-skinned, but not European – the coffee colour of her complexion was natural, not a tan, and that thick black hair, swept back and up into a ponytail, and the bushy eyebrows over coal-black eyes were definitely Indian.

She smiled first at Janaki and then at the girl.

'*Namaste*,' she said, 'You must be Janaki – Dr Nath told me about you. And I see you've already made friends with our little patient here. Hello, *beti*. How are you? I see you have a friend!' She spoke Hindi, and then, seeing that the girl did not understand, English. Janaki translated into Tamil.

'You speak Tamil!' said the woman, and her eyes lit up. 'Wonderful – she's terrified and doesn't understand a word we say. Our Tamil nurses are far too busy to spare a moment to translate. By the way, my name's Gita. I'm a social worker in the hospital, but also a volunteer who works with Dr Nath's patients, in the hospital and out there in the wilds, as we call it. I need to ask her a few questions; can you translate? I take it that this is not the girl you are looking for? What's *her* name again?'

'Asha,' said Janaki, 'and no, this isn't her. Asha is a bit older. This girl's name is Sakhi.'

'You seem to have won her trust,' said Gita. 'I see you've been talking to her already; she seems so much more relaxed now. Well done! I've got some questions I need to ask, for the social services department. Would you translate for me?'

Janaki nodded. 'Of course. I'll try.'

'But not now. Later. When she's at Tulasa House. I'm going there now. Will you come? I'll come back for Sakhi later.'

Janaki nodded, and stood up to leave.

'This is such wonderful work Dr Nath is doing,' said Janaki, as she walked down the corridor with Gita. 'Even if it's a drop in the ocean. To save a child, even if it's just one. To return a child to her parents...'

'Unfortunately, it's not usually a happy ending,' said Gita. 'Very often we can't send a girl like this back to her parents. They won't accept her – after what she has been through, she must expect a further hurt, the hurt of rejection. These girls usually end up in an orphanage. You must ask Dr Nath about Tulasa, the girl he's dedicated his work to. Ask him. I have to go back to my own work now, but ask him. Goodbye, Janaki, and thank you for your help.'

Later that evening, Dr Nath did tell her the story of the Nepali girl to whom he dedicated his work. A story of exploitation and rape and utter depravity. It reduced Janaki to tears.

'We can't let that happen to Asha! Save her, Dr Nath! I beg you, save her!'

Dr Nath laid a hand on Janaki's trembling arm.

'I'll do my best – I promise you that. But, as I have already told you, the reality is that Asha is just one girl out of thousands. Girls are abducted from villages all over India and Nepal, lured away on some pretext or the other: going to movies, cities, temples, making them film stars, lucrative job opportunities, marriage. And then every year thousands of girls are ceremonially dedicated to the goddess Yellamma, and must serve her as child prostitutes. Others are sold to the highest bidder and then turned over to the urban brothels. You've seen Bombay; you've seen the chaos, the crowds. I just want you to know the reality. It won't be easy. You have my help, but I can't do much. The police force isn't going to help at all. You need to brace yourself. I understand your tears, your fears, but wishing and wanting isn't going to help. Your prayers might – prayers provide strength and faith, and you will need both. You will also need a miracle. And all your wits about you. And you seem to have good wits. You got this far. You say that you were able to intercept some emails?'

Janaki wiped her tears on a corner of her *pallu* and tried to steady her voice.

'Yes. I was able to contact Asha when she was still in Madras. I was able to check the emails of the people who had captured her. But those criminals found out and that was the end of that.'

Janaki told him the details of her detective work, her communication with Asha.

'If only I hadn't tried to be so clever. If only I had told her to run! Run away from that house immediately, to not go looking for passwords and things. I was trying to be a smart-aleck and I just made everything worse. It's my fault this happened. All my fault.'

'Blaming yourself isn't going to get you anywhere. I think it's time you called it a day. Tomorrow I'll try to fix you up with a computer and Internet and you can maybe do some more research – you're good at that. Walking the streets of Kamath-ipura isn't going to help. And as you say, tomorrow her parents will be here. It's not good for you to be alone. The three of you, together, will give each other strength. Just don't give up. All right?'

Janaki sniffed. 'All right.'

'Tomorrow is a new day. You look exhausted. I'll get my driver to take you home. Where is your hotel?'

Janaki was sure she would not sleep that night. However, the moment her head touched the pillow she sank into a deep and dreamless sleep.

THIRTY

Asha

Devaki and Asha emerged from the taxi, Devaki's grip firm on Asha's wrist. They were both dressed well, Asha in a shiny red sari, and full make-up. Devaki turned to Asha and said sternly, 'This is your chance. I am warning you, you must talk to him, and be nice and polite. You are very fortunate, because not all girls get such an opportunity. He is very rich and this would be your home. But only if you are pleasant to him today.'

Devaki led her up a path to the front door of a grand mansion and rang the bell. The door opened; a maid in a deep blue sari gestured for them to step inside, and led them into a gaudy reception room, signalled to a gaudy bright red sofa, and left. As they sat down Devaki nervously adjusted Asha's sari, her jewels, her hair.

'I cannot believe you are so stubborn, Kamini. You are such a silly little girl,' she scolded. 'This is your big chance. You will be meeting Mr Chaudhuri in a minute, alone, and you *must* speak to him. You must at least say "Good morning" and smile.

It's not much to ask. Just talk. I did my best to train you. I cannot do more. He insists on seeing you today. So behave.'

The maid re-entered the room. 'Mr Chaudhuri will see the girl now, Madam. She must come with me, alone.'

Devaki pushed Asha to her feet. Asha stumbled, and Devaki got up to steady her.

'You must go, Kamini. Do not be afraid. He is a kind man. He just wants a young companion. Your future hangs on this interview. Remember what I told you? Be good. Be polite. Because where will you go if he rejects you? If you just say "Good morning" that will do for the beginning. Please!'

Asha said nothing. She followed when the maid beckoned and walked off behind her, staring at the ground. Her heart was in her mouth; she could feel it pounding. Her hands trembled. She clasped them tightly to stop the trembling but then the quiver seemed to run up her arms to her jaw, and that began to wobble. Silently, she called out: *Mom! Daddy! Janaki!*

The maid led Asha into an even grander living room. A man sat there, in a plush red velvet armchair, clearly waiting for her. An old man. Asha could not gauge his age but his hair was white, brushed back from his heavy-jowled face, thin strands covering a balding spot. He wore a dazzling white shirt, pulled tight over a large belly, and he wore gold rings on all his fingers. He stood up as Asha entered with the maid and walked forward to greet her. His lips peeled back in a grin that revealed teeth that were abnormally white. It filled Asha with dread rather than welcoming warmth. A strange nausea rose up in her, and she turned her head away. He picked up her hand. It lay limply in his.

'Ah, lovely! Delightful! Even better than in the photos. Absolutely delightful. Hello, Kamini, I've been looking forward to meeting you.'

Asha said nothing. She kept her eyes lowered as Mr Chaudhuri lifted her chin to inspect her face. He turned her face back and forth, exclaiming all the time. His face was so close to hers she could smell his breath, and it was nasty. The sickness in her rose up in her throat. She feared she would vomit. Then what?

'Charming! But you are not going to even greet me? No "Good morning"? That is rather rude, isn't it? They told me you speak English. Is that true?'

Asha looked behind her to see if the maid was still there. She was. The trembling spread to her whole body. She tried to stop, but it only grew worse. She feared her knees would give way and she would fall to the floor. Then what?

'What is this? What's this trembling? You don't have to be afraid of me. I might be an oldish man but I am not dangerous, and I will treat you well when you come to live with me. You will have a nice soft bed and the best food. And you will be happy. This is a good place, and I am a kind man.'

He touched her hair. She flinched. His eyes flashed with anger.

'What rudeness is this? You should be smiling and welcoming me with open arms, instead of sulking. You prefer to speak Hindi?'

He changed from English to Hindi, then back to English.

'I know you are shy but you're taking it too far. Do you know what life I am offering you? Did Devaki not tell you?'

He lifted her little hand again. It lay limply in his, like a wet rag.

'Do you know what it's like out there on the streets? You don't have parents to protect you. Nobody will help you out there. Me, I will protect you. You will live in luxury. My wife won't mind; she'll be delighted not to have to perform her duties anymore. You will be so happy, and yet you treat me like this?'

Asha continued to stare at the carpet, trying with all her might not to tremble, and failing. Mr Chaudhuri grabbed her other hand. He shouted, 'Look at me, girl!'

He grabbed her chin and raised her head so that Asha's eyes

met his. Tears had gathered, and she looked away as she could not bear his gaze. He flung her hand down in disgust and turned to the maid.

'You wait here with her. I need to have a word...'

He stormed off. Asha's face crumpled and she covered it with her hands. The maid tore away her hands and spoke sharply, words Asha did not understand.

Devaki leapt to her feet as Chaudhuri entered the sitting room where she sat waiting. She looked at him nervously.

'So, how was it? Do you like her? Was she polite?'

Mr Chaudhuri slowly shook his head. He slapped his forehead, then flipped out his hands in a clear – and rude – gesture of disapproval. More than disapproval. Of ridicule.

'Did you sew that girl's lips together? She doesn't speak a word.'

Devaki clasped her hands at her breast and put on her most confident smile and her most encouraging voice.

'She's just a bit shy still. She only needs time. She needs to relax. It's because she's so very innocent, Mr Chaudhuri. You won't find another girl like this one. She is very best quality. Very rare to find a girl like this.'

'You claim she speaks English but she didn't speak even Hindi.'

Devaki shrugged, and spread her hands in a gesture that said, *well, what do you expect?*

'She does speak English! She came from a good family and only misfortune brought her to me. She has nobody in the whole world. Only me. She has foreign parents who do not want her. They live abroad. She is Tamil and English speaking. Her foster-parents who were looking after her died recently. She is just upset still. She only needs time. Give me a week more and I will train her to talk.'

'And how you expect to do that? Force the words out of her lips? What do they say, you can lead a horse to water but...'

'...you can't make it drink. I know. But I will scare her. I will show her the alternatives. When she sees the other life waiting for her she will talk. I guarantee one hundred per cent.'

Mr Chaudhuri turned away, walked to the window, was silent in contemplation for a minute, then turned back.

'I hope so. I like her very much but you understand, I do not want to be treated like a monster. I want a girl who will be kind and gentle. A loving girl. That was my specification. You need to train this girl.'

'I will, Mr Chaudhuri. I will. It's a promise. Devaki always keeps her word.' Devaki clasped her hands at her breast and smiled the most winning, the most convincing smile she could conjure up.

'Well, I'll give you another chance. But I want to see results. I give you one more week.'

A few minutes later, Devaki and Asha sat in the back seat of a taxi. Devaki was fuming, her eyes mere slits, her face a mask of such ugliness Asha drew away. Devaki gripped her two forearms and spat the words.

'You stupid, stubborn girl! You've ruined everything! This was the best chance you had and you ruined it! Do you know what you've done? Do you know the consequences?'

Asha turned her face away and stared out the car window, tears running down her cheeks.

'Well, I'll show you where you're going to end up, Little Miss High and Mighty! When you share your dinner with rats you'll know to be grateful!'

Asha continued to stare out the window. She was trembling again and didn't know how to stop it.

'Look at me, you little fool!'

Devaki grabbed Asha by the chin, swung her face around and pinched her cheeks together.

'Such a little fool. Such a waste.'

Her open hand flew out, landed a slap on Asha's cheeks. Left cheek, right cheek. She shoved her away.

'Training? Training, he said. I don't have time for training. You'll soon see what happens to stubborn little girls.'

She leaned forward, talked to the taxi driver, gave him instructions which Asha could not understand. The taxi driver nodded. He sped up a little, veered into a different lane of traffic.

THIRTY-ONE

Janaki

The next morning Janaki arrived at Tulasa House at the break
of dawn; there was no time to be wasted. And indeed, as she sat
at the kitchen table with Dr Nath, drinking coffee and chatting,
the door to the kitchen opened and Kamal stood in the doorway,
Caroline right behind him. Janaki's hand holding the coffee cup
dropped, spilling coffee over the table.

In her mind, up to now, Kamal had still been Kamal Uncle;
a much older man, an uncle after all, a generation above her, an
authority, a father figure, tall and prepossessing. And she had
been the little girl who had looked up to him; the little girl who
had looked after his child, but a little girl all the same, a child.

But in the intervening years she had changed. Grown up.
Become a woman. And he had also changed. Changed, and yet
still the same, the same Kamal. Changed, not so much physically, but in her perception of him. It wasn't just his physical
appearance. No, it was the very *substance* of him, something
that could not be seen but which imparted itself to her through

countless signals, imperceptible to the senses but immediately recognised by the rhythm of her soul.

Kamal wore khaki cotton trousers and a nondescript, faded, striped cotton shirt. He wore cheap flip-flops. He was tall and straight-backed, golden-brown in colour. His face was angular, verging on gaunt, his eyes under thick eyebrows deep-set and large; there was no mistaking the veiled anguish in them. A short beard covered his chin, a moustache his upper lip. He was unsmiling. The overall expression was of distance and authority. He was unapproachable.

Yet still she smiled. 'Hello, Kamal Uncle!' she said.

Kamal did not return her smile, and only vaguely raised his hands in a hasty *namaste*, did not even greet her. It was Caroline who smiled, stepping forward from behind her former husband to sweep Janaki into her arms.

'Janaki!' she said. 'It's so good to see you again! I can't believe how much you've grown – you're a woman now!'

'Yes, Caroline Aunty,' said Janaki, feeling shy all of a sudden. Caroline was so American; in the year she had spent in California she had grown used to the overflowing enthusiasm and friendliness of American women, but here, in Bombay, it seemed all at once alien, out of place, inappropriate even, given the circumstances.

Caroline, in contrast to Kamal, was dressed in casual-but-smart attire: well-cut, obviously expensive trousers and a long floral blouse that would have been more appropriate in the lobby of a luxury hotel than here in this so shabby room. She wore shiny leather sandals with heels and a blue silk scarf around her neck. On her slender fingers she wore rings, clearly expensive; on her wrist was an elegant watch. And from her ears dangled hooped earrings.

Though still beautiful, she had aged, and bore no resemblance at all to the hippie-styled young woman in flowing skirts who had shared her home when Asha was a toddler. This woman was a stranger – strange, smart and incongruous here in the bowels of Bombay.

Caroline, as if recognising that her enthusiastic greeting of Janaki was somehow over the top in this sombre place, loosened her embrace and stepped back, her smile dropping away, her features falling into a grimace.

'I can't believe we're here, doing this,' she said. 'I can't believe that Asha – my baby – is here. What a mess. Do you—'

'Have you any news?' Kamal butted in. He turned to Dr Nath, who now stood up from the table where he had been eating his breakfast.

'Have you made any progress? You must be Dr Nath.'

'No,' said Dr Nath, walking to the sink to wash his hands. 'I was just telling Janaki yesterday. There won't be any miracles. This is slow, tedious, frustrating work and success is not guaranteed. You're looking for a needle in a haystack.'

'A cliché,' said Kamal impatiently. 'Asha is not a needle. She's my daughter and I *will* find her. I'll find her if I have to spend the rest of my life searching.'

'Right,' said Caroline. 'We're here to find her and we won't turn back. I'm not going before I hold her in my arms again.'

Dr Nath, wiping his hands on a towel, only shook his head, imperceptibly, and even Janaki, having recovered most of her equilibrium, felt that both Kamal and Caroline had spoken too hastily, too confidently, too brashly. They had not yet walked the streets of Kamathipura. They seemed naive; such certainty, such cocky presumptuousness, she feared, might jinx the entire mission. She felt the need to put a dampener on their assertiveness.

'Kamal, Caroline,' she said, 'I've made a start. I went out looking yesterday, just walking around the area. And it's... well, it's a bit depressing, really. It really does seem, as Dr Nath says, like a needle in a haystack.'

Only after she'd spoken did she realise: she'd addressed

Kamal and Caroline not as Uncle and Aunty, but as equals, as her peers. She hoped they wouldn't think it rude. Especially Kamal: she wanted to make a good impression on him, and she couldn't put her finger on *why*. Perhaps to break the ice that seemed to have settled around him; he was so austere, so grim, so brusque. How did she appear to him, she wondered. As a little girl? As the precocious teenager he'd treated with kindness but distance in the past? As a grown woman? He seemed hardly to have acknowledged her up to now; his mind was filled with Asha. He had not even greeted her. Disappointment welled up in her, but only for an instant.

Janaki, she told herself sternly, what are you thinking? This is your Kamal Uncle, a much older man. What you are thinking is ridiculous! She remembered Rani, and her outrageous desire to pair her off with Kamal – and Rani's suggestion at the moment didn't seem outrageous in the least. Except that obviously Kamal hardly even saw her. Had she, completely unconsciously, accepted Rani's challenge?

All these thoughts ran through Janaki's head in the space of an instant, and then she came back down to earth. In that one instant she had forgotten Asha, and the direness of her situation. She had, for that moment, forgotten what she was here for, carried away on the wings of – what? A stupid female romantic dream. She physically pinched herself to bring her attention back to the task at hand, which meant aligning herself with the desperation that fired both Kamal and Caroline.

'Look, why don't you just go to Kamathipura now and look around a bit? I mean, I've only been there once myself but you should see the place to get a better idea of how to organise the search.'

'Yes – you do that,' said Dr Nath. 'I'm going to be busy this morning. But at four this afternoon I've scheduled a team meeting – some of the people who work for Safe Haven will be coming around to discuss some urgent matters, and they'll be able to look into the Asha problem, and you'll be able to ask for advice and help, maybe develop a strategy. But remember we're all very busy. After that, if you still have questions, we can have our talk. Now, off you go with Janaki. She's been a great help.'

For the first time, Kamal looked at Janaki with something more than distraction in his eyes, as if he only now acknowledged her presence. He nodded.

'Right,' he said. 'Let's go, Janaki. Let's see this hellhole.'

Janaki looked in panic at him, and then at Dr Nath. 'But is nobody going to come with us? Show us around?' Dr Nath sniffed in exasperation.

'I just explained. We're all much too busy to give guided tours, sorry. Best you just go, plunge in and discover it all by yourself. Get a feel for the place. Later at the meeting you can maybe exchange a few words with someone if you have a lead or if you feel you want a closer look; maybe someone can find the time. But – well, best you just go.'

Just as they were about to leave, Gita arrived with Sakhi in tow. Sakhi was limping, but she seemed much better than yesterday, even managing a half-smile and a *namaste*. Janaki introduced Kamal and Caroline, then looked at Gita with something like desperation.

'We're off to Kamathipura,' she said. 'Yesterday you said you'd show me around a bit – do you – could you – I mean, we're supposed to be going now, and I know you're busy, but...'

Gita looked at her watch. 'I guess I could spare an hour or two,' she said. 'If Dr Nath doesn't mind. We've got the team meeting at four...'

She looked at Dr Nath, who looked at his watch.

'Subhadai will look after Sakhi,' he said. 'I've got some HIV patients at my clinic this morning – I'll be back this afternoon for the team meeting. All right, Gita, go with them. Show them the place.'

Janaki breathed out in relief. It had seemed, for a while, as if

Kamal and Caroline were both relying on her for a guided tour of the city, as if she had been here a year instead of just a day – and expected to find Asha on the way.

The four of them stepped out onto the pavement. Gita went to hail a rickshaw, but then she stopped and turned to Caroline.

'Caroline,' she said, 'it'd be better if you remove your jewellery. Those rings, they look so expensive. You're going to attract attention anyway as a white woman; we're going into a high-crime area. Can you take them off for a while?'

Caroline flinched. 'Oh, sorry. You're right. I hadn't thought of that.'

She took them off, reaching up to her ears for the earrings and slipping the rings off her fingers. Then turned her back to Janaki, lifting the curtain of her blonde hair. 'Janaki – can you undo the clasp on my chain, please? I'll put the rings on it for the time being. The earrings can go in my handbag. And these...' She slipped the bracelet and watch from her wrist, removed her earrings, dropped everything into her handbag.

Janaki opened the clasp, and Caroline hung the two rings through the gold chain on which a single sapphire pendant hung. Janaki remembered that, back in the day, Caroline had told her mother that the pendant had been a gift from Kamal, an heirloom from his family in Chandrapur. She relocked the chain for Caroline. Caroline was still dressed far too smartly for Janaki's liking, but the removal of the rings, bracelet and watch would have to do for now. Gita nodded.

'Much better,' she said, 'now come. Let's find an auto-rickshaw.'

As they drove towards Kamathipura, Gita said, 'It's a pity that you're going to see the worst of Mumbai. It's not all bad, you know. Mumbai is actually a wonderful city, but you have to know it. It's not a place; it's a feeling.'

Janaki nodded. 'I noticed you call it Mumbai – I'm still calling it Bombay. Is that bad?'

'Don't worry about it,' said Gita, flapping her hand in dismissal. 'The city has always been called Mumbai in Marathi, and Bombay in English, Bambai in Hindi. A powerful regional political party called Shiv Sena argued that Bombay was a corrupted English version of Mumbai and an unwanted legacy of British colonial rule and pushed for the name change. In 1995 official agencies and governments were ordered to adopt the change. It's happening gradually. In a few years it will all be Mumbai. But if you still call it Bombay nobody's going to shoot you.'

She peered out of the rickshaw. 'And,' she announced, 'here we are. Kamathipura. The sin-centre of Mumbai.'

THIRTY-TWO

Caroline

Kamathipura.

A day ago, she had never even heard the word. And now it was a synonym for everything that was wrong with the world, and with India. All the ugliness, all the horror, all the filth, compressed into one word. All the evil. Before leaving Madras she had bought a book on Bombay – an older book, so it did not refer to the city as Mumbai. The chapter on the notorious red-light district had, she thought, seemed somewhat sugar-coated, described as a tourist destination for the salaciously curious. She knew it was worse.

Real life, though, was worse than the worst.

I can't do this! I can't go there! screamed a high-pitched, hysterical voice within her. But then another voice, louder, sombre in tone, serious, collected, calm, replied: Asha is there. Asha is there. You must find Asha.

And so she walked on. Instinctively, she reached out for Kamal's hand, and his fingers closed around hers; but then Gita came in from behind them, placed her hand around both their wrists and drew them gently apart.

'Sorry,' she said. 'You two shouldn't hold hands in Kamathipura. It'll give the wrong impression. Remember where you are.'

Janaki must have noticed the little incident and stepped forward on the other side of Caroline and took her hand; Caroline clasped hers as if her life depended on it. She had held Kamal's hand not for affection but for strength; Janaki's hand would do. From it came both strength and comfort.

Kamal and Janaki, Caroline realised, were both Indians; somehow that explained that centred calm that she, now, was desperate for; but there it was, in Janaki's hand, clasped firmly around hers. As if a current ran from Janaki to her, an anchor holding her upright when she would faint, keeping her grounded when she would run away, back to the cool luxury of the Taj Mahal hotel.

She and Kamal had arrived in the wee hours of the morning and gone straight to the Taj. She had persuaded Kamal to spend at least that one night there, instead of going out to look for a more modest hotel.

'It's past midnight,' she said. 'Come on, Kamal. It'll be an hour before you find another place. Just stay here this one night; we need to be rested tomorrow. Let me pay if it's outside your budget.'

Kamal grunted something about it not being about money, but then shrugged and conceded.

And so he'd stayed, in a room of his own, and he had insisted on paying his own way. Kamal was proud like that. But then, he had probably earned well in Dubai and since he lived so modestly... well, she could only guess at his means but no doubt he had savings enough.

And so they had both slept at the Taj – though sleep, at least in her case, meant tossing and turning and obsessing about Asha, and having a thousand million thoughts and fears rushing through her brain all at once. She had needed all the little calming tricks of her own trade to find some modicum of rest: deep breathing and meditation exercises, and calming affirmations. I *will* find Asha. I *will*.

And now here they were, walking into the den of iniquity that was Kamathipura, the place where women were nothing more than chattels, a cheap commodity, their lives bits of detritus in a drain of lost humanity. Here, you could smell the despair. Caroline took a deep breath, but the air was thick with misery and it did not help at all.

Janaki, walking beside her with a firm hold on her hand, did help. How she had grown, in more ways than one; she was a woman now, and a lovely one at that, emitting that serene charm and calm and self-possession that came naturally to so many Indian women. Janaki seemed unperturbed by the horror of Kamathipura; she seemed physically cool and collected, in a simple but somehow stylish blue cotton *shalwar kameez*, her hair tied back in a ponytail, make-up free and smiling. So relaxed, cool.

Ahead of them walked Gita, somehow incongruous in jeans and T-shirt. Though why incongruous, Caroline asked herself, why shouldn't an Indian woman wear Western clothes in India? It just went to show how ingrained the cultural clichés were. She was leading them confidently into a narrow lane lined with ramshackle houses.

Kamal walked with Gita. Why? she thought. Why not with her? Was he avoiding her? He was so stern, still so aloof, at least towards her. Was it because of Asha, or did it have to do with her, Caroline, and his unresolved feelings towards her?

Front doors opened directly onto the small forecourts where people gathered. Women, leaning against the doorjambs, looked up as they walked past. One or two of them waved at Gita. Others sat on worn-out *charpais*. Many looked as if they had just rolled out of bed, though it was already midday.

Some, though, were heavily made-up, their perfume pungent in the congested air, adding its essence to that mélange of smells that formed an olfactory assault on the senses – the tangible smells of cooking, spices, flowers, perfume, hair oil, face powder, incense, rotting fruit, drains, sewage, urine, vomit, sweat and semen, with the intangible ones of fear, loneliness, anguish, hate, hunger, malevolence, abuse, dread and horror. Mingled, coagulated, metamorphosed into that unique and pungent odour Caroline now named 'Bombay sweet-and-sour'. It seeped out like a crawling mist through the lanes and alleys, creeping up the walls and through the windows and lying like a shroud over Kamathipura.

All of Caroline's senses were operating now on crisis frequency. She could hardly think, for the impressions they gathered pelted themselves at her and screamed for attention, a jumble of sound, sight and smell colliding with her own unsorted feelings of disgust, dread, embarrassment and sheer horror. Once again, she wanted to turn and run, but always that cool calm voice – *Asha is here!* – called her back. That, and Janaki's hand around her own.

Gita talked as she walked, sometimes waving at a woman and smiling, sometimes stopping to explain some detail. She stopped to introduce them to a friendly brothel manager, called, she said, a *gharwali*. 'But we call her Bai, like a mother, or an aunt. These women are just doing their jobs. They are not evil.'

Gita turned a corner; they walked down another lane. And another. They were lost in a labyrinth of grimy back streets lined by tall, half-derelict buildings. She shuddered, reining in an imagination that veered in a direction that only amplified the encroaching sense of dread. A black veil creeping through her being.

And yet, the street scenes seemed simultaneously so harmless, so everyday. Just women, standing and sitting around, a few men – where was all the horror? What went on behind those stone walls?

There was the real horror. She glanced up and, yes, there were the notorious cages, barred windows in the upper storeys, some shuttered, some like dark holes into the warrens of vice behind them. Drapes of washed-out laundry hanging out to dry on balcony railings and window bars high above her head.

These homes, she knew, were veritable prisons. At night, the female prisoners would sit behind those bars, all dolled up, tawdry lures for the hungry on the streets. But how desperate must a man be to come here for relief? And yet, here on the street, there was no sense of desperation. It was all so very – normal. Except for one thing: they themselves. *They* were the deviation from the norm.

Caroline felt like an involuntary tourist being led around some noteworthy cultural attraction, except that this attraction was decidedly unattractive. In fact, she felt that she herself was the great attraction. Caroline might have removed her ostentatious jewellery, but it turned out that that was the least of her problems. It was the white skin and light-coloured hair that drew eyes to her; that, and the tailored clothes and obviously expensive shoes. Wherever they walked, people stepped back and stared; not just the unobtrusive glances polite Westerners might throw at a conspicuous stranger, but blatant, in-your-face ogling.

Caroline, already flustered by the knowledge that they were walking through the streets of one of the most notorious red-light districts in the world, grew more nervous by the minute at the attention she was attracting.

The very next thing I'll do, she said to herself, is buy a cheap *shalwar kameez*. I should dye my hair black as well, and colour my skin brown. With bronzer. An internal finger wagged at her: you can't do that. That would be blackface! But Caroline struck it down immediately. This was India, and all internalised concepts brought as baggage from America collapsed in the face of the immediate reality.

The thought again... Asha is here. Somewhere in these labyrinthine lanes is my daughter. Somewhere behind those crumbling facades is the most precious person in my life. I have to find her. But how? And when?

THIRTY-THREE

Caroline

By morning's end Caroline was a walking heap of sweaty exhaustion and desperation.

'Seen enough?' Gita asked, and when she nodded in response, said, 'So, now you know what you're up against.' She looked at her watch. 'It's eleven thirty. Go back to your hotel and rest; but be sure to come to the team meeting at four. We'll have a brainstorming session – if you have any ideas on how to move forward, bring them there. See you!' And she was gone.

'I need a meal and a nap,' said Caroline to the others. 'How about you?' She looked from one to the other.

'I'm going to take a walk,' said Kamal. 'I need to think. I'll see you at Tulasa House at about three forty-five, OK?'

Caroline nodded, disappointed. She had hoped to discuss matters with Kamal over a light lunch, but already he was walking away, melting into the crowds on the Mumbai sidewalk.

'And you, Janaki? Are you going back to your hotel? Where is it, anyway? I'm staying at the Taj.'

Janaki laughed. 'The Taj is way out of my league,' she said.

'I'm at some cheap digs not too far away. But I don't need a rest. I'm going back to Tulasa House. I want to use the computer.'

Janaki hailed two rickshaws, one for Caroline and one for herself; her Hindi, she found, was good enough to bargain down Caroline's taxi fare a little (the Taj, she found, combined with Caroline's white skin, demanded an automatic luxury levy) and so they parted company.

'See you later,' she said, stepping into her own vehicle.

Sleeping during the day always had the effect on Caroline of a heavy drug, knocking her out for hours. She avoided it in America, but here, in India, in combination with jetlag and the sleeplessness of the previous night, it was like opium.

Fortunately she had set the alarm, and it woke her at two-thirty, yet she found she could not get up. The lethargy clung to her like a coarse skin; she lay under the slowly rotating ceiling fan, too lazy even to get up to pour herself a glass of cool water from the flask on the sideboard. The drawn blinds kept out the afternoon sun, and the gloom was like a further narcotic.

'Get up,' she scolded herself. 'Take a shower. There are things to be done. A meeting to attend. Asha to be found.'

And so she forced herself out of the soft lavishness of the bed, into the coolness of the shower where she washed her hair and then dried it. Thank goodness it was so short, cut for convenience just before her flight to India.

Looking at her open suitcase, she remembered her resolve to buy a *shalwar kameez*. She had noticed a boutique down in the hotel foyer; this was a good time to go down and buy herself something suitable. She put on clean trousers and a blouse and made her way down.

The boutique attendant was obsequious in her desire to sell a matching trio of flowing silk tunic, wide trousers and shawl, but Caroline could not make up her mind, and eventually left the shop without a purchase. Those suits were all – well, unsuitable, she thought, wincing at her own bad pun. Far too swish, too shiny, too Taj.

She needed something simple. Something like Janaki had worn. Cotton, not silk. She walked out into the heat of the day, onto the pavement, and hailed a rickshaw. In broken English, and fingering her blouse to demonstrate to the driver, she managed to make her intentions known: *Shalwar kameez* shop? Sari shop? He bobbled his head and drove off.

By three thirty Caroline was the proud owner of five brand-new simple but pretty *shalwar kameezes*. But it was too late to go back to the Taj.

'I'll wear one now,' she had told the shop attendant who had helped her choose. In fact there had been three of them, all male, eager to help her make the right choice, offering her a chair and a cup of tea, which she had gratefully accepted (and when the *chai* came milked and sugared, she held her breath and drank it all up, because that was the Indian way, the polite way, and she was learning), and bending over backwards to help her choose only the best-quality and most expensive suits. But she had gone with her instincts and chosen for practicality, not for fashion.

'Madam, it is not suitable for wearing right away,' said the attendant. 'The fabric is too stiff. You must wash it once before wearing to remove the starch.'

'No, it doesn't matter if it's a bit stiff. I have to wear it now. I'll wear this one: see, the shawl is soft and flowing. I'll put it back on. Thank you for your help.'

'Thank you, madam, no problem. I will write you a bill; you just take it to the cashier at the front of the shop.'

'Can you deliver the other three to me at the Taj Mahal Hotel?'

'Of course, of course, madam!' said the head-bobbing attendant. He took down her name and assured her it would be done, as part of the service.

As she walked away every one of the attendants in the shop – all male – stood back, smiled at her, bowed, bid her farewell and thanked her for her custom.

Americans, she thought, could take some lessons in customer service from the Indians. Once again, she stepped out into the sweltering Mumbai heat. It was now three thirty. She might just make it to Tulasa House in time; she certainly wouldn't make that tentative three forty-five meeting with Kamal. Once more, time had dropped into a hole and the day was more than half over and Asha was still not found.

Basically, she had wasted a day. Wasted a whole day strolling around Kamathipura like some celebrity diva and then sleeping and then shopping, all while Asha was still in jeopardy, still not found.

And time still seemed to be stretching before her, waiting for her to quicken her pace, get back into the rhythm she had once known, that American sense of *time*, a conveyor-belt constantly on the ebb, constantly running away, taking success and achievement and victory with it; and if she did not run in pace all would be lost, forever.

In America, time was something to grab, now, here, before it was too late. In India, time was leisurely and eternal. But it held Asha captive, and that was the problem. She needed to inject a little bit of America into India. This dawdling was not for her. And yet, today, she had subscribed to it completely.

'This won't do,' she told herself. 'I've wasted a day and Asha is out there and nobody seems to see the need to make each moment count. We need to change pace. I need to take control. I'll speak up at that team meeting.'

THIRTY-FOUR

Janaki

I'm addicted, thought Janaki, as she thankfully pressed the *on* button on Dr Nath's computer. Away from the screen for too long and I develop withdrawal tendencies.

But it was more than that, she knew. Asha was out there, somewhere, and Janaki believed with all her heart that all the information they needed to know was swirling around in cyber-space; all she needed was the key to enter that space. Walking through Kamathipura this morning had been a complete waste of time; it had been for Caroline and Kamal's benefit, as she had done that already the day before. The obligatory tourist walk-through that left anyone with a beating heart in distress. Caroline, indeed, had been in tears.

'How will we ever find Asha in that labyrinth?' Caroline had asked her. 'Janaki, it seems impossible!'

'It's not impossible at all,' Janaki had said, thinking of the computer and her itchy fingers. 'We just need a strategy. Come to the meeting this afternoon – we'll share our ideas there. Go home and have a rest now – you look exhausted.'

Caroline had nodded and stepped into the taxi Janaki hailed and negotiated for her.

Caroline shouldn't have come to Kamathipura, Janaki thought. She should have stayed in the luxury of the Taj and let us Indians find Asha. The shock of Kamathipura's reality was too much for her.

Caroline was not ready for this side of India. Gingee had been bad enough; this was so much worse. She should have stayed in her pristine sheltered world and let us do the work, Kamal and me. Both just as desperate to find Asha as Caroline, but better equipped to deal with the squalor and the poverty and the heaving throngs that make up everyday India. We grew up here. We know. We are impervious, better equipped to hold our true inner selves separate from the ugliness without.

And besides, thought Janaki, how on earth could a blonde, white, amber-eyed American be of any earthly help in the quest before them? Someone who couldn't speak a word of an Indian language, a wealthy American who didn't even know it was inappropriate to wear a diamond ring in a slum? Janaki shook her head. She'd have to have a word with Caroline. Persuade her to let her and Kamal do all the searching needed.

Kamal. Janaki smiled as his name once again came to her mind. Yes, Kamal had changed. But so had she. He no more the older uncle, she no more the precocious child – mature enough, back then, to care for his daughter maybe, but still a child. He had been so austere at first, so locked within himself, but she had now found the key to his armour, and the key was Asha.

It was as if their mutual quest had linked them together in some intangible way, beyond the attraction she had initially felt towards him. They were together now, together in their desperation to find his lost daughter, together in their need to save the girl from whatever horrors she faced or – God forbid! – had already been subjected to.

'Dear God, let it not be too late,' Janaki prayed now, as she opened the web browser and tapped in the keyword to Mr Pandian's email account. Let there be some clue, some sign, some hint as to her way forward. Hopefully Mr Pandian had not closed the account, had not, somehow, changed the password...

There. The account opened, along with a list of at least thirty unopened mails. That meant that Mr Pandian was probably still in jail, with no access to his account; hopefully he would stay there, be tried and convicted, and spend the rest of his days in hell. For what he had done to Asha, and most likely other girls like her.

How could men do this thing? How could they? Did they not have daughters, sisters, mothers, wives? If I ever have a son, Janaki swore to herself, I will teach him this: treat every woman as you would wish your mother, sister, daughter to be treated. Let that be your guideline. Then you can do no wrong. Love and respect women as they deserve to be loved and respected – as human beings with lives of their own, and not as property to be used and abused.

If only every mother would teach her son that golden rule. If only every father would live that rule, as an example to their sons, and to show their daughters what a real man is. A real man, like Kamal...

She sighed, shook away those useless reflections, scanned the list of emails, looking for a crumb of a clue. Something to work with. Something that would point her in the direction to be taken next. But the names of the senders, the subject titles all seemed innocuous. Just *Hello!* and *What's up?* and *Can you make it?*

Some in Tamil, some in English. Many, too many, in Hindi, which she could not read. Mostly from men, some from women. Pandian's sister was one of the first, before she knew of his arrest, apparently; reminding him of his niece's tenth birthday and prompting him to visit, or at least call: *You know how much*

Indira loves her favourite uncle! Such words now seemed ominous. Why was Mr Pandian a favourite uncle? Had he oozed himself into Indira's favour, but with an ulterior motive? No, surely not. Not his own niece. Yet, to a man without morals, perhaps even a niece was fair play. Janaki shuddered. It didn't bear thinking about.

The personal emails were interspersed with several ads. Spam, it was called, Janaki had learned in America: spam, like the processed meat. She remembered suddenly that Caroline had craved spam when she had stayed with the Iyengars, when Asha was a baby. Funny how an irrelevant memory could suddenly pop into the mind. She ignored the obvious spam messages and worked her way down the inbox, reading, then marking the messages as unread. Just in case. Covering her tracks. Obviously she was even ahead of the police investigation in this respect at least. If the police were even investigating, which she doubted.

One after the other she rejected the messages as useless. There was talk of a Lotus Pond. It sounded interesting. Was it a bar, a brothel? *You need a password to get in,* someone said. *What is the password? I'd like to join.* The first someone replied: *The password is Dhuan. Smoke.* She added that password to her notebook list. The net was closing; the net she, Janaki, had woven. She opened her notebook and wrote down some of the details, names, numbers. *The Lotus Pond. Rajagopal. Telephone and fax numbers. Email addresses, possibly useful. Dhuan.*

She did an Internet search for a Lotus Pond bar or club in Mumbai, but there seemed not to be one. Maybe it was a secret place where these men met. She found nothing useful.

At one point, Mr Pandian asked for a fax number. *I will send photos of this special girl,* he'd written. *She is truly delight-ful. And she speaks English.*

There. That could only be Asha. So Pandian had been faxing photos of Asha to certain individuals. In some cases, he sent email attachments, secured with passwords. A little fiddling, and Janaki had the password. She opened the attachment. And her heart swelled and sank at the same time. The attachment showed a black-and-white photo of Asha.

Asha, in a black-and-white sari. Asha, her face pale and grey and permeated with fear. Janaki let out a gasp of horror. And yet, and yet. This photo was evidence. And it meant progress.

The next one down, sent four days ago, was from a Mr Chaudhuri. Janaki read it, sat up straight as a bolt, and read it again. It was curt, but compelling. And, thought Janaki in triumph, crucial.

She is lovely. I want her.

Janaki felt a surge of triumph as she printed out the message and the photo. Just a little more fiddling on the computer, a few more of the tricks she had learned over the last few years, a search in the Sent folder, a couple more printouts, opening of attachments (hopefully they did not have a virus) and she was ready for the team meeting. She looked at her watch. Just after 2 p.m. Enough time for a short nap; the team meeting was at four, and she now had delicious juice for them.

Against one wall of the office was a *charpai*. She lay down. Sleep came in an instant.

'Janaki! Janaki, wake up!'

She stirred, grunted and opened her eyes. A face hovered within the half-mist of wake-up. Grunting again, she sat up on the *charpai*, rubbing her eyes.

'I could have slept forever!' she complained. 'Why did you – oh!'

Looking at her watch, she sprang to her feet.

'Exactly!' said Gita. 'Half past four. The rest of the team

has been at it for a while – we've been discussing the HIV patients. But we're moving on to Asha now, and you need to be there. Come on.'

'I need a shower,' Janaki said, 'but I'll make do with a splash. Where's the bathroom in this place?'

They left the room and Gita pointed to the bathroom door. 'When you've finished, join us in the conference room. It's opposite the kitchen,' she said. 'Caroline and Kamal are both there already.'

Freshened up, Janaki returned to the office and collected the printouts before joining the others in the main room at the front of the house. There were about twenty people in the room; Caroline and Kamal sat on a wooden bench at the back. Janaki edged her way in and Caroline moved to the side, making space for her. Dr Nath seemed to be leading a lively discussion, but when Janaki entered he looked up and changed the subject abruptly.

'Here she is!' he said. 'We can move on to Asha now – we'll get back to the mobile clinic schedule tomorrow. Team – I wanted you all to be here to meet our newcomers. This is Janaki, from Tamil Nadu; Caroline from America, and Kamal. And these...'

His arms swept around the room to indicate all the people sitting there, some on chairs, a few on an old sofa, a few on the floor.

'These are the wonderful people working in the field, on the streets, in the brothels, trying to bring a bit of humanity and caring into the profession, a bit of relief into the suffering. Doctors, nurses, social workers... I won't introduce them by name – you won't remember the names. Some are here professionally, many as volunteers, but all fully dedicated. Now, friends, you've all heard the basics: a little girl, Asha, thirteen years old, abducted, lost like so many others and the trail has led to Kamathipura. You know the story. Caroline is her mother and has come all the way from America to find her. Kamal – over there – is her father. She grew up in Tamil Nadu with foster-parents and after their death was abducted and presumably sold to a pimp and she's here, somewhere.

'Now, all of you are active on the streets, in the houses. I want you to keep a sharp lookout for this girl. Ask questions, follow leads, however slight.'

'A needle in a haystack,' said a man near the back.

'Yes, we all know that. But sometimes a miracle occurs, and we find that needle, and we're going to find this one. And now I'd like to know—'

'Any photos?' said a thin girl sitting near the front.

'Yes,' said Caroline, standing up. She passed a manila envelope to Dr Nath. 'These are the most recent photos I have of her, taken a year ago, just before her twelfth birthday. I don't have anything more recent, unfortunately. But—'

Janaki interrupted. 'But I do!' she said triumphantly. 'I have this!'

She held up an A4 sheet of paper. Everyone looked up. The page showed a grainy black-and-white print of a young girl dressed as a woman, a sari wrapped around her, bangles on her arm, dangling hoops hanging from her ears, studs in her nostrils. An ornate necklace lay on her throat. On her face an expression of utter terror. Her eyes, wide open, showed cold, naked fear. Asha, all dolled up. A prostitute in the making. Caroline gasped. Kamal exclaimed, 'Bloody hell!'

The photo was passed around, and when it came into her hands Caroline couldn't help it: she burst into tears.

'Where did you get hold of this photo?' someone asked.

'I did a bit of searching on the computer,' Janaki explained. 'It was easy, basically. I still have that Madras fellow's email sign-in details. I checked his Sent folder. He sent this photo to a Mr Chaudhuri just over a week ago. Mr Chaudhuri replied, saying he wants her. I checked Mr Chaudhuri's IP address: he's in Bombay.'

'Well done, Janaki!' said Dr Nath. 'It's something to go on – not really much, but something.'

'It's a common name,' said the man at the back. 'Do you know how many Chaudhuris are living in Bombay? Hundreds, probably, if not thousands. Do you want to go through the entire telephone book?'

'It would take days!' said someone else.

'What's an IP?' said the same thin girl.

'And how would we go about it?' interjected the man at the back. 'Call them on the phone and ask them if they molested a girl? Oh yes, that would work beautifully!'

Caroline, voice shaking with tears, said: 'Can't we just give this information to the police?' The room exploded into laughter.

'The police? Really?' said someone. 'You believe the police will help find some random girl? How much do you intend to pay them? More than the pimps are surely paying?'

'Police are corrupt,' said someone with finality. 'No help there.'

The discussion swung around to police corruption and how if anything the police were to be avoided. Finding Asha was up to them, the people in this room. Strategies had to be offered, ideas, suggestions.

'What about the American consulate?' asked someone. 'Surely it's their responsibility to step in?'

Caroline, shaking off her emotion, shook her head. She remembered her resolve. She needed wits, and fortitude, not tears.

'No. I already called them yesterday. They won't help because Asha isn't American; I mean, she could be, but I never did the necessary paperwork. She's Indian. So even though her mother is American it's not their job. They said I have to go to the police. They washed their hands of her.'

Everyone in the room groaned or chuckled or shook their heads or rolled their eyes. Holding the printout against her breast, Caroline stood up.

'May I say something, please?' she said, and without waiting for an answer, continued. 'I think we need to step up our game. Put more effort and urgency into it. My daughter is out there, in jeopardy, and I need to find her. I need to find her, like, yesterday—'

'Yesterday?' interjected the thin girl, frowning. 'How can you find her in the past?'

'It's just an expression,' said Caroline impatiently. 'It means we're working against the clock. She's out there, in danger, in someone's hands, and I want her back. It's all so leisurely here in India, people have no sense of time. It's like a go-with-the-flow hippie thing. Lethargic. I'd like to see a bit more dynamism—'

'Why? What's so special about this girl?' said the man at the back.

'She's my daughter and I want her back!'

'Oh, because she's American, white, or half-white, she's special, is she? Actually, every little girl out there is special. Asha is no more special than any other girl. Every girl is some mother's daughter. You're not the only mother who—'

Caroline was silent, but Janaki felt her jerk and cast a surreptitious glance at her; that was harsh. She reached out and took Caroline's hand, lying on the bench between them. Caroline squeezed her hand and Janaki squeezed back.

'Enough, Giri!' said Dr Nath, pushing his palm towards the speaker. 'This isn't the time for argument. Fact is, Caroline's here, now, and we have a lead. There might be hundreds of Chaudhuris in Bombay, but not so many interested in young girls. I want you all to keep your eyes and ears open. Ask questions. Listen. Ask everyone you meet out there if they've heard of this Chaudhuri. Ask about Tamil girls and where they might end up. Keep asking.'

'What I wanted to say just now, but I didn't get to finish,' said Caroline, 'is that we need a strategy, a plan. We need ideas! I'd like to have a brainstorming session, and—'

'What's a brainstorming session?' asked the thin girl.

'Your ideas. All your ideas. For instance, my idea is to dye my hair black and get my skin darkened somehow. There must be a way to do that. Maybe a beautician would know, and—'

'Nobody makes themselves darker in India,' said the man at the back. 'Now, if you want a skin-bleaching treatment...'

'Caroline, why do you want to make yourself dark? I don't understand!' said Janaki.

'Well, it's obvious, isn't it? You saw what it was like. When I go out into the streets I stick out like a sore thumb. I can't go searching for Asha looking like some tourist. I'm trying to *Indianise* myself. I even bought a *shalwar kameez*!'

She plucked at the shoulders of her tunic.

'Yes, I saw that,' said Janaki. 'Very nice. But I still don't understand how looking like an Indian is going to help. You don't speak Hindi or even Tamil. How are you going to search if you can't even talk to people?'

Caroline did not immediately answer, and in the gap Gita spoke up.

'My idea actually is that you stay American, but we give you a *legend*. That's what it's called, isn't it, in your spy novels. We say you're a journalist, and one of us goes with you to the brothels where we know they keep young girls and say you are writing an article for an American magazine and want to talk to people about the work.'

'But why would they talk to us? Surely they would be suspicious and tight-lipped?'

'Not if you pay them! Find the right people, the ladies in

charge of the younger girls, and offer them money. They'll talk. I bet. Just use your wits.'

'That's an excellent idea,' said Dr Nath. 'Anything else? Kamal?'

'I have two ideas,' said Kamal slowly. 'One is to hire a private detective. And the other – well, it's not something I'm keen on doing. But it might work. What if I pose as a client looking for young girls myself? Ask to be put in touch with... girls like Asha?' He grimaced as he said the last words, and Janaki felt for him. Their eyes locked.

'It's a good idea,' she said, 'if you can do it.'

'I must,' he said. 'It's about the only thing I can do.'

'Sudesh, maybe you can help him there. Introduce him to your contacts, let him infiltrate the trade as a client.' The man addressed as Sudesh nodded.

Others from Dr Nath's team offered their own suggestions and wrote down addresses on pieces of paper; the man at the back threw cold water on every suggestion, and the thin girl asked question after question. The team members were to go out there and keep asking, find a lead to Mr Chaudhuri. Kamal would pose as a client looking for a sweet young virgin, superior quality. Caroline would go with Gita, posing as a journalist writing a story on Kamathipura, bribing her way into the brothels, asking for access to the youngest girls. Money, she said, would be no object; her parents stood behind her and would wire her as much as she needed. There were other suggestions. Each one was thoroughly discussed, considered, and either rejected or accepted as a possibility.

'What will you do, Janaki?' asked Caroline.

'Since I don't think I'll be much use on the streets or in the brothels – I don't even speak Hindi,' said Janaki, 'I'll do what I've always done: search the Internet. It's called surfing. Follow links, ask questions, find clues there. I feel a bit cowardly...'

'Janaki, you're the only one here who's made any progress at all,' said Kamal, 'and it's all been at the computer. Don't feel bad; you've been great. Maybe you can crack the code. More and more detectives in America solve problems from the comfort of their own office. You've been great!'

'Thanks.' Janaki's cheeks turned hot at the compliment.

'So I guess that's it. When do we start?' she asked. 'Tonight?'

A murmur of agreement floated through the room.

Dr Nath raised his voice.

'Meeting's over,' he said. 'I'd like to hold a short *puja* before we disperse. That our work may be blessed.'

Several people nodded. Dr Nath lit a small oil lamp at a shrine set into an alcove in the brick wall, and some sticks of incense. People stood up and gathered around him for *arati*, flame-waving worship. Dr Nath raised his voice, strong and deep, in the *arati* hymn, '*Jai Jagadish Hare*'. Others joined in as he lit a piece of camphor on a metal plate, slowly waved the flame before the shrine, passed the plate on to the next person. The plate passed from person to person; each one waved it before the shrine. And then Dr Nath stepped from person to person, allowing each their own personal devotion. Passing her hands across the flame, Janaki closed her eyes and spoke a silent prayer. *Keep Asha Safe.*

The *puja* ceremony ended; people from the team began to mill around, checking their watches, saying their goodbyes. Through the open window the sounds of the Mumbai evening were growing louder: horns honking, sirens, the steady growl of traffic. The day was coming to a close. The team member called Sudesh approached Kamal and spoke a few words with him; Kamal said goodbye to Janaki and Caroline and the two men left together.

Gita said to Caroline, 'Now isn't a good time to start. Their workday is just about to begin; no good asking for interviews now. Go back to your hotel; get all the rest you can and we start work tomorrow.'

Caroline looked relieved, as if released from a nasty obligation. Janaki felt more and more respect for her. Clearly out of her depth in Mumbai, Caroline was still doing her best to overcome her natural revulsion and sense of alienation. It was touching, how she had bought herself a *shalwar kameez*. And now, Janaki saw with a smile, Caroline had even smeared *vibhuti*, sacred ash, on her forehead, and wore a *bindi*, the red dot made of turmeric paste and lime, on her forehead. She was adjusting, adapting, shedding her American alienation to work with them all. The man at the back had been quite rude, and at times Caroline had seemed ready to either explode in anger or break down in tears.

But she had rallied, calmed down, and now she was one of them.

Tomorrow their work would begin.

Their task seemed futile. Impossible. Janaki closed her eyes again. Let the impossible be possible, she prayed. Her fingers itched; she flexed them, clawing the air. Back to the computer.

THIRTY-FIVE

Janaki

Janaki shut down the computer and stood up, stretching her arms and legs. It was no good. She was hungry. She hadn't eaten since breakfast; she had simply forgotten to do so, but hunger now gnawed at her and she could no longer ignore it. She was tired, too. I'll grab a bite, she thought, and then go to the hotel's computer room and do some more research. It was all getting so interesting...

She had noticed a restaurant near her hotel: Ashaak; she'd go there.

Here on the ground floor the house was silent, but a murmur of voices floated down from the upper floor, and the clattering of dishes drifted in from the kitchen. Janaki opened the front door to step into the street, looking at her watch.

'Hey, Janaki, look where you're going!' said a familiar voice, and she looked up. It was Kamal, standing in the street.

'Oh. Hi!' she said. 'Sorry – I – are you back already? I thought...'

'Tomorrow,' said Kamal. 'The fellow we were supposed to

meet is busy tonight. Gives me a bit more time to prepare, I suppose.' He grimaced. 'Where are you off to?'

'Going to grab a bite to eat, then back to my hotel, probably. What about you? What're you doing here?'

'I came to get my bag. I stayed at the Taj last night – Caroline insisted – but I want to move out. What's your hotel like? Do they have available rooms? Is it far away?'

'Probably rooms free,' said Janaki. 'It's about half an hour from here. I'll take you there, if you like, and you can ask.'

'Fine. Let me just get my stuff.'

He slipped into the hallway and kitchen, returning with a small backpack slung over one shoulder.

'Are you hungry? I was just about to go for a meal.'

'Very,' he replied. 'I'll join you – if you don't mind?'

'Of course not,' she said. Quite the contrary, in fact, she thought. Their eyes met, and Janaki had the distinct feeling that Kamal read that thought, because he smiled, and so she smiled back, but he had already turned away and was trying to flag down a taxi on the busy street. And so she did the same. It was a while before an auto-rickshaw stopped, and they both got in.

'Whew,' said Janaki as she slid along the seat to make room for him. 'Bombay traffic is even worse than in Madras. It sounds impossible but it's true.'

She leaned forward and showed the driver her hotel's card. He nodded and drove off.

'We'd probably be there quicker if we walked,' said Kamal, after ten minutes of stop-and-go traffic.

'True – I came this morning early and it wasn't so bad. It took half an hour. With this traffic, though, it'll be twice as long.'

'Well – I suggest we find a place to eat nearby, and then go to the hotel later, when the traffic is maybe a bit better.'

'Yes, let's do that. You talk to the driver, ask him to take us somewhere good nearby.'

Kamal leaned forward and exchanged a few words in Hindi

with the driver, who nodded and turned on his indicator. This new street was less congested, and after a few more traffic lights, a few more minutes of standstill and crawling, they arrived at a brightly lit restaurant. The rickshaw stopped, they emerged, Kamal paid and they entered the restaurant, where a waiter in a white jacket showed them to a free table and handed them menu cards.

'Wow – this is a bit fancier than I expected,' said Janaki.

'My treat,' said Kamal. 'I owe you so much. I can't even begin to thank you. Coming all this way to help...'

'Why should you thank me at all? I love Asha. I am her baby-amma. I raised her like my own child, even though I was really a child myself. I need to find her as much as you and Caroline. I feel terribly responsible for what happened. I should have been more alert, come home immediately after the accident, even though I missed the funeral. Should never have left her with Paruthy Uncle. I never liked or trusted him. I need to find her too!'

Tears stung her eyes, and she raised her menu card so he would not see.

Kamal laid a comforting hand on her wrist.

'We have to. We just have to,' she sobbed.

'We will.'

They were both silent then, inspecting the menu cards.

Then Janaki looked up. 'The thing is, Kamal—' She stopped, chuckled and said, 'I hope you don't mind me calling you Kamal. Somehow I can't call you Kamal Uncle anymore!'

He laughed. And it was the most open, natural, relaxed thing he had done since she'd first seen him here in Mumbai, and she couldn't help but laugh out loud too. And in that moment of laughter their eyes met and all the tension that had held her in its grip fled.

'Don't you ever call me Kamal Uncle again!' said Kamal. They regarded each other with smiling eyes for a moment longer, and then the waiter appeared and took their order and everything was back to normal. Except it wasn't. Kamal had become a friend, and her romantic fantasies had somehow washed away, irrelevant.

They looked at each other again. Janaki thought it was her turn to speak, but she didn't know what to say. Kamal solved the problem by speaking first.

'So what do you do all day on that computer?' he said. 'You're welded together. It's like your best friend.'

She chuckled wryly. 'You're sort of right. I can't stay away from a computer for too long. But you have to admit it's been useful. Look where we are. Everything we know about Asha, we found out through a computer and the Internet.'

'Yes, but what are you actually *doing*?'

'Same thing you all are doing: searching for Asha.'

'In a computer?'

She nodded. 'Digging. Following leads. Analysing. It's quite fascinating what you can find.'

'For instance?'

'Well, for instance, I've tried to access online communities that traffic children in India. I thought maybe I could discreetly ask around for this Mr Chaudhuri. I thought maybe these people know each other, and exchange knowledge. So I managed to get into a chatroom and I am there right now, just listening – I mean, reading – at the moment. It's called lurking, in chatroom language.'

'What's a chatroom?'

'Well, it's what it sounds like – a gathering of people talking, just like in real life, except that you don't see each other, and they chat in writing instead of talking. This one is called the Lotus Pond. Like a secret room, invisible to the public. Sort of floating in space. It was very hard to find, but I did in the end. Everybody in the room has a secret identity and they discuss whatever they want to discuss. You can pretend to be someone quite different. You basically make up a character, give yourself a fictional name, and off you go, chatting away.'

'What do you chat about?'

'In the Lotus Pond? Girls, of course. The younger the better. Occasionally boys. And all for one sordid purpose. It's pretty disgusting, I can tell you.'

'So you have a secret identity in this chatroom?'

'Yes. But I haven't written anything yet. I'm just lurking, eavesdropping. I made myself a male ID. My chatroom name is Foreigner.'

'Why Foreigner?'

She shrugged. 'It's just a stupid ID name, a handle. Everyone has silly handles. One guy calls himself Moviestar, and another is Billionaire. Some just have place-name names like BombayBoy or MrBengal, or even a real name like Ashok. It's play-acting in a way. Foreigner just popped into my head because I feel so foreign here now. This place – what am I doing here? It's not me. But I have to find Asha.'

He nodded. 'I know. I'm a foreigner too, in my own task. It's all so – alien. I'm dreading tomorrow night when I have to do some real-life play-acting.'

'What are you going to be doing?'

'Sudesh has discreetly put me in touch with some fellow who deals in young girls – a pimp, I guess, though they didn't use that word. I'm supposed to be a foreign-returned Indian visiting Bombay who's looking for action with very young girls, preferably foreign-looking, fair-skinned. It's grim. Horrible. But this guy, this pimp, knows all the networks and I'm hoping that this Mr Chaudhuri is one of his contacts and – well, it's all very vague. I'm going to have to play it by ear.'

'What if they take you to a real girl and it's not Asha?'

Kamal shuddered. 'It turns my stomach.'

They were both silent for a moment, contemplating the horror of it all. A young girl, who wasn't Asha, caught up in a net of iniquity. A girl, every bit as precious, every bit as lost, but not Asha. Kamal would have to walk away...

'And that's not the only problem, Kamal.'

She paused.

'Yes?'

'You'd never convince them. You just don't look like that sort of a man.'

'What sort of a man?'

'You know. Rough. Ruthless. A man who would – rape – a young girl. Anyone could tell at a glance.'

'I'll just have to act really well then. I used to be a good amateur actor, back in the day. As for my looks – there's a profession called make-up artist. Actors use them all the time.'

'Still – you can't change your eyes, Kamal. Your eyes show who you are. They show kindness.'

'You're saying I'm a wimp?'

'No. A good man,' she whispered. 'A caring man. A father, who would do anything in the world to save his daughter.'

Again, their eyes met. Again, that sweet warmth washed through her.

'That's not weakness, Kamal,' she added, 'it's strength. A quiet strength, but a strength all the same. The mistake you men make – some of you – is that you think strength is domination, control, bullying, throwing their weight around, establishing themselves as the boss. It's not. Compassion is the true strength.'

'I know that, Janaki. I was just teasing. I know that strength. It's why women are the stronger sex after all. That old, maligned role of nourisher, carer, mother: it's made them so very strong.'

'And you are like that; and you're going to need every bit of it in the role you've chosen to play. Going into the dragon's den, pretending to be a dragon yourself...' She shuddered.

'A man's got to do what a man's got to do, as they say in America.'

'I guess I have the easy task, sitting at a desk tapping stuff into a computer. But I do think that's the best task for me, Kamal. I'm not trying to avoid the real-life things you and Caroline are doing out there. It's just what I'm good at, and it does bring results. Like in this chatroom, if I ever decide to come out of hiding – it's called de-lurking – I can do the same thing you're doing. I can say I'm looking for a foreign-looking young girl, fair-skinned, English-speaking... One of the reasons I chose Foreigner as my nickname is that I don't speak Hindi, and a lot of the chat is in Hindi, or half-Hindi half-English. So if I ever de-lurk I'm going to say I'm foreign-returned and living in Bombay but my native tongue is Tamil and that's why I can only chat in English. English is the one language that connects us all in India, wherever we live. It's the one good thing the Raj left behind.'

'Supposedly,' said Kamal. 'So, basically, we're doing the same thing, just that you're doing it behind a screen, and I have to go out there and face the real horror of Kamathipura.'

Janaki nodded. Once again, she felt tears welling behind her eyes, as if the constant nagging ache in her heart was rising through her being, spilling out through her eyes. Worst of all, her sheer helplessness in the face of a task that seemed quite impossible. Asha, out there, lost, in danger.

'I'm sorry. It sounds so cowardly. But trust me, it works. We wouldn't even be here at all if it wasn't for email and Internet.'

'I'm not blaming you. You're actually getting results, unlike the rest of us. But—'

'Kamal! I just had an idea! A brilliant one!'

'Yes?'

'Why don't we combine tactics? Why doesn't Foreigner come out of lurking, start talking in the chatroom, say that he's a foreign-returned Indian looking for that kind of girl – what if the people behind Asha contact Foreigner, and we set up a date, and then *you* turn up, as Foreigner?'

'But how will we know it's Asha I'm meeting?'

'Trust me, that's how it works. People chat online and make connections and then they connect privately through direct personal messages and arrange meetings and so on. The things I've seen, Kamal – it would make you sick. One man offered his own daughter! Can you believe it?'

'Of course I can. But—'

'Listen, Kamal, it's brilliant. I'll pose as a very rich foreign-returned businessman. OK? Build up a whole identity for Foreigner: back from America, or maybe Dubai. Maybe CEO of an engineering company, as that's your field. Mid-thirties. Single. I'll describe the real-life you. And then I describe the kind of young girl you want. And I bet there aren't many girls like her in Bombay. I bet I'll get some offers. I'll then set up direct messaging. If people offer me girls like that, I'll ask for a snapshot. I can always say I don't like the snaps, until Asha turns up. And when she does, I set up the meeting. And you go and get her. Somehow.'

'It sounds good, Janaki. But it'd take days. Weeks, even!'

'None of us has anything that will be any quicker. Looking through the telephone directory for the right Chaudhuri? Posing as a journalist? Pretending to be a customer? All of those tactics could take days or weeks. My method, at least it sorts the wheat from the chaff in advance. You don't know for sure if this guy you're going to meet has Asha, do you? You're just guessing?'

'Well, yes. But...'

'But my idea is quicker, much quicker. People can hide online the way they can't in real life. I'm telling you, the Internet is going to explode in the next few years with all the possibilities. It's connecting the whole world, strangers chatting and getting to know each other without ever leaving their homes. My way, I can maybe dig right down to the centre of things. These people are savvy, Kamal; they work with the latest methods now because that's where the money is. They are all online. It's huge. Everyone keeps saying that finding Asha is like looking for a needle in a haystack; well, I'll tell you this, if anything can find a needle in a haystack, it's a computer search engine!'

'If you say so. But I still need to keep that appointment tomorrow, right?'

'Of course. And tomorrow I'll get up bright and early, and get moving as Foreigner.'

By now they had finished their meal. Kamal summoned the waiter, and paid.

'So, what are you doing now?'

'Going back to my hotel, I suppose. And you wanted to check in there, didn't you?'

He nodded. 'And then?'

'Well, I was thinking of the Internet shop near the hotel. Do some more research. Maybe Foreigner can casually introduce himself. Come out of lurking.'

'Can't it wait till tomorrow? Have you been to Juhu Beach yet?'

'No, of course not. I basically went straight to Tulasa House when I arrived in Bombay.'

'Shall we go there now? To the beach? Go for a walk, stretch our legs? You need to get away from that computer, Janaki. Let's do that.'

She nodded. 'OK. And anyway, there's something else I wanted to talk to you about.'

'Really? Sounds mysterious. What?'

She shook her head. 'Later. Let's go.'

THIRTY-SIX

Caroline

Despondency clung to Caroline like a shroud as she picked up the receiver and punched in the US number.

'Hi, Mom.'

'Darling, at last! How are you? Where are you? What's going on? Have you found her? Is she OK?'

'Sorry to call you at the office. The time difference makes things difficult, that's why I didn't call sooner.'

'Honey – you can call me any time. Middle of the night, any time. So tell me? How is she? When are you coming home?'

'Oh Mom... sh-she's... No. I haven't found her. Mom, I've lost her. She's lost. I'm in Bombay, trying to find her, but, but... Oh, Mom!' She burst into tears. for the umpteenth time. Her mother waited, making comforting noises. Finally, Caroline was able to speak again.

'She's been abducted. Stolen! She's here in Bombay and they want to sell her as a child prostitute. Oh, Mom! What am I going to do?'

'Oh my God! What...? How...? Honey, listen... Are they

demanding a ransom? You still have a bank account in India, right? Tell me the details. Email them to me. I'll put some money in there – a few hundred grand. Whatever they ask. Just pay it.'

'It's not that easy, Mom. No, they haven't asked for a ransom. We don't know who has her. I can't... I don't...'

'Darling. It will be all right. You'll find her, you will. Just be patient. I'll tell your dad. Are you in a hotel? Give us your phone number. We'll take care of everything. Don't worry, sweetheart.'

'Of course I'm worried, Mom! Money doesn't buy everything, you know.'

'But in this case, it will. Just don't panic.'

A few minutes later, Caroline's dad called, and he was the same, except he had other solutions.

'Pay them whatever they want, honey. Make sure the police are doing their job. Hire a private detective. Don't leave any stone unturned. And I have great contacts. Senators, congressmen. I'll get in touch with the Indian Ambassador over here. And the American consulate. We'll work it out. Send me an email to let me know the details. I'll arrange everything. We'll get her back. Don't worry. Honey, I have to rush now but I'll get my secretary to wire over the money. Bye honey, and don't worry.'

And he was gone. That was Dad all over. Always too busy, too matter-of-fact. Thinking that money and contacts and pulling strings were all that was needed to get through life. But it wasn't. Yet speaking to him had helped. And he was right. Money would speak, to a certain extent. After all, if Asha was to be sold, and to the highest bidder, what was preventing *her*, Caroline, from being the highest bidder?

But she knew exactly what the answer to that was. This wasn't a normal ransom case. If they didn't know *who* was selling Asha, *who* was demanding money, how could they bid?

This was all underground. The whole matter was being conducted in Mumbai's dark underbelly, and time was horrendously against them.

Caroline went to the bathroom and splashed her face with cold water. She looked in the mirror. She looked terrible. But no wonder. She was shattered after today, walking the labyrinthine streets of Kamathipura yet again, this time with Gita. The futile interviews, the fake smiles, the wads of money handed out so that the people would talk. Seeing those women, those girls, some so young, so very young, so resigned to their fate. The blank stares, the hardened faces, the dull eyes; knowing that Asha was lined up to join their ranks or maybe, maybe – she forced herself to think it – maybe *already was* one of them.

It didn't bear thinking about. She wished she had someone to talk to. Janaki. Kamal. Where were those two anyway? Kamal had checked out of the Taj early that morning. To look for a less fancy place, he'd said. Where was he? The three of them should be together, comforting and supporting each other.

This roaring monster of a city – it devoured strangers, and that's what they all were. Here she was, facing the greatest challenge of her life, and she was all alone. Even Gita had disappeared, gone back home to her husband and children. There was no one to talk to.

And she needed desperately to talk. To confess her blistering sense of guilt. Because she was guilty. Completely guilty. This was all her fault. She had abandoned Asha when she was still a toddler; rushed back to America and never returned for her daughter.

She remembered Kamal's words, so many years ago: *We will return to America. I will get a job there, no problem. We'll take Asha and be a real family, anywhere you like. If you prefer to go to work, you can do that and I'll look after her. I know it's hard, but tough it out for a few months more, Caro. Just a few months more.*

But she had gone back home alone and moved in with her parents and left Asha behind. She wondered what would have happened if she'd been a better mother, or if she had liked India more, or if they had moved back to America soon after Asha had been born, after she'd realised she was having problems.

Gone back home, to Mom. And Kamal had come too. What kind of life would they have had? Would Asha have been happier, growing up as an American child?

Or if, when she'd flown home after the food-poisoning drama – if she'd sent for Asha. She could have somehow hired a nanny to bring her daughter, once she'd decided to stay. So many should-haves and could-haves, and with the wisdom of hindsight, she saw now that there *had* been options. But, as her therapist back then had said, she'd been in a deep depression and in no state to make wise decisions. She'd done what had felt right for herself at the time. Had Asha paid the price? She certainly wouldn't be in this situation. What if...?

She'd never know the answers and it was wrong to beat herself up over things that couldn't be changed. You couldn't turn back the clock.

Yet, against her better judgment, Caroline tortured herself with speculation and longed to do just that. She'd done it all wrong. She'd committed adultery. She'd abandoned her daughter. She'd given up, and focused on a new life, a career. Even found a new man, betrayed her loving husband. This was all her fault.

Of course it was her fault.

And there was no one to confess to. No one to grant absolution. She sensed that Kamal blamed her, and that's why he had disappeared. Maybe Janaki blamed her too. Both of them knew what she had done. Both of them must hate her. Because now the little girl they all adored was lost in the worst hellhole on earth. And it was all her fault.

Her clothes stank of Kamathipura. It was in her hair, her

skin. She tore the blue *shalwar kameez* from her body, shoved it into the rubbish bin. Maybe a maid would salvage it tomorrow; she didn't care. But then – no. That was just spoilt behaviour. Entitled. She fished it out again, placed it in the laundry bag supplied by the hotel.

Naked, she stepped into the shower. She stood under the gushing water for ages. Washed her hair, scrubbed her skin. The shower gel and shampoo on offer from the Taj smelt delicious. If only she could wash away her thoughts, make them smell sweet. Maybe she could. She would try to meditate afterwards. She was hungry, but didn't think she could eat. Her stomach was churning; she'd probably throw up everything. She needed to *talk!*

After drying her hair she put on a new *shalwar kameez*, delivered by the sari shop. Feeling freshened up, she made her way down to the hotel lobby and asked for the Internet room. She found a computer, logged in to her mail account and began typing an email. Her father had asked her to write him an account of exactly what had happened, from beginning to end. All the details, all the names, all the information they'd been given by Dr Nath, what they'd seen, what they knew.

She began at the beginning, with the loss of contact with Sundari, with that soul-destroying visit to Gingee, the discovery that Sundari and Vikram had died. By the time she got to the discovery that Asha had been removed from the house in Madras, however, she began to lose control. She wiped away the tears with her *dupatta* and typed on. Tears that rolled down her cheek and quickly dried, leaving tracks like snail-trails. Now and then she sniffed as her nose began to run, but still she typed on.

Someone tapped her on her shoulder. She looked up; it was a man, an Indian man, late thirties, well-dressed, smiling at her. He brandished a crisp, white, folded handkerchief.

'I'm at the next computer,' he said. His accent was British, cut-glass English. 'I hope I'm not being interfering, but I thought you could use this, instead of that lovely shawl.'

She looked up at him with anguish spilling from her eyes, still immersed in her story, not quite hearing.

'What did you say?'

'I thought you might like a hanky,' he said. 'I couldn't help but hear you crying. I'm sorry if...'

'Oh. Thanks.' She took the handkerchief, wiped her eyes and cheeks with it.

'Keep it,' he said, stepping away. Caroline thanked him and turned back to the keyboard and her typing, now crying openly, sniffing and snorting and blowing into the handkerchief, and somehow it all helped, writing everything down, weeping openly and without constraint. It was a release, as was the email. Finally, she pressed Send, and off it went. She stood up, just a little bit unburdened. Maybe she could now eat after all. Just a snack.

She left the computer room. The handkerchief man was waiting for her outside, sitting in a chair beside the door and reading a newspaper.

'Hello again,' he said, smiling. 'I was worried about you. You seem so distressed – is there anything I can do to help?'

'No,' she replied. 'Nobody can help me.'

'But it's not good to be alone with one's distress. Would you join me for a drink? A glass of good wine can work wonders.'

'No,' she said again. 'No thank you. I'm heading for the restaurant, for a snack.'

'Well, may I join you there? I don't like the idea of a lady being alone with so much sorrow.'

Caroline thought for a moment. Why not? All that lay in front of her was food and drink and then bed with the TV on or some novel or other and the anguish gnawing away at her mind preventing her from understanding a word she read or heard. Maybe a little distraction would help.

'OK,' she said.

She had an omelette and a glass of wine, and then another glass, and learned that his name was Hiran and he was a businessman in Mumbai for work and flying home to London a few days later. And he was friendly and ready to listen, so she told him the whole story and he commiserated and comforted and supported her and reassured her that of course she would find Asha, of course she would, and if he could help in any way he would, but in the meantime she needed to take care of herself, seek relief, release the tension. He slipped his business card across the table, gold-rimmed. Hiran Kapur was his full name.

'I have the day off tomorrow, doing some sightseeing,' he said. 'It's my first time in Bombay. I was born and bred in England. Why don't you come with me, relax a bit?'

'No,' said Caroline. 'I've got to look for Asha.'

'You have to think of yourself as well,' he said. 'Take care of yourself. You're a wreck. You need to relax.'

'It's all my fault. That's why I'm a wreck,' mumbled Caroline, sipping her wine. She told him that part of the story, how she had abandoned Asha. She confessed her guilt. It felt good to talk about it, but it wasn't enough. She needed absolution.

'It's not your fault,' said Hiran, but the words sounded hollow, a cliché gleaned from a thousand pseudo-psychological movies. People could repeat a thousand times that it wasn't your fault, but if you *knew* what you'd done, mere words couldn't undo it.

'I need to go to bed,' she said, standing up, swaying slightly.

'Why not come to my room, and enjoy a bit more wine and some music? It will help release the tension.'

'So that's what this was all about,' she said, turned her back and walked off.

Hiram grabbed her elbow. 'Wait!' he cried. 'I didn't mean—'

Caroline shook him off, turned to face him. 'Yes, you did!' she spat. 'Everything else, all that friendliness, was just a run-up to this, wasn't it? Poor needy American lady needs man, right? Easy Western woman, right? Well, not this one!'

She marched off. Men! she thought. That's all they ever think about. She would have liked to give him a slap, but what remained of her dignity would not allow it.

She went back to her room, stripped again and dived between the sheets. No book. No TV. Just sleep and forgetting. Tomorrow Gita would come at daybreak to pick her up. Tomorrow she'd be that fake journalist again. She'd have to get some more cash. Bribing those brothel madams was expensive. She fell asleep the moment her head touched the pillow.

The next day dawned. Gita picked her up as promised and, just as Kamathipura began to come to life, they began the same old routine: stopping at the brothels, introducing Caroline as a journalist, talking to the women, Caroline asking the questions in English and Gita translating into Hindi, and then, when the women talked, the same in reverse. At this time of day there were few men about, and all the more women, women going about their daily routines. They stopped to speak to several madams.

The questions were always the same. First the general introduction and enquiries. How many girls work here? What ages are they? Where do they come from? How long have they been here? And then the specifics. Any Tamil-speaking girls? English speaking? Educated girls? High-class girls? Could Caroline interview any of them? For more cash, of course.

Always cash. One thing Caroline had learned by the end of the day: money talked. The cliché was quite true. But in this case, the talk was invariably useless. Nobody knew anything.

She returned to her hotel more despondent than ever, and as alone as ever. A shower, a meal, a siesta. And then the phone rang.

Her dad, perhaps. He'd have read her email by now, maybe set the ball rolling with his precious but useless 'contacts' back home. Or maybe he had wired over a good chunk of money.

But it wasn't Dad.

It was Janaki, breathless.

THIRTY-SEVEN

Janaki

Mumbai traffic being what it was, it was nearly ten when the auto-rickshaw carrying Janaki and Kamal reached Juhu Beach. Despite the late hour it was still crowded with people enjoying the fresh evening air. The vendors were out, briskly selling veg biryani, samosas, Bombay *chaats* and other local specialities.

'Care for some dessert?' asked Kamal, and when Janaki nodded, bought two ice *golas* and handed her one: a crushed ice lollipop covered with flavoured juices.

All around them, families were out enjoying the night breeze. The beach was well lit, and the women's saris shone in the lamps' glow like bright moving jewels. People sitting, walking, some running; groups of friends, couples canoodling, children playing or sleeping on their mothers' laps. It was hard to believe that this was the same city; that such a relaxed and joyous community could harbour the evil that had swallowed Asha.

That's India, thought Janaki: the juxtaposition of extremes. The highest bliss and the deepest misery. Abject poverty next to fabulous wealth. Shining saintliness next to darkest evil. And everything in between.

Licking their *golas*, they walked out towards the sea; black waves touched with ripples of frothing white surf lapping at the sand; a cool breeze playing with her hair and her *dupatta*.

It was perfect. A bubble of delight stolen from the anguish that defined her life right now, and his.

'So what did you want to talk about?' asked Kamal, after a while.

'Your grandmother,' said Janaki.

He stiffened and looked at her.

'My grandmother? What do you know about my grandmother?'

'I met her,' said Janaki. 'I'm sorry, I haven't had a chance to tell you yet – everything's been about Asha up to now. I was desperate to find you when Asha first went missing and I had no contact details, nothing at all. But I remembered Amma being so impressed that you were actually a prince, and—'

'I'm not,' said Kamal, cutting in. 'Don't go repeating that nonsense.'

'Kamal, I know you reject—'

He stopped walking, turned to her, grabbed her arm. She too stopped, turned to face him. She'd never heard this voice from him before. Sharp, accusatory.

'You listened to her lies? Yes, they are all lies. We are not a royal family. Not a drop of our blood is blue. No maharajas and maharanis. It's all a huge, big lie.'

'Really? Rani said—'

Kamal raised a hand to interrupt. 'What happened is this: we're a very wealthy family. We're from a long line of silk manufacturers and merchants. We must have started out as tailors, because that's what our surname means. We made all kinds of silk, but our speciality was and is patola silk. Patola weaving is a closely guarded family tradition; only a few families know how to do it. It can take six months to one year to make a single sari; that's how precious the silk is. In the past it was only royalty that wore patola silk; it's still only the fabulously wealthy. Anyway. A few generations back one of the Indian royal families was getting poor and so they married one of my ancestors. That's the whole story. And we're not from that line at all – we're just the in-laws. That's our only link to royalty. All this talk of maharajas and the Maharani of Jaipur and her wedding – it's just stupid boasting. Daadi is a fake, Janaki. That's why I cut all ties with her.'

'She said it was because she was trying to arrange your marriage.'

'Nonsense. Why would I be annoyed for that reason? It's normal in India, and all I had to do was ignore her. Which I did. I married Caroline, didn't I? No, Janaki, marriage wasn't the reason. When I was in America, I did the research and discovered who we really are. That she had tried to raise me on a pack of lies. Made my childhood miserable. I was so furious – I wrote her a letter and told her not to contact me ever again. And went my own way. I had a trust fund, still have it, for that matter, though I've not needed it for a long time. It's for Asha. No – I just couldn't deal with the lie. She tried to brainwash me with it when I was just a boy, kept me practically imprisoned in the palace – which by the way was never a real palace. Just a huge luxurious home some ancestor built a long time ago. She fed me all that nonsense about being a prince. Being of royal blood. All those women she tried to marry me off to – she fed them the lie as well. Her dishonesty is what enraged me, and she knows it. She's fixated on that lie and just won't admit to anyone, not even to herself, that she isn't royalty. She's crazy.'

He shook his head as if in dismissal and turned to walk forward again. Janaki walked beside him.

'She's just an old woman who's very lonely, Kamal. I mean, why would she make up such a huge fiction? Surely it can only be because she feels insecure? Who does that, except someone who feels small? She's lonely and desperate for contact with you. Did you know she's been following you around the world, with the help of private detectives, all this time? She knew exactly where to find you. She even called your office in Dubai while I was there. I bet she's got a detective following us right now.'

'She—' Kamal cried out in protest, but Janaki did not let him speak. She simply carried on.

'No, don't say anything. Let me finish. She's obsessed, and she's interested in Asha, too, Kamal. That's what I wanted to say. Asha's her great-granddaughter. Why don't we get this private detective of hers to help in the search? She's dying for you to make contact. And one day she will die, Kamal. Her health isn't at all good. You should make up with her before she dies. You really should. Family is everything.'

The more she spoke, the more impassioned was Janaki's little speech. Yes, she understood Kamal's rejection of his grandmother. Yes, she had resented Rani's wanting to interfere in her own life, and she could understand how much worse it had been for Kamal.

But surely, *surely*, behind it all was only love? The love of a grandmother for her only grandchild. Surely Rani felt much the same anguish at losing Kamal, as Kamal felt at losing Asha? She tried to make this clear to him.

'She loves you, Kamal, and misses you desperately. You're all she has left in the world. You must forgive her. You must!'

She paused slightly now to take a breath, which she knew would give him a chance to speak up, but he didn't, and so she just continued.

'It's not good to harbour resentment for so many years, Kamal. It's not good for your spiritual health. It just gnaws away inside you and it's not good. Like a little leech that won't let go. You should contact her. Reconcile. It would do you good, I promise. You know, this might sound strange, but I feel sorry for her. I really do. She's really lonely, stuck in that palace with her Bollywood movies and her luxury, and not being able to walk and having to be cared for. She's just a sad, obese, lonely, disabled old woman. You shouldn't hate her.'

'I don't hate her. It was anger, not hate, that caused the rift.'

'Well then. If you don't hate her, it's time to cool down the anger. It's high time, Kamal. You shouldn't nurse anger for so many years. It's really unhealthy.'

'You're quite a little guru, aren't you?'

'It's just common sense. That's all it is. Anyone could tell you that.'

'So you take her side, do you?'

There was a smile in his voice now, and Janaki knew she had won. Still, she had to make her point clear.

'It's not a question of taking sides. I'm just telling you what would be good for you.'

'Hmmm. Still, she seems to have won you over. What else did she tell you?'

It was Janaki's turn to smile.

'Promise you won't take this the wrong way?'

'Promise.'

'She thought I should marry you.'

He laughed out loud. 'Typical! So typical. And what did you say to that?'

'I told her you were too old for me.'

'What! Are you out of your mind? Old? Me?'

She chuckled and shrugged. '*Too* old, not old. I also told her I was already engaged.'

'Really? I didn't know that.'

'Well, I was, at the time. He broke it off just after I got to Bombay.'

'He broke it off? Really? Why? Stupid fellow! A lovely

woman like you, caring and wise and educated as well? What more could he want?'

'I guess he was more traditional than I thought. His parents weren't keen anymore. Not since my parents died. They wanted a big wedding, which my parents would have provided, and also the fact that I was actually an orphan – they thought it was bad luck. They talked him into breaking it off.'

'So it was an arranged marriage? I wouldn't have thought...'

'No – it was a love marriage. I mean, it was going to be a love marriage. But of course our parents discussed it and approved and all that Indian stuff. You can never really get away from it. We did care for each other. We were going to get married when I returned from America.'

'So are you very upset?'

'To be honest, no. He told me via email – what a way to break up with someone! And I was already in the throes of the whole drama of Asha so everything else seemed so minor in comparison. It was like water off a duck's back.'

She paused, and they walked in silence for a while, each lost in their thoughts. Then Janaki said, 'And what about you and Caroline? Amma used to say your heart was so thoroughly broken you would never recover. She admired you so much for that.'

'Oh, nonsense. Of course, I was hurt when she dumped me. I loved her, and took my marriage seriously. And I've got that thing called male pride, and that was hurt too. And it was tough for a while. But I'm a realist. I got back on my feet. I went to stay in an ashram for a while, and found my spiritual bearings again, and that helped. And then I simply got on with life. What's the point of nursing a grievance for years and years?'

'Are you sure? You're so cold towards her. At least, what I've seen of you together. As if you're still mad at her. She's trying so hard to be nice to you and you're like a cold fish. It made me think you're still in love with her.'

'A cold fish, am I? I wasn't aware of it. OK, I'll try to be nicer to her in future. But I'm definitely not still in love with her. Not at all.'

'Hmm. Over-protesting, perhaps? Daadi also thinks you're clinging to the past. To her, to Caroline. And that's why you never remarried. Or showed any interest in women.'

'Oh, really? Daadi said that. What else did Daadi say about my marital prospects?'

'For someone so furious at her, you seem very interested.'

'Of course! I want to know what you women get up to when you discuss my possible future marriage. Go on – what else did she say?'

'Well – she said she had arranged for you to meet attractive women again and again. But always you refused. She thought maybe you were gay. Or you were still grieving for Caroline. Or you were a would-be monk. Or something.'

He laughed. 'No to all of that. Those beautiful women who kept bumping into me accidentally-on-purpose – I might have known she was behind it all. But no. I just haven't – hadn't – met the right woman. It's not so easy. Not in India. Not even in the West.'

'*Especially* not in the West. My closest female friend in California, Terri, always used to say I was so lucky to be already engaged. She wanted to find Mr Right but you can't even mention marriage and kids on a first date, she said, when you're trying to suss out the basics, like if the guy is only out for a fun time or if he's serious. And usually it's the former. Just fun. And fun isn't enough, is it? It can get really frustrating, Terri said, because you have to avoid the subject for months and even years and then when you finally find out he's commitment-phobic and doesn't want kids, you've wasted a lot of time and energy and emotional investment, and it all ends in acrimony and leaves you with yet another scar so that you're afraid to trust. But you're a good feminist and so you put on a brave face and pretend to be just as commitment-phobic and you don't need a man, and you don't want kids, and you try again, and it's the same coyness and scars and by the time you're thirty – she's twenty-nine – all you are is one big scar and you can't trust anyone. At least that's how she seems to me, and she admits it too. With us Indians, you know from the very first date that it's all about marriage. Marriage compatibility.'

She stopped for breath and the silence between them was thick as he absorbed what she'd said, and her last two words seemed to echo up to the stars. And it was suddenly embarrassing. Had she been too open? Too... *something*. She'd spoken the M-word, so taboo in the West. The surf splashed and lapped against the beach in frothy gladness, as if laughing at her silly little speech. So revealing, so unnecessary. So un-feminist.

He spoke into her self-recriminations, and it wasn't what she'd expected.

'So, Janaki, does this count as a first date?'

She chuckled. 'Does that count as an expression of interest?'

They both laughed then, and he said, 'I guess it's a *yes* to both questions, then. No coyness.'

Her hand closed around his. A bit immodest, perhaps, but in life you had to take chances.

THIRTY-EIGHT

Janaki

Foreigner:

Let me introduce myself. I'm not really a foreigner, just foreign-returned and foreign-educated. I'm as Indian as all of you. I've been in the USA studying and working for ten years and now I'm back in Bombay. I have certain specific interests and tastes and I would like them to be fulfilled. I've been lurking for one or two days to get the feel of this place and I think you fellows can help me out. I like this group; it seems very open and yet discreet. A trusted friend gave me the password and so I'm here. Obviously no more personal details. In the coming posts I'll tell you more about what I like and what I don't like. I will begin with saying that what I don't like is vulgarity. I don't want one of those cheap girls from the streets. I don't want a Kamath-ipura girl. I want a cultured girl. A virgin if possible but at least inexperienced, as I want to train her myself. I have a nice apartment in Bombay and she will live with me as my maid and companion until I tire of her. So that's enough for now. I am an educated businessman, very wealthy, and I don't like common girls. I will pay for superior quality.

Janaki read it over, made a few adjustments, copied it, took a deep breath and pasted it into the Lotus Pond forum.

There. It was done. Foreigner was part of the conversation.

Replies came thick and fast. Welcome messages, suggestions, men discussing the perfect age: thirteen? ten? five? Men boasting that they raped babies. Tales of this girl and that. Recommendations. Lewd remarks and jokes. Janaki took a deep breath and joined in, as Foreigner. 'Lord forgive me,' she whispered. 'It is for a good cause.'

She played the disgusting game all morning, pausing only to run out and buy herself a cup of coffee. Foreigner grew in popularity. It was possible, on the forum, to add 'reputation points', or, as they were called here, 'likes' to certain messages and his reputation grew stronger and stronger. He was *liked*. A few private messages came through, but none of any consequence. Particularly, a MrBengal shared his taste and understood him perfectly. *Such cultured girls like to play hard to get,* he wrote, *but they are worth it in the end. I have my eye on one myself.*

In the space of a few hours Foreigner became one of a close band of paedophiles and child abusers. Foreigner played the game and knew the deal. He was demanding, yes, but, as he had said, he was willing to pay for superior quality. No cheap slut from the brothels. Only best quality. Fair-skinned. Young, of course (twelve to thirteen was his ideal age), and beautiful. If she could speak English, it was a bonus. He himself was from Tamil Nadu. Madras. That was where he grew up. In a very prosperous family. He himself was very prosperous through hard graft. His family dealt in luxury silk.

Janaki was a little nervous about writing that last; it was a little too close to the truth. Yet, what harm could it do? Nobody had contact with Kamal, Foreigner's alter-ego, and they wouldn't know about his background. It was fine.

Around midday a private message notification popped up on the screen. It was from a member named The Vituperator.

I might be able to help you

How?

Just such a girl. All of your requirements fulfilled. Her native language is Tamil but she speaks English.

Can we take this to email? Can you provide a photo? When can I meet her?

Certainly. If you like the photo I can show you her tomorrow. How much are you willing to pay?

What is the asking price?

She is already being reviewed by someone else. If you can improve on his offer she can be yours tomorrow. Just one thing. She is not compliant. Is that an impediment?

Not at all. So much the better. I will make her compliant. A little discipline and a few slaps never hurt.

Janaki winced as she wrote that. She had to practically steel her body, cut it off from her feelings. *Play the game, play the game,* she kept repeating to herself. Only, it wasn't really a game, was it? It was real life. Horrific, soul-destroying reality.

Very well. Tell me your email address and I will send photo. Once we agree on price I will take you to view her. Only viewing tomorrow. I will meet you at midday tomorrow and take you there. If you like her, same-day delivery to your place.

A minute later an email with an attachment popped into Janaki's Yahoo account, at the email address she had created just for this purpose.

It was the very same photo she had printed out yesterday. It was Asha. Janaki's heart lurched with joy and shattered with despair both at the same time.

> OK OK. Very nice. But tomorrow is no good. I want to see her today.

> Unfortunately, not possible today. Please understand that there is competition for this girl as she is superior quality. We have other bookings tonight.

> If you tell me the address I will go and view myself.

> I am not disclosing address. You will have to wait till tomorrow. But please note that tomorrow she might no longer be available.

> I am telling you I cannot make tomorrow. You absolutely need to prepone the viewing. If you do not tell me the address the deal is off. I just want to ensure the photo is the same girl. I will pay advance for immediate viewing. Money is no object. And if I am liking then delivery tonight to my place. I will make an offer you cannot refuse.

A long pause followed, in which Janaki thought the deal was indeed off, or at least, the immediate viewing. She would have to give in, agree to a meeting tomorrow, but then Asha might be gone forever, sold to a stranger. She was nervous. What to do?

A viewing today would mean she had to find Kamal, and quickly. She wasn't sure she could. Kamal had told her he'd be spending today with Sudesh, the social worker who that coming night would be passing him into the underground, the network that would, hopefully, lead him to Asha.

But now there was no need. Now he could make direct contact; but she had to know the address. Perhaps Kamal could rescue Asha today – *delivery to your place!* All he had to do was outbid the other suitor. Kamal had money, a lot of it; and so did Caroline.

Whatever the price.

The minutes ticked by. Ten. Fifteen. Twenty. Then: *Ping!* A new notification from The Vituperator.

> Very well. I will give you address now. But you must pay in advance. One lakh of rupees advance, only for viewing. You must hand it to the mistress of the house I will send you to. I will inform her that you are coming and of the amount by telephone and she will count it before letting you in. There is a password. It is Aishwarya. If you say the password she will take you to see Kamini. That is the name of the girl. You will view her only through the door, a peephole. No talking and no touching. Tomorrow there will be further price negotiations. As I told you someone has already reserved her for viewing tonight. Whoever offers the better price can have her. If you agree to pay one lakh of rupees, non-refundable, for viewing only I will give you address discreetly. This is very special girl, virgin, superior quality. Wheatish complexion. She is worth the price. You must go between three and four o'clock. After four, deal is off.

Janaki was shaking as she closed down the computer. She'd done it! She'd found Asha, in only one day. She slipped the note with the address into the pocket of her *kurta*. Now to find Kamal. Hopefully, she'd find him in time. She *had* to find him in time. Everything in her laughed as she ran out into the street.

Kamal! she cried silently. We've done it, we've found Asha!

Had they found more than Asha? She smiled to herself as

she flagged down a rickshaw. Kamal... last night...the walk along the beach, holding hands. The taxi drive back to the hotel, again holding hands. Perhaps Daadi was prescient.

But on the other hand...

Caroline. The smile faded from her lips. Kamal had indeed protested too much.

And really, it was *she* who had found Asha. Kamal was still searching. Out there in the hell that was Kamathipura.

It would be a race against time, to find him. If she didn't...

With a shudder, Janaki recalled the words: *Someone has reserved her for viewing tonight.*

It was a race against time, and she had no idea where or how to find Kamal.

THIRTY-NINE

Caroline

'I've found her!' Janaki's voice was so loud Caroline had to hold the phone away from her ear. 'I've found her, Caroline, I know exactly where she is! I've... we've found her!'

'W-where...? H-how...?' Caroline could only stutter.

'She's in a house in Kamathipura. Kamal has to go and look at her between three and four; the trouble is I can't find him anywhere. He's gone out with Sudesh – the social worker – and no one knows where they are. I don't think I'll find him in time. God, how I wish he had one of those mobile phones!'

'If you know where she is, if you have an address, can't you just send in the police? Why do you need Kamal?'

'Caroline! You heard what Dr Nath said. You can't trust the police! They are paid by those pimps. They're absolutely in their pocket – they're all thugs together. If we run to the police I can guarantee that within five minutes they'll put Asha some-where else and we'll never find her again. No, I've set up an appointment for Kamal and he's the one who has to go – I'll explain later how, but now I just wanted to ask if you've seen him? If he's been in touch?'

'No,' said Caroline. 'Kamal hasn't been in touch. The only person I've seen since yesterday is Gita. She's coming to pick me up at two. In fact...' She looked at her watch. 'It's nearly two now. She could be here any time.'

'Damn. Damn. I should have tried to force a night appointment; we'd have had more time to find him.'

'What're you talking about?'

'Just thinking aloud. I need to do something, postpone the appointment. He won't be pleased.'

'Who won't be pleased? What's going on?'

'I'll explain later – it's just that I went to a lot of trouble to get this appointment and Kamal is supposed to go and look at her to confirm he wants her and then he can buy her tomorrow. It's complicated. Like viewing a house you want to buy but others are outbidding you and it's a race against time. We have to negotiate a final price; but he has to make a down payment today, before he views her. One lakh rupees advance today.'

'How much is that in dollars?'

'A lakh is a hundred thousand rupees. At today's rate it's about one thousand five hundred dollars.'

'I'll pay it. I'll go myself. I'll cash in some traveller's cheques and go. Or go to the Bank of India. My dad told me he'd wire money to my account there; it should be there already.'

'Wait. Let me think this through. Someone has to go, but he expects a man. They don't know what Kamal looks like, so any man can go – but the problem is, only Kamal can really identify her. I might be able to get one of Dr Nath's team but they're all out working right now. It's too short notice. The money has to be paid to the brothel madam.'

'Make up some story – tell them Kamal can't come so he sent me instead. Say I'm his secretary. Tell them anything. As long as I hand over the money – just for looking, that's a crazy amount – they shouldn't mind.'

'An American woman instead of an Indian man? He'd never believe me. He'd know something's up.' They both fell silent, thinking. Then Caroline said:

'I know someone who might do it. Since they don't know what Kamal looks like any man will do, right?'

'What man is this, Caroline? You can't just pick a man off the street—'

'No! Somebody I met. An Indian. Same age as Kamal. I told him the story. He knows. He'll help, I'm sure. I just have to ask him.'

Yes, Hiran would help. She'd apologise for walking away last night. For being so rude after he'd been so gallant, so help-ful. She'd beg him to help. He'd been so supportive; of course he'd do it. She'd promise him anything, anything. He'd said he had today free; maybe she'd find him, ask him, offer herself – whatever he wanted. Just let him go and find Asha.

'He'll do it. Janaki. I'm completely sure. He's nice. He's helpful.'

'Well...'

'Janaki, it's our chance! We have to, don't you see? Just give me the address. I'll go and talk to Hiran – that's his name. I'll get the money, and it's done.'

'Well, I guess that's a good enough option. You said he knows the whole story?'

'Yes. I was – I was lonely last night and I told him every-thing. He really cares, Janaki. He'll help, I'm sure. I'll show him some photos of Asha so he can recognise her. Are you sure it's Asha, by the way?'

'Absolutely certain. It's the same photo.'

'Well then, let me do that. I need to do something, Janaki. I feel so helpless. Let me do this. Let me. Please!'

'Hmmm... well, I suppose it would work. He only has to

hand over the money, say the password, look through a peep-hole, and confirm. That's it, really.'

'See? It's not much. He'll do it.'

'OK. I'll give you the address and the password. Have you got something to write with?'

'Hold on a minute... yes. Fire away.'

Janaki dictated the address, spelling out the Hindi words as Caroline wrote them down in her diary.

'And you need a password. It's *Aishwarya*. Like in Aish-warya Rai Bachchan, the Bollywood star.'

Caroline shrugged. 'Never heard of her. Let me write that down and learn it. How's it spelt?'

'This friend of yours will know the name. She's famous and beautiful. It's spelt...'

Janaki spelt out the name. Caroline wrote it down.

'Got it,' said Caroline, folding the note.

'OK then. I guess that's it. Confirm it's her, and tomorrow Kamal buys her back. That part should be simple enough – he's supposed to be buying her as a live-in girlfriend and maid.'

Caroline turned pale. 'How can they do this? How can a grown man...' She couldn't finish.

'I know. And they're all in this together. Pandian and Rajagopal and Chaudhuri and this Vituperator and... Oh!'

She gasped.

'Oh what?'

Janaki was slowly shaking her head, frowning, as if figuring out something.

'I get it now. I get it. This Vituperator—it's Rajagopal. That's his alias in the Lotus Pond. It's all interconnected. As for Chaudhuri—he's plainly MrBengal in the chat. I always suspected that.'

She saw them all, now. Shadow figures behind shadow figures behind names and aliases. But at some point the shadows dissolved away revealing the real humans hiding behind masks. Real men. Real monsters. Real devils. And Asha had fallen into their hands.

Hiran was not in his room. He was not in the dining room either. He had probably gone sightseeing on his own, and now she was stuck with the address: a priceless winning ticket and no one to redeem it.

She had left a note for Gita at reception, and indeed, there was Gita waiting for her, jumping to her feet at her approach.

'Hi,' said Caroline. 'I've got news.'

She gave Gita a quick summary of the situation.

'So either we have to find a man to replace Kamal immediately, or—'

'Or we lose this chance,' Gita finished.

'No. Or I go myself.'

'You must be crazy! It has to be a man!'

'I'll fix that,' said Caroline. She opened her handbag and showed Gita a large wad of banknotes. 'Money speaks. It's just a brothel manager who will show me Asha, not the actual pimp. The madam in charge. I'll give her the money as arranged – see, there it is in the envelope, all counted out – and pay her extra for letting me in instead of a man and keeping her mouth shut. An extra lakh. It's nothing for me, and a fortune for her. She'll do it. I bet she'll do it.'

'Caroline, you're—'

'Brilliant, right?'

'I was going to say crazy. Deranged. But brilliant will do. And brave.'

'Maybe all three. But c'mon. Let's get cracking.'

FORTY

Caroline

The building was hard to find, but after asking directions, they finally stood before it. It was a squalid grey building in one of Kamathipura's narrowest and busiest lanes. Barred windows in its top storey were flanked by ragged scraps of would-be curtains. Between the two narrow holes of windows hung a washing line sagging with the weight of a few nondescript pieces of clothing. A woman stood at the window, screaming down at another woman who sat cross-legged on a *charpai* outside the doorway, nursing a baby and playing cards with a boy of about twelve, and yelling what sounded like abuse back at the woman above.

Gita took Caroline's hand. 'This is it,' she said.

Sensing their presence, the card-playing woman looked up, quickly assessed Gita and Caroline as irrelevant, and returned to her card game and her screaming match. She pulled the baby away from her breast and laid it on the *charpai* behind her, where it began to squall with rage. The boy had his back to them and did not look around. The door was open, offering a glimpse of a long black passage in whose depths blinked a string of red fairy lights, perhaps framing a door, perhaps lighting the way upstairs.

'*Namaste*,' said Gita. The woman on the *charpai* looked up. She stared first at Gita, then at Caroline. Everyone here stared at Caroline and she was getting used to it; she met the woman's gaze steadily, nodded in greeting and turned to Gita.

'OK, can you translate, Gita? Tell her that the fellow who was supposed to come couldn't make it and I came instead. Tell her I have the money for her pimp but also the same again for her if she keeps quiet. Tell her I want to see the girl.' Gita spoke.

'She says she's not interested,' Gita said after a few sentences. 'I think she wants more. She's taking a risk, after all. It's you being a foreigner, I bet. She has her reputation to consider. She can't just go rogue and not follow instructions.'

'But I have the password. That should prove I'm authentic, surely. Tell her I'll pay her more for her help. We have more to lose than she does; all she has to do is let me see Asha. That's it. I don't have a camera. She has nothing to lose, and a lot to gain. See if you can bargain with her. Offer her whatever she wants, within reason.'

'What's within reason?'

'I have the equivalent of four thousand dollars with me. One and a half is for the pimp. You can offer her the rest.'

'Wow! A small fortune!'

'Money speaks.'

Gita, Caroline could tell, was a hard negotiator, but so was the woman, who sent away the boy and gathered up the cards before getting down to what was obviously hard business.

Finally, Gita said, 'She says two lakh to show you the girl and for her silence. But first, the password.'

'Aishwarya,' said Caroline at once. The woman nodded.

The woman got up from the *charpai*, taking her time doing so, as if moving caused her much pain. Once she was standing, she rearranged her sari, tucking in various corners and ends, hawked and spat into the gutter, screamed at a skinny dog that had ventured under the *charpai* foraging for grains of cooked rice, and then gestured to the two women to enter the house behind her.

The corridor, lit only by the red fairy lights, was so dark that Caroline and Gita were forced to walk slowly. It ended in a staircase so narrow, and a ceiling so low, they had to stoop as they ascended. Caroline groped until she felt the wall, cool and dank, covered with what felt like slime. She shuddered but moved on until she stumbled against something like a plank at ankle level; but by now the blackness had lightened to grey and she could see the shadowed outline of a steep staircase.

The building was narrow but tall. The staircase was, in effect, nothing more than an appropriately adjusted ladder, fitted to slant snugly against the wall and upgraded with a precarious banister. She reached the first landing and edged herself along a dimly lit corridor, little more than two feet across and interrupted by several narrow doorways, some open, some curtained.

Glancing through the open doorways Caroline saw tiny cubicles, each one about the length of a human being and the breadth of a human being with an arm stretched out. A cot occupied half of the space, and on each one lay a filthy mattress and crumpled sheet. A rat scurried across the far end of the corridor and Caroline glimpsed the shadow of a human disappearing into a cubicle and heard the *ratch* of a quickly drawn curtain, which still shivered as Gita passed it seconds later.

At the end of the corridor was another flight of stairs. The woman led the way up, Caroline trying her best to keep up.

She reached the second landing, where she stopped for a

moment to draw breath and, literally, sniff the air. The smell was acrid, an alloy of rancid body fluids and other unidentifiable rotting waste. Caroline felt her mind open like a satellite dish, receiving signals imperceptible to the senses: thoughts and feelings, heartbeats and heartaches, and a never-ending, silent wail of terror.

Up the next flight, to the third storey, the woman panting by now. This corridor was identical to the two beneath it, except that the cubicles here had numbered doors, and all the doors were shut – and bolted, with heavy steel padlocks hanging from the bolts.

The woman, panting still, stopped in front of one of the doors and pointed.

'This is the one,' said Gita. The woman reached up to a small curtain at eye level, drew it back. Behind it was a tiny window, the glass smeared, let into the door. Caroline peered through into a box room, little more than a cubicle, lit dimly by a single bulb dangling from the ceiling.

A *charpai* was pushed against the far wall, and on the *charpai* a small girl reclined. There she was, curled up in a foetal position with her back to the door. Her face was not visible, but still, Caroline knew. Perhaps it was her hair – not dead straight as an Indian's might be, but curly, just as in the photos; now, a tangled mop.

'Asha,' breathed Caroline. 'Gita, it's her. It's really her.'

'Let me have a look,' said Gita, and she too looked. She shrugged.

'I can't see her face!'

'It's her all right. I know.'

The woman drew back the curtain so that the peephole was covered once more, and turned to go.

'Stop!' cried Caroline. The woman stopped and looked at her.

'Tell her to open this door,' she said to Gita. She pointed to the bunch of keys dangling from a knot at the end of the woman's sari. 'Those are the keys. Tell her to open it.' She tapped at the door.

Gita spoke to the woman, who replied sharply in Hindi.

'She says that wasn't the deal. The deal was to look only. No opening of doors, no talking, no touching.'

'I need to see the girl's face. That was the deal. The girl's back is facing the door. I will tell her boss she did not show me properly, so the deal is off. I want her to open that door. I need to see the girl's face. Now. Or else.'

At the 'Or else' Gita translated everything. A long conversation ensued, in which it was clear that Gita was threatening something dire.

Finally, the woman shrugged, scowled and fumbled with the knot in her sari, muttering and uttering what could only be foul curses. She held the bunch of keys up nearer to the naked ceiling bulb. She tried various keys in the keyhole. Finally, one fit. She turned it.

The door creaked back, opening into the cubicle.

Caroline entered the room. The girl on the cot sat up, and turned around rubbing her eyes.

'Asha? Asha, it's me. It's me, my darling. It's Mom.'

The girl stared for a moment. Terrified eyes focused in recognition, and the brow above them, creased with a frown of puzzlement, smoothed out.

'Mom? Mom!' she cried.

Caroline, arms held out, rushed forward towards Asha. She was halfway across the room when a loud crash made her stop and swing around. The door to the cubicle had been slammed shut; she heard the rasp of the bolt as it rammed into its slot. The clatter of keys and the click of the padlock snapping shut followed, and the vile cackle of their jailer.

The woman shouted something obviously very rude at them

from beyond the door. There was shouting: Gita's voice, and the woman's, in Hindi.

'I'll get help, Caroline!' shouted Gita.

Steps on the stairs, growing fainter by the second, after which there was silence.

Caroline was locked in with Asha.

FORTY-ONE

Gita

Once out on the street Gita ran. She ran for her life, zigzagging down the crowded lanes, sometimes knocking into people, running without looking back, leaping over a ditch here or a dead dog there. Heads turned as she ran but she tore on until forced to stop for breath, and when she had recovered, she ran on until she reached the edge of Kamathipura. There she flagged down an auto-rickshaw.

'Telephone shop,' she cried. 'Quick!'

They didn't have to drive far; within five minutes the driver found a small shop with the ubiquitous sign *STD International Calls Fax Internet.* Gita leapt from the rickshaw before it had stopped, thrust a 100-rupee note at the driver and plunged into the shop, finally able to stop for breath again.

She nodded to the shop attendant and practically leapt into the telephone cubicle next to the open doorway. She dialled the number of Tulasa House; Subhadai answered. In reply to Gita's breathless demand she said, calmly, 'Doctor is not here. Nobody is here.'

'Damn!' muttered Gita and fumbled in her shoulder bag for her notebook. Finding the number for Dr Nath's office at the hospital, she dialled that. No reply. She dialled a few other numbers of possible contacts, but nobody was available. The person to contact was Kamal, but he was out with Sudesh.

Janaki could not be reached either. By now she could hardly think. But she had to. She sat herself down on the rusty metal chair in the cubicle and buried her face in her hands and thought. A few deep breaths. *Think, Gita, think.*

There remained, of course, the police. But everyone knew what the police would do: nothing at all. Kamathipura was out of bounds as far as a police rescue mission was concerned. Riddled with crime and prostitutes and pimps, it was beyond redemption and a person lost in there, a person imprisoned or abducted, had only themselves to blame. Even if that person was a foreigner, a white-skinned blonde, an American.

An American! Gita gasped. Of course! Yesterday they had discussed contacting the American consulate for help, and the problem had been that Asha was not yet American. But *Caroline* was, and now Caroline, too, was in jeopardy. The American consulate would be bound to help. They'd send in the CIA, the military, a whole arsenal of gun-toting troopers who would march in there and storm the building and pull out both Caroline and Asha.

She needed the number. There was a fat, dirty, seriously dog-eared *Bombay* telephone book on a shelf in the cubicle, dated several years ago. Gita leafed through the chunk of pages under A. Several had been torn out, including, she realised, the pages beginning with Am.

She burst out of the cubicle.

'Computer!' she cried to the assistant. 'Internet!'

He nodded languidly and pointed to a computer station at the back of the shop. Gita swung herself onto the rickety chair, tapped a button and waited impatiently for the computer to boot and connect. The dial-up buzzing took ages, but finally a connection was established. She tapped 'American Consulate' into the search engine.

Eventually the site opened. It showed a number and opening times. She looked at her watch. They would be closed by now, but there was an emergency number. She scribbled it into her notebook, returned to the cubicle and dialled. An impeccably polite, American-accented voice answered.

'How may I help you, ma'am?'

'My friend, an American citizen, has been imprisoned! She's in danger! She needs immediate help.'

'Very well, ma'am. Please describe the circumstances of the emergency. Where is your friend? How did this happen? Have you notified the police?'

The calm voice infuriated rather than calmed her. Gita gave a breathless account of the situation. The woman at the other end asked questions, but the more Gita spoke and the more the woman asked, the more Gita became aware of the scepticism and the doubt, even the reluctance, in the voice.

'So you're saying this friend of yours went voluntarily into a brothel in Kamathipura? And she is locked up in there?'

'Yes, yes, she went to rescue her daughter—'

'Her daughter is a prostitute?'

'Yes – no – her daughter is a child, imprisoned there, she...'

'Ma'am, Kamathipura is an extremely dangerous area. A high-crime area. Was your friend aware of this when she entered? Was she aware of the risk involved?'

'Yes, she knew but her daughter was kidnapped, and—'

'Is the daughter an American citizen?'

'No, Indian. Well, maybe half-American, I'm not sure. But the mother, my friend, is American, and—'

'Have you reported this to the police? You must submit a FIR – a First Information Report. And then—'

'But the police won't bother with me. They're all bribed! Can't you do it? Please, you have to send someone with authority! The Consul himself – or – or...'

'Just give me your name and address, ma'am, and your friend's name and where she is, and I'll see what we can do. But we're closed for the day; I suggest you visit the consulate when we open tomorrow.'

'No! No, it's urgent! You have to contact the police now, and insist they go there! Now! Or – or send your own agents, whatever you can do. It's so urgent!'

'We will certainly do the best we can, after opening hours tomorrow morning.'

Gita cried out: 'No! Not tomorrow! It's an emergency! You have to send someone *now*!'

The voice sounded less calm now. Less calm, but more indifferent.

'I will ensure that the information gets to the Regional Security Officer, ma'am, and we will see what we can do. Now just give me the address, please. Better yet, come yourself to the consulate tomorrow and speak to him in person. But my advice to you, as I said, is to go to the police.'

Gita was in tears of frustration as she dictated the address.

'Please, *please*... can you just send someone to rescue her, right now?'

But the voice on the other end, clearly impatient to end the call, had only platitudes to offer, leaving Gita more frustrated than before the call. She left the cubicle and the shop, slumped into herself, physically and mentally. She had to find someone, someone who understood. She flagged down a rickshaw.

Where would Janaki be? At a computer somewhere, no doubt. She had said there was an Internet shop across the road from her hotel. Gita looked at her watch. Nearly six o'clock, and dusk was approaching. Kamathipura would be coming to life for business. Would Caroline even be there, still? Wouldn't they have removed her straight away? She had to talk to someone, if only to relieve her own distress. She gave Janaki's hotel address to the driver, and he chugged off.

FORTY-TWO

Caroline

Caroline turned back to Asha, to complete her embrace; but Asha, it seemed, had had a change of heart since the door slammed shut and now, instead of coming forward, shrank away, back to the *charpai*, folding her limbs into a huddle.

'Honey, oh honey! Don't be scared – I'm here, and I'll never leave you again. Never. I'm so happy I've found you.'

The girl did not react. She simply sat there, hugging her knees, head burrowed in the sari skirt between them.

'Oh, honey... say you're happy I found you! I love you so much. I'm sorry, so sorry, you're here and I'll do my very best to get us out. I promise. I really promise.'

Asha looked up at last and stared at Caroline. Far from showing happiness at being found, at being with her mother, the spark of animation she had shown on hearing her name, on calling out to her mother, her expression now reflected trepidation and fear. Caroline noticed a tightening of the grasp that held her legs hugged tightly to her body.

Watching her for the first time Caroline took in Asha's

physical appearance. And for the first time she acknowledged Asha's subtle, ethereal beauty, which managed to shine through in spite of the veneer of abject misery that coated her both physically and mentally.

The girl was the personification of distress, and yet instead of distorting her features that distress itself seemed somehow uplifted by resting on this girl; it glowed with a pain so exquisite and poignant Caroline could feel it physically, echoing in her own heart.

Asha's eyes were amber, like her own, but eloquent with an anguish that seemed to have dimension beyond dimension, a universe-sized torment that seemed infinite. A torment so pure it shocked.

Her features seemed etched with that same anguish; her skin, so fair for an Indian, was translucent, as if her soul shone through.

Asha's clothing was ragged and dirty, her hair unkempt. Yet all of this seemed to accentuate her beauty rather than diminish it, to enhance her ethereal purity, rather than besmirch it.

Caroline was reminded of a lotus, so symbolic within the Hindu religion. The lotus grew in the filthiest of trenches, in the deepest, stinking mud; yet remained pure, unaffected by the grime surrounding it. It was light, against the odds, unaffected by darkness. That was Asha's beauty.

'That hag!' said Caroline. 'The awful woman! Listen, Asha, I came here to rescue you, and I will. We've all been looking for you. Not just me: your daddy too, and Janaki. We've been looking for you for ages and now I've found you, I won't let you go again.'

Caroline couldn't be sure, but she thought she saw a flicker of something in the staring eyes at the name 'Janaki'. Certainly, Asha was closest to Janaki, and the fact that Janaki was also nearby must have given her... Hope? Longing? Or simply the absence of terror, a drawing back of shadows? Whatever it was, Caroline was encouraged, and continued.

'Oh, Asha!' she sighed. 'Maybe you think I abandoned you. Maybe you think I didn't love you, and that's why I left you behind. It's not true, my darling. I've always loved you. There hasn't been a day, a minute, a second, that I haven't thought of you in all these years. I left you because – because...'

Because what? Caroline thought. What reason can I give, that she would understand? She stumbled on.

'Because I was ill, Asha. I was lost, just like you are now, just not in a physical sense. I was lost in my mind, in a darkness I could not banish. I wish it wasn't so. I wish it had been different, that we could have been together, that I could have been your mom all your life. But I can't turn back the clock. I can't change the past. But I can change the future, Asha, and I will. I promise. I will be a proper mom from now on.'

She talked. She talked to Asha as the shadows lengthened and the noises outside the room grew louder: female chattering and buckets clanging.

She talked when the door opened about six inches, and a blackened aluminium pot was pushed through the opening at floor level. Caroline caught a glimpse of a tiny hand, the hand of a child, pushing it in, the fingers flicking it forward, and then quickly jerking back to safety. The door was slammed shut again, the latch rasped, the lock snapped.

The pot contained rice soaked in a yellowish liquid. There were neither plates nor cutlery. By now Caroline was ravenous, and she supposed Asha was too. She forced herself to take three mouthfuls, scooping up the rice with her fingers – before giving up and turning away in disgust. Asha ate even less. No wonder she was so thin.

So Caroline continued to talk, in a voice that she hoped was calm, soothing and trust-evoking. She spoke about her life before coming to India, about her family, her dreams, her plans for Asha. Asha seemed not to be listening, but still Caroline talked, because she knew that somewhere, at some level of her consciousness, Asha heard and understood.

While talking Caroline tried to stay calm, but that calmness was filtering away with every passing minute. The endless waiting with no sign that it would ever end. Her ramblings for Asha's benefit now seemed more banal even than the silences they broke; her ears constantly strained to pick up noises from beyond the door. Occasionally she heard voices or footsteps from the bowels of the house, but they never came up to this floor.

Her sense of frustration was like a rising tide of boiling water within her; she wanted to get up, move around, stretch her limbs, aching from so much sitting. Occasionally she did, but the cubicle was too small to bring any relief and every time she simply flung herself back onto the mattress.

Only Asha seemed resigned to this infinity of waiting; or rather, she didn't wait at all, but simply existed, as if her mind had lost the capacity to measure time, to even conceive of a better future, to hope for change. As if she had given up.

Asha huddled in her corner; now and again she fell asleep, even while Caroline talked, her head lolling to one side, her body leaning abjectly against the wall. Even in her sleep she shifted several times, as if unable to find a comfortable position.

Near the door was a rusty pail, which obviously served as a toilet and also had obviously not been changed for a day or two. Caroline had grown used to the stench by now.

Occasionally she stood up and walked to the opening that served as a window to sniff the fresh air that seeped in through the wooden slats. She looked through the windowpane, but it was so smudged that not much could be seen except the vague outline of the opposite building, a grey-and-black tenement with barred windows just like this one.

Caroline inspected the window more closely, to see if there was any chance of opening it, but it was nailed securely shut, and the bars outside it were obviously solid, so that even if she broke a pane of the glass there could be no escape that way; nor would shouting down to the street be of any use, for who would hear them? And who would care? They were caged.

Asha was asleep again, huddled against the wall, and Caroline took the liberty of touching her again, helping her down into a lying position and covering her with one of the torn sheets. Asha did not wake. Caroline longed to partly undress her, to check her for wounds; she longed to stroke her hair.

If there was one thought that made this predicament bearable it was the thought of Asha, right there, in the same room. She, Caroline, may have been impulsive, reckless, headstrong, giddy – but she had been right. She was with Asha. Better that she should be with Asha, than Asha should be alone.

The night seemed even more endless than the day; the sounds filtering in from the street, muffled though they were, helped keep Caroline awake. The street had been quiet during the day; at night it seemed to wake up and the mélange of loudspeaker music, raucous laughter, shouting and a thousand other noises conspired to ensure she could not escape from her carousel of thoughts for even half an hour at a time.

She hugged Asha to her, kissed the top of her head. She stank; she had obviously not had a bath or washed her hair for days. Caroline pulled her closer yet, and closed her eyes, and somehow, perhaps through sheer exhaustion, dozed off.

It seemed only seconds had passed when she was abruptly shaken out of her restless nap. The light bulb glared overhead; there were voices in the cubicle, loud male voices, and, as she saw on rubbing the sleep from her eyes, the men to go with them. Two beefy Indian men, clones of each other, and of every

Bollywood villain who ever scowled on an oversized hoarding on a Bombay street corner: the thick moustaches, the slicked-back greasy hair, the sideburns, the puffy jowls, the hooded long-lashed eyes. Caroline would have laughed at the cliché if she did not feel more like crying.

The woman of yesterday was there too, chattering loudly and coarsely, pointing and glaring at her. She bent over and snatched Caroline's handbag, which was lying on the floor. She opened it, found the purse and took out the rest of the paper money. She threw the bag back onto the floor, counted and folded the hundred-rupee notes and stuck the wad into the neckline of her blouse.

'Don't try any trick, we got knife! We got gun!' said one of the men.

'Who are you?' said the other. 'Why you come here?'

'I'm her mother,' said Caroline, 'and I'm staying with her.'

At that moment, Asha woke up. Rubbing her eyes, she squeaked, 'Mom? Mom? I'm scared!'

'Don't be scared, honey. I'm with you.'

'She talking?' said the first man.

'Of course she's talking. She's my daughter.'

'You going. We not needing you here. She is ours.'

'She's not. She's my daughter and I'm not leaving her anywhere.'

'Mom, Mom!' Asha kept crying, clinging to Caroline.

'Don't worry, sweetheart. I won't let them take you away.'

There followed a conversation in Hindi, of which Caroline understood not a word; except, now and then, 'foreigner', and 'English' and, occasionally, the name Chaudhuri. Chaudhuri, that rang a bell. Wasn't it the name that Janaki had found on one of her Internet searches? The name they'd all grasped at, like drowning people grasped at a lifebuoy, only to discard as useless?

One of the men took out a mobile phone. He pulled out an

antenna, punched one of the keys and spoke some sharp words in Hindi, eyes fixed on her all the time. Caroline could only recognise the word 'Kamini' every now and then. The man listened, nodded, then put away the phone. He spoke to his companion who, abruptly, spat on the floor and, with quick shooing gestures towards the door, said in English:

'You can go. We don't want you. Only girl. You free.'

'No! You're not taking her anywhere!'

Asha clung to Caroline.

'Mom! Mom! Stay with me!' she cried.

'I'm staying with you, honey. They're not taking you away.' To the men, she repeated, 'I'm staying with her. You can't take her.'

One of the men tried to pull Asha away, but she screamed and clung to Caroline. 'Mom! Mom! I'm scared!'

There was a struggle, Caroline holding onto Asha and pulling her away, Asha screaming and clinging. The other man pulled out the phone again and made another quick call.

Putting the phone away, he spoke sharply to his friend, who let go of Asha.

'OK OK. You can come. Both of you can come. You come with girl. But you come quietly otherwise I shoot you. I got gun.' He tapped his pocket, where indeed a gun-shaped bulge was visible.

'Where are you taking us to?'

'You will see. Better place than this, to be sure. We take her, with or without you.'

The man strode over to the *charpai* and made as if to grab Asha again, but she shrieked and clung to her mother. Caroline laid a protective arm around her, hugged Asha against her.

'Don't touch her. We'll come. We can discuss this. I can pay for her, buy her off you. We are wealthy foreigners. Take me to whoever is your boss and I'll talk to him.'

FORTY-THREE

Caroline

They reached the front door and then were out in the street, Asha clinging to Caroline's arm. Caroline felt a tight grip on her other arm; one of the men who appeared to be the senior, the taller, darker, bulkier of the two, had taken hold of her and was urging her forward, up the lane. Glancing to her left, she saw that Asha was being held on her other side by the other man. She looked over her shoulder; the street was half deserted. She saw a few women in bright saris standing in doorways as they passed. Late male stragglers made their way to the end of the lane, where the main thoroughfare – in the daytime a roaring, fuming chaos of motor vehicles – lay quiet and forsaken.

A black car crouched at the roadside. Its back door opened silently at their approach, as if by the hand of a ghost. Caroline and Asha were bundled into the back seat. The car door slammed and they were enclosed in the black, musty interior.

There was a third man already waiting in the driver's seat, reeking of some heavy aftershave and smiling in a manner that made Caroline cringe and draw back in disgust. Their two male escorts slid into the back seat with her and Asha, one on either side, next to the doors. The motor coughed once, twice, then relaxed into a quiet purring. They drove off.

It seemed an endless drive all through the night and into the dawn. It could have been one hour, and it could have been four or even five. Caroline dozed off now and then, Asha sleeping on her lap, only to be startled into wakefulness by a dream or a memory or a sound, then to drift back into sleep. Sometimes, when she was awake, she heard the men talking; sometimes she heard nothing but the hum of the engine. When she woke for the last time the car had stopped, and she felt fresh air on her cheeks and heard raised male voices. She blinked and could make out only the silhouettes of houses and a few male figures. Were they still in Bombay? She could not tell.

Someone pushed her out of the car. Loose gravel crunched beneath her bare feet. She reached for Asha's hand and held it tightly.

'It's OK, honey. I'm here,' she whispered. Yes, she was afraid. But how much more afraid must Asha be? It was her job to calm that fear, to be a mother. In doing so she had to find her own fearlessness. She could see nothing but those dark silhouettes, and here and there a dim light against a building. The tight hold on her arm did not relax for a fraction of a second.

They were at a detached house, set back from the road. They all entered a gate, then walked up a short path. One of the men pressed a buzzer. The door opened with a buzz of its own. He pushed Caroline and Asha into a hallway lit by an overhead lamp, which led to a flight of stairs of bare wood.

The voices around her were loud and crude, the grip on her wrist tight and uncompromising. All that could be seen were walls of a wide hall. The man gestured and let go of her. Caroline walked up, still clinging to Asha's hand. Asha's bare feet padded beside her own. The men, all three of them now, followed.

They reached the top of the stairs and then there was a woman's voice, speaking three or four sharp words, and uncouth hands tugged at her and pushed her and Asha into a brightly lit room.

'Mom, I'm scared!' Asha whimpered. Caroline placed an arm around her and pulled her close.

'Don't worry, darling. I'll protect you,' she said. She blinked at the harsh light, then looked around. The men from the brothel had been joined by a woman.

This woman could have been anything between forty and sixty. She wore a faded beauty with the dignity of a queen, though she was not dressed to fit that role. She had obviously been roused from her bed, for she wore a long neck-to-ankle cylinder of a nightgown in pink nylon, slightly gathered around a buttoned lace bib that rose above a generously loose bosom.

Her skin was the colour of dark honey, and she had high cheekbones and long heavy-lidded eyes that seemed to have slid slightly lower down her cheeks than was originally intended. Her hair hung in a long plait over her right shoulder. She wore several gold rings on her fingers and a small gold stud at the flare of her nostril. She was speaking in Hindi to one of the men, but her gaze flitted now and again from Caroline to Asha, summing them up with cunning expertise. Caroline felt like a collector's doll being offered for sale.

The woman had obviously been unprepared for their coming; she was also clearly of higher rank than the men who had brought Caroline and Asha. She was arguing with them, but Caroline, of course, could not understand a word. Finally the woman addressed her directly, in English.

'You are this girl's mother?'

Caroline nodded. Asha was edging behind her, trying to

hide. The hand in her own trembled like a small, captured bird. The woman addressed Asha now; she reached for her, gripped her by the upper arm and pulled her out from behind Caroline.

'Let me look at you,' she said, and reached out to touch Asha.

'Mom!' cried Asha. 'I don't want her to—'

'Don't touch her!' cried Caroline, pulling Asha closer yet, against herself. The woman ignored them both, grabbed Asha's shoulders and turned her around, forcing her to let go of Caroline's hand.

'You have grown so thin, Kamini. What have they done to you? Did they starve you at that place? Well, now perhaps you can appreciate how lucky you were before.'

Asha did not answer but looked up at Caroline.

'Mom!' she whimpered again.

The woman spoke to the man who appeared to be the senior.

There followed a long conversation in Hindi, in which the man spoke the most, the woman merely shaking her head and saying 'Acha, acha' at intervals. The man took out a bulky mobile phone and spoke into it. He handed the phone to the woman, and she spoke too, belligerently, clearly arguing with someone. Finally, they seemed to reach a sort of agreement, for the tone of voice changed; it became friendly. Almost.

The man and his cronies turned and clattered down the stairs. The woman gestured for Caroline and Asha to follow her and led them a short way down the corridor and through a door. They were in a fairly large room now, sparsely furnished with a double bed, a chest of drawers, a table and chairs, and a wardrobe. It was frugal but, compared to the room they had just left, a queen's chamber – the bed had a sparkling white sheet, and both the windows were open, though barred by wrought-iron patterned grids.

'It's late,' the woman said to Caroline. 'You should go to bed and sleep now and we'll talk in the morning. You are Kamini's mother, and you have caused her to speak again. I am pleased. That is a good thing for Kamini. We only have to decide what to do with you. It is not my decision. If Kamini is speaking it is very good for her. I will explain all in the morning. Now take rest. You will be fine here but don't try any tricks. I'm kind but I don't stand for any nonsense. Don't give me any trouble and I won't give you any. Are you hungry? Shall I bring you some food? There's water in the jug over there.' Another flick of her thumb, this time towards the flask and two glasses on a tray. 'Look, I'm tired and I have to go and finish the business with those men so I'm leaving now. I'll talk to you in the morning. You'll find night garments in the top drawer.' She pointed to the chest of drawers.

Then she was gone, and Caroline's reply, that indeed she was hungry, they were both hungry, and could she have something to eat, died on her lips. The key turned in the lock.

Caroline sighed and, assuming there would be a breakfast within a few hours, helped a passive Asha out of her sari and into one of the nightdresses the woman had indicated were in a drawer. While doing so she had the perfect opportunity to see, for the first time, the three bloodied welts across Asha's thin back.

The vicious witch, Caroline thought angrily. It must be that hag at the brothel. People like her ought to be publicly flogged. One of the wounds seemed to be infected; it ought to be dressed properly, but Caroline knew there would be no help tonight. Tomorrow would have to do.

Caroline then pulled on another nightdress. It was white, starched and ironed, and smelt strongly of washing powder. Whatever the future held, at least their conditions had drastically improved since yesterday. And at least their new jailer spoke English and seemed to have a brain beyond that of a beast.

Caroline thought of her friends. Kamal, and Janaki, and Gita, my assistant. Gita would not know where to find her now. Why, oh why, had she not let Janaki arrange things her own way? Why had she leapt in where angels fear to tread?

I did it for Asha, she said to herself. At least Asha is no longer alone. Words that had been, and would be, her single comfort throughout the ordeal. She thought of her parents, her dad, pulling all kinds of strings in America.

They cannot keep me imprisoned for long, she thought. I am an American citizen. This time, they will have to act. Have to set the police on me to avoid an international incident. Dad had influential friends in government. They would put pressure on whomever it was necessary to put pressure on. Dad would help. She touched the rings on the chain around her neck, the pendant once given her by Kamal.

Kamal is my husband, she thought. He is Asha's father. He will move the earth to find us. So will Janaki. They will rescue us.

She glanced at her watch before turning off the light. It was 3 a.m. She walked to the bed where Asha had lain down and now was fast asleep.

We are a family. Kamal, Asha and me. We belong together.

At that thought she, too, fell asleep.

Caroline awoke to the sound of a key turning, and sat up, still groggy but immediately alert as soon as she saw the woman from last night crossing the room. Behind her followed a maid with a tray, on which were some slices of toast, butter and jam, as well as cups, plates and a steaming pot. The delicious aroma of coffee drifted from the pot, stimulating the hunger accumulated from the previous day. The maid set the tray down on the table and silently left the room. The woman stayed.

'All right,' she said. 'Take food. I want to have a few words with you. What is your good name?'

Caroline told her as she sat down at the table and poured herself a cup of coffee. Asha was still asleep. Let her sleep as long as she can, Caroline thought.

'Well, my name is Devaki and I have to tell you that this girl has been very naughty,' said the woman. 'She refused to speak. Her only chance of a good future is if she is nice and pleasant to our customer. That's why we sent her to that other place. To teach her a lesson. Our customer is a good man. He will treat her well. I want you to encourage this girl to be pleasant towards him.'

'You must be out of your *fucking* mind.' Caroline spat the words. 'Who do you think I am, a monster like you lot?'

'Don't be rude,' said Devaki sharply. 'I told you, don't give me any trouble and I won't give you any trouble. I only know she refused to speak and is thus useless. They say she is now speaking. That changes everything. You can change everything by helping.'

'I'm not changing anything,' Caroline said. 'My daughter will speak if she wants to and be silent if she wants to.'

She wanted to continue but stopped herself. She did not want to provoke Devaki more than necessary. But she couldn't help it. The words burst out of her:

'How can you do this to young girls,' she cried, 'don't you have a heart? She's terrified. Of course she doesn't speak.'

'Pah! She'll just have to put armour around herself and get on with it. It's survival of the fittest in this trade. Otherwise she won't last very long.'

'Not the way she's been whipped, she won't!' Caroline retorted. 'I need something to dress her back with. It's covered in welts.'

'What?' cried Devaki, and hurried over to the bed where Asha still lay in deep sleep. Clearly not worried about waking the girl, she turned her over onto her stomach and pulled at the nightie till Asha's back was exposed. She inspected the welts, running her fingers lightly along them.

'Mom!' cried Asha, rubbing her eyes and reaching out for Caroline. Caroline rushed to sit next to her and hugged her to herself.

'Those scoundrels!' said Devaki. 'They never said... Well, anyway, it doesn't show on her face. She's very beautiful and with a bit of care she will become more beautiful, fill out again and so on. A doctor is coming today to look at both of you. But first you have to be bathed and deloused. Both of you stink to high heaven. This is a respectable house, not like that place you came from. We never beat our girls here. If a girl is so recalcitrant she needs to be beaten she is simply passed on to such houses where beatings take place; Mr Rajagopal doesn't stand for any corporal punishment in his houses. He believes in treating his girls kindly, then they will work willingly, for they know they are in a good position. You are very lucky to come here.'

'You must have lost your mind! Asha is not some whore from the streets! She has parents, she is American. She was stolen from us and we will take her back to America, where she belongs. You cannot have her.'

'You misunderstand. We are not selling her as a whore. Mr Chaudhuri does not want a whore. He wants a mistress. A young, healthy mistress who can be a companion. A cultured girl who speaks English, who he can take out to restaurants and so on. Be seen with. He is married but his wife does not do her duty and she is old, so he wants a lovely young mistress. Kamini is perfect. It's a very good future for her. He is a kind man. But there are other possibilities. Another man has expressed interest and we shall see. A foreigner – I mean, a foreign-returned

Indian. Mr Rajagopal too is a kind man. He takes good care of his girls, finds good places for them.'

'My daughter is not Mr Rajagopal's girl, whoever he is,' Caroline protested loudly. 'And neither am I.'

'Ha!' Devaki cackled. 'Tell that to Mr Rajagopal. I paid for you both and you both belong to me. That is, to Mr Rajagopal. He bought this girl for Mr Chaudhuri, who is very attached to her. I am only doing my job. I have nothing to do with you – what do I care? I only make sure he gets good quality for the price. He trusts me completely, you see. I'm good at my job. But it's only a job. Mr Rajagopal is kind though, or at least as kind as any man. I've seen much worse but not many better. Thank your deity you were brought here. But I'm glad Kamini has been returned, given another chance. She was wasted in Kamathipura. A girl like this needs special care and now she will get it – they don't call me Devaki the Blameless for nothing! It's good you speak English. I can do with some girls speaking English. You sound educated as well, that's a good thing. I can get you some excellent escort work. But Kamini now, she's the real prize. You don't realise how...'

Devaki chattered on as if she hadn't noticed that Caroline had stopped eating long ago and was only fiddling with her food. She had stopped listening too, ever since the words, 'I paid for you both.'

It couldn't be. It just couldn't be. It wasn't possible that she had been sold. She had volunteered to come with Asha, for goodness' sake. She had been set free. She could have gone but had insisted on coming. She knew for a fact that the men had not "bought" her. She could have left at any time before getting into the car with Asha. She had not been bought; so how then could she have been *sold*?

But perhaps such logic did not exist in this business.

Slowly, slowly, it dawned on Caroline that at some point during the drive between the house in Kamathipura and this house she had changed status. She had been transformed from the formerly self-determined, free American individual of the past into a commodity, a marketable ware to be bought and sold at the whim of strangers.

Janaki was perfectly right: she had rushed in like a fool where angels fear to tread. She now, according to the rules of this trade, belonged to Devaki.

FORTY-FOUR

Kamal

'So this is it,' said Sudesh to Kamal, stepping out of the phone cubicle. Kamal stood up from the rickety chair he'd been sitting on in the Internet shop during what seemed an endless wait while Sudesh made his calls. The two of them left the shop and returned to the crowded pavement. Kamal felt lost, disoriented in this behemoth of a city, a city teeming with strangers. Disheartened. How could anyone find anyone here? Where was Caroline, where was Janaki, where was Dr Nath, where was Gita? Most of all: *where was Asha?*

He wished he could talk to the others, somehow make contact; but each one was isolated, each on a separate mission; no way to find out if any one of them, Caroline, or Janaki, or Gita, or someone from Dr Nath's team, was any closer to the goal, or had any news to report.

What we all need, thought Kamal, is a mobile phone. A few people had them already; maybe the day would dawn when such a gadget would be as commonplace and affordable as a wallet, and everyone could have one. But this was now; and this was Mumbai, India's most overcrowded city, and there was no contact, no collaboration. It was each man, each woman, on his or her own.

'This evening, six o'clock,' Sudesh continued, steering him around a dead dog lying on the pavement, 'we are meeting a fellow called Ramsingh in a coffee shop. Ramsingh has contacts in the business. He will introduce us to another fellow. I don't know his name but he's the real thing. A real pimp. He's the one who will take you to the girl believed to be Asha.'

'How certain are you that it's her?'

'Not absolutely, but it sounds like her. Seventy-five per cent certain. In the description it sounds like her.'

'And what then?'

'Then he will take you to a special hotel. After that it's up to you. I cannot plan the rest in advance. If it's her, you can negotiate to buy her. Then she is yours.'

'And if it's not her?'

'If it's not her just say you don't like her, and it's done. No problem. Then you return home and we try again the next night.'

'And keep trying, I suppose. Until the right girl turns up. It could take weeks. I actually think my friend's plan is better. She is going to try and connect me through some Internet chatroom.'

'That's nonsense,' said Sudesh with a dismissive hand gesture. 'Those chatrooms; I know them. People boast a lot and pretend to be who they aren't. Just a lot of overblown egos. I wouldn't trust anyone I met in a chatroom.'

'Well, I guess I'll meet this Ramsingh and see what he has to offer. Did he show you a photograph?'

'No. But the description is fairly accurate.'

'What does "fairly" mean?'

'It means it could very well be her and you need to take a chance.'

'OK then. And until then?'

'Until then I want to show you the inner workings of the trade. Just come around with me today while I work, see what I do. I don't want to send you in there as a total innocent. You look too innocent already.'

'So I've been told.'

'Yes. You need toughening up so you can play the role correctly. You need to change your looks too. You look too clean.'

'So you're going to dirty me up?'

'Right. Not literally. But you'd be surprised what make-up can do. You need to look a little rougher. Haggard. Tough. I will take you to someone who can do the job.'

Kamal shrugged. 'Whatever it takes.'

'Kapoor is my name. Happy to meet you. My task is to ensure your full satisfaction or money back. What languages do you speak?'

'Hindi, Gujarati and English only,' Kamal replied.

'My native tongues are Marathi and Hindi but I also speak English. What language do you prefer to converse in?'

'Either Hindi or English; no Marathi.'

The man wobbled his head in agreement. 'You have the money? I need everything in advance. Ramsingh must have told you the price. Cash of course.'

Kamal handed over the dirty drawstring cotton bag he held. Kapoor looked inside; it was filled to bulging with wads of banknotes, all bundled together with rubber bands, a slip of paper with the rupee amount tucked into the band around each bundle. Indian banks did not provide banknotes larger than five hundred rupees.

'We are going there in a car. While we are driving I will count the money to make sure everything is correct. We will pick up the girl in about half an hour. She will be delivered to the car and then we will take her to a certain hotel. I will wait outside until you are finished and pick her up afterwards. Agreed?'

'Agreed,' said Kamal.

'Very well. Let's go.'

A slick white car with a driver was waiting at the kerb. Kapoor got into the front seat and gestured for Kamal to get in the back, which he did.

'Excuse me while I count this money. It seems correct though. The bag is nice and heavy.' Kapoor, turning to speak to Kamal in the back seat, grinned, bouncing the bag up and down to demonstrate its weight. He then turned around again and started counting. He was halfway through when a phone rang. Kapoor fished a thick black mobile phone out of his bag, held it up to show Kamal.

'These things are so convenient. You must get one.'

He answered the call, listened for a minute and then let out a word that could only be an expletive. Then a cascade of words fell, but in Marathi so that Kamal could not understand what was said. This went on for quite a while. Kapoor was obviously agitated, but after a while seemed to calm down somewhat, bobbed his head, saying 'Acha, acha.' He put away the phone.

'Is there a problem?'

'No problem, sah. No problem at all. Everything fine.'

He spoke to the driver in Marathi, then picked up the phone again and punched in a number.

'Excuse me, I need to make another call.' A few seconds later he was chattering away again in Marathi, excitedly, urgently. Once again he put away the phone, once again he conversed with the driver. The driver reacted by swivelling his head back and forth to assess the traffic, blaring his horn and barging his way through a slight gap in the traffic ahead before making a sudden and swift right turn.

'Just a slight detour,' said Kapoor, turning to grin at Kamal.

'What's wrong?'

'Nothing, nothing at all. Just a slight change in pick-up destination. No problem at all.'

He grinned another white-toothed grin. Kapoor, Kamal thought, could have stepped off an oversized Bollywood hoarding as either a villain or a hero. He was clean-shaven except for a full moustache, and his hair was slicked back; he wore a chequered long-sleeved shirt with the sleeves rolled up and open at the neck down to the third button, revealing an extremely hairy chest. Around his neck was a gold chain, and on his wrist a gold watch.

They had driven for a further half hour when the phone rang yet again. This time, he seemed happy with this conversation, which was very short. But afterwards he turned to Kamal.

'We are nearly there. Just five minutes more. But there has been a slight change of plan. Unfortunately the girl is not available tonight. We have arranged for a replacement, in a slightly younger age group. I am certain you will be completely satisfied with this new arrangement. A very lovely girl.'

'Wait a minute! I don't want a replacement! I gave you the specifications!'

'Yes, sir, calm down. This girl meets your specifications exactly but is slightly younger. No problem. We aim to provide complete satisfaction, your money's worth.'

'Look, I don't want a slightly younger replacement. I want my money back. Give it back, now, and let me out. The deal is off.'

'No, sir. You have paid your money and there is no refund. Ramsingh surely made that clear to you. Now we will provide our side of the deal. We are nearly there. A very nice girl. You will be absolutely two hundred per cent satisfied.'

'Don't you understand? I said I don't want another girl! Come on, give me back the money!' He leaned against the front seat, reaching out for the bag. Kapoor, however, dropped the bag into the footwell of the passenger seat.

'I said no refund! You will take this girl or nothing. One girl is the same as the next and this one is even better because she is younger. A virgin. She is ideal for you. Look, here she comes now.'

They were on a quieter street now. The car slid to a stop beside the curb. A man was walking towards them along the pavement, gripping a child by the upper arm, dragging her along.

The car stopped; the man grinned into the front window. Kapoor opened it and slid a packet of banknotes through. The man glanced at the bundle, grinned again and nodded, after which he opened the back door and thrust the child into the rear seat. She was a girl of, at the most, six years old.

She was snivelling. 'Bapu, Bapu!' she cried to the man who had shoved her in. He patted her on the head, and said, in Hindi, 'Be a good girl, little one, you will be back soon,' and turned away. A moment later he had vanished from sight.

The girl was now sobbing silently, face hidden in her hands.

Kapoor turned around again.

'You see? A lovely girl. You will have a lovely time.'

'Are you out of your mind? This is a child! I didn't ask for a child! That man was her father?'

Kapoor, still twisted around, shrugged. 'Yes, her father. Her mother died a year ago and he lost his job. What can a man do? Life is a struggle.'

'This is insane! She can't be more than five years old!'

'Six, I think. You are being unreasonable, sir. Many men prefer them at this age. It's a very good replacement, much more valuable. You will definitely be getting your money's worth. Her name is Ragi.'

Kamal fell back against the seat as the car drove off. He had no answer. He had no words. The girl was bent forward with her face still buried in her hands, her shoulders shaking as she wept.

If it is not me it would be someone else, he thought. *So it is better that it is me.*

After a moment's thought he spoke again.

'Very well. I've changed my mind. I will take her.'

'Ah, very wise. Very wise,' said Kapoor. 'You will be a very happy man tonight.'

'Indeed,' said Kamal. He wanted to comfort the child but was wary of touching her. Yet he would have to touch her. Scare her. He looked up, at the traffic. They were approaching a traffic light, red. The car stopped. Kamal waited. He waited and waited until he believed the lights were about to change to green. They turned yellow.

He grabbed the girl, flung open the passenger door, leapt out of the car grasping the girl in his arms and ran, leaving the passenger door dangling open.

All around him horns blared. The lights changed and the traffic moved forward. Clutching the child tightly, he dashed between the cars, the girl bouncing in his arms and wailing. From the car he had left came a shout; he didn't look back but the sound of a car door slamming indicated that Kapoor had leapt out after him.

He reached the pavement and ran. He ran and ran. Behind him the traffic was moving on, swifter now. He dared to look behind; Kapoor was stuck now between bumper-to-bumper ranks of traffic – a sea of metal, cars, rickshaws, lorries and motorcycles now moving forward, the car he had vacated standing still as other cars swerved around it, horns blaring, a madness of metal.

Kamal ran on, then glanced back again. Kapoor was leaping Bollywood-style onto the bonnet of a stationary car, about to jump to the next: but that driver jerked forward at the last moment and he stumbled and fell. Slipped between the cars. Right into the path of a motorcycle zipping forward between the lines of traffic. Kamal ran on. There was a loud crash. Kamal stopped, turned and stared; but he could not see much. Just that the motorcycle was no longer zipping and Kapoor was no longer running.

Horns and klaxons blared louder yet; somebody yelled, maybe Kapoor himself, maybe the motorcyclist. Cars stopped and doors opened and people gathered, shouting and gesticulating. 'May you rot in hell,' he said aloud. 'May you never harm another child. May you be reborn as a cockroach.'

Then he strolled away and looked for a taxi, the girl in his arms, leaning over his shoulder, wailing in despair.

Kamal's taxi took him back to the hotel. The child was still weeping silently, her fists dug into her eyes. It was now past ten; Janaki would be in bed. He knocked on her door.

'Janaki – it's me – Kamal!' he said, not too loud, because it was so late. He heard bare feet running across the room to the door, which flew open.

'Kamal! Thank goodness! I've been—'

Janaki, standing in the open doorway in a nightdress, stopped suddenly, and stared.

Kamal thrust the little girl at her.

'Take her. She's scared. Of me and probably all men. I told her I won't hurt her, but she doesn't believe me. It wasn't Asha, it was her. Her name is Ragi.'

'Oh, darling. My sweet. Come to me, *beti*.'

Speaking in broken Hindi, Janaki held out her arms and immediately the little girl leaned forward and swung into her embrace. Hugging her close, Janaki turned away from Kamal.

'Leave me alone with her for the night. She's terrified. You can tell me what happened later. And... oh, I've got news too! I'll tell you tomorrow.'

He nodded and, gently, she closed the door in his face.

FORTY-FIVE

Janaki

They breakfasted together, all three, at a restaurant down the road, and Janaki filled Kamal in on the previous day's events and Caroline's plight.

'So the good news is that she found Asha, the bad news is that now they're *both* captured.'

'For goodness' sake!' Kamal spluttered. 'Why didn't you tell me that last night when I came? I would have gone round there right away and—'

'Kamal, if you remember, we had other problems last night,' said Janaki, glancing at the girl. She was, astonishingly, tucking into her breakfast with appetite. She had calmed down as soon as Kamal had left and fallen asleep curled up in Janaki's arms. Though she had refused to speak a word, she had this morning seemed to have recovered from the shock of last night's events, and allowed Janaki to wash and dress her. Her clothes seemed reasonably clean and in good condition. She and Kamal had to decide what to do next, but first Kamal needed to hear the news about Asha.

'Why didn't you send round the police right away? Why—'

'Kamal, you keep forgetting we're in India, not America. I keep forgetting it too. When Gita came round and told me what had happened that was also my first thought, and she just laughed in scorn. She'd already thought of everything, called the American consulate, who aren't being at all helpful. Kamathipura is the problem. The police don't care, Kamal. They're completely in the pockets of those pimps, and the fact that Caroline is white isn't any help. They'd either stroll around there in two or three days' time and enjoy a cup of coffee with the madam, or not bother at all.'

'Caroline's American. This time the American consulate *has* to help.'

'I told you – Gita already tried them. And again, Kamathipura is the problem. Try explaining why they should rescue an American woman who voluntarily went into the worst area of Bombay, into a brothel, and see how eager they are to help. But I have a plan...'

Kamal interrupted. 'I'm going to call Caroline's father. He'll know what to do. Caroline said he has good contacts; he knows the Ambassador. We need to pull some strings.'

Janaki nodded. 'Yes, do that, call the dad. But, do you really think Caroline and Asha are in the same room still? Surely they have been removed by now? All we can do is hope that Caroline is astute enough to somehow free them both. I don't think wild horses could separate her from Asha now, and unless—'

'My God, Janaki, how can you be so sanguine about all this? Caroline can't deal with being locked up in Kamathipura by a bunch of goons! Caroline can't deal with India at all, much less handle a situation like this. She's a fragile American, used to luxury and people licking her ass! I have to go...'

He leapt to his feet as if to rush off to help Caroline.

'Wait, Kamal, wait! Listen, you unloaded another problem

on us last night and we really, really need to deal with this little girl as well. What do you want me to do with her?'

They both glanced again at the child, who continued to shovel food into her mouth as if she hadn't eaten in a year.

'She's so thin!' said Janaki. 'So now tell me – what happened? How did you get her?'

'It's grim,' said Kamal, sitting down again. 'They offered me her as a substitute for the girl I was supposed to get, and shoved her in the car. I escaped with her. That's it, basically. All I know is that her own father is selling her. I saw it with my own eyes. Her mother is dead, apparently.'

'Gruesome.' Janaki shuddered. 'We should bring her to Dr Nath, so he can take her into his programme. And she needs to go to hospital, Kamal. She needs to be examined and we need to get social services looking into it. If she's being trafficked by her own father she can't go back to him.'

'I agree, absolutely. But, Janaki – can you do that alone? She's terrified of men, and no wonder. And yesterday I kind of grabbed her and ran... it must have been terrifying for her. Look. I'll deal with Caroline and Asha, and you deal with Ragi, OK?'

'You'll be needed, though, Kamal. You'll have to make a police statement at some point, describe what happened.'

'I thought the police didn't care?'

'They don't. But with a child as young as this – well, they can't send her back to her dad and there must be some system set up and they'll have to investigate. Social services, or something. Dr Nath will know.'

'Right. Well, when they need me, I'll come. Right now, I need to go and look for Asha and Caroline. Are you finished? I am. Why don't you stay here while I run off. What's the address again?'

Janaki handed Kamal a slip of paper with the address of Asha's tentative whereabouts on it.

'But she won't be there any longer. I guarantee it. As I said, I have a—'

'I'm going to the American consulate and then I'll call Caroline's father. He'll pull some strings if they aren't helpful; he knows all the right people. His best friend is a senator. That'll do the trick.'

Kamal paid the cashier next to the door and loped out into the morning sunshine. Janaki shook her head. His eagerness and sense of urgency was understandable, but going back to that brothel was nothing more than futile.

Janaki had plans of her own. She'd deliver the child, Ragi, to Dr Nath and then return to the computer at Tulasa House. Talk to The Vituperator, who had been unavailable yesterday afternoon – and somehow bargain with him. Maybe he was the key to rescuing Caroline and Asha. She had an idea about how to do that. But first things first.

The child.

'They tried to sell her to Kamal,' said Janaki to Dr Nath. 'He managed to rescue her.'

'Well done,' said Dr Nath, squatting down to the girl's level, holding out a hand. '*Namaste, beti*. What is your name?'

But the girl recoiled, hid behind Janaki's back, covered her face with the hem of Janaki's *kameez*.

'She's like that with Kamal too,' said Janaki. 'She's scared of all men. Her name is Ragi.'

Dr Nath stood up. 'Right. Understandable. Can you come with her to hospital? Stay with her while she's being examined? She seems to trust you.'

Janaki thought of the computer, but only for a second.

'Of course I'll come. She does seem to like me. Come on, *beti*. Come with Janaki Aunty.'

She held out her hand and the little girl took it and walked with her out of the house. Dr Nath flagged down a taxi and they all three entered. Janaki laid an arm around Ragi and pulled her close. The girl stuck a thumb in her mouth and nuzzled into Janaki's side. Janaki pulled her even closer, and stroked her hair. At the hospital, Dr Nath swept them past the waiting crowds and into a doctor's office, without knocking.

'This is my sister, Pratima,' he said, and to the doctor rising to her feet from behind her desk, 'A new patient for you, Prat. Just rescued... from her own father. Social services need to be called in, but Janaki here will stay with her till she's stable.'

Janaki was sitting at Ragi's bedside – she had by now been transferred to a ward – when a nurse approached and said, 'There's someone outside to see you, ma'am. Are you able to come?'

Janaki glanced at the girl. She was asleep. She could go. She rose from her chair and walked out of the ward. Kamal was waiting for her.

'So?' she asked. 'How did it go? Did you go to the consulate?'

Kamal looked drained, haggard, unkempt, his chin shadowed with dark stubble.

'I went to the police station first and it was like talking to the Great Wall of China. Then I went to the American consulate, and just as I was going in Gita came out and we had lunch together. The consulate isn't interested. Seems they think Caroline put herself deliberately into harm's way by entering a high-crime red-light district. They said the American consulate isn't a nanny; this is a police job. And you know Bombay. Sluggish, indifferent. So...'

He ran his fingers through his hair. 'But I managed to get hold of Caroline's dad on the phone. Mr Mitchell. He already knew it all and he's been active. Can you imagine, the story has gone to the America media. It's all over the USA TV news. It's developing into a big story. And he's getting the next plane out. He's frantic; not only have we *not* found Asha, but we've also lost Caroline.'

His eyes grew eloquent with anguish as he spoke the last words. They welled with something more than tears.

'I *told* her not to go,' said Janaki. 'If she'd only waited, I could somehow have sent you or some other man instead and you could have officially bought Asha the next day. It was all perfectly arranged; she had to go and mess it all up.'

'So now it's Caroline's fault she's been captured? Because she was brave enough to try and rescue her child?'

His voice was so harsh that Janaki looked up. And what she saw told her, without a doubt, that any future with him was gone. That silent anguish spoke now more clearly than tears ever could. The pain of losing Asha had doubled. He had lost his entire family.

Still, Janaki's annoyance at Caroline's interference had another reason. She said: 'So now we have to wait for the Americans to act? But you know, they could both just disappear into a black hole. You know that, right?'

They stared at each other, faces grim. The black hole of hopelessness yawned open.

'I know. So what now?'

'What now? Nothing. It's all a waiting game. It seems that all we ever do in Bombay is wait.'

FORTY-SIX

Up until this point Caroline had successfully kept her fear at bay. It was as if she had worn an armour of invulnerability. On hearing this news, she tried to speak, but the words would not come. Devaki, on the other hand, was still talking away, her back to Caroline, while sorting the clothing from one of the drawers into two piles.

'These are some of the best *kurtas* you can find in Bombay. I still call this place Bombay; old people like me can't suddenly change like that. I think you would look good in a rich emerald green. Kamini would look beautiful in any colour, any style. She has your amber eyes, and everything goes with amber. Look, I have found something suitable for you. I want you both to wash your hair now. Afterwards I will put some ointment on it to get rid of the lice. The best thing is shaving off all the hair but that is too extreme in this case. The bathroom is through that door. Here's a nice red *kurta* for her, but don't get dressed properly until after the lice treatment.'

'Devaki, listen.' Caroline found her voice, and though it

seemed, to her, to be little more than a croak, it was determined. 'I told you – I'm not for sale. Neither of us is for sale. If those men sold me, it was a big mistake. I stayed with Asha voluntarily in order to look after her. I'm her mother. I don't know what's going on but I'm glad you speak English and maybe you can explain—'

'I have no time for explanations. It's quite simple. I work with Mr Rajagopal and this girl had been selected by Mr Chaudhuri who is his wealthy customer. That's all there is to it. You are an older white woman. Mr Rajagopal will decide what to do with you. He might not have any use for you if you say you are unwilling. I don't know. There are certainly men who will enjoy you even if you are unwilling. You know what men are like. Some men like old white women. I don't care. You were cheap. Mr Rajagopal will make the decision. There are several options, but I would strongly suggest that you behave and look your best for him because then you will have a good life in a very good house.'

Caroline's outrage exploded. 'You can't keep me!' she cried. 'I am an American citizen. My father has important contacts. They will come after you for abduction, and there'll be big trouble for you. Prison, for years! You can't mess with an American citizen! You should let us both go, now!'

But Devaki only shrugged. 'How will they find you? This is a huge city. You're like a single ant in an anthill. Of no consequence. Just behave yourself and you'll be fine.'

'You can't honestly expect me to suddenly become a – a *prostitute*? I'm an American! I have rights, important contacts. My father will raise hell!'

Devaki chuckled. 'Oh, so high and mighty! You think you are better than ladies of the night because you never had to sell yourself? Better than me? You privileged white people think you are gods or something. You think you have *rights*? Who gave you those rights? You think anyone here cares about your rights?

Well, let me tell you this, there are people out there who would pay a good price to bring down a white god like you with all your rights. You are valuable even though you are too old really. It's your daughter they want and she's just an ant in an anthill too. They'll probably keep her and let you go.'

'They will find you! My father will find you! I'll make sure that you go to prison for life! I—'

'And *how* will he find me? You don't even know where you are. This is a city of twenty million. They cannot find you. And you'd better explain to Kamini that she needs to be talking. I expect you to encourage her, then she can return to Mr Chaudhuri soon. She will have an excellent career. As for you, you're not bad-looking but you don't have her class – I know of a good place for you but you can't expect luxury. And you're old. Now look... No, don't interrupt me. I haven't much time. I have to see to some other girls upstairs. You get her bathed and put on your nighties again for delousing. I am sending a maid with the bottle. You just massage it into the hair and leave it there for ten minutes. It's a special treatment we import from Germany, very efficient; all the lice and nits are gone afterwards. I call it Devil Juice. When you have done that, you are to wash it out properly again, then dry your hair and hers and get dressed. I'll be back in an hour to see how things are. I want you looking lovely for Mr Rajagopal; he wants to see Kamini for himself and has asked me to bring her over this afternoon. It's all to your advantage. If I were you, I would persuade her to speak to him. He has a bad temper sometimes and if he thinks she is still being stubborn he might just send her back into one of the cheap houses in Kamathipura. You don't want that. You've been there, you know what the houses are like. Both of you could have a better life but you have to behave sensibly. Then all will be well. I have to go now. Do what I said and get yourselves cleaned up. You'll have to wake her; she can't sleep all day. I'll be back in an hour.'

When Devaki had left the room Caroline walked to the

window and looked out, assessing their chances of escape. Her heart sank as she saw that the house was in the middle of a garden, and that garden was surrounded by a high brick wall topped by rolls of barbed wire. There was an iron gate, obviously securely locked, and two sentries in khaki uniforms sitting on metal folding chairs just inside it, to the side of the gravel driveway, smoking and chatting. Though they weren't very alert at the moment, Caroline knew that they would be armed, and that they would be vigilant should she ever manage to leave the house. From this window, at least, there was no escape. It was firmly barred. A prison.

Her panic on realising that she had, in Devaki's eyes at least, been sold into prostitution had settled into a quiet dread and stimulated a wary, high frequency of thought. She had plunged into this predicament without thinking, following only her instinct. The moment Asha had clung to her in fear she had known she could not leave her, ever again. There had been no premeditation. It was that maternal instinct, the one she thought she had lacked, springing up in full force.

Since there could be no escape for the moment, it seemed to Caroline prudent to do as Devaki said. It did not seem as if she and Asha were expected to begin 'work' immediately; in that case going along with Devaki was a play for time. Sooner or later a situation would turn up that would make flight possible. Until then it would be best to keep Devaki's guard down. She would play it by ear. She would wait for the right moment, trusting that at that moment the right means of escape would present itself. More than that she could not do. And anyway, she was dying for a shower.

Her mind firmly made up, she walked over to the bed, gently placed her hand on Asha's shoulder and shook it. 'Asha,' she said softly. 'Wake up.'

FORTY-SEVEN

Caroline

Caroline's head still tingled from the delousing liquid. The instructions on the bottle had been in German, but she had done what Devaki said and doused first Asha's, then her own hair generously, left the liquid to soak in and then washed it out. In Asha's rinse water there had been several dead lice. In her own, none, but it had felt good to know that if any nits had been lurking there, they were now well and truly wiped out. And she had to admit it – the emerald green *shalwar kameez* suited her well.

And Asha looked simply stunning – if one did not look at her eyes. She wore crimson silk, the *kameez* embroidered all the way up a front seam, with a pattern of tiny sequins sewn into the neckline. She looked like a princess.

Asha had submitted willingly to Caroline's handling of her. On awakening, she had followed the bathing, shampooing and delousing routine without a word. Afterwards she had allowed herself to be fed and had drunk from the cup held to her lips. She had stepped into the *shalwar* Caroline had held out for her, right foot, left foot, holding onto Caroline's shoulders for balance, and allowed the drawstring to be tied; she had raised her arms and let Caroline pull the *kameez* over her head and fasten the hooks and eyes at the shoulder. Her hair had been blow-dried and brushed, so that it fell in a thick black curtain halfway down her back.

Now she sat in the chair with her hands in her lap and stared at the wall, and her eyes, large almond eyes that should have been like brilliant amber sequins shining with spirit, were dead.

All this time, Caroline talked to her. Told her again and again she was sorry, so sorry, for leaving her behind as a small child. Sorry, so sorry, for not staying with her. For not coming to visit more often. So very sorry for not coming to get her, taking her to live with her in America, being her mother. So sorry for not knowing that Sundari and Vikram had died, that Asha had no one to care for her, for not protecting her against Paruthy Uncle, for not writing or calling each and every day to tell her how much she loved her.

'But now I'm here, Asha. Now I'm with you and I'll never, ever again let you go until you are ready to go, all grown up and not needing me anymore. I will protect you. I will keep you safe, I promise.'

Asha seemed not to listen, not to hear. But Caroline knew that deep inside, Asha was hearing every word and absorbing every promise, and that deep inside Asha also knew that this time she, Caroline, was here for keeps. And though all of Caroline's efforts to catch those eyes and fan a little life-spark into them simply failed, like flies hitting a pane of glass and falling stunned, somewhere, she knew, somewhere deep inside her daughter's heart a tiny spark still glowed; and it was that spark she spoke to, believed in. It would grow. She knew it.

Caroline now tried to keep up a lively, cheerful banter.

'Asha, it's going to be all right. Don't worry. We're much

better off here, and if I keep my wits about me I'm sure we'll be able to get out soon. And look how clean it is here, and we get fed properly. I think your luck has turned. But I don't know how long it will take. We have to meet the owner of this place in a while, and somehow impress him. I don't want to push you. You can take your own time, but it would be much better if you would speak a word or two; just to keep him from shunting us back into Kamathipura. I'm sure you can do that. Say good morning and try to smile. Just to let him know you speak English; it's a play for time because I don't know when and I don't know how I'm going to get us out, but I will. That's a promise!'

But Asha seemed frozen. All she did, now, was stare, and her lips did not so much as twitch. No more words, no more desperate calls for Mom.

Caroline was beginning to despair of ever coaxing a reaction from Asha when once again the key turned in the lock and Devaki entered, followed by the same maid who had brought their breakfast.

'Oh, you look lovely! Very lovely, both of you. Who would have guessed it – though I certainly knew that beneath all the grime there were two little jewels hiding. Mr Rajagopal will be extremely pleased with you – this girl is simply delightful. She has a very rare beauty. Have you persuaded her to speak?'

'Not yet,' Caroline admitted, 'but I'm sure I will.'

Everything in her rebelled against the role she knew it was necessary to play. She wanted to lash out at Devaki – to dig at her eyes, scratch at her face, bite and kick her before taking flight – but she knew she had only one trump card and had to play it carefully.

The time would come, and the means would not be violent ones, but wily. She would not lose this battle, even if it meant, for a while, playing the mild meek pussycat while a tiger crouched within, waiting to attack... But no. There would be no violent attack. The situation called for cunning.

Devaki impatiently beckoned the maid forward and said something to her in another language.

'What you both need is some jewellery. I will have some costume jewellery sent up. What's that?' She reached out and fingered the rings around Caroline's neck.

'They're my rings.'

'Hmmm. Nice rings. You're right not to wear them on your fingers. And this?'

She fingered Caroline's sapphire pendant. 'Very beautiful. A real sapphire isn't it.'

Caroline nodded.

'It's of sentimental value. Asha's father gave it to me, long ago.'

'Well, I would take it off and hide it if I were you – that's my tip. Because Mr Rajagopal will want it – you need to pay him back the price he paid for you, you know. He is rather greedy. I am sure it is worth several lakhs.'

'Do you think I could buy our freedom with it?'

'With that?' Devaki laughed. 'That's still peanuts to Mr Rajagopal... I know a little about jewellery and I can tell he won't be impressed – it's certainly not enough to offset the amount he intends to make with Kamini. Do you know how much Mr Chaudhuri is paying him for Kamini?'

'How much?'

'Well, I don't know, but it's a lot.'

'I will pay more.'

Devaki laughed. 'How generous! But you know, that's not how this works. It's not *just* about the money. It's about reputation. Mr Chaudhuri is his best customer. If Mr Rajagopal goes behind his back and sells her back to her family, well... Mr Chaudhuri would be very cross indeed. And don't think he wouldn't find out. The streets right now are abuzz with news about this white woman trying to reclaim her daughter. How do you think Mr Rajagopal's customers will feel about him making a deal with her? And Mr Chaudhuri will never trust him again.'

'But why would he need to, once he has Asha? Theoretically of course.'

The words *once he has Asha* were like barbs that stuck in Caroline's throat. It was an outcome too atrocious to even contemplate.

Devaki roared with laughter. 'You think Kamini will be the last?'

'But... you said... she would be like a mistress. Long term.'

Devaki laughed again and shook her head at such silliness.

'Long term, for a young girl, is three, four years at the most. She will grow old and haggard in that time. She will be passed on and Chaudhuri will be back for another. He likes the nymphs.'

'You mean, he wants a *child*? And when she becomes a woman he throws her away?'

Devaki shrugged. 'It is the way of men. Many men. They like the freshness of youth. The perfection.'

FORTY-EIGHT

Caroline was speechless with horror. In this silence Devaki continued as if they were speaking of how best to treat a child with measles.

'These men, they are often sick with some STD or the other. They think a young girl will cure them of AIDS and any number of other diseases. That's life.'

She shrugged and changed the subject while Caroline shook her head in numbed silence.

'As for the jewellery, if you like, you can give them to me for safekeeping. The pendant and the rings. I will keep them safe for you.'

Caroline was sick to her stomach. What Devaki had just told her filled her with a revulsion that was beyond her wildest nightmare. She had to think of something.

It burst from her: 'I will pay double!'

Devaki looked at her with slanted eyes. 'You will pay double?'

'Treble, even! Any price! I want my daughter! I can afford it!'

Devaki laughed. 'Interesting. I will talk to Mr Rajagopal once we are finished here. I don't think he'll be interested but maybe you can do a deal. So will you give me the jewellery? Just for safekeeping?'

'Why should I trust you? Since everyone around here is such a scoundrel. You said so yourself.'

She had to think of something. Had to. Now, the best she could do was keep Devaki talking. Provoke her into talking. She listened with one ear while her mind turned and twisted wildly, trying to think of a solution.

'Oh, I am very trustworthy. Don't think because I am working in this trade I am a thief. You won't find a more honest person than me working in the trade. In fact, I am a very decent woman, my origins are extremely respectable. I used to be a maid for a very high-class English lady. I have a good education; my parents sent me to an English-medium school. And I am a very kind woman; I have never hit any girl working for me in all my life. I only happened into this trade through bad luck.'

Devaki spoke casually, as if she were with a woman friend exchanging intimacies. If there was anything Devaki liked doing, it was talking. The woman seemed under a compulsion to talk, talk, talk, and Caroline realised that the more she kept her talking, the more information she would get out of her, and the better she would be able to figure out an escape plan.

'What happened?' she asked boldly.

'Well, it was that dastardly son of the Englishwoman – James was his name. Very good-looking. I was a young woman of sixteen at the time, very impressionable. He coaxed me into acting immorally, against my conscience – I was a very innocent girl, what did I know of the ways of men? What could I do to repel the advances of a young Englishman? He was younger than me, fifteen.

'Well, all went well for a time but what did I know about the facts of life? Before I knew it, I was expecting a child and his mother threw me out. What could I do? I could not return to my village – what a disgrace for my parents! I found a Catholic home where I could stay until my daughter was born. They wanted me to give her up for adoption, but I would never do that – give up my own flesh and blood! Never.

'So, I put her in the orphanage and went to look for work. Well, what work could I find after that disgrace – me, a girl on her own in such a big city? I was a fallen woman, and I fell still further – how could I not? What a terrible life I was forced to lead! But the worst of it was losing my daughter. Ay! Those nuns found out what I was doing and wouldn't let me near her. They wanted me to sign some papers to take her away from me permanently – in fact they stole her from me. But I wasn't allowing that! And when she was six, I stole her back.'

Devaki opened a plastic box. It was full to the brim of hair-styling apparatus: brushes, combs, ribbons, grips, everything a hairdresser could possibly need. She plunged her hands into Asha's hair, lifted it, let it fall in heavy strands of silk.

'I shall make this hair really beautiful,' she said. 'You won't believe what magic my hands can perform!'

'So how old is your daughter now?' Caroline prompted. She had to keep the woman chatting. She could do both: listen to the chat, and work out a plan.

'About Kamini's age, or a year or two older,' said Devaki. 'Perhaps not as lovely, but to a mother her daughter is always beautiful. She is fair too, of course; her father was an English-man, after all. You must tell me your daughter's story one of these days. I like to hear all your stories – I am like a mother; I really care about my girls.'

'If you really cared about them you'd let them go. You wouldn't be doing this work at all.'

Devaki chuckled.

'But my girls are happy. I can tell you're new at this trade – any girl who's lived for a time in Kamathipura would give her eyes to work for me. You are very ungrateful. I can tell Kamini here thinks differently – she can appreciate it now.' Devaki was now vigorously brushing Asha's hair, and obviously taking great pleasure in it.

'But would you let your own daughter work like this? If she's Asha's age, do you also have her doing this kind of work?'

The woman glanced at Caroline and scowled.

'Of course she isn't working like this, don't even suggest it! That's one of the reasons I used all my cunning to advance in my profession, so I could move out of that hovel I was living in and find a more respectable lodging for me and my daughter. But rents are so expensive in Bombay – all I had was a small room, quite near Kamathipura. The nuns would not tell me where she is but I found out and stole her back. I placed her in a private home for young girls. She goes to a normal school.'

'But if – say she lived with you. Would you allow her to...?'

'Never! Of course not! I would never let her work this way. My daughter is lovely. She is also educated, and in a few years' time she will have finished school.'

'What will she do then?'

'Well, I have to try and find a proper husband for her but it is difficult – I want her to marry decently but how can I prevent the boy's parents from finding out what I do for a living? That is my great sorrow. It is hard enough raising a child alone, but finding a husband for a daughter is near to impossible for a single mother and especially one of my profession. But everybody has their dream.'

Devaki twisted a strand of Asha's hair into a long curl and clipped it to the top of her head. She picked up a second strand and did the same again, over and over, till only one strand was left. This she began to plait with quick, deft fingers. Every now and then she stopped to push the bangles up her arm. Why doesn't she just take them off, Caroline wondered vaguely, since they all keep falling down anyway?

'What is your dream?' she asked.

'My dream? Well, I don't usually tell this to my girls but between you and me, for my daughter's sake it would be necessary to start all over again, in some other city where I can be anonymous. Lucknow: that is my dream. My native village is in the vicinity of Lucknow, and I know the city well. A nice clean little flat for me and my daughter. It doesn't have to be big, but respectable. I don't even mind working as a housekeeper for some rich family – I would not earn as much as I do here, but I would make good contacts that way. My daughter could also find work as a maid – I would train her myself.

'But hairdressing is my real dream. I have a gift for hair-styling. I would like to style the hair of brides – I'm sure I could make a business out of it. And my final dream is to see my daughter as a bride herself, and style her hair for her own wedding. But it is only a dream. How can I start anew? I am trying to save every *paise* I have but life is costly here – money just fritters away and I am struggling even to survive. How can I save anything? You see, we all have our problems, and every-one's problem is a mountain to that person, so you shouldn't complain. Now please don't talk to me anymore, I have to concentrate. When I'm finished you will see why.'

And Caroline did see why. Asha's hair, when finished, was truly fit for a bride: smooth and sleek around her face, and at the back a sculpture of interwoven plaits. It managed to be sophisti-cated and simple at once, every strand placed in exactly the right position, not a single hair out of place.

Pleased with herself, Devaki pushed the bangles up her arms again and turned to Caroline with a smile.

'See! That's how Mr Rajagopal likes hair to be styled. Now it's your turn.'

'You said you'd talk to him about my offer.'

'Oh yes, that's right. He might just take the bait. You never know. Is your family really that rich?'

'My father is a multi-millionaire!' cried Caroline. 'No price is too high for my daughter.'

'Interesting,' is all Devaki said. She picked up a comb and began to fiddle with Caroline's own hair.

Caroline, meanwhile, regretted her outburst. How foolish, to boast of her father's wealth. How mortifying to even offer money for Asha. How shameful, to bargain with a criminal for her daughter's honour. Offering huge amounts of money to buy a girl from a fate worse than death – surely that was in itself supporting the trade. What if it led to more girls with rich fathers being kidnapped? It was a terrible thing to do.

But yes. If it came to that, there was no price that was too high to buy back Asha. Asha, right now, was a commodity. And she might have the means to change that. She did not care one jot about the morality of it. Yes, she'd pay any price.

But maybe there was another way.

A better way.

FORTY-NINE

Caroline

Caroline frowned in contemplation, Devaki's words tumbling through her mind.

Everybody has a dream.

I want to go to Lucknow and live with my daughter.

I want her to marry decently.

I want to be a hairdresser for brides.

'So, that's done,' Devaki said, holding up a mirror so that Caroline could see the back of her head. But Caroline wasn't interested. She was still thinking, thinking, thinking. Slowly, surely, a plan was piecing itself together.

'We will go now to Mr Rajagopal. Once we are there we can discuss your offer. If you're lucky, he will agree. A car is coming to pick us up. It will be here in ten minutes.'

Caroline had not spoken a word since her preposterous and so shameful outburst. She had let Devaki style her hair without comment, murmuring only an 'um' in answer to questions, or nodding when asked for approval. She'd been thinking, planning, plotting. Now it was time to speak up.

'Devaki,' she said, quietly. 'I'm going to make you an offer. Come here; look at me.'

'Yes? What is it?'

Devaki was touching up Asha's face; a little bit more rouge, and a touch more kajal. Asha now looked more like eighteen than thirteen, and Caroline wondered in passing why, if young girls were so coveted in this trade, so much effort was made to make them look older, like grown women.

But other, more important, things were on her mind and so she said, 'Come, Devaki. Leave her and come.'

'Just a little bit more – close your eyes, *beti* – I'm coming. What is it? We have to hurry. The car will be here soon—'

'Never mind the car, Devaki. Listen, how would you like to fulfil your dream now? Right now. Today. I can make your dream come true.'

Devaki's eyes narrowed. 'What do you mean?'

'I mean, like I said, I have money. My family has money. I prefer to give it to you than to Mr Rajagopal. Because you told me your story and I know that once upon a time, you too were a victim of this horrible trade. Listen. I have money right here in my bank in Bombay. I have a bank account here that I use in India, to pay for Asha's maintenance. It is full of money. I will give you enough to buy a little house in Lucknow and set you up independently there. You are so good with hairstyling. You can start your hairstyling business right away. I will help you. I promise. I offer you three *crores* of rupees. A bank draft.'

Devaki's eyes narrowed.

'No draft. Cash. We go to bank and you give me cash.'

'I won't be able to withdraw a large amount in cash. They don't do that. But a bank draft is just like cash. You can deposit it in your own bank and in a few days the money will be yours.'

Devaki frowned, thinking.

'But if I do that and you report me maybe you send police to put me in jail. They will find me through my bank. You will betray me.'

'No, Devaki. I would never do that. I promise. You can trust me.'

'Why should I trust you? No. It is a trick.'

'Look into my eyes, Devaki.'

Caroline took Devaki's hands in hers. They gazed into each other's eyes. Caroline placed all the love, all the hope, all the sincerity she could muster into that gaze.

'I swear,' she said. 'I swear on my daughter's life that I will not betray you.'

'Still. You could. Why would you let me have all that money, if you are both free already?'

Why, indeed? Caroline, the panic rising within her, had to think quickly. It was now or never. She closed her eyes, took a deep breath and cleared her mind.

'Because my daughter's freedom is worth more to me than all the money in the world. All the jewels. I would give all I possess for her.'

Inspiration came to her. She reached up, behind her neck.

'Look, Devaki. This pendant. I lied to you. The rings look flashy, but they are not worth much; the diamonds are not real. It's the pendant that is valuable. It's a real sapphire, and it has historical value. It was a gift from the Rani of Jaipur, Gayatri Devi, to Asha's grandmother, the Rani of Chandrapur. It's an heirloom, precious to me as I am keeping it for Asha. But I will give you the pendant and the rings as a security deposit. Because I trust you. If I can trust you, you can trust me.

'Listen, we will go to my bank now, together. I will give you the pendant and the rings, then I will instruct the bank to transfer the money from my account into yours. You can watch me fill out the forms. You can check that the name and the bank account are yours. In a few days' time you call me at my hotel and we will go together to your bank, to check if the money is in your account. And only once the money is in your account, you return the jewellery to me.

'So it's a deposit of trust. I trust you, and you trust me. The pendant especially is very precious to me as my daughter's heirloom, but I trust you with it. You could sell it for a lot of money, but it would take time. The bank transfer would be easier and much quicker for you. You could be in Lucknow in a week's time. All you have to do is give me back my Asha. I am a mother too, Devaki. As mothers together, let us help each other. Here. Take the jewellery.'

As she spoke, unclasping the chain, she tried to look into Devaki's eye, tried to hold the other woman's fickle, flickering gaze. She slid the two rings and the pendant off their chain and held them out to Devaki. Devaki held out her open palm, her eyes still hesitant, dithering, doubtful. Outside, a car blew its horn. Devaki snapped back her hand as if bitten, wiped it on her *dupatta* as if it were stained.

'No,' she said. 'The driver has come. We have to go. Mr Rajagopal is waiting.'

She turned as if to walk away, but Caroline reached for her, grabbed her shoulder, cried out in desperation:

'Devaki, no! Please, let us go! You will be free and your daughter too. Let's do this! Don't let those criminals win! Free my daughter. Build a life of your own with *your* daughter. Please, Devaki, please!'

Her eyes filled with tears, and that was the moment Devaki could finally look into them, feel their depth and their pain, feel her own pain, her own needs, her own longing for freedom. Devaki's own eyes grew moist, and she reached out and closed her palm over Caroline's hand that still held the jewellery. And finally, their gazes met, connected.

'I do not need your jewels. Keep them. I trust you. We will do it. We will go to the bank.'

. . .

The car slid through the open gate, Devaki in the passenger seat, Asha and Caroline in the back. Caroline held her breath. Would Devaki change her mind? Would she rethink her decision, get cold feet, fear that she would be caught, mistrust her, Caroline, again? The silence was unnerving – but what could she say to break it?

They drove in that uncomfortable silence for half an hour through stop-and-go traffic. Then Devaki, in the front seat, turned to the driver and spoke a few words in Hindi. He bobbed his head in acquiescence.

'The rear doors have a security lock,' she said. 'He has to unlock them for you. I told him we are going for a meal at a restaurant at the next corner. He's a stupid man, and I'm his superior – he will obey me, though it's an unusual request. But he knows I don't fool around. So he'll let you out, and I will get out too. When he has driven off we will get another taxi and go to your bank.'

The car stopped in front of a restaurant. There was a click as the locks were released. Caroline opened her door, and she and Asha stepped out onto the pavement. Devaki's door also opened, and she climbed out to stand beside them.

'Now we all walk calmly towards the restaurant. The chauffeur will have to drive away; he's going to park somewhere nearby and I told him to pick us up in half an hour. When he comes he won't find anybody!'

Devaki could hardly hide her mirth at this thought; she placed a hand over her mouth to suppress a giggle. 'He's very faithful to Mr Rajagopal but he has to obey me. Come on, let's go. Walk in front of me as if I'm the boss!'

They made their way towards the restaurant; the car slid past them.

'All right. He's gone. Now, a taxi!' Devaki flagged down an empty auto-rickshaw, which stopped immediately. The two women and Asha climbed in. Caroline checked the address of her bank's Mumbai branch.

'Central Avenue Road, Chembur,' she said, and Devaki repeated the instructions to the driver. The rickshaw scooted off.

It took an hour to get to the bank, and another half-hour before the forms were filled out for the bank transfer. Identification had to be shown, and there was a lot of paperwork at a desk in a back office. But finally it was all done.

'Just a moment,' said Caroline. 'I need to go to the counter as well.'

'What? What for?' Devaki's eyes narrowed suspiciously.

Caroline laughed. 'No, I'm not going to revoke the transaction! Come with me to the counter, and you'll see.'

She joined the queue at the counter, Asha still clutching her hand. Devaki clung to Asha's other hand, as if afraid of a last-minute change of plan.

Ten minutes later, they left the bank together. On the pavement again, Caroline let go of Asha's hand, fished in her handbag and took out a thick wad of bank notes.

'Here you are. A small bonus, for the trust you gave me. Some cash: two thousand rupees, to tide you over for the next few days, till the three *crores* are in your account. Go to a nice hotel, visit your daughter, have some nice meals. If you need me, if there's any problem, I'll be at the Taj. But this, this is your new life.'

Devaki took the cash and, holding it between her two palms, raised her hand to her forehead and closed her eyes. 'It's the grace of God,' she said. 'You are God in human form.'

Caroline laughed, bowed slightly, and placed her palms in *namaste*.

'No, Devaki, I'm just a mother doing what is right for her child,' she said. 'I wish you well. And your daughter.'

Devaki bowed her head slightly in acknowledgement.

Then, simultaneously, they turned around, parting company. Devaki walked in one direction; Caroline took Asha's hand and walked in another.

She had no idea where she was. Traffic snorted and screeched around her, exhaust fumes belched, the pavement heaved with a stream of humanity that parted at their coming and closed again behind them.

Hardly believing it, Caroline beamed at Asha, took her hand again and walked on. And then she could no longer walk. She ran, laughing, and Asha ran beside her, also laughing.

Hysterical with laughter, Caroline stopped, hugged Asha, and waved at passing taxis.

Eventually, one stopped. They climbed into the back seat.

And only then did Caroline trust her voice.

'Come, Asha. Let's go home. We're free. Forever! And I'll never let you go again.'

She folded Asha into her arms. Clung to her as if she'd never let go, and her laughter turned to sobs, and they both cried all the way to Tulasa House.

FIFTY

'Have you had lunch?' asked Janaki, as she and Kamal emerged from the auto-rickshaw at Tulasa House.

'Yes,' said Kamal. 'I went to a restaurant with Gita and had a bite, but I couldn't eat much. I feel sick. But you must be starving – I take it you haven't eaten all day? It's nearly three. Let's find a restaurant.'

'OK. I just need to check my email first. To see if there are any updates from Rajagopal.' She led the way to the front door.

Kamal sighed. 'Can you spend even one hour, go for one meal, without checking your email?'

Janaki chuckled. 'I'm afraid not. I'm addicted.' She rapped on the door. Subhadai opened it, and they walked in, through to the main room.

'What the...?' Kamal stopped in his tracks, speechless. And then he rushed forward.

Caroline too rushed forward, and fell into his arms, sobbing with relief. Then she pulled away and opened one arm to invite another person to join them.

'Yes! Yes! I found her and we're back. She's safe, Kamal. She's safe. Come on, Asha! You too!'

She gestured for Asha to come forward, to join in the hug. But Asha just stood there, hands behind her back, staring. Kamal let go of Caroline, and, very slowly, smiling, arms held out, walked up to Asha.

'Asha! I've missed you so much!'

Asha backed away.

Caroline moved to her side, put an arm around her shoulders, and bent down to whisper in her ears. Asha smiled, and seemed to relax.

Kamal waited.

And then, Asha rushed forward, into his arms, and as she ran she cried, 'Daddy!' And then they were all in a huddle, Caroline, Kamal, and Asha.

Janaki laughed, and looked beyond them to see Dr Nath, sitting on the sofa at the back, watching. Gita sat next to him, grinning like a Cheshire cat. Janaki stepped around the family group and flung herself down next to Dr Nath.

'I can't believe we've done it, Dr Nath!' she said.

'*You* did it, Janaki!' he replied. '*You* found Asha. And I think we need to talk.'

She looked at him, and at Gita. 'I know. I want to hear the whole story. It doesn't look as if Caroline's going to be telling me it any time soon.'

She sighed. It had been a pleasant dream, while it lasted: her and Kamal. But anyway, she reminded herself, he was too old for her, by far. Though Amma would disagree. An engineer, or a lawyer, or a doctor, Amma had said.

'I don't mean that,' said Dr Nath. 'You'll hear the full story in time. I meant – I wondered if you'd consider working for me. Here, in Bombay. Your detective work – we could really do with more of that. I mean, it would be as a volunteer, and I can't offer you a salary, but...'

'Dr Nath, I'd love to! It's just that...'

'Please. Call me Dilip. And I know. You'll need a proper

job, in the city. But with your talents, the head-hunters will be after you. After this story – even now, the American media is calling you a star detective, a hero. I don't even know if you'll have time for volunteer work. But... maybe...'

Their eyes met. His were warm and his smile even warmer.

Janaki glanced at Kamal, Caroline and Asha, who were still standing together, arms linked, a family, glowing with joy. That look between Caroline and Kamal! The way they both looked down at Asha... The way Asha looked up at them, from one to the other, in adoration.

Janaki looked back at Dr Nath, her eyes brimming with tears, because this outcome was beyond any romantic dreams she'd harboured.

'Yes. Yes. Of course, I'll work for you, Dilip, and with you. But now, I'm really starving. Maybe we can all go somewhere for a meal.'

They went in two taxis – Dr Nath, Gita and Janaki in one, Caroline, Kamal and Asha in the other – back to the Taj for a celebratory dinner.

In the back seat of their car, Caroline and Kamal exchanged another long, lingering look. Caroline's cheeks hurt from all her grinning. Asha, sitting between them, had fallen asleep, and was leaning against Caroline. Kamal said,

'What did you whisper to Asha back then, to put her at ease?'

Caroline laughed out loud.

'Kamal! Have you seen yourself in a mirror of late? You're the image of a Bollywood movie thug! You looked just like the men from that brothel. She didn't recognise you, she was scared. That's all it was. So I told her that it's you, her daddy. I've been telling her about you for days now. I told her you're the best daddy in the world. That you love her.'

Kamal felt his chin, felt the prickly stubble covering it.

'Oh heck! I need a shave. And clean clothes... I can't go to the restaurant like this. We should go to my hotel first, so I can pick up—'

Caroline squeezed his hand and interrupted.

'No. I'll smuggle you up to my room at the Taj. You can have a shower and a shave. And they have a boutique, downstairs, with men's clothing. I'll buy you something decent to change into.'

She squeezed his hand again.

'What do you say, shall I book us all a suite?'

FIFTY-ONE

Kodaikanal

Kamal strode up and down the deck, frowning, gesticulating with one hand and holding a heavy mobile phone to his ear with the other. He spoke in Hindi, and Caroline, sitting in the wicker double swing on the deck, didn't understand a word. She looked down at Asha, cuddled against her, and smiled contentedly, gazing out at the shining mirror of the Kodai Lake.

Visibly annoyed, Kamal pushed the antenna back into the phone, chucked it onto the glass-topped table.

'I need a drink!' he said and poured himself a glass of *nimbu pani* from the jug on the table. He looked glumly at the glass. 'Nothing stronger than this?'

'Not here,' said Caroline, patting the cushion next to her. 'Come, sit down; tell me what that was all about. You shouldn't let her get you so riled up, you know.'

She was used to it now. Kamal had been on the phone with Daadi every single day, one argument after the other. But Caroline knew the arguments weren't serious. From the resigned exasperation in Kamal's voice, and she could feel the fondness from his side of the discussion. She couldn't wait to meet Daadi.

'She just hasn't changed. Not a bit. It's always been that way, since I was a boy, controlling my life. Daadi's just a dragon and now she's old it's worse.'

Caroline knew to take those words with a pinch of salt.

'Yes, but what was it about?'

'A wedding. She wants to organise a wedding. For us.'

He wagged a finger between the two of them as he dropped down to sit on the other side of Asha. Asha slid closer to Caroline to make room for him.

Caroline laughed. 'For us? Not for you and Janaki?'

'Don't tease! Of course for you and me. Now that we're together again, of course for you and me.'

'But we're already married! *Still* married, I should say.'

'Yes, but it doesn't count to her because that was a civil ceremony. She wants a proper wedding with a proper Hindu blessing. From proper Hindu priests. In Sanskrit. She says it's only a proper wedding if there's a blessing, and we didn't have one, and that's why everything went wrong from the start. The *blessing* is what matters.'

'Oh, she wants one of those big Hindu weddings, three days of pomp and ceremony? Where we walk around a fire and throw garlands around each other's head? And you ride up on a white horse, carrying a sword?'

'Yes, yes, that too. And I told her that it's ridiculous and a waste of money since we're married already.'

'Oh, but I would love a wedding like that! I'd wear a beautiful red silk sari and my hands and arms would have intricate henna designs, and I'd have jewels in my ears and nose! Wonderful! And my parents would come, and all my friends, and there'd be a huge feast and three days of celebration and—'

'Just a complete waste of money, a big gala wedding. That's what I told Daadi.'

'If she wants to spend that money, why should we stop her? It's hers to spend.'

'Caroline! You told me you didn't want a big wedding. You hated the idea, back then!'

'Ah, but I was young and foolish back then. And I didn't know how important the blessing was, and we didn't have Asha. She'd love a big wedding, a party, wouldn't you, honey?'

She gave Asha a hug and they looked at each other, smiling.

'Of course, Mom!' said Asha.

Caroline loved to hear that precious word: *Mom.*

Asha had called her that right from the start, seamlessly, as if there'd never been a Mom-less time. As if Asha had always known, but had kept it all inside until the time was right. Now, the time was right.

They had come to the Nilgiri Hills two weeks ago to recover from the whole ordeal. They planned to spend a month in the resort before returning up north to visit Daadi at Chandrapur. A month to recover.

In the meantime, much goodwill had come from the nightmare they'd all lived through. Thanks to Caroline's father, and the huge media coverage in the USA, the story of Janaki, Caroline and Kamal, as well as Dr Nath and Gita, had made international headlines. The TV breakfast shows had all taken up the story; the world had waited with bated breath, and when news broke of the story-book outcome, the world had rejoiced. They were all heroes of the story, as well as Asha and Ragi, the rescued victims.

An embarrassed Mumbai police force, under pressure from 'horrified' Indian political leaders of all parties, had been obliged to take action. Devaki had given a witness statement; Rajagopal, Chaudhuri and Kapoor now languished in jail, as well as the Pandians. There was talk of yet more crackdowns to come, a 'clean-up' in Kamathipura, rescue actions of prostitutes held in cages.

And not only in India, but all over the world. Child trafficking, the prostitution of girls, the horrendous abuse taking place in dark places, was recognised as a scourge that had to be dealt with.

Dr Nath shrugged it all off.

'It's good to see more people waking up,' he said. 'But it'll all return to normal after the headlines stop. Nothing will change. A few girls rescued, perhaps, but nothing lasting. It's everywhere. Mumbai is just a dot on the world map of child trafficking.'

But they could celebrate their own good news. Just a week after Kamal's wedding conversation, a car drew up outside the resort. They were all there to meet it: Caroline, Kamal and Asha. The back passenger doors opened. Out stepped Gita from one, Janaki from the other. Janaki waved, turned, reached into the back seat with both arms. And then she was holding Ragi, and grinning. She put Ragi down to stand beside her, bent over to whisper in Ragi's ear.

By now, both Caroline and Kamal had stepped over to the car, hugging Janaki and Gita, trying not to laugh too loudly so as not to scare Ragi. And then, Ragi placed her hands together at her chest and smiled.

It had taken an age, the formal process of removing her officially from her father's care and appointing Caroline and Kamal as her foster-parents. Later, if all went well, they'd adopt her. There was no reason not to adopt her even now, but Indian bureaucracy moved slowly. It would take time.

And then it would take much more time for her to heal. She'd been badly damaged by the ordeal her father had put her through. But back in Mumbai she had responded well to Caroline, and, after all, healing was Caroline's profession, her skill. Caroline was no longer that bumbling, insecure first-time mother.

Now she knew that all a young child needed was love.

Now, she had confidence and warmth, and all that it took for a child in her care to flourish. She couldn't wait for Ragi to join them, because if ever there was a child needing intensive care and therapy and above all, love, it was Ragi. Caroline shuddered at the thought of what Ragi must have endured at her father's hands.

Asha's healing process wouldn't take as long; she was doing well already, though there were undoubtedly deep wounds. The cruelty she'd endured had left its mark, but the scars were already healing and she responded so well to her parents' love. Of which there was an abundance. And love heals all wounds.

A week later, their last at the resort, they sat in the swing seat again, but now they were four: Caroline, Kamal, arms joined along the back rest, and between them the two girls, chattering together, reading a picture book together. They didn't have a single common language, these two girls, but somehow they communicated perfectly.

These two children, Asha and Ragi, were now Caroline's focus, her only focus. She had already sold the thriving child-therapy practice she'd founded and built up in Cambridge; a close friend and colleague had bought the business and taken over the reins. Caroline now had a different, more personal focus.

Because *this*, now, was her life. Asha, and Ragi. And Kamal. They'd start again. Kamal back at the Aliyar dam. They'd buy or build a home in the scenic valleys near the dam, just as they'd planned so long ago.

This would be the India she'd dreamt of as a child. She pushed the ground gently with her feet so that the swing swayed back and forth.

'Asha, why don't you go to the pond and show Ragi the tadpoles,' she said.

'Sure,' said Asha. 'C'mon, Ragi.' The girls scampered off and Caroline moved closer to Kamal and nestled against him. His arm rested casually on her shoulder, but she could feel the tension within him. She was so looking forward to moving on to Chandrapur, meeting Daadi – but how could she, with this unresolved issue hanging between them, these endless discussions on weddings and money and Daadi's permanent interference?

They'd both been silent for a while, Caroline lost in her dreams and Kamal no doubt arguing with Daadi in his mind. It never stops, Caroline thought to herself. But I think, deep inside, he loves her. Now, he suddenly spoke, cutting into her musings.

'Maybe we can make a deal with Daadi,' he said.

Caroline rubbed her head to bring herself back down to earth. 'What deal? What do you mean?'

'If Daadi wants to spend heaps of money, then let her spend useful money as well,' said Kamal.

'What d'you mean?'

'Remember what Dr Nath told us, when we first met him. That those rescued girls have nowhere to go, because their families, their communities, can't take them back. And that he wants to buy a home for them. A proper home for rescued girls.'

'Oh, Kamal!' Caroline sat up straight in the swing, half turned to face him. Her eyes gleamed as they met his. No words were necessary. The map she was drawing in her mind changed shape; its contours changed, its boundaries expanded.

'Could we? Can we?'

'Yes. We can. Establish a place for India's lost daughters. A beautiful place, a place of healing. A future for them. And you could run it, Caroline. If you'd like to.'

'But of course!'

'There we have it, then. And you know what? That'll be our

bargaining chip. Daadi can have her big gala wedding, but only if we get that home for lost girls.'

She felt his hand on her shoulder, squeezing gently.

She relaxed into it, snuggled up to him.

'The blessing,' she said. 'Our marriage will be blessed this time.'

A LETTER FROM THE AUTHOR

First of all, I want to say a huge thank you for choosing *Girl in a Red Silk Sari*. I hope you enjoyed reading Asha's story just as much as I loved writing it. If you want to join other readers in hearing all about my new releases and bonus content, you can sign up for my newsletter.

www.stormpublishing.co/sharon-maas

If you could also spare a few moments to leave a review that would be hugely appreciated. Even a short review can make all the difference in encouraging a reader to discover my books for the first time. Thank you so much!

If you did enjoy *Girl in a Red Silk Sari*, I would be forever grateful if you'd tell others: readers in your family, friends and social media circles. I think Asha's story needs to be told, and nothing helps a book as much as word of mouth: simply telling others 'You should read this book.'

On a more personal level, there's nothing that makes my day as much as a reader's letter so do please drop me a line, either on my social media pages or through the contact form on my website. I promise to reply!

This particular book is close to my heart, since it addresses a heart-breaking situation that unfortunately is still alive in today's world. At this moment, there are children such as Asha and Ragi who are sold into prostitution like pieces of property, abused, broken. They need our awareness; awareness leads to help. Please go on to read my author notes following this letter.

Thank you so much for your support – until next time.

Sharon Maas

www.sharonmaas.com

AUTHOR NOTES

Asha, Ragi and the other 'lost' girls who appear in *Girl in a Red Silk Sari* might be fictitious, but they are nevertheless real. I first came into contact with the horrendous plight of such girls in the year 2000, during the research for one of my early novels. Like Janaki and Caroline, I walked the streets of Kamathipura, and was able to visit a few brothels and talk to young girls who had been stolen from their homes for the trade.

In my research I was aided by Dr Gilada, the founder of the People's Health Organisation in Mumbai. Dr Nath of *Girl in a Red Silk Sari* is inspired by Dr Gilada. The story Dr Nath tells of the Nepalese girl Tulasa is taken directly from an interview I did with him back in 2000.

Tulasa's story is true. There are still many Tulasas in Mumbai and other Indian and Asian cities today, and all over the world, including right on our doorstep in the West. Her story is shocking, but sometimes we need to be shocked. However, there is at last some good news. Here is that interview, with an update:

Saving Tulasa, Nepalese child forced into prostitution

An Interview with Dr Gilada

Dr Ishwarprasad Gilada, founder, General-Secretary and driving force behind the People's Health Organisation in India, has been fighting against the horrors of the Bombay sex trade for the last two decades.

Sharon: Dr Gilada, your crusade against child prostitution in India began with the rescue of Tulasa in 1982; back then, the story made front page headlines in India and Nepal, and opened a viper's nest of horrors. Who was Tulasa?

Dr I.G.: Tulasa was a twelve-year-old Nepali girl who in 1982 was kidnapped from her village and sold into prostitution in Bombay. She was systematically raped to make her fit for the trade and then forced to entertain an average of eight clients a day. I met her ten months later in the Bombay hospital where I was working at the time. Her tiny body – the body of a child – was completely broken. She was suffering from three types of sexually transmitted diseases (STDs), genital warts and brain tuberculosis, which had left her disabled and wheelchair-bound, and finally killed her. The story she told was horrific. The People's Health Organisation embarked on a fully-fledged 'Save Tulasa' campaign, and with the support of the media managed to rescue her. We located her father – her mother had died shortly after her disappearance – and sent her home.

Sharon: You say with the support of the media. Didn't the police help in the rescue campaign?

Dr I.G.: Police collusion with the flesh trade was a crucial point in Tulasa's revelations. Even today the police and the politicians are in collaboration with the pimps – the profit is huge. Back then, the uproar generated by her story forced the police into action, and in no time thirty-two persons involved were arrested, including the three brothel owners Tulasa had worked for. The police knew exactly what was going on, but only stepped in when forced to do so. It took them eighteen months to ascertain her age and three years to file a charge. And only last January, eighteen years later, did the case finally come to trial. The police were given a month to produce her in court. Only then did we receive a message that Tulasa had died two years previously. Meanwhile, her abusers have been running free.

Sharon: After her rescue didn't she find peace in Nepal?

Dr I.G.: No. At first there had been an outpouring of sympathy for her – offers of adoption and marriage, an invitation to Switzerland, gifts of money and medicine. None of it came to anything. Tulasa was rejected by her father's second wife, and moved into a home. Her father avoided her to keep the family peace. She was in constant pain, but worst of all was the feeling that nobody loved her, that she had been used and abused and finally discarded like a piece of rubbish.

Sharon: Is Tulasa's story typical of child prostitutes in India's megacities?

Dr I.G.: Yes. Soon after Tulasa's rescue the air was abuzz with innumerable stories of girls who were caged and treated like animals in Kamathipura, Bombay's infamous red-light district. They narrated harrowing tales of torture and abuse. The PHO has to-date directly rescued more than 130 girls, and more than 3,000 indirectly. The youngest girl we rescued was only eight years old.

Sharon: Has trafficking of children in Bombay improved since Tulasa's rescue?

Dr I.G.: Horrifying as it is, Tulasa's case has had some positive fallout. The episode threw the spotlight on the appalling practice of child prostitution – the public outcry was tremendous. As a result, the governments of India and Nepal signed a treaty for the rescue and repatriation of Nepali girls from Indian brothels. In India the sentence for trafficking minors has been hiked from seven to thirteen years. Child prostitution has been reduced by about forty per cent.

Sharon: How do children end up as prostitutes in India?

Dr I.G.: About forty per cent of all child prostitutes have been abducted from villages all over India and Nepal. They are lured away on some pretext or other: going to movies, cities, temples, making them film stars, lucrative job opportunities, marriage. Another major source of child prostitutes is the Devadasi system. Every year thousands of girls are ceremonially dedicated to the goddess Yellamma. They are sold to the highest bidder and after a brief period of concubinage turned over to the urban brothels. The system is officially banned but continues to operate clandestinely, contributing up to twenty per cent of urban child prostitutes.

A small proportion of child prostitutes come to the trade after being raped. Others run away from incestuous relationships with family members. Yet others are daughters of prostitutes, who have no other option than to follow their mother's profession.

Sharon: What are their living conditions in the brothels?

Dr I.G.: The girls live in unimaginable squalor, usually about ten–twelve girls in a small room. The brothels are foul, stinking holes, often overrun with rats and vermin. They eat from filthy cafeterias or vendors, and have to pay twice the price for their food and other necessary commodities. Most of them are forced to abuse drugs, alcohol and nicotine. Seventy-five to eighty per cent of the girls suffer from STDs. More than half of the girls are HIV-infected.

Sharon: What is the PHO doing to deal with the situation?

Dr I.G.: The prevention of child prostitution and the containment of AIDS are two of our main aims. We have a mobile clinic – donated by a German organisation – and go out into red-light districts several times a week with a team consisting of health workers, social workers and ex-sex workers. We distribute free condoms, and provide medical check-ups and counselling on specific health or social problems. In many of the brothels there are prostitutes working for us, helping to educate others so as to prevent the spread of AIDS. We have had considerable success in this area.

Sharon: What success have you had with your other main aim, the prevention of child prostitution? Is it possible to rehabilitate the children you rescue from the brothels?

Dr I.G: At the moment, the emphasis is on prevention rather than rescue. The problem is, where can they go after they have been rescued, or when they contract AIDS and are thrown out of the brothels? They are often rejected by their communities and families and cannot return home, and we simply do not have the facilities to look after these girls. We have a twenty-five-acre plot of land on the Bombay–Goa highway, where we had planned to build a home for rescued children, a training centre and a school, but we simply don't have the funds to carry on. The PHO operates on a shoestring.

UPDATE 2025:

Sharon: Dr Gilada, it's good to talk to you again! It's been twenty-five years since our first interview took place. I'd like to know if anything has changed in that time, and especially, if things in Mumbai have improved.

Dr I.G.: Things have indeed changed. Street and brothel prostitution has decreased a great deal, by almost eighty per cent, thanks to the HIV awareness, and HIV affliction among sex workers. New recruitment is less, as their trade/business has taken a beating. Child prostitution, though not extinct, has been reduced to a tiny fraction of what it was then.

Sharon: Did the home for rescued children ever materialise?

Dr I.G.: The planned home for rescued girls who had been trafficked could not come to fruition due to legal tangles and opposition from the villagers surrounding the land.

Sharon: So that's good and bad news at the same time. It's good to know that there are now fewer recruits to the trade, but it's sad that it still continues at all, and that the home could not be established. What does your work consist of now?

Dr I.G.: Most of my time is dedicated to working for HIV/AIDS patients at my clinic. I deal with several young children/adolescents, who have been infected at birth, now at marriageable age. They have their own challenges.

Sharon: Dr Gilada, thank you for this interview and for your help during my research. I wish you much strength, support and success for the future.

Follow Dr Gilada on X: @drgilada